Islands of the Dying Light

Rolf Lappert

Islands of the Dying Light

Translated from the German by
Eugene H. Hayworth

OWL CANYON PRESS, 2012

Original title: *Auf den Inseln des letzten Lichts* by Rolf Lappert
© Carl Hanser Verlag München 2010

Translation Copyright 2011 Eugene H. Hayworth

First Edition, 2012
All Rights Reserved
Library of Congress Cataloging-in-Publication Data

Rolf Lappert.
Island's of the Dying Light—1st ed.
p. cm.
ISBN: 978-0983476412
2011941904

Owl Canyon Press
Boulder, Colorado

I want to be able to be alone,
to find it nourishing —
not just a waiting.
Susan Sontag, *Diaries*

Two can be as bad as one.
It's the loneliest number since the number one.
Aimee Mann, *One is the Loneliest Number*

PROLOGUE

After it had been raining almost all of July, August finally brought warm, dry weather. "Sunshine," the man on the radio said, and Megan whispered the word, because the sound pleased her. *Sunshine.* That was what her mother called her, when it was a good day and her voice was a tender singsong. Megan sat in front of the door of the house, under the canopy where the colorful flowers grew, and held the baby-bottle filled with sweet tea. There were flapjacks and slices of discolored brown apple on a plate. The cackling of the chickens wafted above; now and then the nag Sam snorted when the flies annoyed him too much. Far away, the chugging of a tractor rose into the immeasurable, dazzling blue sky. A gust of wind blew the hot air away from the veranda and cooled the girl's sweating body a little.

The woman in the car looked at the house. Behind the sunglasses her face was blurred by a square of glistening light. When the man started the engine, she rolled down the window and lifted her hand in a tentative wave. But then the car started moving, rode over the empty ochre-colored ground and disappeared behind the trees that lined the dry ditch. When the engine noise died down and the dust settled, the boy's crying rose from inside the house, at first whimpering, questioning, finally with the full volume and strength a half-year old is capable of. Megan listened carefully for a while, waiting to see if someone would come and take care of the annoying creature, but nobody came. All she could hear was the careless flock of chickens and the humming of the tractor, quieter than a bumble-bee.

Then the baby stopped crying. He was probably lying there, staring at the ceiling, eyes as large as Daddy's coat buttons, his face gone all red and more spotted than the skin of the cat. Tobey. A noisemaker and a glutton when he wasn't sleeping. Toto. "Little Brother," Mom always said when Megan looked at him and wished someone would stuff him into the trash, along with the stinky diaper and the rattle—which belonged to her—and the pink blanket she had slept on until he showed up.

Megan put down the baby bottle, turned to the side, put her hands on the wooden planks and pushed herself up. She waited until she no longer wobbled, then she moved toward the front door, which was open like all the other doors and windows of the house. She heard the wailing of the creature, who couldn't do anything for himself except make noise. He couldn't walk; he couldn't hold a spoon or a bottle; and he couldn't even clap his hands. Nevertheless, he spent much more time with Mommy than her, *Megan, Meggie, Sweetie*, who no longer had to be carried around and constantly fed, who could wash her own hands and use the toilet if someone sat her on it.

When she reached the door, something held Megan back. She turned around but there was no one there. Then, while trying to cross the threshold, she felt the slight pressure of the strap around the upper part of her body, covered with a thin camisole. She took a step back and saw the rope that hung from the center of her back, which ran in a curved line starting at the floor boards and ending at one of the railing posts. Megan looked at the knot in the rope, ran her fingers over the straps, and finally sat down. In her small, warm head thoughts circled; short, simple questions, the way they were posed in the books her mother read to her from before she went to sleep sometimes. Where do fish sleep when they are tired? What does the sun do at night? She pulled on the leash. Can a girl turn into a dog the way a frog can turn into a prince? She still had all her fingers on her hands. Her feet had not turned into paws.

Megan looked over the place where the sun had extinguished everything: the stones, the potholes, the tire tracks. It was quiet. The chickens were dozing somewhere in the shadows, Sam had toddled off to the other end of the pasture where a few trees stood. Then, as if she had called to him, the dog appeared.

"Wellie," Megan said softly. She got up and walked a few paces toward the sun-drenched steps of the veranda, until the rope was stretched tight. The Border collie heard her, wagged his tail and wanted to come to her, but the chain attached to the wall of the barn was holding him back. He tugged at it and barked, and after a while he sat down despite the heat that covered the ground with a layer of shimmering air.

"Wellie," Megan said again, a little louder than before. The useless creature in the house began to cry again, and now Megan was crying too.

Part One

HEAT

1

The hull of the ship glistened, a dark animal that had settled on its side, an enormous, arched body swollen by the passing of time. A curved line of portholes ran along the side that faced the light, black, circular wounds framed by scabby rust. On the belly, under a furry coat of seaweed, bowed steel ribs corroded by salt. The swell was barely noticeable, the ocean a stage-set sea of gray cloth which reflected nothing, not even the clouds in the windless sky.

Tobey O'Flynn watched as the boat that had brought him to the island departed. He stood on the strip of dry grass between the shoreline and the gently rising embankment, and listened to the fading chug of the outboard motor. He had not let go of his suitcases during the entire journey and even now clasped the handles. In the distance he thought he could make out sea birds, tiny scissors opening and closing against a yellow horizon. A sense of desolation seized him so intensely that he had to smile. He closed his eyes and hummed the first bars of a song that had accompanied him since his departure. The evening finally brought coolness; his clothes loosened from his damp skin. Although his suitcases were heavy, he did not put them down; the strain in his arms reminded him vaguely of real pain. Tobey O'Flynn imagined himself to be a ship—his burning arms were the chains and the suitcases the anchors that were not allowed to touch the ground. Not yet.

After he had stood there that way for a while he opened his eyes, turned around and walked across the strip of sand, stones, and driftwood over to an elevated field; where dry grass rustled beneath his shoes. Palms and trees with eroded roots leaned toward the sea; the wind had pushed others inland. A worn trail wound its way through the blades of brown, knee-high grass and withered bushes. Soon a forest of smooth, slender trunks appeared. The forest was full of humming and chirping; beetles in flight bumped into leaves like drops of indecisive rain. Swarms of flies the size of pinheads hung like a quivering fabric in the air. When Tobey stood still, he heard a faint crackling and scratching under the leaves that covered the ground. He pushed the palm-sized leaves to the side with his shoe and saw centipedes and worms, as thin as thread. A crab disappeared backwards into a hole. While he walked, Tobey's suitcases struck against the trees. When he emerged from the forest, he raised his eyes. The light faded into gray, enough that the form of the moon had become faintly visible.

After the shipwreck on the shore, the first signs of civilization that Tobey encountered were gas cans and tires. They were lying in a shallow ditch at the edge of the path that continued the worn trail from the far side of the forest. In one of the cans there was a buzzing sound— bees or wasps were flying in and out. A metal sign with an illegible inscription hung on a crooked pole. The shining surface Tobey had taken for a water puddle proved to be a windshield overgrown with pale vines. Roots as thick as fingers grew high up the sides of a barrel; moss covered a tire. Nature worked slowly and silently, growing over the garbage, covering it with leaves: thousands of bright green blankets.

The ground under Tobey's shoes changed from sand to clay. In the tire ruts, where water had collected during the rainy season, the earth was dark and cracked. Trees stood on either side of the path, their leaves shimmering in countless shades of green despite the rapid onset of dusk. Grass grew between the tree trunks, beaten down by the wind that had blown in the night and subsided in the afternoon, the remnants of a storm over Indonesia. Continuing to stand, Tobey peered into the twilight of the tunnel where the path ended. He listened for sounds and heard chirping and a drawn-out humming, and far away, the sea, tossing the waves against the shore in a rhythm lulled by eternity.

The tunnel led to a clearing, a field covered with dry grass, where a corrugated metal shed loomed in front of the dark forest. A road paved with cracked concrete slabs led to the building. Where the clearing ended and the original vegetation was reclaiming the land, a tractor stood decomposing in the damp salty air. The façade of the shed seemed to glow weakly like a screen that had stored up the light of day; insects swirled in front of it. Moths floated slowly down out of the darkness, like heavy snowflakes, carried into the air again and again by a gust of wind that did not exist. Tobey put down his suitcases; his arms were burning. The melody was still circling incessantly through his brain. He was troubled for a moment by the thought that he did not carry a weapon with him, and then he picked up a stone and threw it against the corrugated iron.

The sky turned dark blue. The last glimmer of light, weak as a fire on a distant island, flowed into the sea behind the trees and vanished. Tobey had given up the attempt to open the enormous sliding door at the front of the shed and climbed in through one of the side windows. He had brought two flashlights with him and he aimed the beam of light from the larger one into every corner of the hall, revolving like a lighthouse. Crooked cabinets stood against one wall, their doors partially open. Work benches, open metal barrels, boxes, and parts of a car body were lined up along another wall. Under the roof there were birds' nests in the iron girders; splashes of their white excrement formed patterns on the raw boards of the floor below. At one spot in the gable there was a gaping hole through which Tobey could see the night sky. A woven basket that contained a handful of rusty nails was fastened to one of the ropes that were hanging from the crossbar of the roof. A refrigerator without a door stood on concrete blocks; empty bottles were piled in a corner, their glass tarnished by a brown, powdery dust.

Tobey pushed a work bench away from the wall a bit where the ants were climbing, wiped it with a rag until it was as clean as he could get it, and on top of it he spread out the insulated sleeping pad that had been lying flat as a folded road map in one of his two suitcases. The salesman at the outdoor shop in Manila had advised him to buy an enormous back-pack, but Tobey could not be argued out of the firm conviction that he would continue to carry his belongings in two suitcases. Even though he had only wanted to buy one mosquito net and a sleeping bag, he returned to the hotel an hour later with the sleeping pad, a gas cooker, dishes and pots, two flashlights, and a water purification kit. He had spread out everything he had carried with him from London onto the bed, separated out a down jacket, a pair of leather shoes, a flannel shirt and a towel, and then distributed the rest between the two suitcases. He gave the jacket, shirt, and shoes to the night porter, who seemed more puzzled than pleased about it. He had crumpled the towel and threw it out of the eighth floor window, just to watch it float down into the back courtyard.

Outside, two birds called to each other; the roof beams creaked almost inaudibly. Tobey unrolled his sleeping bag on the surface of the work-bench and regretted having chosen the insulated pad instead of the foam rubber mat, simply because the pad took up less space. It occurred to him that he might toss back and forth fitfully on the hard surface and fall off, but the idea of sleeping on the ground, where all kinds of creatures would no doubt be creeping around under the cover of darkness, seemed far more unpleasant. He assembled the cooker and used the smaller of the two the pots to heat some of the water he had carried along in two plastic bottles. While he waited, he ate salted peanuts from *Singapore Airlines* and listened to the sounds of the night. He thought about the knife, which he had held in his hand at the store and had ultimately put back, so that his luggage would not be even heavier. A knife would have been a wise purchase he now decided, as he listened intently to a faint scratching sound on the corrugated iron. On the other hand, he doubted that it was good for much as a weapon. In order to thrust the blade into the flesh of an attacker, you would have to approach him at arm's length; a distance that Tobey decided was far too close.

When the water boiled, he made himself a cup of precooked noodles and a cup of instant coffee. He could no longer hear the scratching sound, but now a fat beetle was droning throughout the hall and bumping from time to time against a wall. Tobey devoured the noodles ravenously; then he drank the coffee and ate a cookie from a package that had a picture of a Chinese dragon on it. He sat down on the workbench, took off his shoes and placed them by his feet, his head full of stories about scorpions that spent the night looking for a place to rest during the day. He rolled up his shirt and trousers and used the bundle as a pillow. The beetle, a small black helicopter, whirred above him. Perhaps it was looking for the hole in the roof, the way out into the open, where the wind was now beginning to blow.

He was tired, but he could not sleep. The men, whose boat he had arrived in, had warned him in their broken English about the island. One of them talked about lights that could sometimes be seen at night, of smugglers, Islamic extremists and pirates. The oldest of the three had said nothing at all. He had smoked black herbs rolled in newspaper and had simply regarded Tobey the way you look at someone who is doomed and knows it, and doesn't do anything to prevent his impending demise.

Tobey sat up and turned on his flashlight; within seconds the light attracted hundreds of small mosquitoes. It was quiet in the shelter; the beetle had either gone or was resting somewhere. Tobey considered hanging up his mosquito net, but the ceiling beams were high above and he had forgotten to bring rope. The old man crossed his mind again. No doubt he bestowed that look on anyone who was foolish enough to come on board his boat, that look with its cunning wisdom and then, at the blink of an eye, its dull ignorance. The fact that the man repeatedly and without apparent reason grinned or threw up his hands and muttered to himself, as if he was praying that he and his shabby boat would not go under, led you to suspect that he might be crazy, or drunk, or both. Perhaps the men had only wanted to intimidate him; they did not understand what business a pale young European had here, hundreds of miles from Manila and far away from the nearest acceptable hotel. They had been amazed and had joked about their strange passenger, might have even really been worried about his well-being; but they had still taken his money for the trip, and also the advance payment to ensure that they would pick him up again in three days.

Tobey slipped into his shoes, dug the toothbrush out of a suitcase and brushed his teeth. With half a cup of water he rinsed his mouth and drank the rest of the water right out of the pot, even though it was still warm. Suddenly he heard voices, and for a few seconds his heart stopped. He did not breath, did not move; then he became conscious of the glaring light in which he sat, and turned off the flashlight. The voices of two men, speaking Tagalog, came through the metal wall. One of the men called out his sentences in high, melodic tones, almost singing; occasionally the other growled back, deeply and without enthusiasm. Tobey did not budge. His heart pounded so loudly in his head that he was convinced the beating could be heard in the short moments of silence when neither of the two men said anything and the soft ground muffled the sound of their steps. He searched the floorboards for the iron bar that he had stumbled over a while ago and that seemed to be a suitable weapon—more suitable, anyhow, than a knife. The high voice came through the sheet metal from a few meters away; the growling voice was even closer, sounded even more bored than before. The two men moved

20

along the outer wall, slowly, while the insects fell silent and the trees interrupted their rustling and the silence was complete, disturbed only by the chatter of a man who was probably still half a child, the son of the one who growled. Father and son, Tobey thought, experiencing a momentary relief. But he remained seated and stared at the iron bar which lay just a few steps away from him. It was as long as an arm, four-sided, painted black, truly dangerous, but only in the hands of someone who wouldn't hesitate to bash a skull with it.

Eventually, the voices died away. After a while, the creaking and chirping of the insects started again; the beetle took off for a new flight and knocked into the metal wall. Tobey sat still for a few minutes, and then he crept to the window, picked up the iron bar, and looked out into the night. There was nothing more to be heard of the two men; the sounds of nature filled the air. Tiny flies swarmed around Tobey's face. One of them flew into his mouth and he spit it out, shaking his head. He crawled outside, stood there pressed against the wall there for a few breaths, listening and waiting until his eyes had become accustomed to the darkness. A walk around the shed one time would calm him down, he told himself, and started walking.

The last birds had abandoned their singing; only the metallic, gentle rise and fall from the hum of cicadas and crickets remained and, as if it were the echo of a single sound, the croaking of frogs from a pond somewhere among the trees. It seemed to take forever to go around the building; walking slowly with strained muscles was more exhausting than it would be if he had been running. He sat on a tree stump beside the window he had climbed from and pulled off his T-shirt. He thought about the powerful summer rains at home and about how his father, standing with the antiquated tractor in a half-mown field, had cursed the sudden change in the weather. He tried to remember the first snowfall of his life and a motorcycle ride in soaked clothes, but he failed. Bats glided by; their wings were quieter than the sound of the fans and the newspapers that the women used to cool themselves on Manila's public buses.

It was quiet and there was nothing more to be heard from the two men. Tobey guessed it was probably midnight. Although he felt severe fatigue in every limb, he rose. It took all his strength to pick up the iron bar, go back to the shed, and climb in through the window. He groped his way to the workbench and lay down. After a while, he heard the whirring of the beetle, and he was happy to know that he was not alone.

News from Megan

I saw Cait. She went into a supermarket, and I followed her. She seemed
smaller to me after all these years, but that is certainly because I have gotten taller. The supermarket was a huge shining palace, a temple filled with
bright objects. Music wafted above us. You would recognize the song,
even though it was an arrangement made for the bustling consumers lost
in reverie and traipsing through the aisles or rushing past the shelves. She
bought the usual stuff, you know, bread and wine and canned food and
hair spray, and threw everything into the shopping cart and went to the
checkout, where she bit her fingernails and looked so sad and lost, that
for a few seconds I felt sorry for her. I bet if you looked down at her
from above you would see the brown roots of her hair, roots from her
miserable past that grow back again and again. Maybe she wants to be
noticed by the men who go for blondes. By the way, I cut off my hair.
Mick Kavanagh would say I look like a guy, and maybe even Barry would
not think I'm beautiful anymore. Where are you, Tobey? Do you still play
the guitar? I went to an R E.M. concert; it was raining and we were soak-
ing wet and our feet sank into the earth. But I don't like so many people
in a mob; it scares me. There was pushing and shoving, and our bodies
wreaked. A cloud floated over the crowd in the floodlights. Maybe I will
see you on television at some point, standing on stage and playing a solo.
Your band will be called Otter Club or Boys on Booze, and the crowd
will sing along on the chorus, and a beautiful girl sitting on her boy-
friend's shoulders will lift her shirt and show you her breasts—just for

you. I will recognize you, Tobey, even if you look completely different now and you continue to change. Cait looked old and unhappy to me in the holy light of the supermarket, disappointed because the major events that she had expected in life haven't happened. But it probably only seems that way to me because that is exactly what I had wished for her: disappointment and unhappiness. In the parking lot she stood in the shadow of a billboard and smoked a cigarette, and when an airplane appeared in the sky she followed it with her eyes like a child. Then she threw the cigarette butt on the ground and crushed it carefully with her red high heels, as if the parking lot could catch fire, and loaded her purchases into the trunk of a car that was not fit for a blonde at all, not even a dyed one. I thought, at some point I will be a woman like that too, tired and slightly dazed and convinced that everything is only going to get worse. Half of her disappeared into the dark mouth of the trunk and then came out of it again; the sun was as large as the whole sky and for some reason this glove fell to the ground, a white cotton glove, and she didn't notice it, and got in and just sat there, as if she had forgotten how to start a car. I almost went over to her then. I wanted to pick up the glove and give it to her, through the open window, without saying a word and without removing my sunglasses. (A horse just passed by my window, a snow-white one!) I carried the glove around with me for a while, crumpled in my pocket. Sometimes, when I didn't care if I made a fool of myself, I slipped it on. It was dirty, full of stains, and there was a gaping hole in the ring finger. She probably used it when she had to change a tire, although I can't imagine that she has ever done such a thing herself. Do you remember how Dad built a bicycle for me? The frame made out of the guard rails from a road barrier; the handlebars from an old hay rake; the fenders out of rain gutters; the handles from a garden hose. He gathered the rest together from the junkyard: the wheels, the chain, and the pedals. He didn't care about getting his hands dirty. He had simply given it to me, just like that: not as a present for my tenth birthday; not on Christmas;

but right in the middle of the summer he placed it next to my bed, so in the morning I would think that I was still dreaming. But he never taught me how to ride a bicycle. You had to do that, little brother. You were also responsible for showing me how to climb a tree, and how to get back down again, how to steal chewing gum from Tesco's without getting caught, how to open a beer bottle with a coin and how to sit on a hill, letting the world go by and for once just keeping my mouth shut. Eventually, I lost the glove. Dad never wore gloves; his skin was rough and full of cracks where ferns and ivy grew. Why did she marry him? Just so I wasn't illegitimate when I was born? (The horse is back. You should see it—it's old Sam, returned in a white shroud, a radiant beauty!) Are you happy, Tobey? Do you remember when we drove to the sea, my very first time? I had a yellow straw hat on and sunglasses made of cardboard and tinted plastic film. Uncle Aidan brought us to Glenbeigh in his car and I filled a bucket with shells, as if I had to clear the whole beach of them. In the evening when I was lying in bed, I swallowed a snail shell, a tiny, fragile work of art, swirled like the ice cream that came out of a machine in the parking lot. I swallowed it because I knew that the shell would break or I would lose it at some point. For a second I noticed the taste of salt on my tongue; then it was all over: the feeling, the day on the beach, the summer. What's your favorite song? Do you miss me sometimes? Do you hate me for what I did? When I'm alone and everything is quiet around me, I hear you bleating my name through the house, across the yard, across a field. Then there is a terrible pang in my heart and I whisper: Toto . . . I had better stop before I start crying and writing stupid things. I am sending this letter to Barry, just like the other ones, and I hope that i t   r e a c h e s   y o u .

Who loves you?
Megan!

2

Tobey had hardly slept. His bones ached from lying on the hard work bench; something had stung him and the back of his left hand was swollen and it itched. At least it had grown a little cooler; a breeze swept over the island and was softly rustling the tree tops. As Tobey folded the sleeping pad, he wondered whether the two men were still in the area. He remembered the bright, untroubled voice of the young boy and the monotonous bass of the old man, and convinced himself that they were fishermen and would have left the island before sunrise and wouldn't return before dark, if at all. He put his suitcases in a cabinet, covered them with some of the tattered burlap sacks that were lying around, and pushed shut the lopsided cabinet doors that were hanging on their hinges. Then he picked up the iron bar and climbed out the window.

The sky was brighter in some places than in others, a freshly painted wall that was drying quickly. Tobey tilted his head back and looked up helplessly for a while. In Ireland, he had always known exactly how the weather would unfold, which clouds would bring rain and which of them would simply move inland over the hills, when the wind would remain harmless and when it would swell into a storm, whether you would have to endure the effects of a low pressure storm for one day or one week.

His mood fluctuated with the air pressure; something in his head reacted to meteorological changes with the precision of a highly developed instrument. Tobey knew twenty hours in advance when a storm front was approaching, felt the hail that fell on County Cork, and the snow that was accumulating on MacGillycuddy's Reeks. On bright blue afternoons he sometimes made a bet with his sister that in the evening a gale would break the brittle branches off the trees, and each time he was right. Under the astonished gaze of his friends he would hold a newspaper over his head seconds before the thick raindrops of a heavy shower fell from a storm in the supposedly clear sky. And he had secretly laughed at his father, who had taken off half of the barn roof after breakfast in order to mend it, even though it was going to be pouring buckets of rain before lunch.

But in this part of the world Tobey's instrument did not work. Here, he awoke in the mornings with the same dull feeling in his head that he had when he lay down in the evening. He was unable to make rhyme or reason out of the changing colors of the sky. He could make nothing of the ebb and flow of the wind, and he read the clouds the way a five-year old reads the alphabet.

The light made him squint. He rubbed his eyes and walked along the path toward the dark mouth of the shady grove. The animals that had enveloped the island with a carpet of sound during the night were completely quiet. Now and then a bird squawked, unhappy about Tobey's presence, or the humming of insect wings pierced the wall of leaves. Every other living thing seemed to be at rest, exhausted from the heat. Hardly any ray of sunshine struck the ground, which was soft and moist and gave off the sweet smell of decay.

Even before he reached the clearing, he heard the clucking of chickens. He stopped and listened, and for a moment he saw the farm and the house and the barn, and he saw Megan, scampering around among the poultry and singing songs. He heard the lilting slant of her voice, always slightly hoarse, and the high-pitched sound of the hens, false notes in a simple melody. Tobey's heart clenched and he could feel the tears rising. He leaned against one of the dark, smooth tree trunks and closed his eyes. He stood there like that for a while, breathing deeply in and out and waiting until the pressure in his chest subsided and Megan's singsong had died away.

Finally, he found himself at the end of the tunnel where light penetrated the dark green. A breeze caressed his face, barely strong enough to stir the outermost sun-drenched leaves. He stayed under the shelter of the trees and looked out across the surface of the dry earth, at the edges overgrown with tufts of grass where a handful of chickens scratched and pecked—brown, lean birds, each one covered with a light veil of dust. Their clucking sounded like soliloquies; monosyllabic complaints about the heat, the meager food supply, and life in general. Deeply rutted tire tracks cut across the clearing; they ended, about a hundred meters from Tobey, at a towering wooden pole, a tattered tree with dry, rust-red branches, crowned at the top with an antenna. Beside it stood a hut; the door and the windows were missing. There was an overturned chair in front of the shelter; a crooked fence disappeared under the grass and shrubs.

When nobody appeared after a few minutes, Tobey stepped out into the bright light, hurried across the clearing, and crouched beside the pole. He picked up a stone, threw it through one of the windows, and waited. He was thirsty, and thought of the water purification kit and the tablets that he had left behind in the shed. He was convinced that there was fresh water somewhere on the island. The frogs that he had heard croaking must live in a pond, or at least in a pool. According to the words of the salesman at the outdoors shop, and according to the instruction manual, you could extract drinking water even from a stagnant puddle, and Tobey had already seen several of those on the island—remnants of the last rainfall. At the thought of a cup of tea he swallowed, and his

28

parched throat ached.

The flock of chickens had discovered him. They fell silent and gathered together to inspect him more closely. After a short time in which they seemed to think over the danger, the animals returned to scratching at the soil to look for grass seeds and insects. They lapsed again into a monotonous cackling; a ragged bundle of muddy brown feathers, lamenting their fate in a bitter, mocking monologue of never-ending hiccups. Tobey listened to this for a while, and then threw a stone at them. Clucking, the chickens scattered and disappeared into the thicket, where they remained in silence while the dust settled on their heads.

Tobey clasped the iron bar in his fist and entered the hut, which was empty except for a few broken bottles, charred paper, and the back of the chair that was lying in the grass outside. Somebody had smeared the letters M, P, and P on one of the walls with earth or mud. Beneath the gable an abandoned wasp nest clung to one of the rough, arm-sized logs that supported the corrugated metal roof. Daylight penetrated the room through several holes that, Tobey presumed with a queasy feeling, were made by bullets. With his foot he shuffled apart the singed scraps of paper and the soot-covered shards of broken glass. A walnut-sized beetle ran across the floor boards, turned around after a half meter and burrowed itself back into the ash-heap from which it had fled. Tobey crouched down and tried to decipher the typewritten text on a small, half-burned piece of paper.

He heard the floor boards creak and was about to stand up, but then something hit his head and the floor scattered into a million pieces before his eyes and became a black hole into which he plunged deeper and deeper in an endless fall, until he finally hit the bottom and his body was flooded with immense warmth.

News from Megan

As a child I hated the night, Tobey. I wasn't about to lie in bed in my room and sleep while the world continued turning and millions of things happened without me. I could barely stand lying still in the dark, couldn't endure the sound of my own breathing, the beating of my heart, the faint creaking of the bed frame when I turned on my other side so I would finally be able to fall asleep. Now, night is my favorite time. When the rabble and the crowd outside subside and the awful noise dies away, I sit at the kitchen table and read. Almost all of the forty square meters of my apartment are filled with books; they are stacked along the walls up to the ceiling, lying on the window sills, on the kitchen cabinets, under the bed, between my clothes. Visitors would certainly get the impression that I was crazy, or at least very, very strange. But I don't have any visitors. I don't have any friends. I see a handful of people regularly, but none of them have been in my apartment. The only person who has entered it since I moved in is a fat little plumber. The poor guy had to repair the toilet and was rather confused when he entered the hall—a tunnel of books—which forced him to carry his tool box in front of his beer belly, because there wasn't any room on the left or right. He was so short that I could see the red spots dotting his bald head. He took short, waddling steps, and he didn't say a word, and it took no more than the sight of a bathtub filled with books for him to realize that he had entered the world of a madman. (Now, don't think I neglect my personal hygiene! I go to the public swimming pool every day, complete my fifty laps, and shower afterwards!) Through the bathroom window I could see the company logo on his van—a huge pipe wrench that had running legs as hand grips. I offered him a cup of tea, but he politely declined. Maybe he was afraid I would poison him and use his skin to make bindings for the books. He completed the repairs quickly and silently and then almost fled from the apartment. I left the bathroom window open all day to get rid of the man's smell. Until recently, I've been going to the Chinese restaurant on the corner twice a week, always in the early afternoon when there are hardly any guests seated at the five tables. The cook and the waitress came from Hungary; the only thing Asian about them is their wrist watches. They took over the bar from some real Chinese guy, who made enough money from the deal to set up a transportation company in Shanghai. That's what people here say, anyway. The food at the Golden Dragon wasn't anything special, but at least Nandor could make noodles or rice with vegetables and tofu that were okay. When she didn't have anything to do, Lilly—Liliana—sat at my table and talked to me. She was always drinking huge quantities of water because she had read in a women's magazine that Michelle Pfeiffer drinks three liters of water per day. She spoke in short phrases, which made everything sound somehow important. For example, she said: "Happy face when sad is easy. Leave cat in Szolnok is hard." (At first I thought that was a rough translation of a Hungarian proverb, but then I realized that she had to leave her cat behind in the town of Szolnok with her parents.) Lilly had a dream: she wanted to work at the Hotel InterContinental Park Lane as a waitress. Imagine, Tobey, a waitress who doesn't dream about being an actress or singer, or at least the owner of a restaurant, but hopes to continue to be a waitress, but simply, in what she sees, at another, better place. I went there once. For a while I just sat in the lobby and looked at those icy chambers of guarded opulence, that chic museum of antiquated rituals; I had to get back out into the air and the real world. A few days later when I went to eat at the Golden Dragon, there was a piece of paper

31

hanging on the door: *Not here anymore, because world evil.* (Wouldn't that be a great inscription for a grave stone?) Two men had attacked the restaurant, had stolen the day's receipts, and had beaten Nandor with a wooden bat. They hadn't done anything to Lilly; at least that's what it said in the local section of the newspaper. I've never seen the two of them again. The restaurant was sold or rented out. Now it's run by Romanians and it's called Shanghai. And so the circle closes. Sometimes I still think of going into the InterContinental, where Lilly might be working now, but I let it alone. Lilly and Nandor are also siblings; he's her big brother. Maybe you're in London, Tobey, only a few streets away from me, and we don't even know it. Perhaps you have looked for me in the telephone book, in vain. Maybe you miss me like I miss you, maybe not. And maybe you wonder why I'm telling you all this, why I'm telling you about Lilly and Nandor and about a small, fat plumber. While I'm writing to you, Tobey, we're sitting next to each other on the hill and we look at the clouds and the cars, the few that roll away like toys through the greenery and briefly flash when a ray of sunlight hits them. We eat the chocolate I got for my birthday, and I point to the chicken hawk that draws his circles around us. I am seven and you are five and a half, and I know that the raptor up there is at risk of extinction, and you know the price that can be obtained at the slaughterhouse for a full-grown cow. We are talking past each other, so we say sentences, formulas mumbled before falling asleep, which we believe hint at our future. We speak, so we know we're there. Far, far away rain drops glisten, and I tell you that they are thousands of herring falling on the fields and meadows, and you don't know whether you should believe me. We talk about the school and the kindergarten and what we've overheard on the street and on the radio, and Briona and Dad and dear God who is probably too busy to hear our foolish prayers. We never talk about Cait, as if we were keeping to an agreement. We're children, afflicted with the wisdom of adults. They call us the poor children of Seamus O'Flynn; behind our backs rages an up-

32

roar of whispers and rumors and lies. Cait has made us famous, because she is gone forever. The only one who's even more popular in the neighborhood is Briona, and Malcolm Carrick, who takes out his glass eye at the pub and lets it roll across the table when he's drunk. On our paltry mountain we're far away from the idiots and their stupid gossip. Up there, we couldn't care less about them. Sometimes we run home, because the sky over our heads has turned black and a wind has disheveled our beautiful sentences. We stumble down the hill, the clapping sound of fish in our ears, pelting to the earth behind us. I write to you so I am with you, Toto. Did I mention that I feel lonely sometimes?

There was this woman from the country,
who disappeared in the big city;
she loved to read,
but she had decomposed,
when, after weeks, they found her.

Who loves you?
Megan!

3

Tobey tried to open his eyes, but he couldn't. His eyelids felt like they weighed as much as he did; every single eyelash felt heavier than an arm. It seemed like there was a knife stuck in his skull and someone was tugging to pull it out. Flashes erupted on his retina, fireworks of immense pain. He lay on the ground, his arms strangely contorted. The steps that he thought he had heard were only the beating of his own heart and it almost made his head burst. He dozed off and sank into darkness, where images floated like pictures in deep water, blurred, their colors dull because there was no light. He was sitting in the boat with the old man; ahead of them there was an island in the mirror-smooth lake. They headed for the island without coming any closer. A woman stood on the bank, waving; her dress was white and her hair cut short. Tobey wanted to stand up and wave back, but he couldn't. The sky was empty except for a huge moon illuminated in the center by the energy at its core. The old man said something that Tobey didn't understand. The boat sailed on in the same old place and the woman waved, while the moon became a pale disk, then slowly faded away.

When Tobey came to again, he could open his eyes. If it had seemed like there was only a knife stuck in his head before, now there were thousands of needles, live wires, a random circuit of pricks and short, burning spasms. He tried to sit up and realized that his arms were twisted behind his back and his wrists were tied. His cheekbones, which had scraped against the crude wooden floor, hurt badly; his neck was stiff and burned with pain. He wondered where he was, and the only place that he could think of after a while was the wooden hut with the corrugated metal roof riddled with bullets. His wrists burned. He moved his numb fingers until they tingled, and then he rolled onto his back and looked up. The roof loomed above him, a blurry firmament full of bullet holes that sparkled like stars.

The realization that someone had knocked him down and tied him up almost made him burst out laughing. Instead, a groan came from his throat, and seconds later he was crying, overwhelmed by the thought that he was going to die. Outside, the sounds of animals rose toward the sky. A slight wind made the trees rustle.

When Tobey heard footsteps, his heart stopped beating for the length of a breath. He tossed around, tugging at his restraints, and felt the rope chafing the skin of his wrists. Someone seized him under the arms and dragged him across the floor boards. He squirmed; he tried to scream, but his mouth was dry—nothing more than a croak escaped his lips. He wasn't able to raise his head until he sat up and his back touched the wall. The man he saw was young. He wore sandals, wide black pants, and a dark vest with some words printed on it in faded letters that Tobey could not decipher. The man's narrow face was expressionless as he looked at Tobey. Tobey was still breathing violently; his head felt heavy and infinitely fragile, a thin-walled receptacle with an ocean sloshing around inside it. Where he was tied, his skin burned; the slightest movement hurt.

The man reached into the darkness behind him and took out a bottle of water. He uncapped it and put it to Tobey's lips. He had white, crooked teeth and had a sparse beard. Tobey struggled so hard to take the first sip that he choked and coughed, struggling for breath, his lungs full of nails. The man waited; his face remained motionless. Tobey finally drank half the bottle. His eyes became accustomed to the dim light and he saw the bag that lay on the ground. The man took some pita bread out of the bag and held it in front of Tobey's mouth. Tobey shook his head. The man put the bread back in the bag, sat down and looked at his opponent. Tobey guessed he was eighteen or twenty; his beard and the crooked teeth made him look older. His T-shirt was surprisingly clean. The white cursive script across the chest said BARNABY & PHELBS BOOKSHOP LONDON.

They looked at each other. A cricket chirped outside the hut; it sounded like a gentle wind blowing into a tiny metal whistle.

"What do you want?" Tobey said as calmly as possible. Pain trickled down the inside of his skull, a shudder and stinging that caused him to squint.

The man looked at him without moving. His close-cropped hair was black and smooth. He sported a dark, pea-sized birthmark under his right eye. He smelled of sweat and wood smoke.

"Do you speak English?"

In the Philippines, almost all the locals spoke English, some very good, others only a little. At a food stall in Manila, a man had taken a seat beside Tobey and introduced himself as an unemployed teacher, smiling and talkative and too excited to realize that Tobey wanted to be left alone so he could read the newspaper. Tobey had ordered the man some soup and a kebab—the same thing that he was eating. When the man suggested taking a tour of the neighborhood and a visit to a children's home, Tobey declined on the grounds that he had a business meeting. While the man, who was hardly able to hide the shame of his hunger with his desperate loquacity, spooned the soup, Tobey went into the restaurant, paid the bill, disappeared through a rear exit, and took a taxi back to the hotel.

"English?" Tobey repeated. But the man just stared at him with a facial expression that might have been apathetic, arrogant, or simply stupid.

The trilling of the insects was loud and drawn-out. Tobey wanted to scream, to shout at this stupidly staring fellow, but he had no air in his lungs. He closed his eyes. The back of his head struck the wall; something oozed down the muscles of his neck, trickled down his spine and dissolved.

Tobey opened his eyes and blinked at the brightness. His legs felt numb. He moved his feet. Only now did he realize that he was lying with the right side of his face against the ground. He thought about spiders and scorpions, and wanted to stretch out his arms and straighten up, but he could not, because his hands were tied behind his back. For a while he lay on his side, breathing in and out as evenly as possible, and then he began to roll away from the wall toward the door. When he stopped in the middle of the room to catch his breath he saw a piece of pita bread, teaming with ants. So he had not been dreaming, he thought: there really had been a man there. And he had brought him bread and water, had stared at him and then was gone again. And he would return. Tobey did not doubt that for a second. His shoulders hurt so much that tears filled his eyes, and he remained on his belly for a while and watched the ants, forming a faint red column, carrying away the bread crumb by crumb.

Megan had been able to sit anywhere for hours and watch animals. Once she spent four days in the barn, from early morning until late in the evening, just to make sure that she didn't miss the chicks hatching. She was six years old then and she already knew all about the wonders of nature, like the fact that frogs came from tadpoles and butterflies came from caterpillars; she could recognize birds of prey circling high in the sky by shape and some birds' eggs by their color and size. She followed the transformation of a caddis fly larva in a mason jar and the growth of amphipods and she regularly wrote down her findings in an exercise book that she illustrated with drawings and she read it at night in her room, out loud and with a solemn voice, as if she was speaking to a group of scientists and researchers.

How happy he would be just to hear one of her speeches now, thought Tobey. He would give his left leg, which he could no longer feel anyway, in order to listen to her report about the hunting behavior of the dwarf-eared bat, which had won her first prize in her school's science project in the category of nature and animals. Full of shame, he recalled how he had shot her subjects with a slingshot—three animals who slept on the barn wall under the gable roof, and how he had hit one of them and how it had fallen to the ground. The wings felt like the material lining the box where his mother used to keep her things from a happier time and that she had forgotten or left behind, as if the things in it had suddenly become worthless to her.

An ant crawled toward him and he blew it away. His tongue was dry in his mouth; when he tried to swallow, his ears popped. He rolled further, almost to the rectangle of light which fell through the door onto the dusty floor. Outside it was quiet, but perhaps, he thought, it was the pressure in his skull that kept him from hearing anything. The leaves of a palm tree swayed in the light wind; the sky shone blue and empty. Tobey was so moved by the sight and the fact that he was alive that he groaned loudly.

Whimpering, he rolled one last time on his axis toward the door opening. A breeze swept across his face. He rested in a prone position, wondering how long it would take him to roll himself back to the woods he had come through. He was calmed by the fact that the chickens did not show themselves; he did not need spectators. He breathed deeply; the air smelled of grass and heat. He turned on his side and looked at the sky with half-closed eyes. The meager antenna perched on the mast like a fish skeleton that someone might have mounted there as a joke.

Tobey now knew that Megan was not here. There was no one on this island except for the bearded child and the old man with the deep voice—possibly the maniac's father. Perhaps other men came at night, sleeping in one of the empty buildings. Everything Tobey had seen so far seemed to have been abandoned years ago. He believed that there were still research laboratories and a feudal villa somewhere, as the old professor in Manila had described to her, as little as he believed that there was a soul alive who was willing to help him. He had to free himself from his bonds, regain some of his strength and make his way to the beach. If he had not yet lost all sense of time from exhaustion and fear, tomorrow evening the men with the boat would surely be coming to pick him up. *Surely*, Tobey thought. The word was such a joke that he almost had to laugh.

Then he saw the ape. He was startled with a fierceness that ran through his body like an electric shock. It was a bonobo—Tobey knew that much, even if he *was* better versed with cows, cattle and sheep than with primates. The bonobo stepped out of the woods, moved across the open expanse and headed for the hut. When he saw Tobey, he stopped. Only now did Tobey see that he was wearing a pair of pants and a shirt—dark blue, like a uniform. He sat down and looked over. Because of the high grass Tobey could only make out the torso and head of the animal. He wanted to sit up, but he did not have the strength to do it. The bonobo raised his long, thin arm and hesitantly moved his hand back and forth and then suddenly he waved wildly, lowered his arm again and rested his chin on his hands in a thoughtful gesture.

Tobey pulled up his legs and struggled to his knees, but when he finally stood up straight, breathless and shaky, and looked across the lawn, the bonobo was gone. His shoulders ached; the grazed skin around his ankles and wrists itched. Far away birds flew through the matte blue of the sky, a long continuous line of shimmering points. But the bonobo was gone, as if it had never existed.

After he had rested a bit Tobey scampered back into the hut, pushed a piece of glass out of the ash heap with his foot, maneuvered it into a gap between two floorboards, wedged it there and lay down so that he could rub the ropes binding his feet along the edge of the broken glass. Again and again the shard broke and he had to push it back into the crack with the heel of his shoe. He was sweating; his whole body ached. He trembled at every sound that penetrated the hut from outside, and he did not move for several minutes. He imagined that Megan stroked her hand over his forehead and through his dirty hair. He was five years old and lay in bed for several days with summer flu. The window was open; rays of light, saturated with heat and dust, pressed through the curtain. Megan was sitting on a wooden stool singing her songs, and from time to time she wiped a damp strand of hair from his forehead. Her voice buzzed in his glowing skull like a beetle in a mason jar. "Mary had a little lamb, her father shot it dead. Now Mary's little lamb lies between two slices of bread." He bit off large chunks of the bread, filled his mouth with it and chewed greedily. The meat was juicy; the butter sweet. He ran across the field behind the house, throwing clumps of earth at the stupid, staring sheep, and he climbed onto the barn roof, to be even closer to the clouds. The first drops fell, as large and heavy as ripe cherries. Now the sky opened its gates, the patter on the corrugated iron became pandemonium and Tobey watched as the world sank, perished with everything that he hated. An enormous buzzard carried Megan away, and he himself was washed away from the barn roof into the sea, far away, through a night sparkling with stars and beyond the horizon, where he reached the beach of an unnamed island and Megan fell from the sky and landed in his arms and kissed him, in a way that no sister kisses her brother.

When the piece of broken glass came loose again and Tobey saw that the rope was still not even half worn through, he turned on his side, closed his eyes and tried not to cry. Megan had never cried. When an animal was slaughtered at the farm she ran up a hill and screamed her pain out into the world so loud that Feargal Walsh, whose farm was nearly two miles away, closed his windows and turned up the radio.

Her fingers fumbled over the rope that bound his wrists together, then stroked his sweat-soaked head. After a while Tobey calmed down. He swallowed back a sob and opened his eyes. This time he was not frightened when he saw the bonobo. The ape was sitting next to him and slowly withdrew his hand from Tobey's head. His legs, protruding from dark blue trousers, were bent; his knees touched the buttoned shirt made of the same material which covered his chest. He looked at Tobey, pursed his lips and made a noise, quiet and questioning. Finally he got up and walked away, standing upright like a man. Tobey wanted to shout after him and ask him to stay but no sound came out, and the ape walked on without looking back.

News from Megan

Have you ever been in a slaughterhouse, Tobey? I have. Since everything is very clean, you have to imagine a huge bathroom with green tiles. When they are delivered by the truck, the animals first come into a room that the boss calls Pig Heaven. At six o'clock in the morning it begins; it is winter and icy, and when the tailgate slams against the ramp the pigs squeal and roar and you are awake and cold to the bone. Then the hatch is opened, but there is only one way through it—along a barricade of metal poles into the waiting bay. The pigs are exhausted from the long drive through the cold, and they are frightened. In almost every load there are injured animals and if one of them is dead on arrival, you have to go into the trailer and examine the corpse. You write heart failure or circulatory collapse on your form. That's common. Sometimes the farmers shoo the animals through the hatch themselves, but usually the driver does it. Today his name is John and he is a nice guy, not too bright, but he gives you a cigarette and tells you about his children and the garage that he built, and the film he saw on Saturday. He has a piece of garden hose in his hand, about two meters long, which he uses to strike those pigs that are moving too slowly up the ramp. And he yells. You should hear him—you would never forget his voice, his voice and the cries of the animals and the trampling of hooves on the metal ramp—never in your life would you forget that. Sometimes John swears, when the animals at the front of the gangway stop. But mostly he does his job quietly, like everyone here, experienced and tired and bored and so jaded that when a sow slips between the tailgate and the ramp and injures a leg and falls down, he thrashes it on the head until the animal rises and limps along behind the others. It is not so long ago that the drivers had stun guns, but they are prohibited now. John regrets that, he says; now the work is as hard as it was before. But it keeps you warm, he says, laughing; and you laugh too, because after two days in here, you are no longer you, but someone in a dream, someone who watches pigs as they try to return to the hatch and at the same time jump against the barricade, where John is standing and swinging away at them. You watch them, because you must spend the first two weeks here, because you want to be a vet, because you have to do the internship, and because people eat meat. You make the first inspection on the ramp; you bend down over dead pigs and dying cows, you avoid the hooves of the bull that is kicking around in the box until Callum, Brian, or Dariusz puts the stun gun to its forehead and pulls the trigger. Outside is the world and everything you know; you walk past a school and a bookstore, and on a roadside bench sits a man who fondles his dog, and the next moment you enter this building and leave the world. You change your clothes; you are number 38; in your locker hangs a photograph of something beautiful. You walk through the bright hall wearing three layers of clothing and a white helmet and a white apron and rubber boots, and you're freezing. It's the limbo that swallows you up, the green tiled room where the arrival, the waiting, and the farewell all take place. The real hell is waiting for you in the next room. There they float in, hanging upside down by chains, some not yet dead, bellowing and legs flailing, and their blood flutters like a broad red ribbon in the room that was spotlessly clean in the morning, and in the evening the floor and walls are covered with the traces of slaughter, a film of blood and meat and fat and excrement. On your first day in hell you'll puke. That happens to almost everyone; you'll throw up in the hole where the men discard the waste, the jowls, and the genitals, and all the viscera except the heart and liver, lungs and tongue. On your first day you may still

43

be able to watch the animals as they're dismembered; how the hooves, horns, and ears are sliced off the cows, bulls, oxen, and calves; how their eyes are gorged out and thrown into the hole, how they're cut into two halves with enormous power saws that throw off water; and how the skin is pulled away from the body by the power of a machine which produces a raging, smacking noise, which you will perhaps get accustomed to, sometime, and which you will forget as little as John's laughing and cursing and shouting and the clack of hooves on the ramp and the stench of urine and blood and the shit that lands on your tongue and enters your skin and settles inside you forever. On your first day in hell you may see the veterinarian who is working today. His name is Trevor and he hates his job, which does not correspond at all with what he wanted to do once; but it's still better than the occasional weekend jobs at the horse track, where he usually waits in vain for an animal to collapse and he is not allowed to make a bet. He is unmarried and shows you vacation photos, and during breaks he goes outside with the others, even though he doesn't smoke, and he tells jokes, even though he can't. Trevor collects samples of flesh from the animals, to be examined for Trichinella in the laboratory on the upper floor. You have seen Trichinella during your studies, but in the four weeks that you work here you will see more than worms, injuries and ulcers. In these four weeks, that will seem like an eternity to you, you will see old, lean cows, waiting for their deaths patiently and with an empty look, and frightened calves hustled together into the waiting pen and jerking so violently with each crack of the bolt that a few of their thin little legs break and they drop to the concrete floor, which is smeared with excrement. You will see cattle and young bulls whose anesthesia failed, pulled up by the chain fully conscious and slit open; and you will see purgatory—a smelly, sooty chamber where the bristles are burned off the pigs that continue to slide into it in an endless procession. If you go outside to escape the noise and stench for a few minutes, you will see the smoke rising from the chimney, a frayed black lanyard that wafts over the place in bad weather and tinges the rain with gray. Then you will stay inside and sit on the floor in the dressing room so you don't smear the bench with blood, and you smoke a cigarette, even though it is forbidden, just to get rid of the taste in your mouth. You sit there and stare at the wall and you see the cow in front of you, hanging from the ceiling, whose belly is slit open, and a fetus slips out and claps to the floor, as small as a cat, bright, almost transparent, eyes closed, peaceful, as if it was blessed never to have been born into this world. And when it's time you put out the cigarette on your skin, get up, and go back. Again and again you go back. Why am I writing this to you, Tobey? So perhaps you will understand what I still have to tell you.

Who loves you?
Megan!

4

Tobey didn't want to die. He didn't want to die of thirst while he was bound hand and foot, or be killed by the bearded child. He wanted to find Megan, or another trail that would lead to her. In the ashes he found a large piece of broken glass which he jammed into a crack between two floor boards. Again he tried to cut the rope that bound his feet together. Again and again he raised his head and looked through the doorway, but the bonobo did not appear. Flies, so small that their wings produced no audible hum, buzzed around him. It was hot; he was sweating and he knew that he would faint again if he did not drink something soon. Mechanically he moved his legs. His body seemed to have lost the ability to feel pain.

He imagined that he was dead and being eaten by animals, rats and birds, ants, grubs and worms. Perhaps the bonobo would come and take his pants and T-shirt. The idea of lying there in his underwear was disagreeable to him, then it made him panic. As if in a never-ending bad dream, he moved his legs back and forth. His bones shone through the skin; he could see his skeleton under the ridiculously thin layer. Thread by thread the rope came loose and when it split in two Tobey had to control himself to keep from crying. He lay there and felt his heart beating; a rattling sound rose from his throat. The blood on his ankles had dried. Flies sat there, but he did not have the power to scare them away. One final, low note from Megan's sing-song circled in his head and died away.

Finally Tobey stood up, tumbled, and continued to lie on his stomach for several minutes. It was only on his third attempt that he was able to keep standing. He walked a few steps, slowly and uncertainly, and went outside. The sky had given up its brightness; everything was lost in vagueness: the colors, the shapes, and the shadows. Tobey leaned against the wall and looked at the opening that led into the forest. It seemed to be infinitely far away. He waited until a little feeling came back to his legs, and then he walked a few steps across the clearing. Again and again he stumbled and fell, rested for a while, got up and staggered on. His shoulder blades burned like fire, but he no longer felt the hands on his back. In the shed he would try to chafe through the rope on the edge of a sheet of corrugated iron. As soon as his hands were free he would take the water purification kit to a pond, make tea, and eat some cookies. The thought made him move faster, but he stumbled and fell again. Panting and with his eyes closed, he lie there and saw the cookie box in front of him, with a dragon that was spewing the name of the manufacturer from its mouth in a corrugated flame.

Tobey crawled across the last few meters of the clearing, his ears filled with the clucking of chickens that had come to make fun of him. When he turned he did not see any chickens, and he wondered whether or not he was slowly going crazy. Maybe there wasn't even an ape, he thought, as he pushed his upper body into the twilight of the tunnel. Perhaps his brain had responded to dehydration and hypoglycemia with hoaxes, producing images and sounds that it had once stored. He tried to remember when and on what occasion he had seen a bonobo in blue clothes, but soon he gave up.

It was cool and dark in the tunnel. For a while he rested, breathing in the musty air, hoping to draw enough strength to move on. The song came to him again. How simple the melody, he thought, how calm and almost monotonous and barely building up at the end, circling calmly and supporting itself like a buzzard in the perfect thermals of a summer day.

When he woke up and felt how the pain had returned to his body, he could not say whether he had slept for a few minutes or for several hours, and he did not know how he had gotten into the shed. His hands were still tied. He could dimly remember leaning his upper body into the window opening and letting himself fall in. Then he had picked himself up and seen the empty bench and the open cabinet doors. Someone had been here and had taken his belongings, the water purification kit, the sleeping bag, the stove—everything. The two suitcases were gone and with them Megan's letters, only copies, yet the most valuable thing he owned. Incapable of understanding the consequences of this loss because of exhaustion, he had lain down on the bench and had fallen asleep.

Now he was reasonably awake and he forced himself to think. If it wasn't for the fact that he was so weak, he could cut through the rope around his wrists. He knew that a person could survive two or three days without water and then either lost consciousness or became such a lunatic that he drank salt water and died even more quickly. If he were to lie in the grass under the protection of the large cliff near the beach, doing nothing, and just wait for the three men who had promised to pick him up, he might have a chance to leave the island alive, he thought, amazed at how calmly, almost indifferently, he contemplated his possible death. He imagined that he dug a hole in the sand and covered himself with grass and leaves. To make sure that he did not fall asleep and miss the arrival of the boat, he would think about the contents of Megan's letters and silently recite the lyrics of songs from his former band. He would count the stars, beginning over again and again, and prick himself in the skin with a thorn every few minutes. Until he heard the chugging of the engine he would not move, hidden under the grass and the leaves, concealed from the guy who had knocked him down and tied him up and maybe even searched the island for him in order to kill him.

He would turn his back on the last trail that led to Megan, the last evidence of her destiny, to save his own life and spend the rest of it trying to repent for his failure. For several years he would wait for a letter from his sister and eventually forget that he was waiting. After a lapse of time determined by the law, a preposterous civil servant would deliver a form for him to sign, which would indicate that he accepted the death of Megan O'Flynn. There would be a funeral, and he wondered if they would put a coffin in the ground, and if so, whether you were supposed to put something inside it—something that belonged to Megan; her letters, maybe.

He thought about his father's funeral. He, the priest, and old, bloated Feargal Walsh, more dead than alive as he stood beside the open grave, had been the only people in the cemetery. After the clergyman's words a huge rain had fallen, which Tobey had failed to predict. Feargal Walsh cried, because he was drunk in the afternoon; because things had taken a disastrous turn; because he was left alone. Tobey remembered slipping money to his former neighbor at the cemetery gate so he could go drinking without him, and how Feargal had looked at him in stupid amazement, his eyes blank and red with despair and the unbridled howl at the grave that had even irritated Father MacMahon.

The wound on the back of Tobey's head throbbed. He turned on his side and looked out the window. It was still light outside. Here and there an insect began to stir the silence, and an emerging wind rustled the trees. The distant hum of the tractor mingled with the sound of Wellie's barking and the radio in the kitchen, which played until his father entered the house. Tobey sank into his bed, grew heavy and sank deeper, then tumbled, with open eyes and outstretched arms, over the stars, which became smaller and finally disappeared, while the radio played its song and everything grew ever brighter and at some point so white and empty and aching that he had to close his eyes.

News from Megan

Do you know me, Tobey? Do you know who I am? You'd be surprised if I told you certain things, little Toto. Some of it would certainly surprise and frighten you. For example, I wanted to kill Feargal Walsh, our fat, stupid neighbor Feargal, who groped my breasts more than once during hay season with his greasy hands, beat his dog when he was drunk, and burned his rubbish in a hole behind the house. Do you remember how he fell from a ladder and broke his foot? I sawed off the top rung. And guess who replaced the planks over the cesspool with rotten ones? Do you still remember how he had no other topic of conversation for weeks but those boards? He probably asks himself to this very day, how the wood could rot so fast. He didn't fall in—his wheelbarrow saved his miserable life. Now I'm glad that I didn't succeed, but then I had only one thing in mind the whole summer: How do I kill this motherfucker and make it look like an accident? Surely you haven't forgotten the night his kitchen caught on fire and the fire department came flying down the road from Killorglin to prevent the worst. I started the fire. First I let the dog off the chain, mistreated Jack, who wasn't about to leave my side that night and who I had to run away from, back to my bed, past your room, empty, because you, with Jason and Mick and Barry were hanging out and only sobered up when you heard the wailing of the sirens and drove to the Walsh Farm, where everything was long over by the time you arrived, and where Feargal sat half-naked on a chair in front of the house and yelled at the firemen, because they had drenched his kitchen with water, until they disappeared without helping clean up or leaving anyone behind to keep an eye on the fire. At least that's what you told me the next day, anyway. Do you remember? Are you shocked now, Toto? Do you recognize me now, little brother? But I'm not evil, not bad. I have a strong sense of justice—my justice. At the time I was fifteen. Feargal had to die for his actions, that was my sentence, and I didn't have the slightest doubt that I was right. I was judge and executioner; I was a goddess. Were you ever afraid of me, Tobey, I mean, really afraid? When I locked you up in the closet for an entire day, because you threw the crow's nest with the eggs out of the tree. Did you think I would leave you to starve and rot in the closet? Or when you ravaged my pet cemetery, did you believe I would pierce your black heart and bury you next to the raccoon and the rat? Was it hard to have me as a big sister, as we grew older and we withdrew year after year more and more into our own worlds? When we stopped, to climb the hill and watch the clouds together as they crossed the sea, to flood Ireland and to bathe England, and we only said the bare minimum to each other, until we finally fell almost completely silent when we saw ourselves. You, so full of contempt for your life and the farm and Seamus, and at the same time already disappointed with your future, which had not even begun yet, so naive and backwoods and foolishly rebellious, so broken and tired, a master of the weather forecast, no good at guessing anybody's inner feelings. I… What was I, Tobey? The oddball, who talked to the animals, sitting in trees and admiring the architecture of the leaves; who knew every frog in the pond, and none of her classmates; who disappeared in books all night long, and for days in drawings; who wanted to know everything about salamanders and nothing about her mother? Who had lost people, was lost to the world, taciturn and stubborn, but in her secret notebooks eloquent, full of overwhelming love and the deepest, bewildering hate, lonely, wavering in her defiant happiness? Is that me, Tobey? Do you see me that way? What I would give for an afternoon on that hill, one hour! The sun shines on our heads and warms our words before we utter them. Sam is standing next to us, chewing thoughtfully on grass and waiting to grow wings. I tell you where I was during all those years and you listen, and sometimes if I refer to something bad, a cloud hovers over us, and Sam shakes his head sadly. The world is spinning; we can feel it. Our fingers grow into one another through the grass. We are a family tree with two trunks, our crests are glittering galaxies. Your stars shine blue, mine red.

Who loves you?
Megan!

5

The pain was gone. He lay there and felt neither the exposed patches on his ankles and wrists nor the wounds on his neck. His body was light; he floated. The radio in the kitchen had stopped playing; silence filled his head. Consciousness seeped into it, warm light, the smell of soap, the feel of fabric on his skin. There was an emergence and a descent, a gentle rocking in a stream of light and darkness. In the dream he was swimming back and forth between deep sleep and an idea of wakefulness. His fingers twitched.

"Tobey?" The voice glowed in his head, yellow, a warm lantern, and then went out.

He swam faster; his legs kicked. When his head thrust into the dawning light, he ripped open his mouth and filled his lungs with air. A sound escaped his chest. It seemed strange to him, like the sound of an animal.

"Are you awake?" asked a voice that did not belong to Megan.

Tobey closed his eyes and opened them again. He blinked. He saw a wall, a hazy, light-grey surface. A face appeared.

"Welcome!"

A good word, Tobey thought, after he was reasonably sure that he had really heard it. It meant something amicable he said to himself, it expressed the opposite of hostility. Then he remembered his feeling of despondency, the shackles and the pain, and the word took on something wrong, something cynical. Welcome to our violence. Welcome to the place of your death.

He straightened up. The room went black for a few seconds and then turned into a pale vault with warped walls, without contour or depth. Tobey sank back; the ceiling above him flickered—murky water, churned by iridescent, deceptive fish. He was no longer swimming. He went under, abandoned the stratum of cloudy gray, and sank into the blackness. Prickly stars and glowing planets floated in his blood. While drifting down he saw a few bright, dirty spots above him, the bellies of islands, rain clouds, then he reached the ground where a shallow pit in the shape of his body was waiting for him.

The next time, Tobey stayed awake. He lay there for a while with his closed eyes and waited for the voice. Since it was still quiet, he opened his eyes. The room in which he found himself was the size of a prison cell. A fluorescent bulb, recessed in the low concrete ceiling and protected by a grate, gave off a light so weak that it got lost on the way to the floor. Except for the metal cot covered with a white sheet, a small table and chair and a bureau, the room was empty. Tobey sat up. Someone had treated his wounds; bandages decorated his ankles and wrists. He moved his stiff fingers, touched the wound on the back of his head and felt stubble, gauze and tape. He could not feel the sharp pain in his head anymore, and he was not thirsty. A band-aid was stuck on the crook of his left arm; under the bandage the red puncture hole from a needle was visible.

Tobey slipped gently from the bed, and when he realized that his legs could carry him, he went to the bureau and opened the three drawers, only to find that they were empty. He searched the floor and the walls of the room and did not even find a light switch. Behind the glass window in the steel door there was only darkness. Water dripped from a barred opening in the ceiling the size of a saucer, and when Tobey held his breath he believed he could hear the sound of falling rain. For a while he listened to the muffled drums, and it wasn't until it occurred to him that he might never be able to escape this hole and feel the rain on his skin, that anxiety seized him. He closed his eyes, took a few deep breaths and calmed down. If they wanted to kill him, he thought, as he grew more and more awake, they would have hardly taken the time to doctor him. He remembered the voice and the word, which he did not wish to think he had only dreamed. *Welcome.*

He felt rested and wondered, suddenly alarmed, how long he might have slept. Perhaps the boat had come, and the men had been waiting for him beside the ship wreck. He saw the three of them crouching in the sand, smoking cigarettes and puzzling over his fate. He imagined how they sailed away, shaking their heads, perhaps even sad, confirmed in their dark forebodings. He hammered on the door until the skin of his fists threatened to crack, and he cried; his lips touched the glass, but what came out of his lungs, his throat, was only a hoarse croak, painful, as if he coughed up tiny shards.

He sat on the floor, clasped his bent legs with his arms and laid his head down on them. He would have liked to have Megan's letters with him. He would have read individual sentences again and again; read again and again the section where she swallowed the shell.

When the door was unlocked, Tobey remained seated. He saw brown feet in sandals coming toward him, white trousers which were spotted with splashes of mud on the hem, an orange-colored shirt hanging over his hips, and brown hands, as small as a woman's.

"How are you?"

Tobey raised his head. The man smiled, his teeth shining in his dark face. He had a bald head—a mirror-smooth surface, encircled by a wreath of short black hair.

"Can you get up?" The man stretched out an arm.

Only now did Tobey see the other two men who stood at the door, Filipinos, the one forty or fifty, the other one young, twenty at most. The younger man, who was barefoot and wore shorts and a yellow vest, cast furtive glances at him. Tobey thought of the voices he had heard on the first night, the grumpy one and the easygoing one, father and son.

"Who are you?" Tobey asked.

The first man laughed. "Oh, if I only knew," he said, lowering his head for a moment and shaking it. Then he looked at Tobey again. "Excuse me." He cleared his throat and his face grew more serious, without losing the childlike, cheerful look completely. "I know your question wasn't meant philosophically."

Tobey stared at the man. Indian, he supposed, sixty years old, maybe a little older. He did not seem threatening, but considerate, and the fact that his English was perfect, despite rolling Rs and a pleasantly un-British melody, calmed Tobey a bit.

"Tanvir Raihan," said the man and smiled when Tobey ignored his outstretched hand. "A few years ago I would have introduced myself as a doctor, but those days of vanity and labels are over."

"What do you want from me?"

"Oh, nothing." All that Tobey said seemed to cheer Tanvir.

"The question is probably more: What do *you* want on this island?"

"Where is the fellow who struck me down?"

"Nowhere in the vicinity."

"How long have I been lying here?"

"Half the night and almost a day."

Tobey thought. The first night he had slept in the metal shed, spent the second tied up in the wooden hut, and the third in the metal shed and then here. Today had to be his third day on the island. A jolt went through him. "What time is it?" He said, getting up hastily.

Tanvir laughed out loud. Then he held out both of his forearms to Tobey. "My days of measuring time are over."

When Tobey stood up, everything grew black before his eyes. He leaned his hands on the couch.

"Is everything okay?" Tanvir asked.

"Is it morning already?"

Tanvir giggled. "Do you always answer a question with another question?"

Tobey went to the door and was about to enter the dark hallway, but the older of the two Filipinos stood in his way. He wore a faded red T-shirt and long, light brown pants, and sneakers on his feet. He looked over Tobey's shoulder at Tanvir, as if he expected instructions about what to do now. The man was half a head shorter and twenty pounds heavier. Tobey thought about shoving him and running away, but he did not move. He felt dizzy, and in the gloomy hall, he probably would have gone no more than ten yards.

"Where are you going?" asked Tanvir, who had stepped behind Tobey.

"Away," said Tobey.

"But where? And how?"

"I'm going to be picked up. By a boat."

"Who is going to pick you up?"

Tobey said no more. Perhaps he had already revealed too much, he thought. He thought feverishly about what exactly it was that he had arranged with the youngest of the three men, who knew some English, whether they should pick him up on the evening of the third day or at the end of three full days, thus on the fourth day—today—and whether they had understood that he would be waiting next to the wreck on the beach in the evening and not in the morning. He had described a sunset with his hand and had drawn a sun dial in the sand, because days before his watch had been stolen in broad daylight in the bathroom of a bar in Manila. He should have drawn an arrow, he thought, beside the sinking sun, pointing to the horizon. He believed he remembered that all three were wearing watches, and he grew sick with anger at his failure to arrange a date with them.

"You must be hungry," Tanvir said. "And thirsty."

Tobey shook his head, but he didn't resist when the older of the Filipinos took him by the arm and led him slowly down the hall. He heard the sound of their footsteps on the concrete floor, from which rose a cool, earthy smell. From the corner of his eye he saw doors, all closed. After a few meters, the corridor became a dark tunnel of corrugated iron. Water flowed down the walls and disappeared into storm drains. When they came to a staircase, the younger man also linked arms with Tobey and helped him up and through an open hatch into the open. Tanvir came up last, closed the hatch cover and closed it off. The elderly Filipino let go of Tobey and camouflaged the entrance carefully with earth, leaves and twigs. Tobey blinked into the light and saw trees in front of him—thin, bright trunks—and beyond them the pale sky. A gust of wind swept over him, and he inhaled the fresh air deep into his lungs.

After they had walked a few meters between the trees, it became clear to Tobey that they were at the foot of a low hill. For a few seconds he thought he saw the sea between the trees. Again he was seized with fright at the thought that the men might at this moment be pulling their boat to shore and sitting down to wait for him. He wrenched himself from the young man's grip and started to run, but after a few steps he stumbled and fell. Because he did not have the strength in his arms to break his fall, he hit his chin on the ground, which had become wet and slippery from the rain. He felt his teeth dig into the flesh of his tongue, and heard the muffled sound of one jawbone striking the other. Water filled his eyes, and he tasted his own blood in his mouth. Then he was taken by both arms and raised to his feet.

"Where are you going?" Tanvir asked, half amused and half annoyed. "And how? By swimming?"

Tobey did not answer. Tears ran down his face, his tongue throbbed to the frantic pulse of his heart beat.

The two Filipinos were standing beside Tanvir, the younger one help-less and embarrassed, the elder tense and ready to tackle Tobey.

"I propose the following," Tanvir said quietly. "We're now getting to a place where I can doctor you and find you something to eat and drink. When you have rested and you are able to suppress the thought of escape for a moment, you can even tell me why you're on this island, who brought you here and how you imagine you'll make your return journey."

Tanvir waited a moment, and when Tobey didn't lift his head and still did not answer him, the two Filipinos seized his arms, one on either side, and marched off. Occasionally, a bird squawked and flew up fluttering through the leafy branches; small animals rustled in the undergrowth, invisible. There did not seem to be a road, not even a path. Tobey made no effort to keep from falling. He moved his legs, but he relied on the two Filipinos, who supported him and caught him when he slipped on the wet leaves. He trotted between them, his chin on his chest, their breathing in his ears, their smell in his nose, and with every step he made, with every minute that passed, he grew more indifferent to what awaited him. He would not make it to the men with the boat, even if today really was the day that they were coming to pick him up. Almost imperceptibly the light disappeared; there was no sun which could set. A sound that reached his ears from far away might be the chugging of a boat engine or the dull croaking from a frog pond. He told himself that he didn't care. With half-closed eyes he silently repeated that it didn't matter to him anymore.

They reached a plain covered with waist-deep grass and shrubs and stopped to wait for Tanvir, who had paused to shake the stones out of his sandals and had been left behind. The grass waved in the wind. Butterflies hovered over it, dove into the waves of straw or rose high and flew away. The young man let go of Tobey's arm and wiped the sweat from his forehead on his vest, but the old one held his prisoner firmly by the wrist and only loosened his grip a little. The sky was clear above them; there was not even a dash of yellow or red on the horizon. Tobey looked back at the hill that had not seemed very high to him; yet he was surprised that he had not noticed it.

When Tanvir had rejoined them, the young Filipino quickly took Tobey's arm. Tanvir shooed flies from his face, covered with a thin film of sweat. "Soon we'll be there," he said, and went ahead.

News from Megan

I don't have any more books, Tobey. I packed them into boxes and hauled them to the junk shop and sold them. A few of them were worth something; the value of the rest was calculated by the kilo. Then I did the same thing with my furniture and clothes and shoes. I pawned my radio and the toaster and all of the pots and pans and dishes. (Actually, the only thing I kept was your ring, and whatever I could fit into a duffel bag.) I watered my plants for the last time and put them in the backyard. I saw my landlord for the second time, as he walked through the empty apartment and recorded every spot on the walls and every scratch on the doors onto a list. For the first time in my life I have no place to stay. Isn't that great? (More later).

Who loves you?
Megan!

6

The first building Tobey saw was a wooden house, green-painted, with a gable roof made of corrugated iron. The house looked dilapidated: the walls were missing several boards, a rain gutter was hanging loose, and one of the windows had been replaced by a sheet of plywood. Beside the house was a dead straight path lined with stone, leading to a sandy spot. At one of the long sides of the clearing, the length of a football field, there was a tin hut; on the left front side there was a house whose walls had no plaster. The hut, like the other buildings that Tobey saw, was supported on concrete pillars. It was about waist high from the ground, a protective measure against floods and rats, Tobey suspected. On the roof there was a white water tank; next to the building he saw the remains of solar panels lying in the grass. Light penetrated through a few of the windows.

"Welcome to the island's capital," Tanvir cried. He turned around to face Tobey and stretched out his arms.

Tobey was silent. He looked into the night sky, which seemed to be swarming with nothing but moths and bats—a space without distance and without stars.

"Not exactly vibrant, I know," said Tanvir. He lowered his arms. "I hope dinner will be a little consolation for the disappointment." He walked across the square toward the hut. Insects flickered in the lighted windows.

Tobey, still flanked by the two Filipinos, followed him. The room they entered a little later was about ten by ten meters high and the air inside was cool, stirred by four whirring ceiling fans. The light came from a number of fluorescent tubes and landed on a floor made of rough boards, on a long table with eight chairs, on a doorless cupboard full of dishes, and on a red upholstered chair that was pitted with holes. Shelves full of cans, bottles and jars lined the walls; between two refrigerators stood a stove; food steamed in pans and pots. Tanvir settled in the chair, took off his shoes, and motioned for Tobey to sit on one of the chairs.

Tobey had barely taken his seat when he was overcome with an unspeakable weariness. He could only keep his eyes open with effort and rested his arms on the table in order to keep from falling out of the chair. The elderly Filipino took a jug from one of the refrigerators and filled four glasses with water. Tanvir picked up his glass and he was about to start a toast, but when he saw that Tobey was already drinking greedily, he simply grinned and also emptied his glass in one swallow.

Tobey could feel the cold water spread through his body, how it flowed into his stomach and how the pain behind his temples throbbed a little less. His tongue had now become a dead lump that lay swollen and numb in his mouth. He heard Tanvir and the Filipinos talking, all three in a rudimentary English. From time to time a word emerged that Tobey took to be Tagalog. His head was about to sink onto the table when a woman stepped through the door, a Filipina, large and stout, with an ape at each hand. One animal was a bonobo that wore a uniform-like suit made of light blue fabric; the other was a chimpanzee in long green pants and an orange T-shirt. Tobey was suddenly wide awake. He rubbed his eyes and stared at the trio with his mouth open, but he only realized what he was doing when Tanvir laughed.

"Tobey, may I introduce you to Rosalinda? She is the heart and soul of this place and she's also responsible for our well-being."

Rosalinda, who wore a wide, sleeveless dress in a flower-patterned fabric, a similar, colorful headband and plastic sandals on her feet, regarded Tobey with a look that contained surprise and suspicion.

"The two men at her side are Montgomery and Chester."

For a few seconds the chimpanzee twisted his lips into a grin that exposed crooked teeth and bright red, spotted gums, and then he looked at Tobey as trustingly and naively as before. The bonobo let go of Rosalinda's hand, made a few small steps toward Tobey, and held out his arm.

"Montgomery attaches great importance to good behavior," Tanvir said.

Tobey got up, confused, also extended his right arm and shook the hand of the great ape, who looked into his eyes and nodded his head.

Rosalinda had now gone to the stove, stirring the pots while Chester sat near her and held the hem of her skirt with two fingers. Montgomery took the jug of water from the countertop next to the refrigerator, filled two glasses and handed one of them to Tobey.

"Thank you," Tobey murmured.

Montgomery discreetly toasted everyone, sipped his glass and then sat on one of the chairs at the end of the table, as if he didn't want to bother anyone anymore, or simply wanted to be left alone. Tobey was completely astonished, but to the others scenes like this seemed to be part of everyday life. Tanvir wrote something in a small notebook; the two Filipinos set the table, and Rosalinda was busy at the stove. Tobey watched Montgomery from the corner of his eye and would not have been surprised if the bonobo had lit a cigarette and read the newspaper. But he just sat there quietly and slowly unbuttoned his jacket, like a tired museum guard at the end of the workday. Tobey almost nodded off. At some point the food appeared on the table. Rosalinda, who sat between Chester and Tanvir, folded her hands, lowered her head, and said a prayer. Tobey looked around and he could not believe his eyes: everyone, including Montgomery and Chester, seemed to be praying. Chester sat with his back bent, pursed his lips and closed his eyes. A white paper napkin hung around his neck, attached to a string with clothespins. Rosalinda's mealtime prayer was long, and although Tobey didn't understand a word of it, he found it theatrical and full of childlike eagerness. After Rosalinda had grown silent and the two Filipinos had muttered an "Amen" and crossed themselves, Tanvir commenced to speak, something that was short and unemotional and sounded more like a report than a "please" or a "thank you". Then everything was quiet, and Tobey, whose eyes were heavy with fatigue and whose chin had dropped to his chest, looked up and saw six pairs of eyes fixed on him. His dangling arms seemed to weigh tons and he hurried to fold his hands and put them on the table. Rosalinda raised an eyebrow and exhaled noisily.

"Only if you want to," said Tanvir.

Tobey felt a spasm in his bowels. He was six years old, sitting at the table with his father and listening to him speak to God, as he began to rebuke Him, as he lamented with Him and haggled, as he threatened Him. And he heard Megan, sitting on the hill behind the house and crying her heart out, because one of her animals had been slaughtered again, and was now being served on their plates as boiled meat.

"I'd rather not," he said and cleared his throat sheepishly. He had not heard his own voice. "I'd rather not," he repeated a little louder.

"Maybe some other time." Tanvir took a bowl of rice and began to fill his plate and Tobey's.

This was the signal for the others to help themselves as well. The two Filipinos grabbed quickly and concentrated on the meal, and Rosalinda ensured that Chester received something and that the dishes were passed to Montgomery, who sat at the end of the table and waited patiently until it was his turn.

No one spoke during the meal, with only Sam emitting an occasional groan of satisfaction. There was rice, vegetables and chicken and flat bread. Everyone drank ice cold water with ginger. Chester ate with a spoon; Montgomery, whose plate had no chicken, ate with a knife and a fork. Tobey had trouble chewing. His tongue hurt again and got in the way; swollen and numb, it seemed to fill his entire mouth. But he was hungry. He rinsed each bite down with water, and managed to finish the whole plate. The hope that he would not be killed seemed to grow more likely each minute, and he relaxed a little. *Maybe some other time.* The sentence reverberated in Tobey; it sounded like a guarantee for the future.

Later, Tanvir went with Tobey by the light of a kerosene lamp to the infirmary at the other end of the barracks. It consisted of a room with two cots and a doorless storage closet full of boxes, blankets, stretchers and crutches. He gave Tobey a disinfectant solution for rinsing to reduce the inflammation of his tongue, a bottle of mineral water and half a dozen pain pills and sleeping tablets that he counted out into an empty matchbox. He dabbed Tobey's wounds with an alcohol solution, changed the bandages, and stuck fresh plaster on the puncture from the needle.

"So you don't know anything about this, eh?"

Tobey shook his head.

"Saline solution. I gave it to you while you were asleep."

"How did you get me here?" Tobey sounded as if his mouth was still full of rice and stew.

Tanvir smiled. "We found you in the old warehouse. You were unconscious and completely dehydrated."

"Who are those two men?"

"Miguel and Jay Jay. They work here."

"And you?"

Tanvir sealed the bottle with the tincture and went to a cabinet. "Tomorrow we'll take a tour." He put the bottle on a shelf and took another one in hand, transparent, like a medicine bottle. "Do you drink?" He turned around to Tobey and grinned. "Don't worry—it's gin."

Tobey considered it. Then he shook his head.

"Too bad. I'm the only one on the island who indulges in this vice." Tanvir took a glass from the cupboard and carried it with the bottle and the kerosene lamp outside to a kind of veranda, a porch hewn from rough planks with a railing and stairs, where there were three wicker chairs and a table made of bamboo.

"Come, sit down!" Tanvir cried after he had made himself comfortable in one of the chairs. "The mosquito hour is over." He filled his glass half full of gin and pushed the cork back into the bottle.

Tobey grabbed the bottle of mouthwash and the bottle of water, pushed the screen door open and stepped out onto the veranda. It had grown a little cooler and it was dark; the light of the lamp reached only out to the edges of the table on which it stood. Butterflies fluttered in the light; one flew over the opening and scorched its wings in the rising flame, mingling with the oily soot that flowed upward in a straight column. The wooden planks gave off heat and an odor which Tobey recalled from the veranda outside his parents' house. His father had built it because Cait had seen a picture of a mansion in South Carolina in an illustrated magazine. It had to be painted white, with decorations on the supporting beams and the railings. There was also a swing, a padded wooden bench that hung on chains and squealed softly when it was being used.

"Will you tell me why you're here?" Tanvir used his foot to push the empty chair in front of him over a little, an invitation for Tobey to sit down.

Tobey stood there quietly. The song of the insects rose from the forest, and a bird cried. He suddenly had the feeling that he had been on the island for an eternity.

"Take a pill—one of the oval ones."

Tobey took the matchbox from his pocket and opened it.

There were six oval tablets and six round tablets inside.

"They're for pain."

Tobey hesitated, then put a tablet on his fat tongue and drank water from the bottle. Finally he sat down. He did not choose the chair facing Tanvir; instead he chose the one on the other side of the table. When he looked at Tanvir briefly from the corner of his eye, he noticed an amused, slightly mocking smile on his face.

"Wait until the drug takes effect." Tanvir drank a sip of gin, moved the empty chair back toward him and put his bare feet up on it. He folded his arms over his chest and stared into the night, as if there would be something there to see other than the dark pattern formed by the tree trunks and the black of the sky.

"I'm looking for someone," Tobey said after a while. His tongue was still swollen, an obstacle that the words had to force themselves around, losing a few consonants in the process.

"How do you know about this island?"

"From this person."

"Who dropped you off on the island?"

"Three men. I paid them money."

"Are they going to pick you up again?"

Tobey closed his eyes. The air smelled like burned petroleum and something sweet, fermented. It made him think of Jason Dwyer; the fruit in his room had rotted before he did—peaches and apricots and bananas—the only thing that Jason was still eating in the weeks before his death. He opened his eyes and stood up. The pill seemed to work—the pain in his mouth began to subside; the abrasions on his wrists did not burn any more.

"They probably already came, today or yesterday."

"Who are you looking for, Tobey?"

Tobey leaned against the railing, propped his arms on it, and turned his back on Tanvir. "As if you didn't know."

"Why should I?"

"Because you read the letters."

"That's not true," Tanvir took his feet off the chair and took a sip. "I only read one," he said more quietly.

An animal rustled in the wet, heavy leaves that were decaying between the trees, and then Tobey saw a shadow flit past.

"So you're her brother."

Tobey didn't answer. The animal disappeared into the forest; soon after that a bird squawked and fluttered through the trees.

"Megan." Tanvir almost whispered her name.

Tobey turned around slowly. He didn't want to ask the question and instead asked a different one. "When was she here?"

Tanvir rose. It seemed as if he intended to reach out to Tobey, but then he stayed where he was, made a helpless motion with his hands and lowered his eyes.

Tobey had tried to imagine how he would react to the news of Megan's death, and saw now how senseless it had been to play through that moment over and over again, because no one could prepare for it. The air stopped buzzing and his heart stopped beating. His head was empty, then images rushed in him and through him, swirling colored blots, lighting up for a fraction of a second. In his head the uproar increased, a whispering and singing and shouting, the sum of all the voices over all the years. Tobey was cold and heavy; the ground beneath him felt soft, as if it would give way.

"I'm sorry," said Tanvir. It sounded like it came from far away.

Tobey turned and looked at the wall. His hands clasped the railing. If you looked long enough, you could recognize the boundary between the treetops and the sky; discern individual trunks, the bare ground beside the building.

"She's buried on the island."

Tobey didn't say anything. He heard Tanvir settle into the chair, how the rattan crackled, how the screw cap of a bottle untwisted and a glass was filled with liquid. He thought he could smell the gin. He remembered how alcohol worked, how it carried you higher and higher when you were riding on a wave, and how it numbed you when you were down, at the dark bottom of a dream.

"Will you show me the grave?"

"Tomorrow. Now you should get some sleep." Tanvir stood up, took the bottle and the lamp and went to the stairs, where he turned around. "Your room is over there." He pointed to the unplastered buildings.

Tobey followed him. The oval of light cast by the lamp swung back and forth on the well-worn path. A wind rose up and blew leaves over the ground in front of them.

"Rain," said Tanvir. He walked up the five steps in the middle of the high brick building, opened a door and entered an area bathed in yellow-ish neon light. Inside there was an old sofa, a round coffee table, a chair and a vending machine; against the wall there were three chairs, each made from a different material. Two corridors led away from the entrance hall. Tanvir went right and took a bundle of keys out of his pocket. He passed three doors; in front of the fourth one he stopped and unlocked it. "It's not the Royal Orchid, but it's better than a flophouse." He turned a switch and the faint glow from the ceiling lamp, which came on at the same time as a fan, fell onto a large bed, a wardrobe and a chest of drawers. The bed stood on a rug made of sisal. Around that, the bare wood floor gleamed. "I'll get you something cold to drink. For the pills." Tanvir went to the door. "Coke. Sprite. Dr. Pepper?"

Tobey shrugged his shoulders. "Sprite," he said. Now that he no longer wanted to talk, he could move his tongue again. He sat on the bed. At the foot of the bed there was a piece of soap on a folded towel. On the wall across from him hung a framed calendar with a picture that showed a part of the Arctic Ocean and fields of sea ice from the air, a faded print with a blue cast. On a stool that served as a night table, there was a kerosene lamp with a box of matches beside it. Through a door on Tobey's left there was a bathroom, where a white sink shone in the half-darkness. The rustling of palm leaves penetrated through an open window covered with mosquito nets.

"Two. That should be enough." Tanvir put the soda cans, frosted from the cold, on the bureau. "Take one of the round ones immediately. It will help you sleep."

"How did she die?"

Tanvir looked at Tobey and wiped his wet hands on his trousers.

"I'll tell you tomorrow," he said.

They heard steps in the hallway, and seconds later the young Filipino entered the room with Tobey's suitcases. He put the suitcases down, looked at Tanvir and left when he nodded.

"I thought that you'd want to have them with you."

Tobey stared at the suitcases. His uncle, his father's brother, had given them to him. When Tobey told him that he planned to search for Megan, Aidan had taken them down from the attic. They were made of cardboard, covered on the outside with imitation brown leather and lined with plaid fabric.

While Aidan cleaned the bags, he explained that they had belonged to his brother who, after he had taken over their father's farm, announced that he would never leave Ireland again. Tobey did not believe that his father, who had hardly ever taken a trip to Killorglin, let alone Cork or Dublin, had owned anything as adventurous as suitcases, but to prove it Aidan showed him the initials S.O. F. scribbled on the inner fabric with a ball-point pen. The initials stood for Seamus O'Flynn. Aidan said that now that his brother was dead, the suitcases belonged to Tobey, and he should make sure that they saw something of the world.

"Well then, good night," Tanvir said, and left the room.

"Good night," said Tobey, and got up and locked the door. Then he opened both of the suitcases and looked for the letters.

News from Megan

Presumably, since you don't know anything about politics, you've never heard about a group called the Illegal Eagles. (Great name, right? It's mine!) There are about twenty of us, sometimes more, sometimes less, all militant animal rights activists. If you read the newspaper from time to time, you must have noticed something about our actions in the recent months. In the last two weeks we set fire to eighteen refrigerated trucks in one night. They belonged to three meat suppliers. Actually, it should have been twenty, but the group I was in had to knock off, because the security guards showed up earlier than usual. We couldn't take our intended escape route and we ran straight through an industrial district, climbed over the walls and slipped through holes in the chain-link fence that we cut out with pliers. One of us (a guy, of course!) sprained his foot when he jumped off a wall. We had to carry him, and it felt like we were in a war film, only nobody shot at us. (In the meantime the police were behind us, and they were equipped with more than the batons and whistles that the guards carry.) One of our guys is a techie and he supplied us with GPS devices, which made it easy for us to find the stolen pickup truck, two kilometers from the wholesale meat distributor's courtyard, where Paul was waiting for us. (We are named after famous vegetarians. My code name is Linda—you know, Linda McCartney. Paul is Paul McCartney, but we have nothing to do with each another, even though he'd like that. The techie is called Kafka.) We've evolved organically. At first there were five of us—three women and two men. We've all participated in animal welfare groups, distributed brochures on the street and collected signatures, given away tofu burgers and shown films about factory farms, the whole program. Should I let you in on something, Toto? It doesn't matter to most people where their steak comes from and how their eggs are produced. But that shouldn't surprise you. You know me, I'm a peace-loving person, but when, during every street action, ten greasy guys say they need to eat red meat for virility, or that they have a hard sausage in their trousers that you can sample, you'll eventually grow sour. And when every fifth guy asks you whether or not *fucking* Hitler was also a *fucking* vegetarian, at some point you have no desire and no more strength left to make ethical and morally responsible beings out of this self-satisfied pack. Then all you want to do is strike. You'd like to kick them in their fat bellies and clobber them with their full shopping bags; you'd like to lock them up in a tin shed for a week, where they'd stand around on each other's feet because there's no room for so many of them; you want to transport them without water in a truck from Palermo to Hamburg. But we do nothing to them. We let them live their lives. We disturb their system just a little; we spit into their soup. Two months ago we placed fake bombs in the bathrooms of forty branches of McDonald's and Burger King. (If you didn't see anything about that, you're living on the moon, Toto!) We sent a letter claiming responsibility to the *Observer*. No claptrap about improving the world, no accusing drivel. There was just one sentence on the sheet: "We did it." Then, the addresses of the hamburger stores and our logo, an eagle with spread wings, holding a spear in one claw and a pen in the other: combat and enlightenment. Under the eagle there's a flying banner, the ends waving; our name appears in capital letters. The whole thing looks a bit like a family crest, a little old-fashioned, but I like it. It reminds me of the books about knights that you read (or did you only look at the pictures?), Ivanhoe and Prince Valiant, King Arthur. They had a coat of arms like that on their shields and the mantles on their horses. That's how I'd like to see myself, Tobey, as a knight fighting for a just cause. The campaign was a huge success. As a precaution every hamburger store across the country was closed, all day long. Hundreds of police cordoned off the streets and re-routed traffic. The fire department was ready. Explosives experts from the police and the army were called in. They treated each fake like a real bomb, forty times in forty branches and five cities. This has made us famous. You may think I've lost all my marbles, but when I saw our name and the eagle on the front pages of the *Times*, the *Sun* and the *Wall Street Journal*, I had to cry. During every action I had a huge fear of being caught and I have it even now, and certainly it was because of this fear that I cried, but there was also something else, something like relief, amazement, and happiness. And yes, why not—pride. For days on end seventeen people crammed travel alarm clocks, wires and plasticine into transparent Tupperware containers and stashed them in their backpacks. On a Wednesday morning between ten o' clock and noon they put them in the toilet stalls of selected fast food outlets. During the preparations they talked about what it would be like to be caught and imprisoned, and how many years they would get for the crimes they had already committed (criminal association, criminal damage, arson, burglary, disturbing the peace, theft, attempted assault, extortion and so on). It came out to two to ten years, depending on police records; they thought about that for a moment and then took the next Tupperware container out of the box to turn it into a deceptively real-looking bomb. And you know what, Toto? It wouldn't have mattered to any one of them if she was caught and put behind bars. She would have sat all day long in her cell, reading, drawing (the cockroach who lives behind her toilet) and writing letters to her brother, whom she misses and from whom she does not know whether he has forgiven her.

The step of the ant moves the rock.
Lao proverb.

Who loves you?
Megan!

7

Tobey was cold, but he did not get up. Wind blew through his hair. He had not been able to sleep and stared for ages at the tablets in the matchbox and then simply went off, out of the room, the barracks, had followed the first best path and after a while landed on the beach. He lay in the sand and closed his eyes, because there was nothing to see above him anyway, no clouds, no stars, no planes. He thought about the afternoon on the beach in Glenbeigh, about the final hours before his decision to go Dublin, about the minutes in his room, about Megan's attempt to convince him to stay, about his escape, racing and lurching between the hills, shooing away the sheep who were too dumb to recognize his sense of urgency, screaming and cursing at the rain that drummed on the guitar at his back.

When the first drops fell, Tobey smiled. Seconds later he was soaked to the bone and crying. He lay there and screamed her name into the night. He roared with the voice of his father and cursed God. He sang, he screamed his rudest song, sand between his teeth. He recited the names in her pet cemetery, lines from her letters; he prayed. He pulled off all his clothes, rolled over, and buried himself.

He lay still; it had long ago ceased to rain. He trembled; his clothes lay next to him in a wet ball. The sky had moved away a little; between streaks of clouds stars appeared. Crabs scuttled in the dim light; Tobey could see them. He raised his head. The horizon was visible, the sea black, the universe a little brighter. Only now did he notice the volume of the surf; it boomed so suddenly in his ears that he struggled to his feet. A bird with narrow, pointed wings glided above him. On the line between the water and the air a light floated. Shivering, Tobey watched how it moved for a while, infinitely slowly from right to left, from east to west. Finally he gathered up his clothes, put on his underpants and shoes and returned along the path from which he had come.

The door to the infirmary was closed, so he sat down for a while on one of the chairs. He wanted to see if the trembling would disappear, and whether he would be strong enough. Tears ran down his cheeks; there was sand in his eyes. The bandages were completely soaked with water, the plaster long ago dissolved. The wind had become a weak stream; the buzzing of the insects reassured him. In his room was the suitcase with her letters, a bundle of curled pages in a plastic bag from *Super Value*. Megan's writing was round and uniform, stringing together the route between childhood and now, the thread that kept him from being lost. He tried to remember where he had been two years ago and Dublin came to mind. Enormous Dublin, which he had only seen sections of: the neighborhood, the house, the room, the basement where they rehearsed, the pub where they drank and took courage and regularly grew angry because they were too dumb to quit and at last look for a job: garbage man, waiter, wedding musician. He wrapped the shirt around his hand, got up and broke the windowpane next to the door. A bird cried out, followed a moment later by second one. With a piece of wood he broke the remaining glass out of the frame and then climbed into the semi-darkness of the room. On a table there were pencils and old newspapers and plates with the remains of spent candles. He lifted the plates; under the third one was the key. He opened the cupboard, took the bottles in hand one by one, turned the seals, and sniffed the openings. They had never drunk gin; that was reserved for the old English windbags and American tourists. Their drink was whiskey; not when they began drinking, but later, when they were eighteen and had a little money and had grown tired of beer. They mixed it with cola, because it tasted better and moved into the bloodstream faster. Everything had to move faster then: drinking, music, life.

He sat down on one of the folding chairs, held the bottle of gin in his hand and looked at the label, a white, rectangular piece of paper which contained the words NARCOTICUM BRITTANNICUM LIQUIDIUM in fancy letters, undoubtedly a joke by the old Indian. He sat there for a while, his eyes closed, inhaling the smell from the bottle, his swaying barely perceptible. He heard his guitar; he was playing the solo from the song "Sick of Being Homesick," and it sounded good, but he knew it could sound better, dirty and sparkling at the same time.

He played the solo to the end, solid and without the arrogance he had during a club gig; he moved his fingers in a dream. The sound welled up in his skull and it satisfied him. At some point he got up, put the bottle back, locked up the closet and climbed out to the porch. A little light was already pressing through the places where the sky did not rest firmly enough against the sea. There was no wind. Tobey went to the brick building and into his room, quietly, so he wouldn't wake anyone. A lizard slithered across the floor in front of him and disappeared under the refrigerator. He took a shower sitting down, the clothes spread out next to him. The water was warm and smelled like chlorine. Then he stood under the fan and waited until he was dry. He found the sight of the ice floes calming; they cooled down his thoughts. After a while he spotted the shadow of a helicopter on one of the white islands, then the polar bear. Megan would have told him a story about this picture, something beautiful and sad about the eternal ice, whose eternity was transient, a legend about the disappearance. Her voice would have been gentle, measured with wistfulness and unacknowledged bitterness.

When he was dry, Tobey turned the light out and lay down on the bed. The ceiling fan turned and made a slight flapping noise. Outside, an apparatus consisting of millions of legs and wings seemed to be at work, a grinding machine that stopped from time to time and then sluggishly restarted, interrupted occasionally by squawking that sounded like an engine backfiring. Tobey got out of bed, took a can of Sprite from the bureau, popped it open, took a sleeping pill out of the match box and washed it down with the now lukewarm drink. Then he lay back on the bed and looked at the ceiling. Perhaps, he thought, there actually was a heaven, and Megan sat up there and was relieved that he knew about her death.

He woke up with a violence that threw his head back. He was drenched in light, as if it had been poured over him like water; he gasped for air and uttered a sound that was hoarse and throaty. He sat up, rubbed his eyes and scratched his foot where he had been stung by an insect. There was a bitter taste in his mouth. He opened the box of matches and counted five oval pills and five round ones. The Sprite was warm and sweet; the carbonation foamed on his tongue, which no longer felt swollen. He went into the bathroom, washed his face and cleaned his teeth, then took fresh clothes from the suitcase and put them on. On an impulse he hid the stack of Megan's letters under the mattress. For a while he sat on the bed, uncertain whether he should cry. He drank water from the bottle and swallowed an oval pill, although he had no identifiable pain. The curtain over the only window stirred in a light morning breeze. He pushed it aside and looked through the screen out to the place where a few chickens were running and water shimmered in the puddles.

Then he saw the old Indian and the guy who had knocked him down. The two moved quickly on a path that ran along the long side the clearing. From time to time Tanvir stopped and talked to the bearded child, gesturing at the same time with an opened umbrella that protected him from the high sun. When the two disappeared from view, Tobey slipped on his damp shoes, left the room and went over to the building where the kitchen was located.

Rosalinda was not there, and neither were any of the apes. A radio made of yellow plastic played soft music, something cheerful and fast. Tobey found instant coffee, sugar and a thermos of hot water, made himself a cup and then looked in the drawers, clay pots and metal boxes for a knife with a handle that would fit in his fist and a blade that was sharp and pointed and no longer than his hand. He found one in a biscuit tin, between scissors and nutcrackers and tiny graters, wrapped it in a cloth rag and put it in one of the side pockets of his trousers. After he drank the coffee and had rinsed the cup and left it to dry, he went back to his room. There, he cut the towel into strips, tied one of them around his right calf, and slipped the knife under it.

New skin, pink and glistening, had formed over the abrasions on his wrists and ankles. He should have taken along supplies to dress the wounds, he thought, and felt guilty when he remembered the broken window pane. He pulled up the leg of his trousers a few times and took out the knife. He practiced the sequence of movements for a while, slowly at first, then faster, using his left hand to jerk up the leg of his trousers and the right one to grab the knife.

He then devoted himself to the two suitcases. If he sorted out the things he didn't need, which included the insulating mat and the gas stove together with the utensils, one piece of luggage would be enough, even if he stuffed a water bottle and a few cans of Sprite into the suitcase. He folded two strips of the towel to make shoulder straps, which he could use to carry the suitcase on his back. He walked a few steps. The straps held the weight of the suitcase and they did not dig into his flesh the way ropes would. He lay face down on the bed and practiced swimming movements until it seemed ridiculous. In the bath he fingered the laceration on the back of his head and stroked the stubble that grew around the spot. Finally, he pushed the two suitcases under the bed and left the room.

It was hot; the sun shone from a cloudless sky; towels and bed sheets were drying on a clothesline. Tobey walked across the clearing and a meadow, came to a narrow dirt road and ended up at a pond. Rosalinda and the chimpanzee were sitting on the bank in the shade of a tree and shelling peas. The sky and a few trees were reflected in the brackish water; the wings of large dragonflies rattled among the reeds. Rosalinda was wearing her colorful dress and a straw hat with a yellow ribbon; Chester wore short blue pants and a striped shirt. They sat on a blanket; between the two of them there was a bowl filled with peas. Tobey watched them for a while and then went back. He followed the path that Tanvir and the bearded child had taken and arrived—after he had already convinced himself that he was lost in the sparse forest—at a one-story building that was about thirty meters long and stood on brick columns. Narrow windows ran along the length of the façade; the panes were all broken. Under the building, where hardly anything grew, there were car tires, barrels, wire mesh, and corrugated metal parts.

Tobey went to the distant end of the building, squeezed through a gap in the fence and found himself in a kind of courtyard. Here, in the shadows, there were empty cages, each about five meters wide and three meters high. Plants grew in from the outside, pencil-thin spiral vines with oval leaves, sparkling light green where the sun hit them. Each cage was connected to the courtyard by a door and half covered by the building's roof. Moss grew on the edges of the walls and over the flagstones. Leaves had accumulated in the corners of the cages and the tiled floors were covered with a layer of dirt. The bars were covered with rust that had affected the metal like a disease and was making them come apart. Tobey noticed a small red ball and a single plastic cup full of yellow water that contained a dark sediment formed of countless dead insects.

Despite the broken windows, the air inside the building was still. Before Tobey went inside he stamped his foot a few times to scare away rats and other animals. Tables had been assembled along the windows; you could raise the Formica tops to make more space. In the twilight Tobey saw office chairs. They were black padded swivel chairs and some of them were missing back supports and some of them were missing arm rests. On one seat there was an empty bird's nest. Between two of the tables there was a metal filing cabinet, painted green: a hollow tower surrounded by empty drawers. Without knowing what he was looking for, Tobey rummaged through documents, but all he found were lined notebook pages speckled with animal excrement, torn calendar pages, candy wrappers and half-decomposed scraps of paper.

In the courtyard it was cool; the plants gave off moisture and a smell that Tobey inhaled greedily. He should have brought along the water bottle, he thought, as he walked over the flagstones. Between the flagstones the grass grew rampantly. At the end of the courtyard he found a large cage, more of an aviary for birds of prey like the ones he had seen in the zoo, but made of metal rods instead of wire mesh. There was a tree in the middle of the cage. It was stripped; in the weak light that penetrated through the blanket of leaves, its wood shone yellow like the belly of a fish. Tobey discovered a hole in the dirt that he decided must be used by some animal to get into the building.

Beside the cage there was a brick compartment with a roof, a door, and a window. Inside there was a table and a folding chair; an electric wire with an empty socket hung from the ceiling. The wood of the folding chair was rotted and the table was covered with a thin, furry film. A stairway led down several steps and ended at a door which had a viewing window and which was slightly open. When a spider crawled out of the keyhole and ran across the unplastered walls, Toby made sure to return to the light quickly.

He looked for the way to the beach, but he did not find it. Finally he came to a path that led a little further through mown grass and a coconut grove. He was thirsty, but he did not know how you got to the liquid inside the coconut. His knife hardly seemed to be a suitable tool. He saw a chicken among the tree trunks, then another one. A bird, unlike anything Tobey had ever heard before, sang somewhere in a tree. Ten meters away from him a black snake was sunning itself on the path, and he stopped. He picked up a rock and threw it at the creature. Flies buzzed around it. After a while he realized that it was not a snake but a piece of inner tube from a bicycle. The path suddenly grew wider and a matted lawn appeared behind a dip, the edges surrounded by white-painted stones. In round beds filled with seashells there were bushes growing that no one had taken care of in a long time. The course of the former path was visible in the withered grass.

Then he saw the villa. The two-story wooden house, painted light blue and white, stood on the suggestion of a hill and shared the place with two trees whose branches cast shadows on the roof. On the first floor there was a veranda which you could access from the inside through a set of French doors. Similar double doors were located on each side; at the entrance they opened onto a set of stairs that led down from the veranda to the front yard. One path, wide enough for two cars and now completely overgrown, must have been the driveway once. The path, only intermittently bordered by stones, led around a circular flower bed planted with shrubs and a dried ornamental tree and lost itself between knee-high grass and sparse shrubs.

Tobey was about to approach the house when someone stepped out on the veranda. He ducked behind a bush and saw Miguel, who shook out a sheet or a tablecloth and then returned to the darkness of the room from which he had come. Tobey sat up and went to the path that led in a wide arc past the house through a grove of trees each as thick as an arm. He thought they were bamboo. He crossed a dry stream bed and battled his way through the undergrowth and reed-like thickets until, after a slight rise, he stood sweating on the summit and saw the sea before him. A gust of wind swept over him and rustled the dry grass, and then it was hot and still again. Sunlight sparkled on the wave crests; the smell of seaweed hung in the air. A few seabirds floated far out in the distance; on the horizon there were clean white clouds. Tobey wondered how wise it would be to go back and get something to drink, but then he ran the two hundred meters down to the beach, removed everything but his underwear, took out the knife and put it on the bundle of clothes. It wasn't until he hit the water that he remembered the articles he had read that warned about sea urchins, snakes, jellyfish and fish with poisonous spines that hid in the sand. He noticed a shadow on the light-colored sea bottom, not five meters in front of him. He swam to shore and sat in the trails of the gentle surf. The dark blotch turned out to be palm fronds, black and half rotted, that bobbed up and down in the current. Tobey narrowed his eyes and saw tiny fish whose bodies glittered with silver when they changed direction. At the foot of a crag crabs stirred; insects whirred over a shallow pool where sea water had collected.

Tobey followed the beach several hundred yards but then turned around because it was too far to the next bend. The sun was burning; he carried the bundle of clothes on his head and the shoes, laces tied together, in his hand. When he reached the path from which he had come, he hesitated. In the shade of a group of trees he got dressed and then decided to walk a little further between the sea and the embankment and to look for the path that led from the bunkhouse to the beach. He remembered smooth rocks as tall as a man and was confident of finding them. While he walked he was on the lookout for boats that might be sailing near the island, but saw only one ship, a freighter or tanker, that floated like a dark joist between the sky and the water.

It made him think of the movie "Papillon." The prisoner in the movie, played by Steve McQueen, tied coconuts together to escape from the island. It occurred to him that the tires under the building, connected with a few boards or bamboo poles, would make an acceptable raft. It shouldn't be difficult to find ropes, he thought, and if he couldn't, he could make some out of gunnysacks. When he noticed the trail he stopped. The embankment was clear of debris, beach grass and withered plants for a width of about two meters. Further above, where the border between the beach and the overgrown heart of the island continued, there was a gap between the bushes and the pathetic little saplings. At one spot, seldom touched by the swell of the waves, there was a boulder half sunk in the sand, covered in seaweed, with a rope tied around it. Tobey followed the path, entered the twilight of a grove, came to a fork and selected the path to the left, in the direction where he suspected the barracks were.

After a while he was back on the beach. He saw the rock where he had been sitting, the tree that was lying on the shore, bone-white and the bottom filled with shells after a long journey at sea. He walked along the path, took the almost imperceptible slope and crossed the strip of sparse vegetation; behind that the lowlands stretched, flat land covered with large areas of grass where stunted trees grew. Apparently the trees got along without water and leaves. The path, and every few yards a stone, formed the dividing line between the flatlands and the clearing around which the buildings stood. It appeared that someone regularly pulled out the clumps of grass that wanted to keep growing out of the flat earth, as well as the first tendrils of the bushes, gnarled shoots that looked dead in the harsh sunlight. It was not immediately clear to Tobey why this area was so well groomed. There were no vehicles on the island, and he doubted that someone went to all this trouble just for the sake of appearances. He looked into the sky, imagined a helicopter sinking down to the landing, heard the engine noise and protected his eyes from the dust kicked up by the rotors.

"Tobey!"

Tobey opened his eyes. Tanvir came around the corner of the building that contained the kitchen and waved. Tobey briefly lifted his hand. He pretended to wipe off the leg of his pants and checked to make sure that the knife was secure. Then he sat up and walked a few steps toward the Indian.

"Where were you? I looked everywhere." Tanvir was a little out of breath. Despite the scorching sun, he had closed the umbrella and used it as a cane.

"I was stretching my legs a little," Tobey said.

"In this heat?" As if to prove that it was hot Tanvir wiped the sweat from his brow with a handkerchief and extended the umbrella. A bloom of delicate wooden spokes and white fabric opened and Tanvir found a place for his body in the round shadow that hovered over the ground.

"I was swimming."

"Swimming," repeated Tanvir. In his mouth the word sounded absurd, became the grotesque activity of naive people doing pointless things.

"I was hot," Tobey said.

"Come on." Tanvir jabbed his umbrella at the sky and walked away.

"I'm thirsty," Tobey said. But Tanvir went on, without slowing or turning around. Tobey thought about leaving him and going to his room, but then followed the old man.

They left the buildings behind and crossed a meadow where dead trees loomed. Locusts flew in front of them, whirred through the air like wind-up toys and fell between the trunks. The path made a curve fringed by palms. Even more coconuts for a raft, Tobey thought. He would have to attach a net, he decided; his foot got caught on a root and he stumbled. He swore softly, thinking about the soda machine that sometimes began to vibrate as if it was shivering with cold. Tanvir hurried ahead, a black-clad monk brandishing a white mushroom. Water had gathered in a shallow hole; animal tracks crisscrossed the mud. Tanvir disappeared behind a bend and as Tobey reached him he saw the cemetery. A closely-trimmed, amazingly green meadow lay before them, perhaps twenty by twenty yards. A gravel path divided the area into two halves; in each half there were three gravestones. At the end of the path there rose a wooden cross, as tall as a man and painted white. Around it hung a chain of artificial flowers and at its base there were saucers and jam jars containing the remnants of candles. A tool shed, only slightly larger than a phone booth, leaned against a tree.

Tanvir laid the umbrella on the ground and slipped out of his sandals before he stepped on the gravel path. He stopped at one of the graves, crouched down and touched the stone. Then he got up and walked, head down, ten, twelve steps back, put his sandals on again, took the umbrella and walked past Tobey.

"Take your time," he added and was gone.

Tobey sat on the wooden bench, flanked by two small trees with light brown, shiny bark, and took off his shoes. The sky was empty, a tidy room with blue wallpaper. Father McMahon had said that the dead dwelt up there, and that Seamus O'Flynn was not alone. God was with him, and his father Cormac and his mother Maeve and his grandparents, Joseph and Claire. After the funeral Tobey got drunk alone in the room of a B & B outside of town. He lay down on a bed that was too soft and too large, staring at a ceiling decorated with stucco and he had imagined that his father occupied a room in heaven next to Jimi Hendrix, who played guitar day and night and cried his soul out to the heavens. Then he remembered that Hendrix had killed himself with drugs and had, according to Catholic law, ended up in hell.

Tobey stood in front of the grave stone and placed both hands on it. The stone had stored the heat of the sun, which had disappeared suddenly, like Tanvir. Megan hummed, a clear voice among a chorus of insects, and Tobey closed his eyes.

News from Megan

We are not here anymore, Tobey. In Socrates' dream we were arrested.
We are scattered to the winds. Grass will grow. My hair will grow. It's
easy to travel with empty hands. I'm in the country, far from everyone,
and soon I will be completely gone. I'll fly through a nightmare with my
eyes closed and land on an island. Like an angel. I will have a different
name—my husband's name. Benson. Cummings. Dempsey. (After the
grass has grown for a year, I'll tell you.) The minister was almost blind;
the man who witnessed the marriage was a philosophy professor from
the Ukraine, whose food cart was stolen the night before. The wedding
march was played on a cassette recorder, and the minister's shirt sleeve
caught fire on a candle flame. I still wonder to this day if that was sad or
funny. (There are no photos.) The landscape here differs little from
where I was three years ago. The horse in the meadow is black instead of
white, no Sam in his shroud, and the next town is sixteen miles instead of
twelve. Sometimes I miss the city, the crowd of people. When you are in
their midst, loneliness has a different weight. Here it doesn't weigh anything; it is the dress that I wear. London makes you mad and angry; here
you become gentle and sleepy. I can hear the grass grow; it has almost
covered my name. I'm sitting in a valley and I create the time and the
light. Sometimes I miss my books. I imagine them standing on people's
shelves, in small dark homes. I would like to get them, to steal every single one and bring them right here. I would leave a gap where I had removed a book. People would look at the empty place and ask themselves

which book was missing. I sit at a table at the window of a house full of books which I will not read. The choice of selecting a book overwhelms me. So many thoughts, ideas, insights; so many words, sentences, chapters. I am two years old and I wonder what the bear dreams about in the winter. I know everything that those at school want to know. I'm going to grow up quickly. The picture of my world is the view from this window. There is no television here (an age-related malfunction, not ideological), and only one radio in the living room. Because a strange fatigue seized me some time ago, I do not listen to music. On some days, my head is so heavy that I have to lay it down like a bleary-eyed child. Then it burns out, an old device, for which there are no more spare parts. On other days it is light; then the memories abandon it. Do you remember when I unscrewed the fuses from the refrigerated storage unit at the butcher shop that belonged to Barry Spillane's parents, and the meat almost spoiled? We did something like that a few weeks ago at the largest chicken farm in Yorkshire. We waited for the day when the fattest animals are driven to the slaughterhouse and fresh chicks are delivered, and we broke into the room where everything is controlled—the lighting of the halls, the ventilation, the feeding—we smashed the whole place to pieces, doused it with gasoline and set it on fire. There were four of us; Paul waited in the getaway car. Everything went smoothly. They had to take the chicks somewhere else. (Maybe they were killed, or disposed of, as they call it.) The next day the newspaper reported that one of the fire trucks sent to the scene of the fire had an accident on the way. It went into a spin and plunged down a hillside. One of the firemen was killed; the other five were injured: bruises, fractures, concussions. Alan was thrown out of the truck and died at the scene. Alan James Woodgate. Thirty-eight years old, married, with one daughter. I was at his grave, two days after the funeral. Photos in the newspaper: the men in uniform; Bernice and Jodie Woodgate hand in hand; a fire helmet on the coffin. The truck wasn't even necessary any more—the others had long

since put out the fire. (Shutdown of the mass chicken production operation: three weeks.) The man who sat next to the driver (Edward Miles
Brolin, twenty-six), said in the newspaper that he had seen a cow on the
road; the driver (Richard Kenneth Webber, forty-three) tried to dodge
it. The driver cannot remember anything. A cow, Tobey. Was she really
there, in the middle of the street? Or did Eddie Brolin only dream
it? There is a curve there. Paul (McCartney) and I drove it, again and
again, faster and faster, until I felt sick. There was a wooden cross stuck
in the grass; there were flowers, still partially wrapped in foil. I cried and
Paul hugged me and kissed me. Then I puked, fifty meters from the place
where Alan James Woodgate hit his head so hard that his neck
broke. Since then, I dream of this cow. It is smeared with feces; flies buzz
around it; there is black smoke. It devours the grass which is supposed to
grow over everything.

Memory is the boat that picks you up
at night and carries you up the river,
against the current, time, and your will.
Jasper Algonquin, *Tracks, Poems*, Pluto Press, Glasgow, 1974

Given away, like all the books. Brought back in thoughts from a flat in
Notting Hill. Slight damage from hasty, inattentive browsing and incom-
prehension of beauty.

Who loves you?
Megan!

90

8

Tobey stood on the porch and watched Jay Jay as he put a new window-pane in the door. He had offered his help, but Jay Jay declined. The sun did not fall directly on the veranda anymore, but it was hot; every now and then a breeze caressed the tops of the nearby trees.

Tanvir sat on one of the chairs and dabbed his brow with a handker-chief. On the table in front of him stood a pitcher with ice-cold water, where pieces of ginger and slices of lemon floated. "Maybe it had a crack and the wind broke it," he said.

"No," Jay Jay said firmly. "Wind?" He shook his head.

Under the porch an animal rustled—a lizard or mouse. Tobey paid no attention to the noise. He leaned against the railing and looked into the room, where coiled ropes hung on a wall.

"A bird," said Tanvir. "It crashed into the pane, was unconscious for a while, and then fluttered away."

"No," said Jay Jay. He took putty out of a can with his knife and smeared it into a frame. "I say it was a burglar."

"But nothing was stolen," cried Tanvir. "Not even gin!"

"Perhaps the burglar didn't find what he was looking for." Jay Jay put down the putty knife thoughtfully, and then nodded to his mirror image in the pane.

Tanvir looked at Tobey and raised his eyebrows.

"A bird sounds plausible," Tobey said.

As if to confirm this thesis, a large flock of birds the size of finches flew over the building and disappeared noisily into the woods.

Tanvir nodded. They watched Jay Jay, who filled the remaining frames with putty and then stashed the tool and the can into a wooden box that had a shoulder strap attached. They also watched him as he swept the floor again. Shards of glass fell into the darkness through the cracks between the boards.

"Well done," said Tanvir.

Jay Jay drained his glass and put it on the table. "Yes." He hung the box on his shoulders and walked to the stairs. "But birds? No." He went down the steps and disappeared around the corner.

Tanvir picked a piece of ginger from his glass and threw it over the railing. For a while neither of them said anything. The birds shot from the trees and scattered away, silently, as if something terrible had frightened them. High above an airplane glided past and Tobey examined it, because it was the first one he had seen in several days.

"Rosalinda takes care of the graves," Tanvir finally said. He had finished his glass and put his feet on the chair in front of him. "She's very religious. Very Catholic."

"How did Megan die?"

Tanvir looked at Tobey, and then he turned his eyes away and seemed to fix them on a point somewhere above the tree tops. "She drowned," he said softly.

Tobey stared at Tanvir. "Drowned? That's impossible! She was a good swimmer!" As a child she swam in ponds, Tobey could have said, in lakes, and in the sea. Megan wanted to be a frog, a fish, a seal. But he said nothing more.

"There are jellyfish in these waters . . . " Tanvir made a vague gesture with his hand and took a deep breath in and out before he went on.

"Their poison can kill a person within minutes."

Tobey sat on the floor. He was sweating; he wiped his shirt sleeve over his face.

"We buried your sister according to Catholic custom. I hope that is what Megan would have wanted."

Tobey raised his head; he nodded. He didn't think it was necessary to tell the Indian that Megan had left the Church when she came of legal age. He had learned about it at the time from Barry Spillane, who heard his mother shock a client with the news.

Tanvir pointed to Tobey's empty glass, which stood on the railing, but Tobey shook his head.

"I lied to you," Tanvir said abruptly. He took his feet off the chair and slipped them into his sandals. "I didn't read just one letter."

Tobey thought about this confession. "I wouldn't have stopped after one, either," he said.

A smile flitted over Tanvir's face. He leaned back and looked at his hands, which were folded across his stomach. Tobey was tired. He had been in the sun too long; the skin of his face had grown a little tight. A fine powder of salt covered his arms. They both grew silent again, each one lost in his own thoughts. Now and then Tanvir sipped his glass or dabbed his forehead with a handkerchief. You could see the way the light became fainter, with each minute the sky lost brightness. Only the heat remained unchanged and the air was almost completely still.

Tobey laid his head on a railing post. With the notion that Megan lay in a grave not even a thousand steps away, forever dead and silent, that he would never be able to speak to her again, would never hear her voice again, that her flesh dissolved, her legs and breasts and lips vanished and her bones appeared, her skull, with holes where her eyes once were, all this was wretched to him, and he gulped down the grief and rage, closed his eyes and buried his head in his arms.

"She often sat in her room and wrote."

93

Tobey opened his eyes. For a few seconds, black spots danced in the air in front of him. He stretched, took the glass from the railing and held it out to Tanvir, who filled it quickly.

"What did she write?"

"Everything. Observations. Poems. Letters."

"Did she send the letters?"

"I don't know."

"Is there a post office?"

"Every now and then a boat comes; it brings things and takes things, including mail." Tobey emptied the glass in one swallow, and then he chewed on a piece of ginger. The sharp flavor pierced his tongue and caused a pleasant burning sensation. "Do you have any of her stuff? What she wrote or anything else?"

"I have a few of her observations about nature. Drawings. Notes."

"And the rest?"

Tanvir looked toward the sea. "There isn't anything else. She must have destroyed everything."

"What? Why would she do that?"

"She had . . . " Tanvir looked at Tobey. "Megan had these phases." He twisted his hands; his ocher-colored palms shone in the light of dusk. "Mood swings."

"I don't understand."

"Your sister was a strong, idealistic woman, exceptionally intelligent. She was interested in everything; her mind was committed to understanding the ways of the world, her heart to the beetle that landed on her notepad. But her time passed in waves. At one moment she was radiant with joy; in the next, she crawled into her very own misfortune."

"What do you mean? That she was depressed?"

Tanvir brushed invisible dirt from his pants. A sort of sigh escaped his lips. "I'm a doctor. I studied philosophy for one semester; I don't understand very much about psychology. I just noticed that your sister lived in

94

cycles of great heights and deep lows."

Tobey rose. A mosquito buzzed in his ear.

"Should I put on new bandages?"

Tobey looked at his wrists. The spots that had bled seemed to have healed well. "Maybe later," he said. "First, I want to shower."

"Supper is at seven."

Tobey nodded. When he was at the stairs, he turned around. "Who found her?"

Tanvir pushed himself out of the chair. He had put on a few extra pounds; a film of sweat covered his face. He exhaled loudly, as if rising exerted him. "Montgomery," he said.

"The ape?"

"Please, never use that word in his presence."

Questions whirled around in Tobey's head, but he was suddenly so exhausted that he turned around, grabbed the railing, and descended the steps one by one, like a child.

Rosalinda waited until everyone was seated at the table, clasped her hands, closed her eyes, and recited a prayer with unshakeable conviction from deep inside her and a camera-ready lack of restraint, as though she was applying for the position of television evangelist. Her words, heated by the fire of her faith, mixed with the steam of the food and filled the room, rose up, were seized by the ceiling fans and blew through the screen door into the open, where they grazed the ear of a toad or a lizard, were drowned out by the din of cicadas and lost in the blackness of the night. As if trying to cool down the heat in the room, Tanvir trotted out a few emotionless phrases in a language foreign to Tobey, and then everyone served themselves from the full pots and bowls. Rosalinda had fried fish and she had cooked sweet potatoes and a leafy vegetable that Tobey did not recognize. Montgomery ate no fish, but lots of bread that the cook had baked in the afternoon. He rubbed each thick slice with butter and sprinkled it with coconut flakes. He was dressed in black knee-length pants, a gray short-sleeved shirt, and a black baseball cap, which he had removed on the doorstep, as if he was entering a church. He looked like a postman. Chester was once again absorbed in gulping down his food. He ate with concentrated haste and he was not as well-mannered as Montgomery, and every few minutes he let out a sigh of satisfaction. Again, no one spoke during the meal. Tanvir praised Rosalinda's culinary skills, and Tobey, Miguel, and Jay Jay muttered hasty confirmation. Rosalinda scowled disparagingly at Tobey once, but then she did not dignify him with another glance for the rest of the evening.

After the meal, Tanvir bandaged Tobey's wounds, although Tobey insisted that it was no longer necessary. He hardly felt the scraped spots on his hands and ankles anymore; a thin, pink skin had begun to form. It was only the injury to the back of his head that would still bleed when Tobey took a shower and the fresh scab came off. He felt uncomfortable in the infirmary; it smelled like wet putty and the gin in Tanvir's glass. One broken piece of glass, which Jay Jay had overlooked, lay on the floor. Tobey looked up. A large gray-brown moth buzzed around the ceiling light; dust from its wings, glittering in the light, trickled to the floor.

"Rosalinda asked me today whether or not you're a wicked man."

"A what?"

"You can't blame her. She is, as you have already noticed, a very religious woman."

Tobey pushed himself off the treatment table with both hands and went to the door; countless insects crawled and fluttered at the mesh screen. The last time he had been in a church was when his father was buried.

"You could even recite a poem instead of a prayer. Or something in your Irish tongue."

"I don't speak Gaelic."

"Can't every Irishman speak Gaelic?"

96

"No."

Tanvir was silent, as if he would have to reassemble his entire conception of the world due to this realization. He sipped his gin and looked at the veranda. He wore his usual sandals, wide black pants and a shirt with a white collar and embroidered cuffs. Around his neck hung a necklace of wooden beads with an amulet attached, a wooden disk of about five centimeters in diameter, decorated with characters and symbols. Suddenly a jolt shot through him. He made two or three strides, pushed open the screen door, and went outside. "Shall we sit down?" he shouted and gestured toward the table and the chairs with his arm. In the light of the petroleum lamp the furniture formed a picture which, according to your mood, could be called romantic or shabby.

Tobey took a seat on one of the chairs.

"Do you have something to drink?"

Tobey raised the half-full can of lukewarm cola he had taken from the bunkhouse. "Yes."

Tanvir also sat down. With the onset of the night, it had become much cooler. A breeze swept across the island, strong enough to make the small forest in front of the veranda rustle.

Tanvir picked up his glass. "What should we drink to?"

"I have no idea."

"To chance?"

"What chance?"

"Like the one that brought you to this lonely island."

"That wasn't chance."

Tanvir looked down and nodded. Finally, he gave Tobey a serious look.

"Then perhaps to the memory of your sister?"

Tobey raised his can. "To Megan," he said softly, and then both drank a sip.

Tanvir exhaled deeply and it was impossible to say whether the sound expressed satisfaction or melancholy. He seemed tired; the skin under his eyes was dark and wrinkled.

Tobey placed the can on the table; in his hands the drink was growing warmer and warmer and was no longer enjoyable. "What are you doing here?" He shooed away an insect. "Where are the others?"

"The others?"

"The scientists. Your colleagues—the ones who conducted research with you here. Where are they?"

Tanvir turned his glass in his hands, staring at the two fingers of gin, and sighed. "All gone, I'm afraid."

"Why?"

Tanvir laughed—a tired laugh. "Look around. Would you want to work here?"

"It wasn't always like this."

"No." Tanvir drained the glass and filled it halfway again. "Long ago there was much more happening on the islands."

"There are more islands?"

"There are two. This one and the one where we found you."

"I was on another island?"

"Did I forget to tell you that?"

"Yes." Now it was clear to Tobey why he had climbed down a hill the other day that he had never seen on the island where the men dropped him off.

"How did . . . How did Montgomery get to the other island?"

"He was there with Jay Jay. They cross over on the boat from time to time and pick coconuts."

"Is it far away?"

"Ten, twenty minutes, depending on the boat. In rough seas it takes longer."

"Why two islands?"

"Fourteen years ago, when I arrived here, there was a lot of activity on both islands. There were eight scientists and five assistants. In addition to the employees there were locals who kept house, cooked, and cultivated vegetables. On the other island there were greenhouses, a few solar panels, and a sea water desalination plant, neither very big, but quite efficient. We had two boats: a small one with an outboard motor and a former fishing trawler." Tanvir scratched his head, a wistful smile on his face.

"You've been on this island for the last fourteen years?"

The doubting tone in Tobey's voice made Tanvir laugh.

Then he let out a long sigh. "Oh yes," he said. And then, after a pause, he spoke again more quietly. "Oh yes." He took a long drink of gin and leaned back. "Not that I was a young man fourteen years ago. But I had ambitions. Dreams. If someone had said to me then that I would still be sitting here today, I would have laughed, probably even cursed." He passed his hand several times over his bald head, as if to console himself.

"Then there was no one here but you when Megan arrived?"

Tanvir seemed to be thinking. He put his hand on the armrest and looked at a moth that sailed over the heat jet of the lamp and fell on the table, its scorched belly turned up and its legs flailing more and more slowly. He sipped his gin and cleared his throat. "No," he finally said, "I was the only one here. And the others that you met."

For a while they were both silent. They could hear the rustle of insect wings, the constant humming and the chirping in the background that rose from the trees that Tobey hardly noticed anymore, in the same way he no longer noticed the hum of a refrigerator.

"What are you researching?" he asked into the apparent silence.

Tanvir laughed again, again only briefly, as if he was amused by the misguided question of a child. The gin seemed to make him equally cheerful and melancholy. "I'm not even looking for the meaning of life anymore, Tobey."

"Why are you still here?"

"Think of me as the administrator of a disbanded operation."

"Who pays you?"

"The foundation. Soon there will be no more money, but it's enough, if nobody has any large expenses."

Tobey drank the rest of the cola. For the first time in a long time he felt a strong desire for whiskey. He was sitting on an island so small that it wouldn't even be recorded on any commercial map; he didn't know if he should think of himself as a prisoner or a guest, and whether or not what Tanvir told him was the truth or a lie, or something in between. He stretched out his arm and crushed the half-dead moth with his thumb. Then he got up and walked to the railing. A handful of stars twinkled above him; he could not see the moon.

"What kind of research took place when there were still people here?"

"Simply put, it was about improving communication between humans and primates; to take it to another dimension."

"Montgomery and Chester can talk?"

"Well, not *talk*. They communicate with us. They use their hands, and cards that contain pictures of things. In the past we even had computers, virtual dictionaries, and mobile keyboards with symbols; but that was a long time ago. Now we hardly practice with the two of them. Chester's ability to communicate is regressing. But Montgomery still has a considerable vocabulary. You can actually carry on something like a conversation with him."

"But isn't that a phenomenon?"

Tanvir nodded. He made a thoughtful face and his eyes rested on the glass in his hand, which was now empty. "You bet," he said. "Montgomery could be famous."

"You too."

Tanvir chuckled, and then he rubbed his bald head with a sigh. "Should I barnstorm around the world with him? From university to university, talk show to talk show?" He looked at Tobey and shook his head. "No. That wouldn't be good for either of us."

Tobey fingered the bandage on his head. The wound itched a little. A fly landed on the cola can; it flew away slowly when he shook it. "How did Megan come to the island?"

"Just like you. On a boat."

"What boat?"

"That's beyond my knowledge. Maybe it was the same men whose services you took advantage of, fishermen who earn a little extra money by dropping off adventurous children on lonely islands." Tanvir smiled and raised his hand. "Forgive me. I'm an old man; I think of all people under forty as children."

"Before she took up an alliance with you, did she ask if anyone here had work for her?"

"No. It just happened. Just like you."

"Who told her about the island?"

"You've got me there. Who told *you* about the island?"

"Megan. In a letter."

"That she sent from here?"

Tobey looked into the dark screen of trees. He felt a desire to hurl the can at it, but placed it on the railing instead. The conversation had exhausted him; he wanted to shower and to lie down on the bed and sleep, without dreaming, for a long time. "What kind of jellyfish did you say killed Megan?"

"I didn't name the exact species. I suspect, however, that it was a sea wasp."

"Are there many of them in these waters?"

"Jellyfish drift with the flow. Their behavior is dependent on the seasons, meteorological conditions, food supply, and reproductive behavior."

"By chance, you mean."

"By chance. Yes."

Tobey turned around. "Well, I'm going to bed now," he said. "I'm

101

tired."

"Sleep well." Tanvir raised his hand in a short wave, and then put his feet up. "I'm going to stay here for a while."

"Thank you for doctoring my wounds."

"Don't mention it."

At the steps, Tobey stopped. "Who is the guy that knocked me down?"

"Oh, him. A hothead with less sense than Chester. His uncle owns the boat that brings us food and fuel. He hangs around now and then on the other island."

"Does he come to this island, too?"

"Don't worry; he hasn't lost anything here."

"What did he want from me?"

"Who knows? He probably thought you were an intruder. Or a spy." Tanvir giggled.

"There's nothing to spy on here."

"Exactly." Tanvir poured some gin into the glass. "As I said, he's hot-headed and not very intelligent."

Tobey slapped his hand on his cheek to kill a mosquito. "So he never comes here."

"No."

The two men looked at each other directly in the eyes for a moment.

"Well then, good night."

Tanvir toasted Tobey. "Good night."

Tobey went down the stairs and across the clearing. The lights outside of the bunkhouse were just bright enough to help him find the entrance. In his room, he looked to see if the knife was still behind the boiler where he had hidden it a few hours ago, and then he took the letters out from under the mattress.

News from Megan

Tomorrow I fly to Borneo. How does that sound, Tobey? My husband
(how odd THAT sounds!) is taking me with him. He is considered one of
the leading European experts in the field of primate research (that is the
third unbelievable sentence in this letter!) and he is supposed to lead a
catch and release center for orangutans there. On Borneo the virgin forests, the habitat of the orangutans, have been cleared, and we, the good
people of the world, are flying there to prevent the worst, although it
happened long ago and happens every day. I'm so excited that I could
hardly sleep or eat for a week. Have I told you about my fear of flying? I
flew from London to Dublin some time ago (Cait in the supermarket; not
a chance encounter by the way), and nearly died of panic. At first, I sat in
my seat and I read the information that tells you what you should do in
an emergency, how to put on the life jacket and the oxygen mask and all
the things that you would really rather not know about. That made me a
bit nervous, and then the flight attendants explained everything to us
again, as if we were not here to fly, but to crash. I asked one of them
whether or not it was too late to get off, but the engine was already accel-
erating, and I closed my eyes and clung to the seat back. I was probably
hyperventilating because my neighbor asked me if everything was okay,
and I certainly seemed frightened to him when I didn't answer and grew
as pale and stiff as a board. My heart almost exploded; it roared in my
head and, when we took off, my stomach churned. (Fortunately, it was
empty.) Tomorrow I fly from London to Jakarta! And if that isn't

enough, I'll also be flying in a helicopter from Jakarta to a nest in the east of the island, where they have finished building the station, and everyone is waiting for the scientists. And for me, who has not completed my veterinarian training, who is only there because her husband cannot be without her. They will hate me, Tobey. They'll whisper behind my back and avoid me, smiling politely. They'll shake their heads when they see me, as I sketch the millipede that has rolled itself up on the floor of the community kitchen. They'll invent stories about me, because I stay in my room all day long and read (a suitcase full of books!); because I sit somewhere and write (useless stuff); because I wear leather boots (fear of flying and of snakes!). What are you afraid of, Toto? That you are as lonely as Seamus? As sad as Cait? That we will never meet again? That we will meet again? Should I send you a photo of myself? Do you want to know what I look like now, eleven years later? Are you ready for the dissolution of the great mystery, Toto, little brother? No, you're not. Let time pass. Wait. Seamus waited for you. In vain. Cait waited for me. In vain. So we spend our lives. We forfeit each other; we go past each other on the zigzag path of our endless search. We miss each other. We avoid each other. Did you cry at Seamus's grave? If yes: What were you crying about? The wasted years? About the words that passed between you? About the unspoken words? About the fact that he is gone, too far away to hear you anymore? I cried after I saw Cait. The light in the supermarket is supposed to make you happy - it depressed me deeply. I took the ferry back to London (to sink instead of crash) and in my apartment I discovered that the glove was gone. Her white gloves with the black spots (Wellie's fur), which she lost in the supermarket parking lot. What is the most important thing that you've ever lost, Tobey? Is it me? I wish that it was true for my sake, but not for yours.

Who loves you?
Megan!

104

9

The next day, Tobey woke up shortly after sunrise. He drank the water bottle empty, went into the bathroom, washed and dressed. He took the knife from its hiding place behind the boiler and slid it under the strip of cloth around his calf. When he sat on the rattan chair and tied his shoelaces, he noticed that the top of the bureau had a small gap at the corner. He gently raised the board, as thick as a thumb, and because it was not attached, he took it off completely and put it on the floor. Under the panel dusty plywood appeared, framed by timber boards nailed to the bureau. Tobey got toilet paper, wet it and wiped the dust from the plywood. The gap between the plywood and the top panel was about two inches wide, enough space for all of Megan's letters, his passport, and fifteen hundred dollars. He had stored the passport in one of the suitcases, in a package that had once contained a ready-to-serve meal, and which he (so it really felt genuine), had partially filled with rice and sealed. The money, divided into two bundles and wrapped in foil, had been hidden under the insoles of his shoes, but he thought it was time for a new repository. He wondered if Tanvir had discovered the passport, but he doubted it, because the bag looked untouched. He lay on the bed and thought about his host. The man, who seemed so friendly, had lied to him about the bearded child, and when it came to Megan and the circumstances of her death, he did not seem very credible to Tobey. He fumbled for the knife, got up and left the room.

Jay Jay was sitting on the sofa next to the refrigerator and reading a magazine which he had pulled apart. Tobey nodded to him, and Jay Jay nodded back. When Tobey was at the door, he heard Jay Jay whistle. It sounded like the chirping of the bird that sat in the tree in front of Tobey's window in the morning. When he turned around, Jay Jay stopped and raised the magazine in front of his face.

Rosalinda was standing at the stove and scooped cut-up vegetables from a wooden board into a pot. Chester sat on the floor beside her, clinging to the hem of her skirt with one hand and a carrot with the other. The radio was on; the music sounded like a military band playing a tango. Tobey greeted the cook in Tagalog. He had learned phrases like *good day*, *goodbye* and *thank you* by heart on the flight from London to Manila, and even knew how to ask about the nearest hospital or doctor in the national language. Rosalinda did not even look at him. She stirred the pot, put a lid on it, and then noisily opened one of the two refrigerators.

Tobey went to the table, where he found half a loaf of bread and some bananas. Chester looked up at him, chewing and with a distant gaze, the fingers of his left hand still clutching the hem of Rosalinda's dress. Rosalinda closed the refrigerator; in her hand she held a big yellow pumpkin.

"Coffee?" Tobey used the English word and when Rosalinda did not respond, he tried the Spanish. He saw the pitcher on the stove; the smell was still strong enough that it was not quite overpowered by the fumes of boiling vegetables.

Rosalinda reached for a kind of machete and cut the pumpkin into two halves, then quarters, a heaving goddess who took her bad mood out on one of the planets.

"I'm Catholic," said Tobey. "All of Ireland is Catholic." It did not matter that he had to exaggerate and lie; his desire for a cup of coffee was too great.

Rosalinda touched the pot briefly, then peeled the pumpkin with a knife and put the flesh in a bowl. Chester put the final piece of carrot in his mouth and looked around for more goodies. When he did not find anything, he tugged at Rosalinda's dress and let out a grunting noise. The cook gave him a cookie, which she took from a tin, and said something to the ape that sounded like a reprimand.

Tobey stood up, rolled up the sleeves of his shirt and showed Rosalinda the cross that he had had tattooed in Dublin, drunk and accompanied by Jason Dwyer, who had chosen a flaming skull for himself.

"Catholic," he said, hoping the barbed wire that was wound around the cross would not deter Rosalinda from recognizing him as a true Christian.

Rosalinda looked at the tattoo with a serious expression. She had large brown retinas and anyone who dared to look her in the eye saw the tiny green flecks inside them. She smelled of food and soap and sweat, and she breathed with a slight gasp, even when she was not moving.

"God," Tobey said after a while, when the cook made no attempt to include him in her church and to welcome him with a cup of coffee. "Dios."

Finally Rosalinda said something in her own language, a murmur, and Tobey could not tell whether it was disparaging or approving. When Chester pulled on her skirt, she reprimanded him with a single word. Then she pointed a finger at Tobey and asked in broken English:

"Do you believe in God?"

Tobey nodded vigorously. "Yes!" Maybe she had interpreted the barbed wire as a crown of thorns, he thought, and cried: "Jesus Christ!" If the woman still did not understand that he was one of them, he would give up and wash down the bread with water.

Rosalinda looked at him skeptically, her mind working to weigh the charges against the exculpatory evidence. Between her two upper incisors

107

a cavity gaped, the entrance to a narrow lane in a row of gleaming white houses. Tobey was warm. None of the ceiling fans were turning. He thought of Father MacMahon, who dedicated his life to God and the church, and he was ashamed of what he had done, all for a cup of coffee and to win the favor of a religious housekeeper.

Chester, who wore jeans severed above the knees and a kind of Hawaiian shirt, straightened up and reached for a piece of pumpkin. Rosalinda struck him lightly on the fingers; her warning was rich with vowels and full of dramatic melodies. Just as she was about to turn to Tobey again, to grant him absolution or to condemn him for eternity, the door opened and Miguel entered the room. He stopped a little too abruptly and looked at Rosalinda and Tobey, as if he had burst in on something extremely intimate. He closed the door, muttering with a wry smile on his face, took a cup from a shelf and poured himself coffee. Rosalinda said something to him, and after a short hesitation he handed the cup to Tobey, who had moved a few steps away from Rosalinda, and then took a new one from the shelf and filled it with coffee.

After a breakfast of coffee, bread, honey, bananas, hard boiled eggs and stale yellow cheese, Tobey went to the cemetery. On the way he had picked flowers; now he was sitting on the bench, which smelled like freshly cut wood. The sun had to be out somewhere; the two trees cast shadow patterns on the ground. Tobey had been crying. He had tried to remember a prayer or at least a few words from the minister during his father's funeral, but he could not even recall the first sentences of the Lord's Prayer. Then he had spoken to Megan about his journey, his quest, and he had grown calmer.

While deep in thought, he heard a noise behind him, the cracking of branches, footsteps. His torso snapped forward; he pulled out the knife and sprang from the bench. The bonobo, dressed in his tropical postman's uniform, stood stock still and stared at the knife in Tobey's outstretched hand. He had removed the cap; he held it in front of his chest with his thin fingers. Tobey lowered his arm, overcome by a wave of shame. The two stood facing each other, motionless, as if exhausted after a day in leaden heat. It was quiet around them; Tobey believed he could hear his heart beating. Montgomery, his eyes still wide open, clung to his cap like a driver to a steering wheel that was the only part left intact after a bizarre accident.

"I'm sorry," Tobey murmured after a while, which he could not say had lasted seconds or minutes. The knife suddenly weighed heavy in his hand. As if performing some obscene act, he turned away, pulled up his trouser leg and pushed the weapon under the strap.

Montgomery blinked and began to move. He went to the bench and looked at Tobey; he seemed to be waiting for him to sit down beside him. Tobey hesitated, and then he took a place beside the bonobo, insecure and shy. He was five and had to sit next to his father in church; he was twelve and sank beside Keira Fitzpatrick, who took his hand and told him they were now engaged; he was twenty and settled down on the sofa, where his friend lay quietly and invited death with a gently singing voice.

For a long time they sat there. Once Montgomery shooed away an insect by blowing it from his arm. Tobey relaxed. At some point he leaned back and noticed how sleepy he was.

When Tobey opened his eyes, the sun had completely disappeared from the small cemetery and a dull, heavy light remained over everything. The cap was lying next to him. He had dreamed, he remembered, that he had been swimming. He had seen lights—stars that were reflected in the water, glowing jellyfish. His left hand was asleep. He shook it.

Montgomery stood in front of Megan's grave, and only now did Tobey realize that he had removed his cap out of respect for the dead. For a long time the bonobo did not move, then he got down on his knees, pulled out the weeds by hand and arranged some of the sea-polished stones that surrounded the grave. Finally, he got up, stopped for a moment with bowed head, and then went to another grave.

Tobey felt strangely light in this shady square of grass and trees, mourning and comfort, remembrance and farewell. He had the feeling of having arrived at the end of his journey. Montgomery came to him and put his hand on Tobey's for a moment. Then he put on his cap and signaled for Tobey to follow him.

They entered the kitchen hut through the back door, where the shadows from a few trees fell. Montgomery went first. They came to a room with four upholstered chairs, an empty bookcase and a television. On the wall behind the chairs there was a picture that showed the nocturnal skyline of New York. Montgomery opened the door and stepped aside to let Tobey enter first.

The room was surprisingly large and bright and furnished with a single bed, a closet, a bureau, a bookshelf, a desk, a stool and an armchair. Part of the floor was covered with a sisal carpet; beside the bed there was a blue wool carpet, an oval lake, where two slippers lay on its banks like barges. On the free areas of the wall hung framed photos: the Eiffel Tower, the Golden Gate Bridge, the Kremlin, and the Pyramids. A colorful bedspread decorated with floral motifs was spread over the bed; on a green pillow *Mr. M* was embroidered with yellow thread. The patina of old age lay over everything; each object was worn out and bleached by the light that penetrated through the thin curtains. The room of a man, Tobey thought, a retired teacher (geography and history), unmarried, lonely.

Montgomery closed the door. He stood, hands intertwined behind his back, two steps away from Tobey, a reserved, polite old man who gives his guest time to look around.

"Nice," said Tobey. He raised the thumb of his right hand and repeated the word.

Montgomery nodded. Then he went to the bookshelf, where there were children's books, illustrated books, and file folders. He took a folder from a shelf and handed it to Tobey. The folder contained about fifty pages. On each sheet there were four words. For every word there was a photo of the concept and illustrations with the appropriate hand signs. *Arm*, Tobey read. *Eye. Ball. Belly.* The illustrations were very simple, black and white graphics.

"Belly," said Tobey. After the concept there were photos of a man and an ape, whose bellies were framed by a red rectangle.

Montgomery went to the desk, took a piece of cardboard the size of a playing card out of a file index box and handed it to Tobey. On one side of the cardboard there were two photos; on the other side there was an illustration, a line drawing that was neither man nor ape, with a head, a torso, two arms and two legs. A hand, consisting entirely of lines, touched the figure's belly. Montgomery rested a hand on his own belly.

Tobey could not prevent the astonished grin that spread across his face. He wanted to applaud, but he realized how inappropriate it would be. He continued to leaf through the pages and read *banana* and *beetles, lamp* and *lion, water* and *worm, fence* and *funny.* Further back in the folder were more difficult concepts: *reject, alone, think, help, sick, air, tired, music, peace, punishment, death, forget, injury, anger, show.* On the last two pages there were names: *Chester. Gwendolyn. Jay Jay. Maxwell. Miguel. Minnie. Nelson. Rosalinda. Tanvir. Wesley.* At the very end, also handwritten but in a different lettering that was intimate to him, Tobey read: *Megan.* Below each of the names a large passport photo was pasted. Maxwell and Minnie were chimpanzees; and Gwendolyn and Wesley bonobos; Nelson an orangutan.

"Megan," Tobey muttered. Tears filled his eyes. Megan's hair was short and bleached by the sun, much brighter than before. She faced the camera, looking the viewer straight in the eye. There was a smile on her face like the pale, dusky evening light that would disappear in the next instant.

Montgomery sat at his desk and took several more cards out of the index file. Then he signed to Tobey. He had laid out four cards.

Megan. Dead. I. Sorry.

Montgomery sat on the chair and looked at the floor. With his crooked back, the crumpled shirt and a pencil stub in his hand, he looked like a tired official in the godforsaken province of a hot, insignificant country. Tobey wanted to put a hand on his shoulder, but he did not; he shut the folder and put it back on the shelf.

The ceiling fan turned; waves of cool air swept over Tobey's naked torso. He lay on the bed and flipped through the folder that Montgomery had given him. A color photograph pasted on the first page showed the bonobo. He was wearing a white shirt and a blue tie with white stripes, and it was hard for Tobey to say whether he was looking into the camera with simple self-confidence, or if he was completely expressionless. The text under the picture said: "ME" and, in brackets: "MONTGOMERY."

After a while Tobey put the folder under the pillow and put on a shirt and shoes. Despite the incident with Montgomery, he strapped the knife to his calf. He left the room and the bunkhouse and went to the beach. The sky was overcast; a slight wind drove the clouds from a direction that Tobey assumed was east. When he reached the sea, he sat on a rock and watched as it grew dark, hardly surprised by the speed with which the sun disappeared behind the horizon.

Then he saw the light. It was white and far away and died away suddenly. Tobey jumped down from the rock, although he was sure he could not be seen in his dark clothing. He stood in the shelter of the rock and listened to the quiet hum of the engine, which slowly came closer. As the noise grew louder, he ran back the way he had come and took the path that led along the beach toward the villa. Where two paths crossed, he ran up the embankment; behind it he saw the sea. Before he reached the top, he slowed his pace and finally stopped. The engine noise was clearly audible, the chugging mingled with the sound of waves that rolled gently onto the beach without breaking. Tobey lay down and peered between the tufts of yellow, dry grass to the point where the stone rose up out of the sand. The sea was a darkly designed, flickering ribbon, which merged with the deep sky. The strip between the sparsely vegetated embankment where Tobey lay and the sluggish heaving sea was just bright enough to make the boat a recognizable object. Four figures emerged from the darkness, swirling points that grew larger and took on shape, like the open wooden boat that they pulled ashore. Their voices, at first a diffuse snarl, stood out gradually against the breaking noise of the surf.

Tobey now thought it best to make himself invisible. He turned around and ran, ducking, down the embankment, followed the path for a bit and disappeared into a grove; between the tree trunks the air was so lightless and substantial that he felt he had to swallow it. When he heard the voices come closer, Tobey went into a crouch. The reed-like grass that lined the path stood waist-deep and dense; when the men emerged a little later, he could only see their heads. He could not see one of them at all. They no longer talked, but one of them swore softly when he dropped something heavy and then groaned as he lifted it. Somewhere a bird sounded an alarm; far away another cawed. The cicadas stopped their shrill singing, only to cry out more violently a moment later.

Tobey waited until the men were gone, then followed them. For a moment he toyed with the idea of taking the boat and sailing it away, only to dismiss it, because he needed his suitcases, money, Megan's letters, and water. He also did not know which direction he needed to take and how much gas there was in the tank of motorboat. He did not want to leave the island without taking something of Megan's, one of the smooth polished stones from her grave, perhaps, or the notes and drawings that Tanvir had mentioned.

First he heard the voices, and then he saw the pale glimmer of light. He crouched down and listened. Reaching for the knife should have calmed him down, but it had the opposite effect. After a short time, while his heart was beating in his throat, he crept forward to a place from which, concealed behind bushes and grass, he could see a small clearing where six men stood, among them the bearded child. Tobey also saw Miguel and Jay Jay, who were talking to one of the men from the boat. Yellow light from several oil lamps fell on the sandy soil; he saw half a dozen canisters and wooden boxes and two containers made of bright plastic, as large as refrigerators, with handles at the ends. The men drank from a bottle they were passing around; two smoked. They spoke in short sentences; no one laughed or raised his voice. When the bottle was empty, the four men who had come by boat lifted the two plastic containers and headed back to the beach.

Tobey forgot everything he had ever read about snakes and crawled through the dry grass in a thicket of bamboo-like trunks, as thick as arms, where he laid on the cool earth that smelled of rot and decomposing leaves and waited until Miguel and Jay Jay had carried the boxes away in their wheelbarrows and all was quiet again.

In his room, he washed his hands and face and lifted up the lid on the chest of drawers to see if everything was still there. Then he went over to the kitchen hut. He peered through the window and saw Rosalinda and Chester, who were sitting at the table and shucking corn. The radio was playing; the sound of violins and a high, sad female voice penetrated through the screen door. Chester was chewing on something and worked slowly; Rosalinda plucked the leaves and fibers from the cobs with an expert hand.

Although Tobey was hungry, he took the smaller of the two flashlights from his room, (the flashlights that the salesman had forced upon him as indispensable), and walked across the field in the direction where he suspected he would find the hill. The cloud cover had broken; now and then moonlight shone through a gap. He turned on the flashlight every few meters so he would not trip, then he continued in the darkness. He got lost, eventually found himself at the field in front of the huts again, turned around, took a different route, and came onto a slightly rising path which he followed. When he passed an uprooted tree, he was sure he had gone in a circle. He sat down, took off his shirt and cursed himself for not having drunk anything in advance.

Megan sat next to him; together they waited for the rain that he had predicted. They talked about the things that had occurred in their lives, about the new teacher from Dublin who drove an old VW Beetle and listened to *Pink Floyd*; about the dead badger in the ditch, whose swollen body was crawling with thousands of maggots; about Megan's essay on the subject of volcanoes, so good that her classmates claimed she had copied it; about Patrick Weelan, who Tobey had thrashed because he had called him a fag; about Ruby, the three-year-old cow that Megan wanted to buy from her father with her allowance, to protect her from the slaughterhouse.

When Tobey heard the voices, he stood up and ducked behind chest-high bushes, whose greenery was just sufficient enough to hide him. He held his breath and listened until he was sure that the men had moved somewhere in front of him and were not behind him. After he put his shirt on again and sat down, he rubbed the bandages on his wrists with moist dirt, because they glowed in the dark. Then he waited.

Miguel, a flashlight in one hand and a bucket in the other, came first. Tanvir was in the middle, and although he wasn't carrying anything, Tobey heard him gasping for breath. Jay Jay, the most heavily loaded with two buckets, followed at a distance of several yards. Like a child who gives himself courage in the forest at night, he talked continuously. His white waistcoat glimmered when the moonlight broke through the clouds for a short moment, then it grew pale and disappeared between the trees like his voice.

Tobey counted to a hundred, then stood up and walked in the direction from which the men had come. When he was sure that he could not be seen, he turned on the flashlight. After a while, he found an air duct pro-truding from a hollow tree trunk which released an unpleasant, acrid odor. The stone that he dropped into the duct struck a grate after half a yard and got stuck. Tobey walked around for a while and scraped the earth with his foot, and then he broke a branch off a tree and brushed the ground with it.

Minutes later he struck metal. He swept the leaves and soil to the side and looked at the padlock. Just to try it, he poked around the key hole with the knife blade, and then he began to loosen the screws on both the hinges which secured the cover to the metal frame. The screws were rusty, and it took forever for Tobey to remove them. Finally, he heaved the cover up and put it on the ground. He shone the flashlight into the shaft, listening one last time for sounds, and then climbed down the steps into the tunnel.

News from Megan

No letter from Megan for such a long time. So many days, weeks, months. The island, the destruction, death. Should I tell you about it, Tobey? Would you want to know how the orangutan babies looked when they were brought to camp from the place where an organized, profitable riot occurred and smoke rose into the sky like that from a slaughter house? Do I have to describe their burnt hands and feet to you; the singed fur; their eyes? Or how they clung to the nurses; how they were doctored and fed by hand so they would not die immediately, but a few days or weeks later; perfect, beautiful creatures with a soul; a tray full of bones and skin; a name on a list; waste. Did you think I would want to tell you about it, Toto? Or—and now comedy comes into the tragedy— about how Stuart (now you know the name!) cheated on me with a journalist? Would you be interested to learn that my husband, who I will never see again and who, I hope, will press ahead with the divorce as soon as he is back in England, after four weeks in Borneo (two of which we spent, like all newcomers, in the quarantine station), arrived at the conclusion that the marriage to me had been a terrible mistake? Should I have told you that after eight weeks he had found Vivienne more attractive than me; less odd, less troubled, less sad, less withdrawn? Should I have entrusted to you that Stuart sought relief in the boat house with Vivienne; a relief that I could not provide to him because I dreamed of blisters and bizarre funerals (initially, small coffins made of wooden crates; later a piece of tent cloth), and government officials, who visited our station, shook hands and then drove to the logging companies and palm oil plantations and cattle ranches in their Range Rovers? Wasn't it better to save you from the description of my premature departure, to spare you the details? (Tears, curses, half a bottle of rum, three torn men's shirts, bribery of a local driver, several dilapidated bridges, a night at the Hotel Imperial in a nameless hick town, an eight-hour bus ride, a night at the Hotel Royal in another nameless hick town, four days in Jakarta, the flight over Kuala Lumpur to Manila.) Manila. I've been here almost three weeks. The Hotel Excelsior. (I remain faithful to anything fantastic and snobbish.) Imagine it like this: a rundown house in a district that has seen better times, but has also seen worse times; eleven rooms, a fat owner named Pablo with two fat girlfriends who always wears the same facial expression (bored), and who everyone secretly calls Papa Botox; a varying number of crazy people (including me!); a dog named Suki and a swimming pool, empty and covered with boards because a guest drowned in it two years ago (there are various stories about what happened in circulation, one more unbelievable than the next). I have a job. I work five mornings a week for an Australian professor; I handle his correspondence, search for articles on the Internet, make coffee, accompany him to the park and the doctor, etc. Jeffrey Salter is a former professor of anthropology and psychology (an interesting combination), who will be seventy-eight next year and spends six months each year in Manila and six in his home town of Darwin. There is a huge library in the apartment and when it is too hot in the early afternoon to go back to the hotel, I stay there and read, well into the evening hours. Although his main interest is people, Jeffrey has numerous books about animals. As a psychologist and a former dog owner, he worries over the question of whether or not animals can think and feel—whether, for example, they grieve and love and sense desire. What do you think Tobey? Did Sam long for his mother? Was he able to remember his time as a colt? Did Wellie love us? What did Holly think about, when someone took her from her pen in the early morning and took her to the rear, where it still smelled of Emma's blood and where they tied up her legs and pushed her onto the concrete floor and a knife was thrust into her large heart, even though she had whelped numerous piglets over many years, had always been good natured and modest and had cried so pitifully for her life? Were the chickens stupid, gently cooing to themselves as father carried them to the wood block? Am I stupid because I ask such questions? Do you remember the book that I carried around for so long it fell apart? Where do the fish sleep when they are tired? What do the bears dream about in hibernation? Where does the sun go when it gets dark?

Who loves you?
Megan!

10

The odor was pungent, but dissipated quickly through the open shaft. Tobey was reminded of the chemistry class at school: of blue flames and clouds of white, of watery eyes and windows hastily flung open. He remembered Sheila Laverty, who had fainted because she could not tolerate the smell of sulfur. The boys in the class had gathered around her to give her mouth-to-mouth resuscitation, but she came to her senses again all by herself. Tobey went through the corrugated iron tunnel and the corridor and rattled the handles of five doors, which were all locked. Shining the flashlight through the window to light up the dark rooms did not illuminate anything; the only thing he saw was a shelf on a wall, where bottles stood and reflected the beams of light. The hallway ended at a steel door and a concrete wall, where someone had scrawled the word JESUS.

When he went back to the exit, he saw the pill lying on the ground. He picked it up, smelled it, and put it in his pocket. Then he climbed the steps, closed the door, and replaced the screws. To conceal the marks from the knife blade, he rubbed damp soil on the screw heads. Finally, he covered the door with soil, leaves, and branches, and then made his way back.

In his room, Tobey took the pill from his pocket and placed it under the pillow. Then he undressed, slipped the knife into the hiding place behind the boiler, showered and took the clothes from the previous day out of the closet. They were not fresh, but they were still clean. He washed the dirty pants and the sweaty shirt in the washbasin with soap and hung them both on the shower curtain rod. After he was dressed, he put the pill in his pocket and went out of the room over to the kitchen hut.

Rosalinda was sitting at the table with a cup of coffee, reading a book. Although she seemed to be in a bad mood, she answered Tobey's greeting. Chester was lying on the floor. He picked little scraps from a slice of bread, rolled them into balls and put them in his mouth. In his right foot he held the hem of Rosalinda's skirt. He looked at Tobey through half-open lids, pursed his lips and made one of those sounds that expressed well-being.

Tobey sat at the table across from Rosalinda. Out of the radio came something muted that sounded like salsa played by a string orchestra. Like the giant hands of a clock moving much too quickly, the blades of the ceiling fans turned, but time seemed to stand still.

The cook looked up. "Wait," she said, pointing to the dainty watch which cut into the flesh of her forearm. She pushed a basket full of bread in Tobey's direction, and then went back to her book.

The bread was dry and heavily salted. Tobey poured water from the jug into his glass and drank it all. When Rosalinda turned a page she sighed heavily, as if it exerted her or as if she lamented the implications of the reading. As far as Tobey could tell, it was a religious book. On every other page color illustrations were printed, which showed creatures that wore crowns of glistening halos, cloud covered mountain peaks where golden crosses stood, angels with flaming swords in their hands. Tobey saw the devil: a red, horned figure, piercing a spear through the chest of a man who was dressed in a suit and hat. At the sight of Satan, Rosalinda crossed herself, muttered something like a short prayer, a formula for the banishment of evil, and turned the pages more quickly. She moved her lips while she read and wrinkled her forehead, and now and then she whispered a word that probably seemed particularly significant to her. Tobey's presence was obviously unimportant to her. When she rose to stir the pots, she dignified him with just as little a glance as when she sat down again. Nevertheless, Tobey had the feeling that the icy disapproval of the first day had given way to a reserved affection, or at least a large-hearted toleration.

Every few minutes, Chester's outstretched arm appeared next to Rosalinda like the periscope of a submarine. Then, without taking her eyes from her reading, the cook grabbed a slice of bread and pressed it into the chimpanzee's hand, whereupon the arm descended and a comforting grunt rose up.

When the three men entered the kitchen, Tobey woke from his comatose state with a start. Miguel and Jay Jay brought in firewood and a dead chicken; Tanvir placed a gas cylinder on the floor. Rosalinda took deep breath, let out a sigh, placed a piece of string between the pages and closed the book noisily.

"I'm sorry," said Tanvir. "It lasted a little longer than planned."

Rosalinda mumbled something, got up and took the pot from the heat. Miguel and Jay Jay went into the next room, where you could wash your hands before eating.

Tanvir looked at Tobey. He wore long, sand-colored pants and a dark blue short-sleeved shirt with thin black stripes. "I thought you left us without saying goodbye."

"How could I?" said Tobey.

"Yes, how could you?" Tanvir smiled and followed the two Filipinos.

Chester's arm appeared next to Rosalinda's empty chair, and when no one gave him a slice of bread he got up and peered over the table top. Rosalinda did not have time for him; she sprinkled spices into a pot full of vegetables and with her knee she banged shut the door of oven, from which she had just removed a grill with baked ears of corn.

The idea to give Chester the pill just came to Tobey. He did not want to hurt the chimpanzee, but he did not want to test it on himself either. While he was forming a ball of soft bread, he told himself that the pill was too small to be seriously dangerous to the portly animal. Maybe it was just a remedy, he thought half-heartedly, for cholera or malaria, diseases that existed in this area, or for pain, diarrhea, fever, or cabin fever. They looked like vitamin tablets, he told himself, but of course he knew that was nonsense. In the pale yellow oval pill there was a synthetic drug. He had seen hundreds of them, in all colors and shapes. For a time he had taken them himself: for stimulation, for reward, for comfort.

What he could not predict was the strength of the drug that he was holding between his thumb and index finger like a lackluster diamond. Nevertheless, he stuck the pill into the pliant dough and he was startled when Rosalinda rattled a pot lid. An opera played on the radio; in the cold dark belly of the refrigerator bottles jingled softly when the motor started up with a violent shiver.

Just as Tobey offered the bread ball to Chester, Montgomery entered the room. Tobey was about to withdraw his hand, but Chester had already seized the ball in his fingers, sniffed it, and put it in his mouth. Montgomery was wearing light gray pants and a shirt of the same color, which made him look like a prison inmate. He sat down in his chair, smoothed the plastic table cloth, and polished his spoon with a paper napkin. Then he sat there, motionless, with his shoulders slumped, as if lost in contemplation of the salt shaker, an expression of indifference and grief on his dark, flat face.

When Tanvir, Miguel, and Jay Jay came from washing their hands, all of the pots, bowls and jugs were on the table. Rosalinda stayed back and finished her prayer after about two minutes, which Tanvir, who seemed restless and tired, repeated.

"Oh, Lord," Tobey said in the ticking silence that followed, between the alternating murmurs of the *Amens* and the backs of chair, rattling cutlery and the satisfied moans of Chester's anticipation, and everyone, including the bonobo and the chimpanzee, stopped in their tracks. The motion which Rosalinda used to guide the ladle froze over a bowl; Tanvir's napkin hung in the air between the edge of the table and his chin; Jay Jay's empty plate floated above the clouds of steam from an open pot. "We thank you for your grace and the abundance of your gifts to us." Forks were gently returned to their places, glasses put down, hands folded. "We pray that all those we love and who cannot be here with us today, may find peace in your care. We also ask you, oh Lord, to help us in our efforts to fight evil, falsehood and lies. Blessed be your name, forever. Amen."

For a moment there was silence in the kitchen. No one moved; only the blades of the ceiling fans circled.

"Amen," Rosalinda said at last, crossed herself, and let the ladle sink into the bowl with the cooked vegetables.

Now the three men came out of their stupor, repeated an "Amen" and began to fill their plates.

"Do you go to church often, Tobey?" Tanvir looked for the largest piece of chicken in the pot and put it on his plate.

"I haven't been in a church for years."

"But it sounded very convincing."

"That wasn't my intention."

Tanvir loaded his plate with rice and vegetables and took a slice of bread from the basket. "Fighting against evil, Tobey? Falsehood?"

Tobey had no desire for a conversation. He chewed and took a long sig of water. "If I can," he said finally.

"Evil." Tanvir paused, to let Tobey take in the significance of his words. "That is a powerful opponent."

Tobey did not say anything else. For a while they all ate in silence. Occasionally Chester made a sound, a long, drawn out sigh comprised of several pitches that was accompanied by a high, fluttery growl.

When the pots and pans were all empty and everyone was full, Rosalinda put on the water for coffee and placed a large plate with watermelon slices in the middle of the table. The plate was the size of a hubcap. She scolded Chester, who was about to serve himself, and took away his paper napkin before he could stuff it into his ears.

"Were you swimming today?" Tanvir asked, after he had reprimanded Chester with a few hand signals.

"Yes."

"Nobody has seen you all day."

"Was somebody looking for me?"

Tanvir smiled and dabbed his mouth with the napkin. "The island is small; encounters are almost inevitable."

"I wanted to be alone."

"I understand." Tanvir put two pieces of melon on his plate. "But on the beach, in the heat?" He clicked his tongue. "You'll get a heat stroke."

"I was in the cemetery."

"Oh, the cemetery." Tanvir picked the seeds from the melon and lined them up on the edge of his plate. "A wonderful place. One would like to stay there forever in its shady coolness."

Rosalinda brought the coffee and poured for those who held out their cups. Chester grabbed the pocket of her dress with both hands and tried to poke his head inside it. The cook placed the coffee pot on the table, grabbed Chester's arms and pushed him back into his chair. At the same time she scolded him quietly, which sounded more threatening than if she had shouted.

"What's wrong with him?" asked Tanvir.

"I don't know," Rosalinda said. "He's acting strange all of a sudden."

Chester stretched out his arms, waved his hands in the air and flung open his mouth, but no sound came from his throat. He rolled his head

125

back and his pupils disappeared beneath his trembling eyelids. His fingers moved as if he was playing a piano, then he waved his arms like a mad conductor, or a drowning man. Rosalinda gave him a pat on the head and scolded him loudly. Now Chester began to howl. He swayed his upper body back and forth and finally fell off the chair and rolled on the ground and continued to lie on his back with outstretched arms and legs, his fingers and toes fluttering.

Tanvir and Miguel jumped up as Chester toppled from the chair. Miguel said something, again and again the same three words, and held Chester's head with both hands. Tanvir stared down at the animal, which rolled around on the wooden planks as if in a terrible dream. Then he turned to Rosalinda and shouted something in Tagalog, which sounded to Tobey's ears like a question or an allegation. The cook shook her head vigorously and defended herself, and when Miguel spoke to her, she began to cry. Then she grabbed the dish towel that hung over her shoulder and threw it at him.

Tobey rose. He looked Chester in the eye and the chimp returned his gaze for a few moments. It seemed like an eternity to Tobey. The animal stuck out his tongue, which was flecked with white spots, and moved his head slowly back and forth. The sounds that poured from his mouth varied between cheerfulness and a deep mumbling misery, and ended with a long droning sigh. Tanvir knelt down beside Chester; he felt his pulse and then shouted something to Jay Jay, who took a flashlight from a shelf and ran out of the kitchen. Rosalinda sat on her chair and sobbed into the dish towel that Miguel had given back to her. Tobey felt terrible, and he suddenly felt nauseous. He gripped the armrest of his chair tightly with both hands and avoided looking at Chester. Once he turned his head to the side and winced when he realized that Montgomery's gaze rested on him.

Two hours later, Tobey was in Tanvir's room at the end of the bunkhouse, far away from the noisy diesel engine, drinking sweet, ice-cold black tea. Tanvir had opened two double doors which led to a narrow veranda. Clay pots stood on the rough wooden planks; between large stones the skull of an animal shimmered in white. Tobey had taken a seat on the sofa. Tanvir sat in a chair whose brown leather was scuffed and cracked. Half an hour earlier they had put Chester to bed. The chimpanzee inhabited a room in the kitchen hut next to Rosalinda's, just a few steps from Montgomery. Because Chester could not be alone, the door between his room and Rosalinda's had been removed years ago and replaced by a curtain. Tobey, plagued by a guilty conscience and yet reasonably calm, because he saw that Chester was slowly recovering, had gone along with them when they carried the sleeping chimpanzee from the kitchen into his room. While Rosalinda was putting a blanket over Chester, Tobey had a look around. Illustrated photos hung on the bright blue walls, a patchwork of mountains, meadows and lakes, automobiles, animals, movie stars, airplanes, tractors and illustrated recipes. The shelves were full of picture books and stuffed animals; in one corner stood a white rocking horse. Montgomery lived in the room of an old man; Chester's room was that of a small child.

"Just a few years ago we had equipment for blood tests here." Tanvir had finished two glasses of iced tea; now he poured himself a gin. He looked even more tired than he had at dinner and nearly sank into the chair, the backrest protruding far above his head. "Now all I can do is speculate."

"I think your guess about a poisonous fruit or plant is the most plausible," Tobey said. A ceiling fan ensured that the stuffy air kept moving, but he was sweating anyway. At Chester's bedside he had held the chimpanzee's hand, just for a moment, and he felt horrible. He had wondered about the after-effects of the drug, whatever it was, and he remembered entire days in bed, a head full of cotton wool and needles and numb fingers.

127

"That would be very strange. Chester is a glutton, but he would never eat anything he didn't recognize."

"Maybe he found something."

"What?"

"I don't know."

Tanvir looked at Tobey blankly. "Puzzling," he said.

A larger beetle crashed into a window and fell to the ground, where he spun around in circles, buzzing.

"Where are Montgomery and Chester from?" Tobey asked to change the subject.

Tanvir looked at Tobey with a slightly confused expression, as if he had never questioned the origin of the primates until now. "I don't know," he said. "They were here when I came."

"It never interested you?"

"Well, I know that they were both born in captivity and raised by humans."

Tobey looked outside. They sat in the dark, so the insects would not come into the room. There were questions he wanted to ask, but they had nothing to do with the primates. He wanted to know if he was being held prisoner here, if drugs were manufactured here, and how Megan had really lost her life. But he was silent. He looked out into the night and imagined himself lying in a boat, on a morning after an endless night, floating on a river, farther and farther, toward an unknown destination.

"Chester and Montgomery don't seem like animals, if that's what you mean." Tanvir's voice was muted, as if from far away, from the distant bank of the river. "They probably think they're people."

"But they're not," Tobey said, drowsy and at the same time awakened by a sudden aversion to this conversation. He reached for his glass and did not notice that it was empty until he held it in his hand. "They belong in Africa. In a jungle, with their own kind."

Tanvir burst out laughing, a short, hoarse cough, which he soothed

128

with a drink of gin. "Very good! And us? Do we belong in caves, dressed in skins and armed with spears? Riding in donkey carts? Or in carriages?"

"I'm serious." Tobey slammed the glass on the table, but the gesture did not have the impact he had hoped for.

"Oh, of course you're serious! Because you're a romantic, Tobey. Have you ever been to Africa? I have. The jungle . . ." Tanvir laughed again, chuckling, slowly shaking his head. "A dreamer and a Christian to boot. Heaven forbid!"

Tobey wanted to get up and leave, but he was worn out and sank into the soft sofa.

"Am I your prisoner?" he asked, so suddenly that the four words surprised him.

Tanvir, whose chin was resting on his chest, raised his head. "What?"

"You heard me. Are you keeping me locked up here?"

Tanvir seemed too tired to laugh. His upper body twitched almost imperceptibly; some air escaped from his mouth. "Did I forget to mention it? The day after tomorrow the supply boat is coming. You can leave on it."

Tobey suddenly felt very uncomfortable. Under his shirt, he could feel the sweat that ran from his pores; his head was empty and it weighed as much as two full suitcases. He wanted to say something, something conciliatory, or something that would have justified his question, but he could not think of anything. He sat on the edge of the sofa and looked into the yellow flicker of a lamp on the veranda.

For the next few minutes the two men sat in silence, each lost in his own thoughts, plunging into an internal lake without light or reason.

"It was a long day," Tanvir finally said, draining his glass and rising from the chair. "If you don't mind, I'll retire now."

"Of course." Tobey also stood up.

Tanvir closed the two doors and bolted them. "Oh, that reminds me. I have something for you." He went to a bureau made of wood as black as coal, decorated with flower blossoms and birds, took an envelope from the top drawer, and gave it to Tobey.

"What is it?"

"You could say that it's Megan's will and testament."

Tobey looked at the brown paper envelope, only a few millimeters thick but weighed heavily in his hand.

"I'm sure she would have wanted you to have her things," Tanvir said as he opened the door.

Tobey stepped into the corridor, which was lit by a fluorescent bulb. He wanted to say something, but he could not think of anything, so he remained silent.

"Good night, Tobey," said Tanvir, who looked even older and more tired in the neon light.

"Good night." Tobey took a few steps, turned around and said, "Thank you." But Tanvir had already closed the door.

Tobey lay on the bed and opened the envelope. He counted eighteen sheets of paper and an oval label from a beer bottle. On the back of the label Megan had drawn a curled up centipede. Eleven of the pages were covered on both sides with sketches of animals and plants; four were portraits of Montgomery and Chester and one was a bonobo with his foot in a plaster cast. Two pages contained poems and one, crumpled and then smoothed out again, was a letter to him.

News from Megan

Today there are no memories, no words, no dreams, no remorse, no despair, no confessions, no happiness, no travel, no childhood, no moments, no sadness, no reconciliation, no cries, no breath, no goodbyes, no stars, no sea, no lies, no pain, no misunderstandings, no places, no songs, no joy, no heaven, no desires, no steps, no sun, no embraces, no questions, no strength, no courage, no rebellion, no pausing, no illusions, no fear, no excuses, no me, no escape, no wonder, no self-reproach, no thoughts, no animals, no tears, no hope, no anger, no soul, no persuasion, no light, no hills, no mercy.

No love.
No Megan.

11

Tobey waded through hip-deep water. With both hands, he gripped a bamboo rod that had a net fastened to its end. He scooped jellyfish from the water with the net and threw them on the beach behind him. The sea and the sky were dark; the jellyfish translucent, luminous muscles that formed pulsing lumps in the sand. Tobey was panting from the effort; with each full net his arms grew heavier. Megan swam far out, where there were no jellyfish. Now and then she raised her arm and waved. He wanted to call out to her—to let her know she must not swim to him— but no sound came out of his mouth. His heart was beating so loudly he could hear it.

When Tobey woke up, his arms felt like lead. He lay there for a while, staring at the ceiling, where the fan was turning on the slowest setting. Outside, it was still dark and almost quiet. He turned on his side and closed his eyes. Then he heard the knock. He sat up and listened. He wanted to shout "Who's there?" but it came out as a whisper. He reached for the water bottle; it was empty. There was another knock. Tobey climbed out of bed, put on shorts and a T-shirt, and opened the door. In that moment it occurred to him that he should get the knife from the bathroom, but then he saw that it was only Montgomery, standing in front of him in his gray uniform. He felt his heart pounding, and forced himself to smile. Montgomery used his hands to form a rectangle, and turned the invisible pages.

"The folder?" Tobey stepped aside and let Montgomery come into the room. He took the folder from the bureau and gave it to the orangutan.

Montgomery put his finger on his picture on the first page, went to the fourth page from the end and tapped on the words *room* and then *show*.

"Do you want to show me something?" Tobey asked.

Montgomery struck the last page and pointed to Megan's photo, then pointed to the words *pen* and *paper*.

Tobey was too sleepy to make a rhyme out of them. He searched for the word *wait*, pointed to the chair, and went to the bathroom to wash his face. Then he got dressed and followed Montgomery, who was carrying the folder, to his room. There Montgomery tipped over the armchair, loosened the horizontal fabric straps that were stretched tightly across the bottom, and pulled out a bundle of paper wrapped in plastic film and held together with string. He went behind the bed with it, settled down on the floor, and waited until Tobey sat on his knees beside him with the folder. The film was worn out and gray, the string frayed and in some places so thin it was almost severed. Like a conservator handling precious documents, Montgomery took page after page in his hand and placed them gently on the closed folder.

On the first three pages there were tables with lists of blood types, numbers, medical-sounding terms, abbreviations and handwritten notes: all sorts of things that Tobey couldn't figure out.

Next there were lists with codes composed of letters and numbers, and entries that looked to Tobey like findings or medical records. He skimmed over four such lists and understood nothing, except that they obviously dealt with blood tests and the status of test subjects, who he suspected were linked to the codes. At the end of some lines he saw the word EXITUS and a date.

Montgomery pulled two photos out of the stack. The black and white photographs showed an emaciated chimpanzee standing against a white wall, and a bonobo, connected to an intravenous drip, who was lying on a cot. Slips of adhesive paper had been stuck to the back of the photos, where data like the day, month, and year of birth, the sex, weight, and blood type had been entered. The last column had been designated for the date of death. There was a code at the top of each slip of paper: B 91-3728 F-and C-89-2935-M. Tobey suspected that the numbers were used to identify the two animals instead of a name.

Montgomery pointed to the folder, and Tobey lifted the stack of paper. The bonobo put the folder on his lap, leafed through the pages and put his finger on a word.

"Dead," Tobey said.

Montgomery pointed to a different word.

"Pain." Tobey almost whispered the word.

Montgomery took out a piece of paper, a folded page from a science magazine that contained an article about a laboratory in Edinburgh specializing in genetic research. A color photograph showed two men, their names written in a caption below; one sounded English and the other sounded Scandinavian. Both were young, not more than forty, and both were smiling. Tobey skimmed the article. It talked about the work of the research laboratories. Montgomery put his finger on one of the faces. According to the caption, the man was Torben Raske, and he was Norwegian.

"Was he here?" Tobey tapped the thin blond man's head, then pointed to the ground, and hoped the bonobo would understand that he was referring to the island.

Montgomery picked out another photo. There were four men and two women in this one, standing in front of a building that Tobey did not recognize. Each of them held a chimpanzee and a bonobo by the hand. One of the men was the Norwegian; another one, in Tobey's opinion, looked very similar to Tanvir, if you imagined him ten years younger. In the background were trees like the ones that grew on the island, and white clouds in a blue sky. One of the two women was tall and dark-haired; the other, small and blond. The taller, older one wore a khaki-colored pants suit. The shorter one wore the white smock of a doctor. Tobey turned the picture over, but, except for a few stains, the back was empty.

The next twenty pages contained even more lists with numerous codes, findings about test subjects, statistics, evaluations of blood analysis, reports about the progress and failures of experiments with new test procedures, about the need for so-called research material: chimpanzees and bonobos, but also rhesus, cynomolgus monkeys, and pigs.

"Who is that?" Tobey held a Polaroid photograph in his hand. It showed a dark-skinned girl, about ten years old, naked and dirty, with matted hair, who squatted on the floor and was eating something. On the back someone had written the name: LARA.

"Who is Lara?"

Montgomery shook his head.

Tobey opened the folder and pointed to the word *look,* and then pointed to Montgomery and the photograph. The bonobo shook his head again and refused to tell Tobey whether he did not know who the girl was, or did not understand what Tobey was asking him.

The next page, crumpled and covered with stains, was the sketch of an island that seemed familiar to Tobey, although it was not the one he was on now. He looked in vain for a hill, but at the lower edge of the island, drawn in green crayon, where it bordered the sea, he discovered a black circle. Beside it was the word SHIPWRECK. Tobey immediately knew that this was the spot where the three men with the boat had let him off. He found the warehouse where he had slept, and the hut where he had been knocked unconscious. In a large rectangle was the word WORKSHOP. This had to be the second, tall corrugated iron shed with the tractor in front—the tractor that had broken down into its individual parts. There were other rectangles, drawn and crossed out, not with black ink, but with a red ball-point pen. LABORATORY was written on one; VISITORS CENTER on another. Slightly apart from this collection of buildings, in a forest suggested by a circle of bright green, Tobey found ten small black rectangles, with the words PRIMATES and CARE-TAKER written underneath. He remembered the remains of the buildings: the concrete foundations, collapsed walls, bricks and beams, which had almost vanished beneath the wildly growing plants. He had apparently overlooked the two houses in the forest during his exploration of the island.

Montgomery put another list of codes and other unintelligible entries in front of him, still more documents whose contents were a mystery to him, test reports teeming with even more technical terms, which seemed to deal with blood, and even more statistics, tables, and footnotes.

After Tobey had turned the last page, a map of Africa with hundreds of colored points which did not have a legend to explain them, the bonobo got up, took the pile, wrapped it in foil, wound the string around it and put it back in the hiding place in the bottom of the chair. Tobey also stood up. He stretched, and noticed how sleepy and thirsty he was. A dull light shone through the window. He closed his eyes for a moment. Words flickered through his head—phrases, codes— and then, bright as the lightning that lit everything for just a second, images: the girl huddled on the floor; the smiling blonde man; the emaciated chimpanzee.

When Montgomery took him by the hand and led him from the room he went along, forgetting his fatigue and thirst; a sleepy child, confused by a story that he did not understand.

In the pale morning light the house seemed a little more shabby than it had on the day that Tobey had first seen it. It seemed like a faded photograph, torn and reassembled; like a bad reproduction of a plantation house from the Deep South, nailed together by bunglers and children.

Almost everything about the building was lopsided, unfinished, or broken. The chimney, protruding from the middle of the roof, was wrapped with black plastic that had been battered by storms. The white metal rain gutters were warped; in some places parts of them hung free or were missing completely. The red tar paper, meant to simulate a tile roof, was marked with ugly spots where it had been replaced with gray patches. The closer Tobey got to the building, the more clearly he could see the consequences of shoddy construction and decay. Palm-sized patches of white paint were peeling away from the window frames, the porch railings were missing rungs, and the boards of the stair steps were bowed. Even the lawn, which had been mowed but did not seem to be maintained, looked more pathetic this morning than it had a few days ago, when the sunlight had overpowered many of its flaws.

Montgomery went up the front steps, cupped both hands around his eyes, and peered into the window of the front door. Inside the villa it was quiet—nothing stirred. Somewhere nearby there was a pond; Tobey heard the faint croaking of frogs. He was thirsty and hungry and sorry that he had followed Montgomery without question. They could have had breakfast first and then headed out, he thought sullenly, wondering, yet again, what on earth he was actually doing here, in this house, on this island, in this country. Then he thought about what Tanvir had said— that a boat would be coming the next day and would take him away—and he calmed down a little. Montgomery turned the doorknob and entered the house. Tobey followed him, in the vague hope of having a cup of coffee and a slice of toast.

They walked through a hallway, where there was a small bureau without drawers. On one wall hung a stained mirror, on a hook there was a single straw hat. The floorboards creaked under Tobey's steps until he entered the next room, reached through an open door, where there was a carpet. Montgomery stopped and took his cap off. The room seemed small and cramped to Tobey. The feeble daylight was dimmed by the curtains, creating a diffuse brightness that reflected on the furniture like a gleaming matte finish. A fan hung from the high ceiling but it was not moving, probably because two blades were missing. On the oriental carpet that was worn and full of holes and covered most of the hallway floor, there were countless crates and boxes, and in between them there were clothes, shoes, books, magazines, loose sheets, pillows, hat boxes, and an umbrella. A painting hung on the wall, in a monstrous pitch-black frame carved with bulging, twisted tendrils and calyx. Some of the calyx blossoms were closed and some were wide open. The canvas depicted a painted landscape in dark colors, dark woods and hills under a stormy sky with tumultuous clouds. An ape sat in the center, a thin, long-limbed animal with a dark coat and a tall black top hat on his head—the kind gravediggers wore. In the ape's hands there was something that Tobey mistook for a bird with bright, outspread wings, but then he realized that it was an open book. A glimmer of light came from its sides, and the source seemed to be the book itself. Below the painting, flanked by two tables, each large enough for a dozen people and crammed with books, bottles, crockery and candles, there was a bed.

"Who's there?" The woman's voice, thin and quite clear, came from under the blankets and pillows that formed a mountain at the foot of the bed.

Montgomery stepped between one of the tables and the bed. Again and again he presented a new image. Now Tobey saw him as a boy scout in uniform, visiting his ailing grandmother.

"Oh, the ape." A skinny pale arm with long, thin fingers hanging at the end of a hand stretched out toward Montgomery, and, to Tobey's surprise, the bonobo took the hand in his and kissed it. "Did the newspaper finally come today?" the woman asked. Because of the mountain of covers, Tobey couldn't see anything of her except her arm, which slowly withdrew.

Montgomery beckoned Tobey. Tobey shook his head and mouthed the

138

word "No." He wanted to get some fresh air; the room seemed like a chamber that stored not only countless things, but also smells, one of which he was absolutely certain came from human excrement.

"Are you there too, Diego?" The voice was louder now. "Diego?" Montgomery was beside him so quickly and grabbed his arm so swiftly that Tobey could not react. The next moment he was standing beside the bed, looking down at a woman who was perhaps seventy, maybe eighty years old. She was wearing a beige-colored, stained raincoat, a nightgown and fuzzy light blue socks. She was lying on a sheet which could hardly be called white because of all the crumbs and ashes, unused tea bags, crumpled scraps of paper and paper tissues, books, candy, cookies, matchboxes, pens, playing cards, scraps of newspaper, and countless other things as difficult to detect as the color white. She regarded Tobey with a look that contained slight displeasure and fatigue, but no fear whatsoever.

"Hello," Tobey said. The light, the smells, the woman's eyes— everything reminded him of a winter's day from his childhood, endless hours at the hospital bedside of a neighbor who had taken care of him and Megan when they were small and had been devastated by a lung dis- ease. His father had dragged him along so he wouldn't have to go alone. Tobey had stood there, embarrassed and confused, and had smelled Briona Fanning's perspiration, listened to her quiet, irregular breathing and wished that she would either become healthy immediately or die, so he could leave that frightening place and look for Megan, who had been hiding on the farm so she wouldn't have to go along. While he stared at his shoes, he had pictured how he would yank the crosses she had crafted from branches and string out of the earth in the animal ceme- tery and how his sister would pounce on him in a violent rage, how they would both struggle and roll over the rain-soaked soil and eventually would lie there and stare at the sky, panting from barely exhausted rage, directed against themselves and something that they could not name.

139

The woman struggled up and stuffed two pillows under the small of her back. "Where's Diego?" she asked in a tone that dispelled any lingering doubt that she might be concerned for her safety.

"I don't know," Tobey said.

"Who are you? Have I seen you before?" The woman had surprisingly long, thick hair piled on her head in a blond-gray mass. A solitary hairclip dangled from a strand of hair over her ear, the sign of a feeble attempt to restrain the disheveled luxuriance. She put on the glasses hanging from a chain of rhinestones around her neck, and looked at Tobey with narrowed eyes.

"My name's O'Flynn," Tobey said so he would not seem impolite. He thought about opening the door to the veranda to let in some air, but he didn't move.

"Did you bring the newspaper? I've been waiting on it for ages."

"No, ma'am."

"O'Flynn, you say? Are you Irish?"

"Yes." Tobey freed his arm from Montgomery's grip and took a step to the side. Because the woman was blatantly looking him over, he avoided her gaze. In addition to the top hat, the ape in the oil painting was wearing a red collar or a tie.

"Good people, the Irish. Very reliable." The woman unwrapped a bonbon and stuffed it into her mouth. "Have you seen Bobbie?"

"Who?"

"Bobbie," the woman said. "My husband." She dropped the candy wrapper on the sheet, where it got lost in the rest of the debris. "Are you new?"

"Yes," said Tobey. In a sense it was true.

"Are you from here?"

"No, ma'am—from Ireland."

The woman looked into the emptiness beyond Tobey for a few seconds with a strained neck and an arduous expression, as if she was concentrating on sounds that only she could hear. Then she let herself sink back into the pillows that supported her back, and fished an open pack of cigarettes out of all the garbage.

Montgomery poked Tobey lightly in his side.

"Where is Diego?" the woman asked.

"No idea." Tobey wondered who this Diego was and why he had not set eyes on him if he really existed. While he looked around, he noticed a barely touched plate of rice and chicken on the table beside him and the wide-open door to the bathroom. A cloud of fruit flies were circling over a bowl of bananas, and there was a cheese sandwich in a woven wastebasket.

"Do you smoke?"

"No."

"Never smoked?" The woman felt around the mattress for something and looked under the covers, which she lifted with her feet.

"Yes. A long time ago."

"Are you one of those?" She found a single match and was now apparently looking for a match box.

"One of what?" Tobey puzzled over what kind of dialect the old lady was speaking. American in any case, and Texan seemed to be the most likely one.

"One of those who hate smoking. Who would put all smokers in a camp."

"No, ma'am." Tobey began to like the woman; she reminded him of a neighbor in Dublin, who had cooked soup for him and Jason two, sometimes three times a week, and left it in a pot in front of their door. There was always a note tucked between the pot and lid, containing the word "EAT!" written in a spidery script.

"Good," said the woman, who had now found the matchbox.

Montgomery tugged on Tobey's shirt. When the match was finally burning, the woman shook the pack with her free hand and a dozen cigarettes dropped onto the sheet. She picked one of them up, put it between her lips and lit it. After she inhaled deeply, she threw the burning match to the floor with a slow, casual flick of her wrist. It landed in front of Tobey's feet. Montgomery picked it up hastily, though it had extinguished in flight, and put it on one of the many empty plates.

"You don't have a newspaper?" The woman looked at Tobey through a cloud of smoke that enveloped her head like a mountain mist.

"No. I'm sorry." There was a figure hidden in the bushes and trees on the left edge of the painting. Slightly hunched and almost hidden by leaves, she focused her attention on the seated ape.

"Of course, I get a whole stack of them at once," the woman said and flicked the ashes into a dish that Montgomery had quickly passed to her. "For weeks I don't get any, and then there are ten at one time."

"What newspaper is that?" Tobey asked and resolved to stay another two minutes and then go or else open the veranda door. He wondered how often the woman bathed and whether she could even leave the bed without help.

"The *New York Times*, of course!" The woman made a swinging motion with the hand that held the cigarette, and ash fell on the raincoat, which was littered with small burn holes.

Montgomery made a startled sound and swept away the ashes, beat on the coat and then wiped his hands on his shirt.

The woman seemed not to have noticed the incident. "Oh, the ape," she said dreamily, patting the air around Montgomery's arm. Then she turned to Tobey. "Are you from this neck of the woods?"

For Tobey, conversations of this kind were not unusual. Daphne Maloney, the neighbor who made the soup, lived with her demented sister, Audrey. On some days, Audrey could list the names of all her former students, and tell stories about school trips; on other days she didn't even know who Daphne was. "No, ma'am, from Ireland."

"Good people, the Irish," the woman said and thoughtfully sucked

142

smoke into her lungs. "Hardworking and honest." She stubbed the cigarette out in the plate, which Montgomery took away and put on the table, found another bonbon in the folds of the sheet and unwrapped the foil.

Tobey cleared a path through the crates and boxes that seemed to be filled with all sorts of rubbish, pulled back a curtain and opened the veranda door. The air that streamed in was warm and smelled of grass and sea and sun; but perhaps he only imagined it, because he had spent so long in the stuffy room. He took a deep breath and thought of the wonderful smell of the coffee that Rosalinda was probably brewing right now in the kitchen hut.

"Who gave you permission to open the window?"

Tobey turned around. The rays of pale light that fell across the room through the curtains, interspersed with dust, illuminated a few articles that were scattered around out of the semi-darkness, and rested over the woman's legs like a bright cloth. "I thought a little air would . . . "

"Drafts are very bad for me!" The woman pulled up her blanket. "Where is Diego?"

"He's coming in a moment." Tobey closed the door. When he walked over to Montgomery he tripped over one of the sofa cushions that were lying on the floor. Audrey Maloney had berated him on the stairs once because he had not greeted her the way she had been accustomed to from her students for forty years.

"I've never seen you here before," the woman cried, pointing a finger at Tobey.

Montgomery took a step away from the bed.

'I'm new here," Tobey said. He smiled, even though he didn't feel like it. The morning air seemed to revive the staleness in the room instead of driving it away; it seemed to Tobey that the stench had grown even more intense. He was tired and thirsty and a little angry at Montgomery, who had dragged him here, and just wanted to return to Rosalinda and her coffee and her reliable silence.

"Where in the world is Diego?" The woman banged her palms on the mattress—a little girl in the body of an old woman.

"I'll look for him," Tobey said and hurried out.

In the shadow of the trees it was rather cool. Now and then there was a slight breeze from the sea, just strong enough to easily stir the unmowed blades of grass. Tobey leaned his back against the tree trunk, but then ants ran over his arm. He took off his shirt and shook it. He sat in the grass a few meters from the tree and waited for Montgomery, who had remained in the house. His head was heavy with all of the information that had rained down on him since he landed on the island, and he could do as little with the information as he could with pages ripped out of a book whose contents he did not know. He knew that Tanvir had deceived him and was producing synthetic drugs in the bunker under the hill, that until recently experiments had been carried out here with apes and that an old demented Texan woman lived in the dilapidated villa. And that Megan had died here and was buried in the cemetery—he knew that, too. But the list of things he did not know was even longer. He spread his shirt out on the grass and lay down. A few clouds shimmered white in a sky of blue that had grown noticeably richer. The wind finally stopped blowing; now heat filled the air. A handful of birds shot by like a load of buckshot in an animated film. From time to time an insect buzzed. When it got too close, Tobey waved his hand through the air. When he closed his eyes dark stains spread over the inside of his eyelids like ink on a blotter. He heard Megan's voice; she was humming a nursery rhyme instead of telling him what had happened.

A beetle landed on Tobey's stomach; the tiny hooks of its feet pinched his flesh. Tobey sat up quickly and the beetle fell into the grass, a polished black ball the size of a hazel nut. Tobey rubbed his eyes. He looked up at the sky where the clouds had not changed shape, and he knew that he could not have nodded off for very long. Then he saw Montgomery, who stood near an open window on the upper floor of the villa and beckoned him. Tobey groaned, got up, put on his shirt and went to the house.

Outside the door, he wondered whether or not it would be better to turn around and finally have breakfast, but he simply sighed and went inside. In the vestibule he stopped, listened for sounds behind the closed door and then quietly climbed up the stairs. Montgomery was waiting for him at the top. Tobey pointed to his stomach and lifted an imaginary glass to his lips, but Montgomery took no notice and opened one of four doors. Tobey cursed quietly and followed him.

The walls of the room he had entered were made of white painted wood and the floor of dark, lacquered boards, just like the ground floor. Through a window you could see part of a meadow and the tree whose shade Tobey had rested under. The room was empty except for a bed frame, two chairs and a rolled carpet. A loose cable hung from the ceiling and a cracked windowpane leaned against a wall.

"Now what? What am I doing here?" Tobey didn't even bother to lower his voice. He stood between the two chairs at the window, raised his arms and lowered them again. There were dead insects on the windowsill and the floor.

Montgomery placed the index finger of his right hand to his lips, went to the bundled roll of carpet, put his arm in up to his shoulder and pulled out a bundle wrapped in brown paper. He sat down, put the bundle in the bowl of his crossed legs, and waited for Tobey to sit down with him.

"What's that? A bunch of schedules and charts?"

Montgomery broke the string and unfolded the wrapping paper, as deliberate and orderly as a disciplined child opening a gift whose contents have long been known. Then he raised a sheet of paper with two fingers and held it out to Tobey.

In the second that Tobey recognized Megan's handwriting, he heard knocking on the door below them and a moment later the old woman's voice.

"Diego? Is that you?"

"No, Misses Preston!" Rosalinda's voice was unmistakable. The floor-boards creaked under the woman's heavy steps; a little later the door opened. "It's me, Rosa!"

"Do you have my newspaper?"

"No. But I brought breakfast."

"Oh, is it morning already?"

The door was closed, and the voices could barely be heard from above. Montgomery put his finger to his lips. Tobey nodded and sat down carefully on the roll of carpet and took the paper in his hand. On the crumpled, slightly yellowed paper Megan had drawn a lizard with crayons and below it one of those beetles that Tobey had often noticed because their armor gleamed with a dark blue like the paint of the Nor-ton's *Bantam*, now growing rusty in a shed beside the butcher's shop that belonged to Barry Spillane's parents. Below the drawing there was a story, less than twenty sentences long (which was typical of Megan), about a dung beetle who falls in love with the glass eye of a doll. The second page Montgomery gave him was full of pencil sketches, involving the mechanics of a locust's legs. On the back, Megan had scrawled an eight-line poem that was crossed out and illegible.

On the ground floor someone turned on a radio and not two minutes later turned it off again. The woman said something unintelligible and Rosalinda growled back. For a while there was a soft rustling under the roof where the water tank was; water trickled gently through the pipes. When it was quiet again, Montgomery took another page from the stack and handed it to Tobey.

News from Megan

I am writing a book, Tobey. In the afternoon, when I'm done working for Jeffrey, I sit in the library and I write. I am allowed to use Jeffrey's type-writer, a manual Remington, whose keys are pale yellow like worn ivory. I sit at a long table, where I have cleared some space for myself. I have a view of the courtyard—nothing beautiful, three walls, a blue-painted wooden gate, a series of flower pots with half withered plants, a bicycle, and garbage cans. When I type, it creates an infernal racket, which I love, and Jeffrey claims that it has a calming effect on him. (Jeffrey is deaf.) It is easy to say that you are writing a book when you have just started and you've completed the first twenty pages. It's not at all easy to say something about the content. It's about me and the world. It's about crickets and blindworms, about magpies and pigs and horses. Wellie has a place in it, and Sam. And Ruby, whose life was worth more than my entire allow-ance. Father haunts the story and mother is a distant ghost. I refuse to include Feargal Walsh—there are no words that can describe my disgust for him. I want to sit in Manila with my eyes closed and stumble through my childhood; I want to see the farm and the hills and the sea. I am the young girl Megan with the eyes of the adult, the adult with the eyes of the young girl. Perhaps the book begins on the day I decide not to eat meat, never again. Perhaps it begins when I see the way my father and fat Fear-gal Walsh (now he has forced his way into the story) slaughter a pig. The two of them have tied the bellowing pig Holly by the hind legs and dragged her into the dark part of the house—you know the corner, where the floor is made of concrete and metal hooks hang from the ceiling beams. They kneel down over her trembling body and thrust a long knife into her chest. I scream, and my screams mix with those from the pig. The men don't hear it; I'm not there—I'm lying in my bed and dreaming about flowers and the sun that waits for me behind the horizon. Holly was my friend, Tobey. (Maybe you don't laugh about it anymore.) Enormous, lazy Holly with the black spot on her snout, who grunted with joy each time I visited her in her dark pen, where she had to lie with her young until they were strong enough to go outside, into the walled corral, the only piece of earth that they would ever see in their lives, ground that had been plowed a thousand times and yet the whole world. My years in London will be included in the book, the days and nights in my cozy, shabby apartment, my little room that I insulated so well from the cold with books and newspapers. Should I write that now, at this moment, the blue wooden door opens and two men in red overalls drag a giant letter O (O' Flynn or Zero?) into the yard? Should I save this event for later on, when I have arrived at this point in the story, here, today? Should I open a notebook and record such incidents like this one with the Zero that now stands abandoned in the yard, as if the men have gone through it and disappeared into a parallel world? Or the one about the boy, who stood outside my bedroom door last week and tried to sell me a puppy, a tiny white dog with closed eyes, which would fit into a child's hand? (I gave the boy money and sent him away.) What should I collect? Archive? What is it worth to be picked up and remembered? The newspaper story about the accident in Singapore, where a man was run over by a truck full of brake pads, because its brakes failed? The seven minutes that it took for the doctor in Jakarta to remove a shard of glass from my foot? The two seconds when I thought I saw Jason as he crossed the street outside the hotel and got on a bus? The moment when I found father in the barn? (A chicken, I think it was Rita, was asleep between his boots.) Sam's smell when I put him in the barn on a summer evening? Holly's

148

eyes when I sang for her? (While you secretly watched.) You jumped out of the barn to scare me; you threw stones at me from your hiding place; you made fun of me, Megan O'Flynn, who everyone called smart, and who played the *White Album* for a dog and told chickens about distant continents, held eulogies over the graves of sparrows and wasted verses on pigs. Do you want to be in my book, Tobey? (You're in it!)

Who loves you?
Megan!

12

Tobey lay on the rolled carpet and looked at the ceiling, watching how the shadow of the lamp cord moved as the light changed. A fly strayed into the room, turning circles and bumping against the window panes again and again, helpless and stubborn. Montgomery was still sitting there, cross-legged, arms resting on his thighs like a meditating monk. Below them it was quiet, but a few times a noise made its way up to them, when a door closed or someone put a metal bucket down. Tobey squinted at the brightness that flowed into the room through the window. The bonobo appeared to be asleep; from time to time a whimpering gasp escaped his lips. He had handed Tobey one page of the letter after another and finally an envelope which, as usual, contained Barry Spillane's address. The envelope was from a hotel in midtown Manila. The lettering covered half the front and there was no stamp. On the back of the second and third pages Megan had drawn butterflies and a gecko. Tobey wondered why she did not put the letter in the mail and satisfied himself with the explanation that she had forgotten about it, and later, when she was on the island, could no longer send it and used the back for sketching. The idea of appearing in her book seemed strange and unreal to him. His sister had already made him a character in her earlier stories: a dwarf, a goblin or a gnome. Sometimes he had become a worm or a beetle and had to atone for his sins—for emptying a bird's nest or smoking out a mouse hole.

Montgomery tugged on the leg of his trousers and put a hand to his ear. Now Tobey could also hear the footsteps on the stairs. Seconds later the front door opened and a moment later the door to the living room.

"Nancy, how are you today?" Tanvir's voice was loud when he talked to someone who had trouble hearing.

"Do you have a newspaper?"

"Of course, Nancy. And look what I've brought for you!"

"What should I do with them? Those flowers are ugly."

Tanvir laughed. "Today is the day. Did you forget it?"

"What day? Where is Diego?"

"He's out there and he's preparing everything. For your message. Do you remember?"

It was quiet for a moment, as the woman deliberated. There was a sound of water being poured into a metal bucket; in the pipes over Tobey's head it softly rustled.

"Where's Bobbie?"

"Nancy, you know that your husband died a long time." Tanvir sounded slightly impatient, but at the same time tried to give his voice a warm tone.

The woman seemed to be thinking again.

"He left us eight years ago, remember?"

"I know he's dead!"

"Shall we go? It's a beautiful day."

"Where is Diego?"

"Outside. He's waiting for you."

"I need to use the bathroom."

"But everything has already been prepared."

A little later a door was shut and locked.

"She should have had her hair washed."

151

"I tried, but she didn't want me to."

"She looks like she's been neglected."

"I take care of Miss Preston. I give her good food. I bathe her." Rosalinda sounded upset and defiant.

"What is she doing in there?"

"Was big mess again. I want to know what she doing all night long. All the boxes open, everything on the floor."

"Hopefully she's not putting on make-up."

The floorboards creaked softly under Rosalinda's weight. "Miss Preston? You okay?"

"Nancy? We're all waiting for you!"

A little later the bathroom door was opened.

"You look absolutely adorable, Nancy! Shall we go?" Tanvir sounded cheerful again. Tobey could almost picture how he took the old lady by the arm and led her across the veranda into the open.

Nancy Preston sat in a wicker chair in the shade of the trees where Tobey had been an hour ago. She wore a flowing, frilly dress and a sombrero hat trimmed with fabric flowers. On a small table beside her were a book and a pair of sunglasses. Rosalinda leaned over her and patted a little rouge on her pale cheeks. Tanvir and Miguel were busy fastening a camera to a tripod. Clouds filled the sky; Tanvir raised his head again and again and looked anxiously upward.

Tobey and Montgomery had crept down the stairs and they were now sitting behind a bush at the back of the house where they could watch the performance on the lawn. After a while Montgomery had taken two candies from his pocket and offered Tobey one. Although the circumstances already seemed rather absurd to him and he hated candy, Tobey took the garish green ball from Montgomery's hand, gently unwrapped it from the transparent foil, and placed it in his mouth. With each breath he could feel the bundle that contained Megan's drawings and letters, lying against his chest between his shirt and his skin.

"We're ready," Tanvir said after Miguel had finished setting up the tripod in front of Nancy Preston. "Rosa?"

"Moment. Not easy." Rosalinda applied lipstick to the old woman's lips, shoved two unruly strands of hair under her hat, straightened the fabric flowers and then stepped away carefully and with half raised hands like someone who has just built a pyramid of champagne glasses.

"The first run through is without the camera," Tanvir said and took the glass and the full carafe out of Nancy's hands before she spilled everything. "Where is Jay Jay?"

Tobey winced. He had completely forgotten about Jay Jay.

"He's coming soon," Miguel said. "I know."

Montgomery looked around as if it had also suddenly occurred to him that Jay Jay could appear at any moment. Tobey pointed to the path. "Jay Jay?" he whispered. Montgomery nodded and then shook his head. Tobey was not reassured.

"I'm thirsty," Nancy protested. Tobey had not noticed until now that she was barefoot. Her slippers were lying in the grass in front of her.

Tanvir filled her glass with water and let her drink, and then he put the glass and the carafe on the table out of her reach. "Nancy?" He bent down to her. "Jay Jay is bringing the newspaper in a little while. Then you can read a bit and we can have a chat. Agreed?"

"Where are my cigarettes?"

"We'll get them soon. Do you want to practice your message?" Tanvir pulled a piece of paper from his back pocket and unfolded it. "It's roughly the same text as a year ago."

Nancy looked blankly at Tanvir, reached for the sunglasses and put them on. "My husband is dead."

Tanvir seemed to reflect on this statement for a moment. "The message isn't for Robert," he said as calmly as possible. "You're addressing the members of the board. Your foundation, Nancy."

153

Nancy searched in the pockets of her dress. "I don't have any candy."

Tanvir stood up, arched his back and took a deep breath, only to tilt his head back and expel it a small eternity later.

"I'll get cigarettes," Miguel said and hurried into the house without waiting for Tanvir's permission.

Tanvir turned away from Nancy and looked at the sheet of paper in his hand, as if it was the map of a city he was lost in. He seemed small and tired and looked up sadly as a cloud cast its shadow on him.

Montgomery pinched Tobey's side and pointed his chin toward the path where Jay Jay and Chester were coming very slowly hand in hand. Tobey moved closer to the bush, crouching lower, even though it was impossible for Jay Jay to see him. Rosalinda approached the two of them and seized Chester's free hand. They ran that way across the meadow—lean, lanky Jay Jay, big, plump Rosalinda, and Chester, who hung his head down and made small, shuffling steps. Hot waves of guilt flooded through Tobey when he looked at Chester.

"Do you have the newspaper?" Tanvir had stepped forward a few meters to meet the trio.

"No newspaper," Jay Jay said. His hair was sweaty; the white bib clung to his body.

"What? Why not?"

"Nobody came."

"But we need a newspaper!" Tanvir cried and spread out his arms in a desperate sweeping gesture, as if to encompass the setting for a production that would fail because of the missing prop. "They have to see a date! A headline!" He dropped his arms and walked around, moving in widening circles.

Miguel walked over to Nancy and gave her a cigarette and a light. Nancy had taken off her hat, and in the process a barrette got tangled in her hair, turned sideways now like after a storm.

"Thank you, Diego." Nancy inhaled the smoke as if it was her first dose of nicotine in days. She held the cigarette between her thumb and index finger like a joint and groaned with every drag. Miguel continued to stand beside her and collected the embers in the palm of his hand, before they could catch her dress on fire. When Nancy saw Chester coming, she took off her sunglasses and stretched out her hand to him. "Oh, the ape," she said in a fleeting fit of enthusiasm; then she returned to her cigarette, smoking like a chimney.

"Maybe we could use old newspaper," said Jay Jay.

"Oh, the last one is at least two months old." Tanvir put up the umbrella and stood there with drooping shoulders, a man waiting for the bus in the London rain.

"Does it really make a big difference?" Miguel asked.

"Yes. Big." Tanvir was thinking. "Well," he finally said, "maybe even an old one will work."

"There aren't any more newspapers. I burned them all." Rosalinda was sitting in the grass with Chester. The chimpanzee had put his head in her lap and let her stroke it. Tobey could not remember ever having seen the animal when he wasn't chewing on something or begging for food.

Tanvir sighed. "Well, that's it for today, then," he said, turning his back to the others. The shadow of the umbrella looked like a hole which floated above him. "If we're lucky, the bastards will deliver a newspaper tomorrow."

"Bastards," Jay Jay repeated and giggled.

Tanvir laboriously brought himself to an upright position and closed the umbrella. Miguel carried the table into the house; Jay Jay tucked the camera into a red Puma gym bag and then folded the tripod together into a handy bundle. Rosalinda stood up, smoothed her wrinkled dress and took the sleepy Chester by the hand. Nancy had been dozing; her head hung to one side and her mouth was slightly open. When Tanvir woke her, addressing her quietly, she looked up at him with a straight face and said, "Is it morning already?"

Within the next five minutes the group broke up. Somnambulistic and calm as they were, they reminded Tobey of a picnic party, who, disappointed by the entertainment value of their outing, clear the field. Tanvir went first, his umbrella open again and his steps indecisive. Rosalinda and Jay Jay took Chester between them and waited for Miguel, who brought Nancy into the house and then ran across the field toward them, as if there was a ghost after him.

Tobey sat on the bench and watched Montgomery, who was watering the lawn of the cemetery. The sky had darkened with clouds, but Tobey wouldn't have bet one cent that it would rain in the next few hours. Although there was almost no wind, in the shade of the trees there was a pleasant coolness. Above the pool that supplied Montgomery with water, dragonflies hovered.

Tobey had not gotten enough sleep; fragments of dreams mixed with images from the morning. He had contemplated Megan's drawings and the letter for a long time in his room and then put them with the other things under the top panel of the bureau. He didn't want to speculate about the reasons for the absurd antics in front of the villa, but it had confirmed his wariness of Tanvir. He wondered whether the boat would come and if Tanvir would actually let him go. Another question concerned him even more, namely whether or not he wanted to go at all; he didn't even know where. When he thought of Dublin, it made him sick. There was nothing left in the city worth returning for. Jason Dwyer was dead; the band was history. Cait would eventually die, alone, or in the company of the fellow who allegedly made her happy. The prospect of no longer having a mother left Tobey almost cold. He had paid a visit to a strange woman in an apartment in Glasnevin a few months ago, not knowing what he should feel or say. He never wanted to see the farm again. Even Megan had gone away—from her home, her pets—two days after the death of her father, as if she had longed for that moment.

156

He looked over at the graves. The wooden cross at the end of the path reminded him of Megan's pet cemetery. He imagined the skeletons, all the bones that formed a design in the dark earth, a secret alphabet. Before she disappeared forever, Megan had burned almost all of her belongings. After Seamus died, she had carried her notebooks and books and her childhood toys and most of her clothes to the fire pit next to the apple tree and set them on fire. Nobody saw her leave the yard, the county, the country. In Tobey's imagination she had left the beaten track to go through the hills and meadows to the sea, and she swam to England like the dolphin they had seen on a trip to Dingle Bay with Uncle Aidan. On hot summer days, when she had been splashing in the pond for hours, Seamus always claimed she would one day grow webbed fingers and toes, and she could hardly wait for that day.

And now she had somehow drowned.

Montgomery put the watering cans back in the wood shed, where the empty flower pots and tools were. With a rake and a bucket he set about gathering up the leaves.

Tobey got up and went to the shed. He did not want to think about what he was doing. He took the shovel, went to Megan's grave, cleared the stones away and began in a feverish haste to dig away the earth that was covered by a thin layer of grass, and with a silent roar in his skull that wiped out any thought. Someone tried to snatch the shovel away from him, a small, amazingly powerful man in a gray uniform, a peculiar caretaker who never uttered a sound. Tobey struck him on the head with his hand and shouted at him, seized the shovel and drove the blade into the soft ground with the soft sole of his shoe. The attacker jumped on his back, clutching his right arm. Tobey shook it off and gave him a kick with his foot. The air was filled with heat and Tobey's voice and the cawing of birds and the flutter of wings. As he fell on his back, the small figure let out a long, drawn out sound—a stunned, terrible sigh.

Then it was quiet.

News from Megan

Do you remember when we were on Valencia Island with Uncle Aidan, Tobey? You were maybe five and thought that we were travelling to another country. The captain of the ferry put his cap on your head and you almost burst with pride. Aidan took a picture—you beaming, gulls flying over your head. (Guess who has the photo!) The island where I will hopefully land soon is not much larger than Valencia Island, but flatter, and lonelier and has no lighthouse. (How I know that it exists is another long story I will tell you when we meet again.) It's night and the three fishermen—the only ones who were willing to bring me here despite the good pay—smoke nasty cigarettes and continue to laugh about the headlamp I switched on an hour ago in order to write this. (Excuse the shaky script.) I will stick the letter in the stamped envelope and give it to them. I don't know if they will take it to the post office. I hope so. I will spend the night on the beach, in my sleeping bag, under a gigantic sky. I have four liters of drinking water, ten cereal bars and a pack of vitamin tablets. That's enough for two days, but if my information is correct, there are people living on this island. I think of you every day, Tobey, and I miss you very much. I hope you are well and these lines reach you somehow, someday. The men have turned off the engine and the two younger ones are rowing now. I have no idea whether they are doing that because of the shallows or on account of the pirates, which they have warned me about. That is also the reason the trip is so expensive. The old man is a strange fellow. He sits in the bow and mutters to himself, and sometimes he looks at me, grinning and waving one hand around. Now I can see the island. I can see the bright strip of the beach and the dark shapes of trees. The men lay the oars in the boat; we let the waves carry us to the shore. I have to stop. I embrace you, Toto, forever.

Who loves you?
Megan!

13

Tobey was sitting beside the open grave when Tanvir arrived. The brightness had diminished by a few degrees; a light wind grazed the treetops and disappeared between the trees. Tanvir sat across the grass from Tobey, exhausted and breathless from running. He saw the vomit on the ground and noticed that Tobey had been crying, so he said nothing. Megan's body, wrapped in a cloth, lay in the pit. He could not tell whether Tobey had removed it and unwrapped it from its surprisingly well-preserved white fabric. Flies buzzed around.

"Why did you do that, Tobey?" he asked after a while and dabbed his damp forehead with a handkerchief.

Tobey did not answer. Hanging his head, he stared at the handle of the shovel lying in front of him. He was wet with sweat; there was dried earth on his hands.

"Didn't you believe that it's Megan?"

Tobey raised his head. His eyes were red; there were traces of vomit in the corners of his mouth and on his chin. "You lied to me," he said in a low, fragile voice.

"But that is Megan—I swear."

"She didn't drown; she was set on fire."

"Oh, Tobey . . . " Tanvir sighed. "I can explain it to you. But I doubt you want to hear it."

"I do want to hear it."

Tanvir sighed again. "When Megan didn't come to dinner that evening, we looked for her," he said. "Late into the night. But without success. The next day, Montgomery found her on the beach. The climate here is very unfavorable, it's . . . " Tanvir tried to find words; his hand grasped the emptiness. "We wanted to cremate your sister, but good firewood is very scarce on the island. When we began the cremation that afternoon, a storm broke out and . . . " He paused again, avoiding Tobey's eyes.

"You didn't finish cremating her?"

Tanvir lowered his head and nodded. "Instead of waiting and looking for more wood, we buried her the next day."

Tobey thought for a while longer. "Why didn't you tell me?" he asked.

"It was all very tragic. I thought I'd spare you."

Tobey looked at Tanvir, as if trying to read his face to see whether he was telling the truth or lying. After a while he looked down and opened his right fist, black with soot. He was holding a ring. Tobey rubbed it on his shirt until it was clean, but the blue color of the stone in the round setting was barely visible.

Tanvir bent his torso forward. "I considered taking it off her finger and keeping it," he finally said. "But then I thought, it belonged to her; she should take it with her."

Tobey looked at the ring a long time. "I helped a neighbor with the potato harvest," he finally began. "I was eight. Actually, I wanted to use the money to buy a box of miscellaneous comics at Sheehan's for three pounds. That was a lot of money. Then I saw the ring. It was in a display case at the cash register, and I bought it. Old man Sheehan gave me a special price. On the way home I cried because I felt so stupid. I had bought a ring. Was I beyond hope?" Tobey looked up, shook his head and dropped it again. "Two weeks later Megan had a birthday."

161

"March thirty-first."

Tobey lifted his head again.

"We celebrated." Tanvir smiled; his fingers played uneasily with the handle of the umbrella.

"You should have seen her face when she unwrapped the ring." Tobey smiled and his lips trembled. Tears ran down his cheeks; he wiped them away with his shirt sleeves. "She had to have it adjusted years later, so she could still wear it."

"What kind of stone is it?" Tanvir asked.

"A semi-precious stone—nothing special. I liked the name. It sounded magical coming from old Sheehan's mouth. Rainbow Obsidian."

For a time they were both silent. Dusk began to fall. Tanvir chased away a few flies from time to time with the umbrella. Suddenly a chicken appeared on the path and ran across the grass to the grave. It stopped a few meters before the grave and looked at the two men, and then it came closer and began to scratch around in the piled earth. It let out faint sounds, short exclamations of surprise at the things it unearthed with its claws.

"Is it one of yours?" Tobey asked softly.

"I don't have any idea. Probably a wild one."

"Megan knew every chicken on the farm. They all looked alike tp me, but she knew them all by name. Lucy. Prudence. Rita. Eleanor. Martha.

"They're all names from Beatles songs."

Tobey smiled. "When she was seven she didn't listen to anything else."

"What was Megan like as a child?"

Tobey looked at the ring in his palm, and then closed his eyes. He was walking across the yard. Wellie rested in the shade of the barn and looked at him without raising his head. The sun was shining; the light was a bit too bright and the contours of things dissolved. He ran through the tall grass meadow behind the house, ducked under the clothesline, picked up a stocking. He knew where he would find her—he heard her war-

162

bling. She sat on the log beside the stone wall and seemed to be waiting for him. She was small, maybe six years old, and wore a floor-length white dress. He wanted to ask her why she was wearing this dress, but he couldn't speak. She got up and gave him a sheet of paper. It was empty, and when Tobey looked up, Megan was gone.

Tobey opened his eyes. Tanvir had folded his hands over the knob of the umbrella and rested his chin on his upper hand. The tip of the umbrella was stuck in the ground. The chicken was gone.

"I don't know," Tobey said. "She loved everything. Animals. Trees. Flowers. Everything equally. Except maybe people. She was very picky about people."

"What about you? Did Megan love you?"

"I think so. Yes. At least that's what she wrote to me in every letter."

Tanvir breathed in and out noisily. Then he braced himself, balanced himself with the umbrella, and wiped the earth and grass from his pants. "Should we fill in the grave and come back tomorrow? We could hold a small ceremony. Nothing Catholic."

Tobey put the ring in his pocket and stood up too. His legs felt numb; his shirt stuck to his back. He picked up the shovel and saw that he had blisters on his hands. "Don't worry; I'll take care of this. You can go on ahead."

Tanvir watched Tobey shovel the earth into the grave. "Are you sure?" He looked up. "It's going to rain."

"Just go. I'd like to be alone for a while."

Tanvir stood there indecisively. "If that's what you want," he said and then turned around and stepped onto the gravel path. "We'll wait for you to return before we have dinner." Before he disappeared around the bend, he opened the umbrella. Seconds later the first drops fell.

Tobey showered so long there was no hot water left, and scrubbed his hands with a brush, even though the blisters had popped. He had thrown his pants and his T-shirt out the window, where they landed in a deep puddle. The rain pelted down on them. He wept again, and, while the cold water flowed over his head, he took the ring from the edge of the sink and cleaned it with the brush. Tanvir knocked on the door and yelled that Rosalinda was insisting he eat something. Tobey promised to come, even though he wasn't hungry.

Rosalinda filled his plate and told him to eat. Apparently, Tanvir had not told her about the incident at the cemetery, because she would have hardly let someone who had desecrated a grave into her kitchen, let alone served them. So as not to anger her, Tobey ate half the rice and beans; he didn't touch the fried chicken leg. While he was chewing halfheartedly, he repeatedly cast furtive glances at Montgomery, who was sitting at his seat in his fresh blue clothes and hardly ever raised his head. Tobey vaguely remembered that he had struck the bonobo and looked for an injury on his head, but didn't see anything. When he turned away, ashamed, he saw Chester, who had indeed recovered to the point that he wanted to eat again, but still looked tired and nervous and sometimes regarded Tobey with thoughtful eyes that were full of disbelief and accusation. Tobey felt horrible, and when Rosalinda planted a plate of fried bananas in front of him, he mumbled an apology and ran outside.

The storm front had passed over. In the far distance it rose like a black wall above the sea, joined by a high, vertical column of fog. The sea currents, illuminated by the moon, were wafting channels composed of a billion tiny beads of glittering fish. Tobey sat on a rock on the beach and looked at the horizon where the sky had cleared, the air liberated from the oppressive rain. There were still clouds floating above his head, pale, frayed stragglers so thin the moonlight passed through them. If he didn't fix his eyes on a point, or a fleck of light on the sea, or a crest of waves, or a piece of driftwood, he saw Megan's charred arm in the darkness in front of him, her hand, the finger where the ring had grown intertwined with the decomposing flesh. When he had freed the arm from the cloth, he had to throw up. He had not looked at the rest of the dead body—wasn't even disturbed by it. He had pried the ring from her finger with a tree branch, and had used the shovel to roll the corpse back into the cloth again.

He took the ring out of his pocket. You could now see that the color of the stone was blue, but metal was still cloudy with the patina from the fire. He would buy a chain, he thought, and wear the ring around his neck. But then he rejected the idea when he remembered that for years his father had hung his wedding ring around his neck on a leather strap, thin as a string, until it fell off one day and was never found, even though he and Megan were forced to search for it for an entire day. He put the ring in his pocket and climbed off the rock. After the rain, the sand was firm and lined with hollows like small craters. Leaves covered the ground where the embankment faded into the forest. The croaking of frogs rose from old and new pools; sporadically the chirping of a cricket could be heard. Tobey walked across the clearing, fished his clothes out of the puddle, squeezed the water out of them and threw them in the shower in his room. Then he took a sheet of paper from one of the suitcases, sat down at the table, and wrote an obituary for his sister.

An hour later he was done. He folded the paper and put it in his back pocket. Then he washed the socks, pants and shirt in the sink and hung everything over the shower curtain rod. He looked in the mirror. The skin was peeling on his nose, his lips were cracked, and he needed a shave. He examined himself for a while, looking for similarities to Megan. He decided to ask Montgomery if he had any other photographs of her. That would give him an opportunity to apologize. He thought about the knife behind the water heater, but left it there and walked out of the room.

Miguel was sitting on the floor next to the sofa, tinkering with the plug on the refrigerator, which he had pulled away from the wall. The refrigerator door was open. There were three cans of soda and a piece of watermelon lost inside.

"Is it broken?" Tobey asked. The question hung in the silence of the hallway like the failed punch line of a joke.

"Yes," Miguel said. He pried apart the two halves of the plastic plug and examined the contents for a long time. "That's not the problem." He took out the cable, turned it in his fingers, and pushed it back into the housing.

Tobey felt obliged to stay a while and watch. "Maybe it's the motor?"

Miguel screwed the halves of the plug together again. "Maybe. Maybe the cable. Maybe the circuit in here." He knocked on the wall.

Tobey nodded. He looked at the covers of the magazines that were on the table, tabloids, some of them so worn out that the titles were barely legible. "Well, good luck," he finally said, and went to the door.

"Tobey?"

Tobey stopped and turned around. "Yes?"

"May I call you Tobey?"

"Yes, of course."

"You're Megan's brother, right?"

"Yes."

Miguel smiled. "Megan was a very good person."

Tobey could not help but smile, too. "Yes, she was." He turned and opened the door and stepped out into the night air, which was full of warmth and moisture. He went to the kitchen hut and looked in the window. Rosalinda was washing the dishes. Chester was sitting beside her on the ground and held her skirt with one hand. The radio was playing; Tobey heard trumpets, saxophones and trombones. On the way to the back door he had to dodge puddles that had formed in the shallow depressions and where the moonlight lay like matt gloss on the sheet metal of a car. The light above the door wasn't on, and Tobey was frightened when

166

an animal jumped in front of him from the top step, a frog or a toad. He walked down the hall to Montgomery's room and knocked, waited, and knocked again. No light penetrated through the gap between the door and the floor; the room was quiet. He called softly, but Montgomery wasn't there, he was sleeping, or he did not want to see him. After a moment's hesitation he turned the doorknob, but the door was locked.

Because he didn't want to lie on the bed in his room staring at the ceiling, he took a walk around the clearing. The kitchen windows were still lit. The clouds had broken up, in between blinking stars. The insects were making noise, as if they were assuring each other that they had not drowned. He had circled the clearing once when he saw a figure emerge from the darkness.

"Tobey." Tanvir came from the direction of the infirmary. He motioned; with his other hand he was holding something.

Tobey waited. Bats sailed just above his head.

"I had to get myself some medicine!" Tanvir called from a distance, and waved a bottle. When he was standing in front of Tobey, he breathed heavily and grinned. "I think I have an upset stomach."

They went across the clearing. Tobey avoided every puddle. Tanvir, who was barefoot and had rolled up his pant legs, marched right through them. He talked about a giant grasshopper on the stair railing of the infirmary, and Tobey noted that he had been drinking.

The doors to the veranda were open again, and again there was ice cold, sweet black tea. Tanvir excused himself and disappeared into the bathroom to wash his feet. Earlier, he had turned on the old record player that he kept in the dark cabinet, and Tobey had been surprised when he heard Van Morrison's voice. He looked at the map of an island that was hanging in a frame above the bureau, and it was only when he read in cursive lettering ISLAND 2, that he realized it was a map of the island where he was. Now he saw the clearing and the barracks, and after a while he discovered the villa. He searched in vain for the building with the cages. The map was drawn in a style that Tobey was familiar with from old books. Giant fish swam in the sea, an octopus wrapped his tentacles around a sailing ship and on the island palm trees grew as tall as skyscrapers. The hill was included—an oval covered with green shrubs—but there was no reference to the bunker. Left of the hill, near a small forest and at the end of a vast empty space, stood a tower, which was drawn so that it loomed toward the viewer.

Tobey sat on the sofa, sipped tea, and listened to the music. He recalled a concert in Dublin, the first since he had left the farm. Jason was smoking dope in those days and popping pills, instead of injecting poison into his veins; Mick studied at a music school in Cork, and Barry stood behind a meat counter smiling and hated his life. Tobey leaned back, a sense of loss and foolish longing flooding through him. He could sing along with every song, but he just sat there and listened. The only thing lighting up the room was a small lamp on the table beside Tanvir's chair. The fan turned too slowly, the tea was too sweet. The open sores on his palms were burning. He had danced to *Tupelo Honey* with a girl who had been standing next to him since the beginning of the concert. After the first few bars she had suddenly clung to him, swaying to the wonderfully slow pace of the music, her breath warm against his chest, and had released him only when the last notes died away, the people clapping and the guitarist already hinting at the opening chord of the next piece. In the heart of this surging mass, Tobey felt like a heated, blissful idiot—like the innocent, hopeful, dumb country boy he was. After the concert the girl had vanished and the night was twilight gray and as warm as beer and had tipped over into the day onto a park bench, decorated with doves and bums.

Tanvir came out of the bathroom and took a seat in the chair. He poured gin into his glass, toasted Tobey and took a sip. Then he leaned back and closed his eyes, rocking from time to time with his feet.

Tobey lay down. Time passed, slowed by the lethargic pace of the music. Every note seemed like a weight that gently pulled him down into the wide-awake, dreaming darkness.

When the record ended, Tanvir stood up and walked to the bureau. "Unfortunately, the second side is scratched," he said. After he closed the cabinet doors, he sat in his chair again and put his feet up.

"Where did you buy the record?" Tobey asked.

"In New York."

"When?"

"It must have been in the late seventies."

"I've always wanted to go to America."

"You should do it. Absolutely. And do it while you're still young." Tanvir emptied the glass in one swig and filled it up again. "How old are you, Tobey? Mid-twenties?"

Tobey nodded.

Tanvir let out a loud moan. "Not thirty yet!" he said, tilting his head back and staring at the ceiling as if he could see a film about his own youth there. "By then, I had quite a lot behind me. By thirty, I was divorced for the second time." He looked at Tobey. "Are you married, Tobey?"

"No."

"Then make sure it stays that way. Marriage isn't a suitable way to achieve happiness." He sighed and took a sip from the glass.

"Why are you here?"

Tanvir let out a laugh that ended in a kind of elongated whimper. "Do you want to hear the long version or the short one?"

Tobey sat up. "Is gin all you've got to drink?"

"Do you always answer a question with a question?"

I haven't had any alcohol to drink in a long time, but today I wouldn't mind a sip of whiskey. Do you have some? Or vodka, for all I care."

169

"Sorry. Just gin."

"Today wasn't so special."

"Tell me about it."

"Then gin it is."

Tanvir jumped to his feet, took a glass from a cabinet, filled it to the brim with gin and gave it to Tobey. "Wait!" He took his glass and held it up. "Here's to knowing that I'm no longer the only corrupt person on this island!" He took a long sip and then looked at Tobey, who was staring into his glass. "What?"

"I shouldn't drink this."

"Why not? It's good English gin."

"Still."

"It's Beefeater's!"

"I do believe you that it's good gin."

"Then why aren't you drinking it?"

"I don't like gin—that's why. I can't even smell it." Tobey put the glass on the table and pushed it away.

Tanvir looked at his half-full glass as if he was suddenly wondering whether or not there was something wrong with the drink. Then he drank it all, went back to his chair, and filled the glass to the brim.

"I'm sorry," said Tobey.

"Oh, well." Tanvir put his legs on the stool. "I'm sorry that I don't have any whiskey."

"It's probably better that way."

For the next few minutes they were both silent. A moth strayed into the room and landed in the cone of light cast on the wall by the lamp. Tobey stretched out full length on the sofa. He was glad he had not taken a drink, and at the same time it felt miserable. One glass, he thought, and the day would have dissolved in it; he would have been able to forget the open, desolate grave; Megan's arm; kicking Montgomery. A single glass. All he had to do was stretch out his hand for it.

170

"Do you still want to hear my story?"

"What? Oh. Of course."

"The long version or the short one?"

"The long one."

Tanvir cleared his throat. "So. I was born many, many years ago, in a small town in the province of Chittagong in Pakistan. I didn't have any brothers or sisters, which was fine with me. I spent a lot of time in my room. I read a lot. I didn't mind being alone. When I was five, my parents moved to the capital. My father had received a better paying job as a teacher there; he taught English and history at a secondary school. My mother worked in the then fledgling Ministry of Agriculture. She was one of the first female officers. She hated offices and everything theoretical; she would rather go to the villages and explain to them how they could increase their income. We weren't rich, but not poor. I went to school. I enjoyed going to school, although everything happened too slowly for me; the lessons seemed to be designed for lazy thinking laggards. On the way to school every day I got myself a banana or an orange from a market stall. I loved one of the women there—she was a little plump and beautiful; at night I dreamed about her." Tanvir chuckled softly and took a sip of gin. His voice sounded darker now; he spoke more slowly. "I was a good student; I completed my degree. Then I studied medicine; in addition to literature natural sciences had always been my passion— biology, chemistry, physics—what lightning is, how the human brain functions. I wanted to conduct research, to discover something great; but above all I wanted to get away from Pakistan, away from my life, which seemed to me, despite the world of knowledge that had opened up to me at the university, narrow and limited. My mother died when I was twenty-six and close to completing my doctorate. During one of her classes she was bitten by a snake in a one-horse town where there was no doctor and no serum. A year later this catastrophe occurred across the land—you may have heard about it. But no, you're too young for that. A cyclone, devastating floods, tens of thousands dead. Our house was built on a hill; below there was nothing, no houses, no pastures, no roads. The country was literally sinking into chaos and destruction; it had finally become a madhouse. The political conflict escalated, we Bengali wanted our own state. Not me, but us. War ensued; that was in March seventy-one, and you weren't even a thought in your mother's head yet. My father sent me to India where one of his sisters lived, and I went, even though I knew that I would never see him again. Two weeks later he was killed, beaten to death, one of countless Bengalis during this terrible time. Khan's henchmen especially had it in for the educated, intellectual elite, and also for the small teacher, the passionate badminton player, dreamy rose growers, inconsolable widowers." He sipped from the glass and groaned. "Tell me if I'm being too long-winded. Or too boring."

"No, no. Tell me more." Tobey adjusted the pillow under his head, and hoped the scar on the back of his head was no longer bleeding. He liked to listen to Tanvir, liked lying on the sofa, distracted by words from this day, which had meanwhile become night.

"So I was, at one blow, not only a complete orphan," Tanvir continued, "but also in a foreign land. And a war was raging in my home. It was possible that our house had been destroyed—I didn't know. I worked as a doctor in a hospital in Delhi—no picnic; you can believe me—a stronghold of viruses and bacteria. Healthy people died there from a scraped knee; it was all very unpleasant. Eventually, I got tired of this madness— the noise in the hall, three crowded rooms, narrow corridors, and the canteen food. I took all my savings and opened a shop. Guess what kind!"

"Liquor?"

Tanvir snorted indignantly. "Oh, listen to you. Liquor!" he said. "Books! I sold books in my tiny, dark shop, wedged between a cobbler and a hole in the wall where you could get anything, from nails to dried tiger penis! But what did I sell? I sold nothing, not a single book. I didn't carry junk, of course, but people probably had other things in mind than Proust and Tolstoy. After a month I was broke. That's how life punished the aesthetic simpleton. On the day I was packing the last books in boxes, to sell them at a loss to a real bookstore in a better neighborhood, a man walked into the place where I had failed—white, tall, well dressed—truly an alien presence in this lightless chamber and this poor district. As he told me later, he had dropped off his housekeeper, who was visiting her parents a street away. He has been waiting for her and was walking around—imagine it—he was roaming around in this neighborhood with expensive, clean shoes on his feet! Excuse me a moment." Tanvir took his legs off the stool, went to the bathroom and came back with a wet towel around his neck. He increased the speed of the fan and sat down again. "Well, my beautiful sign still hung on the shop door, proclaiming in starry-eyed disregard of the circumstances, "Reader's Refuge", which encouraged the courageous man to dare and step over the threshold. He wanted to know whether I had just opened the store or closed it, and we started talking. In short, when he heard that I was a doctor he offered me a job, and two days later I was living in a building that my new employer called the pool house. It was about ten times larger than my former store. And cleaner and brighter, if I may say so myself. A few steps away from my living quarters was a swimming pool, which was completely filled with sand. Frank and Muriel Bennett, whose family I now served as house doctor, had a seven-year-old daughter who suffered from epilepsy."

"That's why there was sand in the pool," Tobey muttered.

"You're still awake! Good. That's exactly why there was sand. Bridget, the girl, was a lively, intelligent, and happy child; totally normal, if you overlooked her disease. But Bridget wasn't in school, the risk was too high, so the child was taught at home, by me, among others. As I mentioned before, I read a lot as a boy. I knew all the American and Russian novels that my father had somehow been able to procure at that time,

173

and that could not cause any serious moral damage in a boy of my age. Bridget and I read *Winnie the Pooh*, and *The Wind in the Willows*, *The Jungle Book*, *Treasure Island*, and *Anna Karenina*. The inventory from my shop was an inexhaustible source."

"You read *Anna Karenina* with a seven year old child?"

"Why not? I read *War and Peace* when I was six! Bridget was also an unusually bright child." Tanvir took a sip. "Anyway, I spent four happy months with the Bennetts, and if it hadn't been for these tragic events, it would have probably lasted a few more months." He looked at Tobey. "Can you endure a little bit of tragedy?"

"Today, in a fit of madness, I excavated my sister's body," Tobey said. "I don't think it can get any more tragic than that."

"Wait and see. —Now, it all happened on a normal day. I had just finished the class with Bridget when Muriel came into the living room and told me that she felt unwell. She turned Bridget over to the housekeeper and begged me to feel her pulse, which of course I did without, however, finding anything abnormal. Muriel said she was hot, and before I knew it, she wrapped her arms around me and kissed me on the mouth. It may surprise you, Tobey, but I was once a young man, and at the risk you might think I'm vain, I must mention that I was considered somewhat handsome at the time. Of course, there's not much to look at anymore. —Anyway, Muriel clasped me in her arms, and I didn't know how I should behave. She was very attractive—no stunning beauty, but very delicate and sensual. I must confess that before that fateful day I had asked myself more than once how good her skin felt, and now, as she pressed herself against me, I was not strong enough to push her away and to put the matter to an end before something happened that we would both regret. —In my defense, perhaps I should say that I was young and rather inexperienced in matters of love. I don't mean to suggest that I was a virgin, not exactly, but I would be lying if I said that I was a man of experience in terms of sexual intercourse at that time. Now, you may be asking yourself how to reconcile that with the fact that I was a very handsome fellow—I really was—even if you can't possibly imagine it." He waited a moment and permitted himself a sip. "Do you want me to answer the question?"

"Yes, I do."

"It was because of talking."

Tobey waited, but Tanvir didn't say anything. He sat up and took a sip of iced tea, now lukewarm, which made it taste even sweeter. "Talking?"

I couldn't talk to girls. I fell silent in their presence—I was paralyzed. And language is really a tool for communication; for advances, for courtship."

"Talk helps," agreed Tobey. He was tired and suppressed a yawn. Perhaps he should have opted for the short version of Tanvir's story.

"It's the key, Tobey. Words open doors, hearts. I was, figuratively speaking, standing in front of locked doors. And so, when Muriel Bennett approached me with her erotic intentions, I was on one hand extremely confused by her breezy manner, and on the other hand I was also highly agitated and aroused by the close proximity of her body. I'll spare us both the details of this clash between two unstable people and come directly to the tragic part that began with the unexpected return of her husband, a scene that was so cliché it was something almost comical, but in this case was the prelude to a sequence of dreadful events. Frank Bennett was an engineer and managed the construction of a factory that would, after its completion, produce prefabricated houses for an English company. For various reasons there had been delays and slip-ups with the construction, and on that very afternoon Frank Bennett was dismissed and replaced by someone who, in the opinion of the firm's leader, would do a better job. As the police investigation later showed, Frank Bennett got drunk after he was fired and had then gone back to the company, where he proceeded to tear apart his former office until he could be subdued. Humiliated and desperate, Frank Bennett found himself out on the road again, eventually driving home to seek comfort from his wife, who he discovered, naked and panting, entwined with a Bengalese doctor on the sofa of his living room. You just have to imagine it." Tanvir took a sip of gin, giving Tobey a little time to form a picture of the scene. "I can only remember fragments of the events that followed. There was a huge outcry, curses and tears, and then Frank Bennett, summarily dismissed and shamefully deceived, stormed out of the room, which gave Muriel and me time to get dressed. A little later the housekeeper came out of the children's room and wanted to know why there had been so much noise, but before Muriel could shoo her back to Bridget, her husband was standing in the room with the gun that he kept stashed between his shirts in case he needed to defend his home and family; he shot once at me and twice at Muriel and then he ran away." Tanvir got up and went to a filing cabinet, opened the top drawer and took out a tin box which he opened and held out Tobey. "Biscuit?"

Tobey, who had expected the tin box to contain the murder weapon, or at least the bullet that had been removed from Tanvir, declined. How Tanvir could have an appetite after such a story was a mystery to him. He sat up, took a sip of tea, and noticed that he was wide awake again.

"The shot hit me in the side here." Tanvir lifted his shirt, revealing a round, hairy belly and, a few inches from his navel, a recessed scar. "It grazed my liver and came back out again." He turned around and displayed the spot where the bullet had left his body. Then he sat back in his chair. "I didn't feel any pain, but, as a doctor, I knew the situation was serious. I was lying on the floor, expecting to die within the next few minutes. When I opened my eyes I saw Muriel beside me in a pool of blood. She wasn't breathing. I was just about to pass out again when there was a shot fired in the garden. When I woke up in the hospital the next day, I was told that Frank Bennett had shot himself in the head in his daughter's sandbox and was as dead as his wife." Tanvir bit into a biscuit and chewed a long time. "How do you think I felt?"

"Like shit?"

"That's the understatement of the century."

"How old was she?"

"Muriel? Thirty-eight."

"She seduced you."

"That takes two." Tanvir dipped a biscuit in gin and slipped it into his mouth. He looked at the veranda, where one of the lamps had gone out. He ran his hand over his bald head.

"What happened to the girl?"

For a while Tanvir didn't say anything, and then, quietly, he said "Bridget." He laid his head on the back of the chair and closed his eyes. "The housekeeper took care of her until Muriel's sister came to fetch the child. Her name was Leslie. She was older than Muriel—forty-three. She visited me at the hospital and I thought she had come to curse me, to blame me for the death of her sister and her brother-in-law, but she did nothing of the sort. She had no idea what had happened between me and Muriel in the half hour before the bloodbath. There was nothing in the police report about adultery or sexual contact."

"Didn't they examine Muriel's body?"

"Yes, but they didn't find anything, because there wasn't anything there. We rolled around on the couch and peeled off each other's clothes, we panted and sweated, but we didn't go all the way."

"The housekeeper saw you."

"When she came in, we were already dressed."

"She heard the screams."

She and the police came to the conclusion that Frank Bennett was yelling like that because he was beside himself about being fired and he was still under the influence of alcohol."

"Why would he want to kill you?"

"I was at the wrong place at the wrong time."

177

Tobey took a sip of iced tea. He wondered how it would taste with a dash of gin, and imagined it was disgusting enough not to try it out. "Didn't you want to tell me how you ended up here?"

"That's exactly what I'm doing. You wanted the long version."

"Yes." Tobey lay down again. "It's hard to believe that you used to be reserved."

"Oh, that was in my youth! In America I quickly learned the art of talking."

'When did you go to America?"

"Not so quick. First there was the trip to England. Leslie had asked me to accompany her and Bridget as soon as I was healthy enough to do so. Bridget was in a very precarious state of mind, as you can imagine, and Leslie thought it was good for the child to have a familiar person nearby. I don't know if you can understand, but I felt guilty for the death of Bridget's parents, and although seeing the girl constantly reminded me of this debt, I could not turn down Leslie's request. She procured all the necessary papers, and soon I was on my way to Blackburn, Great Britain, to a different world." Tanvir looked at the glass as if the gin inside it was the only thing that bound him still with England. "Leslie adopted Bridget; there were no other relatives. For four months I lived a few houses away from them, worked in the shipping division of a department store and taught Bridget three days a week. We read books together and went to the museum or the zoo. I told her everything I knew about Monet and van Gogh and ant-eaters, and she listened to me, but I noticed that she had changed, that she was no longer the same child she had been before that horrible day in Delhi. It grieved me very much and increased my feeling of guilt, which I tried to get rid of by spending more time with her, which only led to the fact that I blamed myself even more vehemently. Her epileptic seizures grew more frequent, and once when she was unsupervised, she fell and hit her head on a stair. We took her to the hospital where a young, extremely nice female doctor took care of her. —

Are you still listening to me?"

"A young, very nice female doctor."

"I don't want to bore you any longer, so I'll get ahead of myself and tell you that I fell in love with this doctor, and she fell in love with me, and that she became my first wife. I would like to skip over the eleven very happy and three very unpleasant months and an ugly divorce, and pick up where I moved to London."

"Not to America?"

"In a little while. First, a summary of my time in London. —A chain of coincidences and a handful of useful acquaintances helped me find a job as a doctor in a shelter for homeless men. Six months later I received a call from Leslie, who told me that Bridget had died. The girl had suffered an epileptic seizure during the night. Vomit had gotten into her lungs, which caused pneumonia. I went to the funeral and stayed a few days to provide Leslie with emotional support. I lived in her house, slept in Bridget's former room, which still contained the packing boxes with her toys. Leslie was really suffering; four years earlier she had lost her husband in a car accident, and now fate had snatched her niece from her. She cried a lot and one day, when I no longer knew what else to do, I took her in my arms. You guessed it: one thing led to another. I stayed in Blackburn and Leslie became my second wife. We were married for almost two years, and I won't diminish the value of marriage by saying that I was not in love with Leslie, but I want to be honest and confess that the relationship was based very strongly on my tendency to console Leslie and my inability to leave her alone with her pain. Far be it from me to conceal that I also hoped through this marriage to erase a part of the debt that I had acquired in Delhi. Well, we lived together; I gave her what encouragement and assistance I could, and she did her best to offer me what she thought a man needed. There was something touching about her almost desperate attempts, and, although we both probably already sensed the futility of our pact, we stubbornly kept it going. She worked

179

for the city government and gave me a job as head of the first aid classes, which were visited regularly by officials. I had a lot of free time and I spent it in the library, where I read medical books higgledy-piggledy— whatever I got my hands on. Leslie was a member of the Ornithological Society, which her husband had presided over until his death. To be honest, I found less pleasure in the feathered birds available for study than with their movement in the wild, and so we wandered many a weekend through forests and fields and observed nesting wrens and black grouse courting. Nearly two years passed like that. And then one day in June, while I was sitting in the library, I realized that I had to go home and tell Leslie that the time for our separation had come. She reacted very calmly, and by winter we were divorced."

"And then you went to America."

"You've got it. However, there were some detours. I was nearly thirty and wanted to get away from England, but before that I had to return to my old home again, to Bangladesh. My uncle, my mother's brother, had taken care of my father's funeral and I went to him and thanked him for it. My father's youngest sister now lived in our former home with her family. I stayed with them for two months and then flew by way of Mumbai to New York."

"America," said Tobey.

"And it welcomed me with harassment and humiliation, in spite of my British passport, which the Empire had generously granted to me after my second marriage. But I was allowed to stay; a stamp gave me the right to stay temporarily in the blessed land. I visited a second cousin who was living in Baltimore. He gave me a job as a nurse in a nursing home, a fairly dreary institution in a neighborhood of warehouses and carpet wholesalers. I could tell you some unpleasant stories about the everyday life of this custodial institution, but I'd rather spare us. I grew somewhat friendly with one of the unfortunate inmates; he was nearly eighty and sat in a wheelchair, but his mind was still as active as mine is now, so he was reasonably sane. When I said that I was a doctor, he told me his whole life story. Don't worry; I won't repeat it now, even though it's an amazing biography, worth passing on. —Anyway, Gregory told me that he had been one of the leading American experts in primate research; in the fifties and sixties he had participated in pioneering studies in America and Europe and published numerous articles on the topic. He showed me a shoe box full of yellowed science magazines and a book that a university press had published in the late sixties. He said that the rest of his books and documents had been lost over time. —Well, I became interested in this man and his work and I searched for information about him in the library. I even went to Washington for a few days to look for information at the Library of Congress. In the course of my investigation I read anything related to primate research, the works of Gregory, of course, which I tracked down in the catacombs of the Library of Congress and freed from decades of dust. And so it happened that within two years, without ever having come across a living chimpanzee (not counting visits to the zoo), I was an expert in this field. Then one day, during the coldest winter I have ever experienced, Gregory died, and his only son came to pick up his things. When I told him that his father had awakened this passion for primate research in me, he invited me to accompany him and to inspect Gregory's estate. Ben, who worked for Texaco in Guatemala, drove me to the house where his parents had lived until his mother died and his father, unable to walk after a fall, was forced to move into the nursing home. The house was small and shabby, the front yard completely overgrown. Although it had been up for sale for two years, Ben would not get rid of it. It was ice cold inside, but the way everything looked suggested the residents had just left and would return at any moment. I was allowed to take anything that I wanted from Gregory's things, and then Ben drove me with all that stuff back to my two-room apartment, which was so narrow that we had to put some of the boxes into the Dodge that I had bought for four hundred dollars, now parked behind the house because the transmission had failed. I remember that the doors were frozen shut and I had to fetch a bucket of hot water so we could get them open." Tanvir giggled. Despite the considerable amount of alcohol in his blood stream, he was in reasonable condition and only sometimes, when he tackled a sentence too quickly, did he mumble a little. "After three years I had enough of Baltimore and its suburbs, and the desolate and icy winters, so I repaired the Dodge and drove to Mexico. I rented a shack in a hick town by the sea (population two hundred), and a Swede who lived in a trailer and painted, taught me how to swim. I spent about a year there; I sold the Dodge in order to stay as long as possible. When I ran out of money I hitchhiked back to Baltimore and worked for six months in a carpenter's workshop, illegally, of course, and for starvation wages. Before it was winter, I got on the bus to Miami, where I washed dishes and scrubbed the floor in the kitchen of a seafood restaurant for almost a year. The next five years followed a similar pattern. I traveled around, worked for a while and then travelled on: San Diego, Los Angeles, San Francisco, Seattle, Las Vegas, New York. Until I ended up in Baltimore again, where my third cousin told me that I could no longer stay in his daughter's room because she had just left her husband and moved back in with her parents. He loaned me five hundred dollars and wished me good luck. I believe that his wife was not unhappy about getting rid of me; I once heard her say to a friend on the phone that I was a pitiful rascal." Tanvir giggled again, choked on the gin and coughed. "Be that as it may, I bought a Toyota minibus with the money, loaded it with my belongings and drove off, down to South Carolina, then to the Gulf of Mexico and New Orleans. I slept on an air mattress in the bus, surrounded by the boxes with Gregory's legacy, and at night, in the light of a camping lamp, I read the documents." Tanvir took a cookie out of the box, looked at it as if it was something whose appearance did not agree with him, and put it back. "And there I found information about the Robert and Nancy Preston foundation, headquartered in Texas. I stayed in the area around New Orleans for a few months and then drove to Fort Worth, where I arrived just a day before Robert Preston's funeral. The building magnate had died of a heart attack on a business trip to Russia, in the arms of a prostitute, as it was later alleged. An ugly story, proving that some members of the press act on the premise that "the defendant is presumed guilty" whether or not innocent people get harmed. —Well, in any case, he left his wife a fortune. They didn't have any children. The foundation focuses on social, cultural, and scientific projects, including IPREC—the International Primate Research Center. You've seen the sad remains."

"And this foundation is still paying? For the place here?"

"You need to know that I have very close personal ties to Nancy Preston. I wasn't admitted to the circle of mourners at the time of the funeral, but then, a few weeks later, I managed to speak to her on the occasion of the inauguration of a home for unwed mothers in Austin. I introduced myself to her as a physician who had a passion for primate research, and asked her to help me with my plan to work for IPREC in one way or another. To my surprise, a few days later she invited me to her home, and over the following weeks and months, we became friends. Very good friends, if I may say so."

"Why does Nancy Preston live on the island?"

Tanvir looked at Tobey with surprise. "Were you in the villa?"

"Yes. And I didn't get the impression that the old woman is taken care of very well here in this dump."

Tanvir let out one of his long sighs. "I agree with you completely, Tobey," he said. "But I can assure you that this admittedly problematic arrangement corresponds entirely to Nancy's wishes. A year ago, after she had set her carpet on fire with a cigarette butt, we housed her here in these rooms and I moved into the room that you now inhabit. But that didn't suit her at all. Nancy Preston is a very friendly and cultured lady, but she has her quirks, and one of them is that she can't bear to have anyone around her most times of the day. Another is that she turns night into day, listening to loud music, and doesn't quiet down until the morning hours. She wanted to return to the villa that, incidentally, used to be on the other island and was rebuilt here at great expense, and we have complied with her wishes. She feels very comfortable there, believe me."

"She's not right in the head. She belongs in a nursing home. I'm sure she'd be taken care of better in America than here."

"So, very slowly and in sequence." Tanvir rubbed his face and took a deep breath in and out. "Nancy is in the early stages of a mild dementia. She's a little confused, but for a seventy-eight year old she is still in quite sound mental condition. I need hardly tell you what I think of nursing homes. And she doesn't want to go back to America. The rumors in connection with the death of her husband have not interested anyone for a long time, but Nancy is convinced that everyone there is pointing the finger at her."

"She forgets that her husband is dead and can torch a house with a burning match. And she remembers the story about the Russian whore?"

"Picture the human brain as a giant filing cabinet, Tobey—thousands of index cards may grow empty as a result of age and disease, the entries rubbed out, but some are labeled forever, and you wonder what is erased and what is saved."

"Why is she even on the island?"

"She accompanied me. Or I her—as you like. The foundation had already paid over a million dollars to IPREC, and yet Nancy only knew about the center from photos in the annual reports. So I suggested that once and for all she see everything on site. That was on a Monday. On Friday we were sitting in the plane to Manila."

"And she's been here since then?"

Tanvir laughed. "What an idea! She stayed for ten days. *I 'm* the one who's been doing time on this wretched island ever since that day!"

"But that was what you wanted."

184

"Yeah, sure. But to pretend I had been welcomed by the scientists with open arms would be an exaggeration. If anything, the small troop had a hostile, frosty attitude toward me. I gained nothing by showing up as a protégé of the great financial donor. Quite the opposite. Nancy was barely sitting in the helicopter before they made it clear to me how things on the island ran. There was a doctor—they did not need a second one, and my reading knowledge in the field of primate research, which I tried to assert, provoked only derision and laughter."

"What did you do?"

"For five weeks I twirled my thumbs, collected mussels, and studied the behavior of the gecko that lived in my bathroom. And then, when I seriously considered leaving the island, Nancy came back. A Russian reporter, allegedly with the best connection to the St. Petersburg police, had sold the story about the prostitute to a British tabloid and, in addition, delivered the lady in question. Although the whole thing may have only been invented to pay off the reporter's debts and to satisfy the prostitute's desire for recognition, a few rogue newspapers in the U.S. picked up the story, and for Nancy the nightmare began. After three days she was at the end of her rope, put all her business in order and headed out of Texas in the direction of the Philippines."

"And she's been here since then?"

"In between times she flew to Manila or to Singapore, Hong Kong, Dubai. But she's lived on the island for eight years."

"Who is Diego?"

"Oh, Nancy's gardener in Texas. Mexican, a nice guy. Now she thinks Miguel is Diego, and he plays along." Tanvir rose sluggishly and stashed the cookie jar in the cupboard.

"Why two islands?"

"I'll tell you that another time, if you don't mind. This journey into the past has really exhausted me."

"Sure." Tobey got up. "Good night, then."

"Good night. Sleep well." Tanvir opened the door. The whites of his eyes looked like they were inflamed, the odor of gin wafted over him.

"You too." Tobey had barely entered the hall before the door closed behind him.

The next day Tobey rose with the first light. He washed, dressed, and went to the kitchen hut, but it was locked. A drowsy silence lay over the research station; the only sound came from the center of the island, where sporadic bird calls rose from the heart of the forest. Tobey looked through a window into the kitchen, where there was a half loaf of bread and cooked eggs in a basket on the table, then he went on his way, hungry, to the cemetery.

Megan's grave still looked awful; the rain had contributed its part to the devastation. The bright, sea-polished stones were scattered everywhere; the grave stone, a piece of rock from the beach coarsely carved into a rectangular shape, protruded crookedly from the raised earth, the lawn around the poorly filled hole disappeared in places under clods of earth and tufts of grass. Tobey took the shovel from the shed and began to work. The open blisters on his palms ached, but he gritted his teeth. He pounded the earth flat over the grave, raked the lawn, and tossed the grass tufts into the woods. He went to the beach three times with a bucket and collected dark stones that he arranged into a pattern together with the light ones. On his knees, he slid along the gravel path and freed it from the lumps of earth and weeds. Last, he cut large purple flowers from a tree and placed them in a water-filled glass.

Then he washed his hands in the water basin and sat on the bench. The coolness of the night began to give way to the warmth of day; the sky brightened along the edges. Tobey rested and took a deep breath. When he was ready, he went to Megan's grave, took the sheet of paper from his pocket and unfolded it. Except for the chirping of the first insects it was quiet; in gusts the emerging wind carried the calls of birds closer.

186

"That's for you, Megan," said Tobey. "You know, I was never as clever as you with words, but listen to it anyway, okay?" He cleared his throat, and then he read what he had written the night before. "Megan O'Flynn never needed much to be happy. When she was small, a box of crayons was enough, a jump rope, a plastic hair clip in the shape of a butterfly that she stuck into the horse's mane instead of her own hair. She could spend half the day building a house for a homeless beetle, and the other half with the solemn funeral for a pied wagtail chick. Out of empty matchboxes and scraps of fabric she constructed beds that she slipped into mouse holes. She read to the cows out loud from the local newspaper and to the crows and magpies from poetry books. She gave each animal a name, from beetles to the chicken to the dog, which she christened Wellie, because he had chewed through a pair of the breeder's rubber boots. When it rained, she played in her room or in the barn with a cloth monkey named Joe, who wore yellow trousers and spoke with a deep, raspy voice. Megan O'Flynn ceased to believe in God when she found a dying blackbird in the garden behind the house and prayed for it in vain. She was three years old then, and neither her father's threats nor the appeals of the priest got her to her change her mind. When she was four she stopped eating meat; at eleven, she won a national short story competition; at fifteen she won the state record in swimming the butterfly over two hundred meters; at eighteen she left the church; at twenty she went to England; at twenty-four, she gave up the study of veterinary medicine; at twenty-six she disappeared forever. It's hard to say why she became a restless soul, because as a child she could sit all day on the trunk of a felled beech and watch ants or write a story about a worm that falls in love with a caterpillar and must watch as it turns into a butterfly and flies away. She wanted to know more than other children; she also wanted to know the other side of all that she was told—the secret treasure, or the terrible secret. If Megan O'Flynn was wrong and there really is a God, it would be nice if He did not turn her away. Perhaps there are forests and

187

meadows and lakes and a sea for all the animals in the afterlife. She would definitely feel at home in such a place."

Tobey stayed in front of the grave for a while, and then he folded the paper, pocketed it and walked away.

After the second knock, Montgomery opened the door. He was wearing slippers and a sort of dressing gown, which was held together by a belt. The white of a T-shirt glowed underneath it. One hand rested on the doorknob; the other was holding a hairbrush.

"Hello," said Tobey.

Montgomery nodded. His face expressed nothing: no joy, no surprise, no hostility. He seemed tired and distracted, thought Tobey, but that was certainly because he had just gotten up.

"Am I disturbing you?" Tobey knew that the bonobo did not understand. Then he remembered the folder, and he described a rectangle with his hands and flipped through invisible pages.

Montgomery stepped aside and let Tobey into the room. The bed was neatly made; long blue pants and a matching shirt lay on the bedspread. Tobey waited for Montgomery to take the folder from the shelf, but the bonobo was still standing at the door, his hand on the handle. Tobey reached for the folder and looked for the word *apology* but he didn't find it, and pointed instead at himself and then at the word *bad*. He looked for *embarrassed*, but that was also missing; then he came across *sad* and again pointed to himself and then to the concept, illustrated with the dot-dot-comma-dash-face with a turned down mouth. He found the word *hit* and formed a sentence, which he held out to Montgomery.

I. Hit. Montgomery. Pain. I. Sorry.

Montgomery closed the door and took the folder from Tobey's hand. He sat in the chair, lay the folder down on his knees and pointed his finger at a word.

Tobey looked at the word. "Understand," he said, smiling. He crouched down beside the chair, took Montgomery's hand and placed it in his, and because he did not know what else to say after a while, he stroked it. Eventually Montgomery leafed through the folder, pointing to the word *eat*.

"Eat," Tobey said, and nodded. "Very good." He searched for the word *hunger*, rubbing his stomach.

Montgomery pointed to the pants and shirt on the bed.

"You're getting dressed. I understand." Tobey got up, pointed to himself, then to the concept *wait* and to the window.

Montgomery nodded.

Tobey left the room, shut the door and stood outside in the shade of trees. The puddles had dried, the hollows in the ground now only dark, damp earth covered with small, lead-gray flies. He could not stand still; he walked back and forth, then picked up a stone and threw it at a tree without hitting it. He thought about what had just happened, and shook his head. He had communicated with an ape, had apologized to him because he had beaten him, and the bonobo had understood him, perhaps even forgiven him. Tobey turned in circles, threw his head back and laughed. He circled the tree, and before he began to dance, Montgomery came and they walked side by side to the kitchen hut.

Chester was squatting on the floor and spooned something out of a bowl as Tobey and Montgomery entered the room. He stopped moving for a moment, and then he dipped the spoon back into the bowl. Rosalinda welcomed Tobey and Montgomery, while Jay Jay, who sat at the table over a plate of scrambled eggs and bacon, briefly raised his head and nodded to Tobey. The fan slowly turned, the kitchen was still cool from the night, and there was a song playing on the radio that Tobey eventually recognized as "Danny Boy", interpreted in Asian by a Filipino singer whose thin voice was almost lost in the bombast of the string-heavy orchestra. He would like to have asked Rosalinda if the Philippine text corresponded to the original, but then the cook placed the bread, butter, cheese, tomatoes and a pot of hot porridge on the table, and he began to eat. In between, he exchanged glances with Montgomery, and happy feelings flowed through him.

After he had finished eating and drinking the last sip of coffee, Jay Jay got up. "Montgomery, Coco," he said, and carried his dishes to the sink.

Montgomery let out a sound, stood up and cleared away his plate and the glass, too. He briefly touched Tobey's arm with his hand and followed Jay Jay outside.

"Where are they going?" Tobey asked after the two were gone.

"Other island. Pick coconuts." Rosalinda sat across from Tobey. She wore a scarf wound into a turban and a colorful dress that was cut wide at the shoulders and a revealing neckline that reminded Tobey of what he would miss about this island at some point, if he did not miss it already.

"With the boat?" Tobey had avoided looking at Rosalinda longer than a second during breakfast, and even now lifted his head only briefly.

The cook nodded. "You saw Tanvir today?" she asked.

"What?" Tobey had been following the path of a bead of sweat that trickled down Rosalinda's neck.

"Mr. Tanvir. You saw him today?"

"No. Not today."

"He's drunk, for sure."

Tobey poured the rest of the porridge into his bowl. "Maybe."

"Is from the devil, alcohol," Rosalinda said and crossed herself with a flying motion of her right hand. "Men come from the devil." Again, she crossed herself.

Tobey wondered what she meant by that. "The men in the boat?" he asked.

Rosalinda nodded and looked at Tobey through the narrow slits of her eyes.

"Bad men. Muslim." She pushed the last word through her teeth, her

190

lips twisted with scorn. She got up, took her plate and cup and put both noisily into the sink.

Tobey was about to ask her something else, but Rosalinda was handling the dishes so loudly that he gave it up. "See you later," he murmured and left the kitchen.

In his room, Tobey took Megan's letters, the money and the passport out of hiding in the bureau, wrapped the letters in two garbage bags, tied them up and placed them with the clean laundry, the ground pad, the water purification equipment, the pot and the two flashlights into the suitcase he had converted into a backpack. He put the bundle of money into his right shoe and the passport into the left. He put the sleeping bag and the kettle on the bureau; perhaps Miguel and Jay Jay had use for it. He took the knife out of the bathroom and tied it around his calf, and then he pushed the suitcase toward the other one under the bed and left the room. The lizard, whose territory apparently included the area in front of his door, skidded across the floor and disappeared behind the refrigerator. In addition to the magazines on the table there was a pencil stub. Tobey stuck it in his pocket and walked out.

He saw the sun, clear and bright for the first time in a long while, not half-hidden under the vague haze of a weather front that he could not interpret. The sky around him was blue, nothing more than parcels of clouds entrenched on the horizon, billowing cirrus formations, whose color and lack of motion concealed their intentions from Tobey. A wind blew, scattered a handful of dry leaves over the clearing and abated after that for several minutes, then pounced down in a gust, rattled the crowns of the trees and died away before it reached the ground and Tobey could tell from which direction it had come and whether it carried the smell of rain.

He went to the beach and searched among the driftwood for a board and found a slightly curved piece of a ship's plank. Sitting in the shade, he used a knife to clean away the spots that were covered with algae and clam shells the size of wheat kernels, took the pencil from his pocket and wrote MEGAN O'FLYNN on the sun-warmed surface. With the knife point he carved the outlines into the wood and finally began to cut away a contour for each letter about two millimeters deep. In the process, a thousand stories went through his head. Images emerged, blurred and shaky; they were clear for a few seconds and then disappeared into the darkness from where new pictures arose, pale at first and then with blazing colors, screen size and crowded, glistening at the edges. The approaching waves rolled and broke almost silently on the flat beach, and he thought about the day he had to go to school for the first time and went holding Megan's hand to the bus stop, where he let it go, because other kids were there and could have taken him for a scaredy-cat, and he remembered the feeling he had after this letting go, the feeling of hot burning shame and emptiness after a heartbreaking betrayal that never again and by nothing could ever make amends. He thought of Dennis Fahy, who had beaten him up after school because he felt like it and was stronger, and whose nose Megan broke with a single punch. He saw himself hanging from the branch of a tree and Megan running across the meadow, carrying a ladder with both arms over her head that looked like the bare bones of a pair of wings. He saw her walking slowly across the courtyard in the nightgown that their mother had left behind, hunched over, moonlight on her shoulders. He saw her sobbing, sitting at the fresh grave of a mole. He saw her naked on the shore of the pond in the evening sun. He found himself reading her notebooks, proud and jealous, because he did not have his own language yet. He saw her next to their father on the tractor, sitting and waving as if she would not be coming back. He saw himself walking through shoulder-high grass, following the winding path of her body, breathless with fear and curiosity. He saw her on the hill above the sea, sitting and waiting for him. He saw her face hovering above his, heard her whispering.

When the name was engraved in the wood, Tobey got up and went to the cemetery. The wind was strong, a rising breath of air pushing and pulling lightly from all sides. The backdrop of clouds had been cleared away, the horizon a straight line ascending behind the dark light. Tobey saw Miguel, who was bolting the diesel generator to the engine. Rosalinda sat in the shade beside him, sewing, with Chester at her feet. Tobey heard her speaking; he waved, but she did not notice him. He walked across the field and through the coconut grove and thought about the raft that he wanted to build. While he made his way to the spot behind the valley where the path turned off to the cemetery, he imagined himself drifting on the sea, nothing beneath him but a net filled with empty coconuts, and wondered how long he would survive. He would have taken along water in plastic bottles and food, stored in several garbage bags, and a handkerchief to protect against the sun. In his suitcase, which would have been tied to the raft, he would have packed two flashlights, the ground pad and the water purification equipment. Out of rope and string and a bamboo pole he would have built a mast and used the mat as a sail. At night he would have been tied to the mast, so as not to roll into the water. Because the silver-coated mat gleamed in the sunlight, at some point a ship would have seen him and saved him. They would have pressed him with questions and brought him to the Irish ambassador in Manila, if there was one, and perhaps he would have told his story.

The gravel crunched beneath his feet. He went to Megan's grave, touched the stone with his hand. Then he placed the piece of wood with her name on it between the stones from the sea.

The heat was oppressive, the air palpable. The machinery of the insects had abated, the birds sat silently in the trees. Tobey had taken a shower— even the cold water was lukewarm. Now he lay on his bed; above him the fan turned. He had been to the kitchen hut, but had not found Tanvir either there or in his room. He had knocked in vain for Montgomery, who still seemed to be away with Jay Jay. He wondered when the boat was coming and what he would do if it did not come. He thought about the ropes in the infirmary and the gas cans in the shed next to the generator, which, empty, were definitely suitable flotation devices for a raft, even better than tires or coconuts. If Tanvir had lied to him about the boat, he would take the cans to the beach and assemble them there. To get to the ropes from the infirmary, he would clear away the putty which had not yet set with a knife, carefully remove the windowpane and set it against the wall. The thought of Jay Jay's face made him smile involuntarily, but the traces of his good mood wore off when he pictured himself spending even one day at sea, at the mercy of the weather and the random tide, between himself and the terrible depths nothing but sheet metal canisters, held together by thin ropes. Then it occurred to him that he could lay boards over the canisters, and thought about the top of the dresser and the back wall and doors of the closet. From the blades of the fan and a shovel he could make a paddle. When he started to think about taking the bed apart, he realized how absurd it would be to escape on a homemade raft. He had no hammer and no nails, and even if he found tools somewhere, he could not work with them on the beach at night, because the noise would wake everyone on the island. He wondered where the boat Jay Jay cruised around in was kept, and why they didn't carry him away from the island in it. He got up, got dressed, strapped the knife to his calf and went out.

No wind blew; the clearing was still, immersed in purple-colored light. He crossed it and followed the path to the pond, curved where the path forked, he followed a vague recollection and took a left and walked toward the hill that loomed before him as he reached the end of the valley. He continued going left, running now and leaving a broad, uncultivated expanse behind him, and fell again into a walking pace when he reached the woods. There was no longer a trail, only dark soil from rotting leaves, and Tobey walked quickly between the tree trunks in order to reach daylight again. He jumped over a small brook with marshy banks and avoided rocks and the thicket bushes, was sometimes convinced that he had gotten lost, and then stood suddenly in the meadow. The hill was right behind him; its slope looked gray and bare. Tobey took a breath of air and ran again, hard dry grass slapping against his legs.

The tower was twelve, maybe fifteen meters high. Tobey kicked one of the bars that was connected to the concrete foundation and formed the square parameter, five layers high, from which four tree trunks loomed, stripped of bark and painted the color of tar. The tree trunks were all about eight inches and braced on one side with timber beams. The ladder inside the tower felt solid, and although the nails were rusty and it was missing a few rungs, Tobey took a chance on climbing it. As a child he had advised Megan never to look down when she climbed a tree, but now, halfway up, he did exactly that, and he pressed himself against the ladder, closed his eyes and counted to ten before he attacked the rest. At the top, he sat down and breathed.

The floor boards of the platform were thick and in good condition. The railing appeared to be stable. Tobey did not even get up to survey the island. The railing was made of vertical bars which supported the handrail, and between the bars there were large gaps that he could look through. The hill looked even smaller from up here. The paths that led to the bunker were not recognizable from this distance. An empty, pale spot with straight edges had to be the clearing, but where the barracks stood, Tobey could only guess. He saw the beach; behind a bend was the rock where he sometimes sat. The sea spread out before him and encircled him. He should have bought a pair of binoculars, he thought. The shop in Manila had several models; some were the size of a fist, wrapped in a soft green rubber skin and almost weightless.

Even up here no wind blew. Tobey took off his shirt, laid it on the boards, and cursed himself once more for not bringing any water along. He turned; every two minutes he looked in another direction: north, east, south, west, and then north again. Once he saw an airplane in the distance, a silver needle in the fabric of the sky, the vapor trail like a thread dragging itself behind. His eyes were tired and he closed them every few minutes for a moment or rubbed them, which really didn't help. He imagined the people in the plane, and the thought that they all had a history and desires triggered a strange feeling of sadness and emotion in him. That they had a destination troubled him even more.

He looked at the sea, thinking of a letter from Megan. It was his favorite letter: he knew it by heart.

News from Megan

Life can be beautiful, Tobey. Do you know that? (Of course you know it!) Leaving London was the best thing I could do. I live on the coast, in an old stone house, and when I go out the door on a stormy day and call a name—yours, for example—into the wind, it blows me a handful of sea, and I can taste salt on my lips. I have no neighbors, only the mad Padraig Halligan, who is not at all crazy, at least no crazier than I am. His parents had an accident on the way to Cardiff by car, when he was fifteen. Now he is fifty and is building something in the barn that the people in town claim is a time machine which he wants to use to go back in time and prevent his parents from taking that trip. But Padraig told me he just wants to build a beautiful machine that moves and flashes and makes sounds. I draw too much. Sometimes seals come to the pebble beach and lie in the sun. I particularly like to draw crabs and clams. Three days a week I work in the city in a stationery store. The owners are nice; they give me a discount on watercolor paints and brushes. In my kitchen there is a radio that I have set to a French radio station, so I don't understand anything. Sometimes I ride the bus into town and borrow a book from the library. I read a lot less than before. But I walk for hours. In London, I sat in my apartment most of the time; here, I am outside whenever possible. I can't swim anywhere; the sea is too cold, and there isn't a swimming pool. Maybe I'll buy a wet suit like the surfers wear, and throw myself into the waves at the beach by my house! Once I was at the movies, but I found it strange to sit in the dark with all those people and laugh or wince at the same time they did. Sometimes, when I sit in front of the house, a cat comes by and sits beside me for a while. The sky here has a beautiful color, different every day and every hour, and I do not even try to mix it in the watercolor box. This is currently my life, Tobey. I'm as happy as I can be, and I hope that you are too.

Who loves you?
Megan!

14

After the plane disappeared, he turned in the direction he thought was south and saw the boat. Actually, he first noticed the foaming "V" that the motor's propeller wrote in the water. The boat moved along the beach at its crest, slowly, and too small for Tobey to see who was on board. Since the boat was holding its course he climbed down the ladder but he was too fast and heard a rung break under his weight. His hands slipped and he fell, landed on his feet and fell backwards. Slightly dazed, he lay there and looked up where the broken rung hung on the nails, two, maybe three meters off the ground.

He groaned and sat up. Then he realized that he had left his shirt on the platform, and wanted to get it. As he struggled to his feet, a searing pain shot through his right foot. He let out a cry, held on to the ladder and took the weight off his leg. He stood there for a while quietly whimpering and cursing, and felt all the blood rush to his foot, causing it to swell. He waited with closed eyes, but knew that he would not be able to go far. Standing on one leg, he dropped to his side, put his hands on the sandy, warm soil and brought himself to a kneeling position. After his experience with shackled ankles, he knew he was faster and could move forward more easily on all fours instead of hopping. Before he thought too long about his fate and the question of why it had turned against him again, he crawled toward the woods.

Nearly two hours passed before his hands touched the cool forest floor. He had counted out loud, which was better than cursing and whining. Every ten minutes he had rested for a moment while trying not to think of water. First he had counted normally—a conscientious surveyor—then he had started to recite or to whisper the numbers in different pitches. Eventually he had shouted them out into the countryside, a child playing hide and seek; finally, he had sung them, lyrics replaced by numbers, and dashed toward the forest which had become visible in the infinitely far distance. When he had rested, lying like a dog on his side, the question had gone through his head if madness had begun, if reason had gone astray, when one repeatedly chanted the numbers from one to sixty, on all fours, crawling across a field.

Now he sat there leaning against a log and trimmed the branch of a tree with a knife, to use it as a crutch. Beside him there was one already finished. He was not crazy; he felt miserable, but at least he had not cried. His foot was swollen; his ankle was turning blue. He loosened his laces, but did not take off his shoe. The knife blade was dull and he sharpened it as best he could on the surface of a stone. When he was twelve he had broken his right leg in a fall from the barn roof and after that moved around for weeks on crutches. From this experience he knew that he could not walk with just one crutch, even though Megan had shown him how to do it and had laughed at him because he had fallen incessantly.

After another hour Tobey limped away. The branch forks pinched into the flesh under his arms and he thought for one moment about going back to the tower to get the shirt, but then he changed his mind. The ground in the forest was soft from the rain and the ends of the crutches sank into it centimeters deep. Once he slipped and fell, but he did not swear or complain. And he did not start to count again.

It was dark night when Tobey saw the light of the kitchen hut. He was surprised that someone was there so late; it had to be well after ten. At the clearing he stopped and took a breath. The skin under his armpits was chafed, his partially healed palms were bleeding again, and his arms felt as if he had rowed here from Ireland. It was just the foot that he hardly felt, the bloated lump hung at the end of his leg like a foreign object throbbing with the rhythm of a heart. He pulled the knife out from under the leg of his trousers and put it in the side pocket of his pants. Then he hobbled to the door and when he opened it and entered the kitchen Rosalinda jumped with fright, gaped at him and crossed herself, muttering softly. She sat at the table; in front of her there was a bowl, half-filled with ice cubes. A folded towel lay across her shoulder, a hand on her quivering bosom.

"Hello, Rosalinda," said Tobey, hoping the woman would not take him for a ghost.

Rosalinda actually seemed to have regained her composure. "What happened?" she asked, getting up and placing a chair in front of Tobey. She wore a floor-length blue dress and rubber slippers; her hair was coiled into a bun, wooden sticks protruding like knitting needles in a ball of wool. She looked tired; the whites of her eyes were red.

"Thanks." Tobey sat down and took the glass which the cook gave him, emptied it in one gulp, and let her fill it up again. "Accident," he said. "Ladder." He made a dismissive gesture, as if the whole thing wasn't even worth mentioning.

"Blood," said Rosalinda, pointing to Tobey hands.

"Yes." Tobey shrugged his shoulders. "It's not so bad." The kitchen seemed strangely alien, and he wondered why that would be. Then he realized that the fans were still and the radio wasn't playing.

Rosalinda took the towel from her shoulder, soaked it with water at the sink and gave it to Tobey. Because she looked at him and seemed to be waiting for him to do something with the towel, he wiped his face with it. Rosalinda pulled a plastic bag from the closet, filled it with two hands full of ice cubes, put her chair in front of Tobey, pulled his leg forward, took off his shoe and covered the foot with the ice pack.

Tobey let these things happen with a delicious self-pity and wondered how Rosalinda could have known he would arrive at this hour with a sprained foot, for which she had already put ice in a bowl.

"Wait," Rosalinda said, took Tobey's hand and laid it on the bag filled with ice. "Hungry?"

Tobey nodded. "A little." He imagined himself naked in front of Rosalinda, but then he was ashamed of it and kept his eyes focused on his foot, which awoke from the cold and began to throb and tingle, as if it had been numb for hours.

Rosalinda prepared a plate of bread, cheese, onion rings and olives for him and put it on the table together with the fruit bowl.

"Thanks." Tobey wiped his hands clean with the cloth and began to eat.

"Is for Tanvir," Rosalinda said, took the bowl with the ice cubes in hand, got a fresh dish towel and went to the door. "You okay, yes?"

Yes. Thank you."

Rosalinda opened the door. "I come back soon."

"Rosalinda?"

"Yes?"

"Was the boat here?"

"Yes, was there," Rosalinda said, went out and shut the door.

Although it made him angry to have missed the boat, he devoured the food ravenously and emptied the whole water pitcher. Music, he thought, might comfort him a little, but he was reasonably comfortable and did not get up to turn on the radio. He put the wet towel around his neck and closed his eyes. After a while he took the ice pack from his foot and held it alternately against one shoulder and then the other. He felt heavy and tired and wanted to let himself fall to the floor and sleep, but he also wanted to shower and to lie on a soft mattress. He took the glass in hand to drink the last sip of water when he remembered that Tanvir never took ice in his gin. He got up, tucked his crutches under his arms, poured the water and the half-melted ice cubes into the sink and left the kitchen.

Because he had been sitting so long, everything hurt even more, his arms, his hands, his legs, and the foot that was hanging naked from his trouser leg. The night was as black as ever and strangely still, the air damp and barely cooler. He limped the few meters around the barracks, labored up the stairs and walked through the lighted hallway to Tanvir's room. Raising the crutch to knock, he heard Rosalinda's excited voice, which sounded as if she had been crying or would soon start. From time to time Tanvir's bass growled in between, slowly and conciliatory. After it had grown quiet for a long time, Tobey knocked.

"Who's there?" said Tanvir, just as Tobey, balancing on one leg, decided to knock a second time.

"It's me, Tobey!"

"Come in!" Tanvir said a few seconds later.

Tobey entered the living room. On the table beside the sofa there was a crumpled towel; beside it stood one of the bottles from the infirmary.

"We're here, in the bedroom!"

The room was next to the bathroom and it was so small that a bedside table and a wooden chest would not fit in addition to the bed. On the wall above the bed hung a black and white poster of London in the fog and on another the poster for the film *Moby Dick*. The umbrella leaned against one corner; in front of that there was a plastic bucket and a pair of sandals. A naked light bulb, sticking out of a cube-shaped wooden lamp base, immersed everything in a chalky 30-watt light.

"Oh, Tobey." Tanvir lay on the bed, dressed in a kind of pajamas; Rosalinda sat at the foot of the bed with the bowl of ice cubes on her lap.

"Am I disturbing you?" Tobey hesitated in the doorway.

"No, no. Come in." Tanvir beckoned Tobey inside. "Unfortunately, I can't offer you a chair." He held a dish towel filled with ice against his left cheek, where a dark blue discoloration was forming around his eye. Tobey limped closer to the bed. "What happened?"

Tanvir said something to Rosalinda in Tagalog, and after a short back and forth the cook stood up and pressed the cold bowl into Tobey's free hand. "Ice," she said, and went out.

"Where the hell were you?" Tanvir exclaimed after Rosalinda had closed the door to the hallway behind her.

"Do you always answer a question with another question?" Tobey said, trying to be funny, but quickly realized that he had chosen the wrong moment.

"I want to know where you were, Lord God!" Tanvir shouted. "And what are those sticks for?" He sat up halfway and pushed the pillow behind the small of his back.

"Crutches," Tobey said, a little disconcerted by the volume of Tanvir's voice. "I had an accident." He lifted his leg and showed Tanvir his swollen foot.

Tanvir groaned and it was hard to tell whether the reason was his own pain or the sight of Tobey's foot. He took the ice pack from his face and wiped his sleeve across his damp, purple-stained cheek.

"And how did *that* happen?" Tobey wondered whether he should sit on the end of the bed, but then decided to take a seat on the trunk that was on a sisal rug under the film poster.

"Another accident. What were you driving?"

"I was walking. What other accident?"

"I crashed. You were walking?"

"Not a good idea, I know. Where did you crash?" Tanvir seemed to have realized the futility of this conversation, and grew silent. He pressed the cloth with the ice cubes against his cheek and sighed again.

"Looks more like you got punched," Tobey said after a while. He dipped both his hands into the ice water for a moment and looked out the window. There was only one opening, with a mosquito net; countless butterflies had settled on the outside of it.

"The boat was here," Tanvir said flatly. The soles of his feet were an ochre color. They reminded Tobey of the color of his guitar, which he had sold much too cheaply before his departure.

Tobey said nothing.

"You wanted to get away and then you take a walk. You're a strange man, Tobey."

"Maybe I don't really want to go away." The icy water hurt his fingers, but it helped soothe the burning of his palms.

"Did I just understand you correctly? You don't want to leave?"

"I don't know."

"What are you doing here?" Tanvir shouted. "You don't even drink!"

"I don't know." Tobey took his hands out of the water and wiped them off with the towel that had been hanging around his shoulder. "I don't know where to go."

For a time both were silent. A very large butterfly landed on the window screen. The two bright spots on its wings looked like a pair of eyes.

"You can't stay here, Tobey." Tanvir put the soaked towel in the dish that stood on the bedside table.

"Why not?"

"It won't work. The reasons don't matter."

"They matter to me. Is it because I don't drink? Can I stay if I start to booze it up?"

"Oh, just stop." The spot on Tanvir's cheek looked, from a distance, like a wine stain.

"Was it the men from the boat?"

"What?"

"Who beat you up."

"I tell you I fell last night. You saw that I had a little too much to drink."

"Where did you fall?"

"Here."

"What did you hit your head on?"

"Is this an interrogation?" Tanvir looked around. "There," he said, "the chest you're sitting on."

"Nonsense." Tobey put down the bowl, propped himself up on his crutches and hobbled to the door.

"Where are you going?"

"I'm going to ask Rosalinda." Tobey left the room.

"Wait!"

Tobey had crossed half the living room and stopped.

"Come back, damn it!" Tanvir mumbled something unintelligible. "And bring the bottle with you—the one on the table beside the sofa!"

"There's no bottle here." The towel and the bottle were gone; the only thing on the table was a pack of matches.

Tanvir muttered something else that Tobey didn't understand, but he thought it might be Bengali. "On the porch you'll find a bottle in a bucket, under the folding chair!"

Tobey got the gin and a glass and brought both of them into the bedroom, which, on crutches, was no easy task. He sat down at the foot of the bed, filled the glass halfway and handed it to Tanvir, who accepted it with a surly grunt, emptied it, and held it out again to Tobey.

"Man, do you actually know how poisonous that stuff is?"

"Oh, don't bore me with your blabber about health! So what? Do I have to ask you for it?"

Tobey again poured gin into the glass.

"Poisonous," muttered Tanvir, and took a sip. "I can only hope!"

Tobey rose.

"Where are you going *now*?"

"I'm going to sit down on the chest."

"All right. But leave the bottle here."

Tobey gave the bottle to Tanvir, limped to the chest, sat down and put his foot on the bed. His ankle was now the same color as Tanvir's cheek.

"So, do you want the short version or the long one?"

"The short one." Tanvir sat up. He looked into his glass for a few seconds, and then looked Tobey in the eye. "Surely you know how intelligent Montgomery is, right?"

Tobey nodded.

"There are people who want to make money off this intelligence. They ask me to perform with Montgomery. To organize a show with him. But I refuse."

"And these people were here today and did that to you?"

"That's right."

"Why not simply snatch Montgomery and go ahead with the whole thing without you?"

"Montgomery is fixated on me; he doesn't communicate with strangers."

"He does with me."

"You're an exception. I'm astonished."

"Who are these people?"

"A fellow from Manila; evil scum."

"And they would have taken me with them today?"

Tanvir looked into his glass again and nodded.

"Then who are the guys I saw the night before last? Three men, one of them your friend, who knocked me down and allegedly never comes to this island. They met with Miguel and Jay Jay and hauled crates to their boat."

Tanvir tried in vain to hide his amazement. "The night before last, you say?"

"Or the night before that. I can't keep track of time anymore."

Tanvir snorted as he laughed. "Very good." He took a sip of gin. "Now I know what you're talking about. That was a delivery. I told you about it. The men bring food, diesel fuel, whatever we need."

"In the middle of the night."

"The sea is often much quieter at night than during the day."

"And what do they take back with them in the boxes? Coconuts?"

"The boxes are empty and set aside for the next delivery." Tobey laughed. "What a bunch of crap," he said, took his leg off the bed and stood up. When he put weight on his foot the pain hurt like hell; tears filled his eyes.

Tanvir pressed himself against the pillow in alarm. "Are you okay?"

Tobey grabbed his crutches and leaned on them. "There are drugs in the crates," he yelled. "Your damn pills are in there! I was in the bunker, man!" He swung a crutch and hit the screen door; the butterfly flew away. "Why do you think Chester was so freaked out? Because of one of your damn pills. You asshole!"

Tanvir stared at Tobey, his eyes wide open.

"You're flabbergasted? And you sit there and tell me this shit about Montgomery and what a good person you are!"

There was a hole in the screen; the little butterfly flew through it and whirled around the room, casting shadows on the walls and the ceiling as it circled around the light bulb. Tobey could have closed the curtain, a faded black piece of cloth on a string, but he left it alone and sat down again. His foot throbbed and he put the bowl on the floor and plunged it into the water, which was still cold but no longer icy. It wasn't until he sat down that he noticed he was breathing heavily.

"Well," said Tanvir after a short time, which he had used to recover from Tobey's performance, then fell silent again for several minutes, emptied his glass and filled it again, staring blankly at the poster above Tobey, lazily brushed a butterfly from his sleeves and rubbed his bald head like a magic lamp from which he expected no more miracles. "Well," he said again. "What happens now?"

Tobey didn't even shrug his shoulders.

Tanvir put the bottle and glass on the bedside table, rose with a groan and closed the curtain. Then he sat down on the bed and tried to catch a few butterflies, but grasped only into the emptiness. "It looks like neither of us has a future on this island." At this realization he took a long gulp.

"Why did the men beat you?"

Tanvir chuckled. "Take a guess."

"Because of me?"

"Does it surprise you to hear that my business partners are bastards? Unscrupulous scoundrels? Murderers?" Tanvir caught a moth, crushed it in his fist and wiped his palm on the sheet. "Oh, and don't forget religious fanatics."

"And what do they want from me?"

"You can guess."

Tobey thought, only for a second, then the knowledge spread through his skull and it felt like carbon dioxide that tingled under his scalp and trickled down his spine, ice cold and debilitating. "You holy shit . . . "He muttered.

"That's pretty much it."

Tobey sat there and looked at a butterfly drawing circles on the ceiling, as if it wanted to encourage the fan to turn. The air was stale and smelled stuffy. More and more butterflies, moths and mosquitoes came through the hole; the shimmering reminded him of the transparent plastic balls, filled with water, that you shook to make the Styrofoam snow fall on the Eiffel Tower or the Statue of Liberty.

"Why isn't the damn fan running?"

"Because the damn fan is broken."

"Have you ever thought about repairing it?"

"It's not that easy to find an electrician here."

"What about Miguel?"

"Yes, he's good at opening things."

"If I had been here a few hours ago, your friends would have killed

209

me." Tobey did not know whether that was an assumption or an observation.

Tanvir did not answer. A butterfly perched on his head, spreading its wings apart and back together again. It looked as if a space probe had landed on a planet and was checking its solar panels. Tanvir didn't notice it, or he didn't care. He stared at his feet, one hand placed over the glass.

"You fucking bastard," Tobey said quietly and dispassionately. He wondered if he wanted to hit Tanvir, imagined himself thrashing him with a crutch, but realized that he had neither the desire nor the power required to pounce on the old man. The idea that he could have been dead a few hours ago was so grotesque that he could not think it through. Each time, when the bullet hit him, his imagination could go no further; he did not fall down and breathe his last breath, but stood there and looked himself in the face, motionless, until the image turned white.

"What would you say if I suggested that we leave the island together? Tonight."

Tobey emerged from his thoughts, as if out of heavy dark water. "I say, I don't give a damn about you."

"Would you rather wait for the bastards and ship out with them?"

"Was that the plan? To throw me into the sea?"

Tanvir took a sip. "Yes."

A thought flashed through Tobey so suddenly and violently that he thought he felt a blow on the head. "Did they kill Megan?"

Tanvir looked down and shook his head slowly.

"Did these bastards throw her into the sea? With your knowledge? Your consent?"

Tanvir still shook his head. "No, no, no . . . " he whispered, his eyes closed. A breeze came through the hole in the screen, gently moving the curtain.

Tobey got up and pulled the curtain down. Then he left the room, crossed the living room and used the crutch to smash everything in sight. His foot was a volcano; lava flowed up his leg into his skull; lightning flashed before his eyes. He opened the door, staggered down the hall and tumbled down the stairs. Fine soil stuck to the wounds of his palms as he struggled to his feet. He limped across the square to the infirmary, smashed in the windowpane and took a pair of metal crutches and all the rope and twine he could find in the dark, went to the shed next to the generator and dragged a dozen empty gas cans outside, tied the handles together with a rope and dragged them to the beach. He was struck by a wind that came from the sea and pushed the fibrous clouds ahead of it. It was pitch dark, but Tobey knew the way, and now and then the moon threw a little light through a gap in the clouds and illuminated the sand.

Next he took the suitcase out of the room. He washed himself hastily and took two pain pills from the matchbox. Then he filled two plastic bottles with water and placed them into the suitcase with his right shoe. He tucked the money wrapped in foil into the passport in his left shoe. After he had put on a shirt and strapped the suitcase to his back, he tore the sheet off the mattress and threw it over his shoulders. He thought about taking the top panel from the chest of drawers in order to attach it to the canisters somehow, but to haul it to the beach seemed impossible so he left it where it was.

When he stepped into the hallway, Jay Jay came out of his room and looked at him with small, red eyes. "What's wrong?"

"Nothing. I can't sleep." Tobey walked past him and went outside. He knew what a sight he made, and did not want to think about the fact that Jay Jay could still make trouble for him. The wind had again increased in strength. When he walked beneath the treetops, it sounded as if hundreds of birds were shaking their feathers. With a piece of twine Tobey attached the small flashlight to one of the crutches so that its beam of light fell on the ground in front of him.

On the beach he sat down in the light of the large flashlight, threw the rope around the cans and tied them together with twine, two rows of six cans, an unstable structure, but at least long enough for him to lie down on. He pulled the raft—which did not deserve the name—into the water to see if it could float. The waves lifted it up, the cans rattling against one another and against the leg Tobey was standing on, fighting for his balance. He dragged it out further, beyond the line where the waves broke, and somehow managed to lie down on it. The sea water burned his hands and his sore armpits; it lapped against the raft and against his legs, which were hanging half in the water, and it was burning in his eyes, which soon saw nothing and only detected something again when he was thrown back onto the beach by a tumbling wave only a few meters away from the glow of his flashlight, and just in front of Tanvir's and Jay Jay's feet. He came out of the sea-spray coughing and spitting, crawled to where the sand was dry, and rolled onto his back.

"Are you okay?" Tanvir asked and stretched out his hand to Tobey. Tobey smacked Tanvir's hand away, pulled the raft from the surf and limped to the suitcase, which lay in the sand next to the flashlight. The pills began to work; slowly the pain subsided.

"So you want to take that out on the sea?" Tanvir kicked a can with his foot.

Tobey turned off the flashlight and put it in the suitcase. Now only the kerosene lantern in Jay Jay's hand was burning.

"I cannot possibly allow that," said Tanvir.

"You go to hell." Tobey shut the suitcase and hung it on his back.

"Well, I'm afraid I'm there already." Tanvir took the pistol from the pocket of his knee-length shirt like a gift that he wanted to give to Tobey, slowly and almost solemnly.

Tobey sat on Tanvir's sofa, his hands and ankles bound, and watched a moth that fluttered out of the bedroom, attracted by the only light source in the room, the light next to Tanvir's chair. He had been allowed to wash his face and hands in the bathroom, and now there was a glass of water in front of him, from which a drinking straw protruded. The patio doors were closed; gusts of wind, one more violent then the next, pushed against it. The suitcase with the harness was on the floor beside the table, sand clung to the damp spots. Tanvir and Jay Jay stood behind the slightly open door in the hallway and talked, hardly intent on being quiet. Jay Jay sounded excited and urgent, Tanvir calm and sooth-ing. Although they spoke their limited English interspersed with Tagalog, Tobey understood hardly anything. The thought that he must soon die flickered through his consciousness at regular intervals. Phases of fierce panic and desperation were replaced by clear moments in which he sifted through the possible forms of his death and planned to ask Tanvir for sleeping pills before being tossed into the sea. He imagined how he sank to the bottom, swarmed by tiny fish, and settled there in the lightless cold, where transparent crabs and blind, arm-length worms lived. Then he could not breathe and tugged at the ropes, calmed down after a while, watched the butterfly that collided with the lamp shade, and tried to re-member Father MacMahon's speech, which had consoled the survivors, that in the afterlife the dead would see their next-of-kin again: grandpar-ents, parents, siblings, and friends. Megan was waiting for him, Tobey told himself, so he would not scream out or weep, now that he had every reason to.

The door swung open and Tanvir, pistol in hand, entered the room. Jay Jay looked at Tobey and walked away. Tanvir shut the door, put the gun on the bureau, poured gin into a glass and drank it. Then he turned around and looked at Tobey, nodded almost imperceptibly a few times. He looked tired; his eyes were empty.

"You have cost us a lot of valuable time," he said finally, nodding vio-lently. "In four, maybe five hours, it will be light. Jay Jay and Miguel will be up." He emptied the glass. "And the storm will probably break up before the sun comes up." He touched the blue spot on his cheek, squinting his eyes.

"Can I have sleeping pills?"

"What?"

"I'm scared shitless of dying, but even more of drowning, so can I take some sleeping pills?"

Tanvir laughed. "What kind of nonsense are you talking? If I wanted you to drown, I would have let you put out to sea on your raft! That thing wouldn't have supported you in the water for an hour!" He sat in his chair and, instead of nodding, he now shook his head. "Good God! If you were as smart as you are stubborn, you'd be a genius! A few hours ago I made you an offer that you and I disappear from here together, but you, you had to give your anger free rein and stomp through my living room in a triumphal procession of outrage and destruction and tie gas cans together like a little boy who wants to play pirate on the duck pond!" From the floor he picked up a piece of the clay fruit bowl that Tobey had smashed with the crutch, and threw it against the bureau.

"Can I take the damn pills now or not?" Listening and speaking exerted Tobey; most of all he would have liked to have had sleeping pills in his stomach already and watched as the colors around him grew pale and the outlines became more indistinct.

"Maybe that would be best," said Tanvir, who had again calmed down. "Then I wouldn't have to listen to your nonsense and your cursing. But I would also have to carry you to the boat, and I am definitely too old for that."

"What kind of a boat are you rambling on about?"

Tanvir took a seat in his chair. "About the boat we would be sitting in now, if you were a grown man and not a prepubescent, irascible, self-righteous boor."

"Just suck me," Tobey said quietly. "You're a lousy old bastard, a drunk and probably a murderer, so spare me your pseudo-psychological bull-

214

shit."

Tanvir seemed to consider whether it was worth the effort to respond to what Tobey had said. He looked at the floor between his feet, picked up a shard, looked at it for a while and let it fall again, absentmindedly stroked his bald head and then leaned back, put up his feet and sighed.

Tobey tried to reach into the side pocket of his pants where the knife was, but Jay Jay had tied his hands tightly and crosswise, so he could not even touch the strap with the Velcro fastener.

"You're right about everything." Tanvir's voice was low; he coughed and groaned. "I'm a lousy old sod and a drunkard. And I've already admitted that my knowledge of psychology is not very profound. But I'm not a murderer."

"Of course you are!" Tobey wanted to roar, but lacked the strength to do it. "If I hadn't sprained my damn foot, I'd be dead now!"

"Is the person who hands over the condemned one to the executioner a murderer?"

Tobey laughed raucously. "You damn hypocrite! They wanted to kill me, so you can continue to pursue your business! I should have beaten you to death with the crutches a few hours ago! I would have freed the world from a cancer!"

"Freed. From a cancer. The world." Tanvir expelled a grunt of air. "Don't be ridiculous. You're a musician? And you didn't try all the drugs you could get?"

"I've never taken heroin!"

"But synthetic drugs, right?"

"Leave me alone."

"In a minute. First, answer me one question: Where do all these powders and pills come from? What do you think Tobey? The stuff falls from the sky? It grows on trees?"

Tobey was silent. His head felt large and heavy, something inside it seemed to expand, his brain was a sponge which soaked up Tanvir's

215

words and pressed against the inside of his skull. He shifted his wrists, but all that he achieved was rubbing his skin sore.

"I'm not proud of what I do, not really. Life on the island isn't bad; it could be worse. But in a few years I'll be seventy, and there are better places in the world for an old man than this one. I earn my pension by manufacturing drugs; yes, well, guilty as charged. The point goes to you, the brilliant young lawyer for morality and justice. But I'll tell you something." Tanvir got up groaning, went to the bureau, took the bottle and the glass and let himself fall back into the chair. "There wouldn't be any drugs, if there weren't any consumers." He poured gin into the glass and emptied it in one gulp. "Have you ever thought about that, Toto?"

"I'd be really happy if you would just sit there, drink your gin and keep your mouth shut," Tobey said, although he had resolved to remain silent. "Today you would have watched as I was being killed. So spare me your shitty attempts at justification."

"Then just one more question." Tanvir looked at Tobey. "What would you have done in my place?"

"How do I know? Maybe I would have said: Hey, Tobey, there are some guys who want to kill you because they think you'll go to the police, but here's a boat so you can get out; have a good trip!"

"A boat? What boat?"

"Lord God, the boat that Jay Jay uses to go back and forth between the islands!"

"That's a rubber dinghy!" cried Tanvir. "An unseaworthy toy with a two-horsepower engine!"

"So what? Better than being killed!"

"Better? It would only take longer for you to die! There is just enough gas for the trip to another island! Which brings me to the next point; namely that you don't know which direction you need to take to get away from here!"

"I don't give a damn! The only important thing is that I actually get away! Once I'm out there far enough, they'll eventually find me!"

"That's right; the bastards will find you and sink you. They go on patrols here every day! And as for the nearest waterway, which is almost a hundred miles away, you couldn't make it there in ten years!"

"I'd go at night," Tobey said more quietly.

"Believe me, the rubber dinghy is a nutshell. Even with enough fuel on board, you would capsize at sea in the first large wave. And this thing had at least a dozen holes that could only be inadequately repaired. Why do you think I'm still here?"

"You want to get away?"

Tanvir sighed, rubbed both hands over his bald head and folded them behind his neck. "I haven't been here voluntarily for a long time. Don't get the idea that this is an attempt to exonerate myself, but if the bastards didn't have me by the collar, I'd be long gone."

"Who are these guys anyway?"

"A bunch of crooks. Rabble. The scum of the sea. Take your pick."

"Business partners."

"Yes. Another point for you. At that time I did not suspect what I had gotten myself mixed up in. Hindsight is always wiser."

"You said something about religious fanatics."

"Oh yes, in addition to their flat panel TVs and digital cameras, they financed their little holy war with drug money. They want to rule the land, but they can't even agree on whether they should call themselves 'Muslim Movement of the Philippines' or 'Muslim Power of the Philippines'. I haven't given up the hope that someday they will bash in each other's heads."

"Drug money for terrorists. You should really be proud of yourself."

"When the business started, these would-be holy warriors didn't have their hands in the game; they only wanted to get involved later."

"Did Megan know it?"

"No. Unless she broke into the bunker and sniffed around, like you. In

217

any case, she never gave Chester a pill."

"If that's an attempt to make me feel guilty, you can go fuck yourself."

For a while neither of them said anything. Now and then a violent gust of wind shook the patio doors and made the corrugated iron roof crackle. More butterflies flew out of the bedroom and danced around the lamp like elves around a fire. The air in the room, stirred by the fan but not cooled, was warm and sticky.

"Have you at least gotten rich off it?"

Tanvir snorted, as if the question had frightened him from sleep. "Well . . . " He cleared his throat. "It might be enough for a small house without a pool in the San Diego area." He got up, cautiously opened the door and stepped into the hallway. Shortly after that he came back and closed the door. "There aren't any lights burning in the bunkhouse. In a quarter of an hour I think we can go."

"Go? With what?"

"With the boat."

"What boat?"

"The second one." Tanvir disappeared into the bedroom and returned a moment later with a gym shoe in each hand. "Now, please don't be angry again. I couldn't lend this boat to you. It's my life insurance."

"Do Miguel and Jay Jay know about it?"

"No. Just me." Tanvir sat on the stool, took off his sandals and put on the sneakers. "You'll wonder what kind of a boat. —Well, almost exactly four months ago I took an evening stroll on the beach."

Tobey groaned loudly.

"Beach walks are not exactly my preferred evening activity," Tanvir continued undeterred, "and it was more than just a coincidence that of all things I. . . "

"The short version!" Tobey cried, unnerved. "If you have to babble at me, then compose yourself and keep it damn short!"

"There's no reason to be rude again. Miguel and Jay Jay might be lying in their beds, but it may take a while before they're asleep. It would be foolish to go to the boat now. So listen and don't interrupt me." Tanvir breathed once in and out deeply. "May I continue?"

Tobey did not answer. He lay down, trying in vain to stretch his hand toward the knife, and closed his eyes.

"I'll take that as a 'yes'," Tanvir said. "Well, as I said, it was more than coincidence that just that evening I walked along the sea. It was destiny. The day before a storm had raged, the beach was covered with driftwood and debris. I was lost in thought, and suddenly, behind a bend, I saw it. At first I thought it was a hallucination; well, it was late evening, I had already enjoyed an aperitif—I usually do before dinner—but it was really there. It lay in front of me in the sand like a giant white shell; I could touch it; it was a boat, a rescue boat at that. You have to imagine it. A gift from the heavens. I was shaking with excitement. Probably lost by a yacht, maybe a ferry or a fishing boat. Three pairs of oars were fastened on the inside, always two together and . . . "

"Wait a minute." Tobey sat up and looked at Tanvir. "A row boat? You want to get away from here in a row boat?"

"Of course," Tanvir cried, and it was hard to tell whether his boost of enthusiasm was inspired by confidence or alcohol. "I can understand your skepticism and assure you that it is completely unfounded! Think about it . . . " He stood up suddenly and crept to the door, listened at it and opened it softly, peered into the dark hallway and closed the door again. "Think about it; an engine makes noise and needs fuel, and if something is broken, I have to tell you honestly that I'm not the right man to repair it. And don't get mad at me, but after I saw your raft, I doubt that you are any more technically gifted."

"But you said yourself that where the ships sail through is a hundred miles away! And look at my hands!" He turned his palms outward as far as he possibly could with the ropes around his hands.

We don't have to row a hundred miles away. There's an island, about thirty miles away, where there are fishermen who will take us to the mainland for a fee. I have ointment and bandages for your hands. I can stock up on painkillers for you, too."

Tobey slumped against the back of the sofa and looked at the ceiling.

"What is it? What is there to think about? This is your only chance!"

Tobey looked at Tanvir. "What about Montgomery and Chester?"

Tanvir sat down, laid his folded arms on his legs, bent his torso forward and hung his head, as if he was trying to read something in small print down on the floor in front of him.

"Montgomery and Chester . . . " he muttered.

"We'll leave them here, right?"

Tanvir nodded. "Yes, we'll leave them here," he said softly.

There was silence in the room for the length of a few breaths.

"It's certainly better for them," Tobey said finally. "They feel comfortable on the island."

"Yes." Tanvir stood up, but his back was crooked, his head lowered.

"Miguel, Jay Jay and Rosalinda will take care of them."

Tanvir raised his head, arched his back and beat his palms on his thighs. "Sure!" he cried. "They will both be fine!" He got up, went to the bureau and took a shoe box out of it. "There is money inside, quite enough for a while. Chester and Montgomery are no longer the youngest." He laughed nervously, and then coughed. Then he placed the box on the bureau, went into the bedroom and came back with two charcoal gray hard shell suitcases. He stopped in front of the sofa and raised his shoulders, as if to examine the weight of the suitcase. "A strange feeling," he said smiling, "to carry your past and future in two suitcases."

"Is the money in there?"

"The money, and a few things that I would not want to part with." He put down the suitcase, took a pair of scissors from a bureau drawer and stepped in front of Tobey. "It's time," he said. He first cut the ropes on his hands and then the ones on his feet, and put the scissors back in the drawer.

Tobey stood up. Wind beat against the windows, traveled under the roof and made the beams creak.

Tanvir lifted the suitcase from the floor and gave it Tobey, who hung it on his back, then handed him the crutches. "We'll go out back," he said, took both his suitcases and went into the bedroom. "You're already pre- pared," he said, and giggled. He enlarged the hole in the screen so he could pass through, hoisted the bags through the opening and climbed out into the open air. After Tobey was also outside, the two went to the medical building where Tanvir filled a plastic bag with drugs and retrieved from the closet a few ropes and balls of twine that Tobey had over- looked.

"I only have two liters of water," Tobey said, when he saw the bottles in the cupboard. He whispered that that was absurd, given the volume of the wind.

"Don't worry; there are twenty in the boat."

The boat was between trees, covered more symbolically with branches than really camouflaged, half of it sticking out of the pit it was in. Tobey estimated its length to be about five meters, the width barely two. It was white and had three dark brown banks of oars. On both sides of the bow HELENA was printed in blue letters.

"Isn't she a beauty?" said Tanvir. He had placed his bags in the sand and began to remove the branches.

Tobey sat down. Walking in the sand had exerted him; his arm muscles were burning. Above him was a single churning and seething, wind bat- tered the trees and whirled up withered driftwood and dry strands of sea- weed; approaching waves rolled and broke with a crash; dirty, frothy sea foam sprayed.

Tanvir stood beside him and handed him a tube. "Smear it on your palms and wrap your hands and wrists with this." He gave him two rolls of bandages and a roll of brown tape. "But not too tight; you still have to be able to grip the oars."

Tobey unscrewed the tube and rubbed his hands with the greasy ointment. "Did you see the waves? How are we going to get out of there?"

"Take a deep breath and go, I'd say," Tanvir cried and proceeded to drag the last branches off the boat.

Tobey bandaged his hands and wrapped a few layers of tape around the loose ends.

In the meantime, Tanvir had dug away the sand in front of the boat with an oar. He took the rope, which was attached to a metal ring on the bow, placed it over his shoulder and leaned forward, seeking support in the sand with his feet, and then began to pull the boat out of the trough. Tobey got up and hopped toward him on one leg.

"Leave it alone!" Tanvir said through the surf noise. "She's made of fiberglass! Weighs practically nothing," As if to prove it, he pulled the boat effortlessly several meters toward the water.

Tobey stood on one leg and thought about whether the lightness of the boat was something good or bad.

Tanvir got his bags, put them into the boat, climbed in after them and began to fasten the bags with ropes to the braces on the inner sides. "Better fasten your suitcase too," he called out to Tobey. "There's a good possibility that we may capsize in the surf!"

"I'll keep it on!"

"And what about this here?" Tanvir lifted the lid of the storage compartment in the rear of the boat and waved an orange life jacket, still in the plastic cover. "I thought you had a fear of drowning!"

Tobey limped to the boat, took the vest and ripped it from its packaging.

"When we're over the first two waves, we've as good as made it!" Tanvir had lashed one of the suitcases and started the other.

"Is this thing even fit for a storm?" Tobey stripped the suitcase off his back and put on a life jacket.

"We'll know in a moment!" Tanvir disengaged two pairs of oars from the sides.

Tobey wrapped a rope several times around the suitcase, the loose end knotted to his belt.

Tanvir tied on his life jacket. "Can it get loose?" he said.

"Yes," Tobey threw the crutches into the boat.

Tanvir jumped into the sand, seized the rope with both hands and pulled the boat into the water. An outgoing wave engulfed it and threw it back onto the sand. Tanvir clung to it like a shying horse. "Get inside, lie flat on the floor and hold the four oars!"

"Shouldn't I help?"

"On one leg? Get in!"

Tobey climbed into the boat. Tanvir helped him with the suitcase, and as Tobey lay down, he went to the rear and pushed the boat into deeper water. The flat tail of a wave lifted the boat almost gently and turned it easily to one side. The next wave struck the bow and rumbled under Tobey. Tobey raised his head and called out to Tanvir. At this moment it began to rain. Thick, warm drops flew in with the wind; within seconds Tobey could only see a few meters.

Tanvir appeared on the left side, both hands holding on to the edge of the boat and his eyes fixed on the wave that was pushing in. "Any more, and we're through," he said. He breathed heavily; a scrap of seaweed stuck to his wet, bald head.

The wave carried the boat up, but it was calm and smooth like the back of a whale, then the boat sank into the valley in front of the next dark rise, and Tanvir lifted himself up and rolled across the side of the boat, tore two oars from Tobey's hand and shouted something that Tobey did not understand, sat on the front bench and put his oar in the brackets. Another mountain grew under the boat and let it slide along on its flank in the deep. Everything was wet and slippery, and Tobey had trouble climbing up onto his feet, sitting on the middle bench and bringing the oar into position.

"Row!" Tanvir yelled.

Tobey put his healthy left foot against the crossbar on the bottom of the boat and tried to pull the oar blades uniformly, but he invariably submerged them too early or they only struck the top of the water. The last time he had been sitting in a rowing boat he was fourteen, on a school trip, but he could not remember how he had done then.

"Push and pull!" Tanvir shouted against the wind. " Push and pull! Come on!"

After a while it was easier. Tobey lowered his head, hunched his back and gradually fell in with Tanvir's rhythm. He imagined the oars as extensions of his arms, the blades as his hands. The bandages were soaked by the rain, but they held. Tanvir's voice, the sea and the storm roared in his head; Tanvir's three words were a prayer and a battle cry. Around him the world dissolved; the sea towered into the sky; the sky fell into the sea. It was dark and there was no horizon, Tobey saw only the bright spot of the boat's bottom in front of him clouded by veils of rain and spume. He thought of the trip to Skellig, where they got caught in a storm on the way back; everyone on board, except perhaps the captain and two sailors, struck by fear of death. The cruise ship had been a converted fishing boat, heavy and sturdy, not a plastic shell, open and light as a feather and not much bigger than two coffins.

Tobey lay under the benches on the floor. There were two plastic containers attached to chains, which he and Tanvir had used to scoop water from the boat. Now they were resting as best they could under the raging storm, tossed by the raging sea. Tanvir sat huddled in the rear, where he had settled after crawling under the benches past Tobey. He had tied himself to the bench with a rope and stared for several minutes at the compass, which he had taken out of the box he was reclining against. There was a pair of oars on the ground next to Tobey; the other two were fastened to the side of the boat with leather straps. Rowing was useless on these waves, trying to keep a course absurd. They had drunk water and eaten some bread and a banana; Tobey had swallowed two painkillers. Rain continued to fall incessantly and in a dense spray, tossed about by wind gusts so hard that the drops glanced off the skin like grains of sand. Now and then, when an enormous wave seized the boat and lifted it and pressed it against the pulsating clouds, Tobey ventured a glance over the edge of the boat and saw nothing but darkness and foaming water, pummeled by the rain. Then he lay down again, closed his eyes and listened to the rumble and pitch beneath him.

After a period of time which Tobey could not measure, because it had passed as if in a waking dream, infinitely slowly and yet rapidly, everything was quiet around him. The wind speed decreased, the waves lost their power and menace. The rain let up, the clouds had lifted, and the sky seemed to be higher and farther away.

Tanvir looked around him, and then raised his eyes as if he was looking for stars.

"Have we made it?" Tobey asked and sat up. The noise of the wind had grown weaker; now he only had to talk very loudly instead of yelling.

"I don't know. It strikes me as peculiar."

"But the storm is over, right?"

"Maybe," said Tanvir. "Maybe not. I, in any case, have never experienced a storm here that was over so soon."

"But everything is peaceful. And soon it will have to be light."

"I don't trust the situation." Tanvir rubbed his bald head. "On the island there were also storms that abated suddenly and an hour later broke out again, often more violent than before. As if the forces of nature only needed a brief rest."

"I think it's behind us," Tobey said, and sat on the bench.

"Anyway. We should use the time and strengthen ourselves." Tanvir unlocked the lid of the box and pulled a plastic container out of it, which contained peeled, hard-boiled eggs. He took off the lid and held the container out to Tobey. Tobey took an egg, even though he wasn't hungry. "When did you put all that stuff in the boat?"

Tanvir grinned. "While you were building your fanciful raft." He took a bite of the egg, chewed for a long time and took a sip of water from the plastic bottle.

"My departure wasn't really planned for tonight," he finally said. "But all of this has been packed in its hiding place for months." He pointed to the two suitcases. "And I had gathered the water and the food together quickly. The biggest problem was Jay Jay."

"Was he searching for me?"

"Well, for the person who had smashed in the window. He was walking around with the lantern, and I pretended that I had just gotten out of bed. Which did indeed correspond in some ways with the facts."

"And the gun?" Tobey ate the egg in small bites.

"That was always under my mattress. I took it out after Jay Jay told me about the window. I had a hunch that was your doing, but I wasn't sure. When we found the empty cans in front of the shed, I knew what you were doing."

"Why didn't you let me go? That would have solved all your problems."

"First, because I had promised the bastards from the MMP or the MPP that I would turn you over to them. I never believed that you were so crazy and that you would flee in the middle of the night, under a gathering storm, on a raft made of gas cans. They would have asserted that I had hidden you, and they would have given me a few more of these to figure out where." Tanvir tapped his finger against his cheek. "And second, I wanted to get away, and quickly. I realized that I have had enough of living on the island. Everything seemed suddenly so sad, so pathetic and futile. The whole day was nothing but an unmitigated disaster, marked by abject failure."

"The filming with Nancy?"

Tanvir stopped chewing and looked at Tobey blankly.

"Montgomery and I were onlookers."

Tanvir expelled air through his nose and shook his head. He swallowed the bite and washed it down with water. "A small fire in the lab, because I wasn't paying attention. The Muslim bastards who suddenly behave like they're the masters of the world and let me know that I'm at their mercy, for better or for worse. The whole situation with you. Loud hints that it was time to leave."

"Without saying goodbye."

Tanvir looked at the bottom where the water sloshed, ankle high, and nodded. "Well, obviously I would not have been able to say goodbye officially, but it would have been nice to have a few days left to wind things up and let everything go. And I would have had no objection to a little less hectic departure." He chuckled, sealed the container and put it back in the box.

The wind picked up again, the rain grew thicker. Tobey looked around; above and behind them dark gray clouds hung from a black, rolling sky into the ocean; on both sides of the horizon, indistinct and faint, was a strip of visible light, dirty yellow, like a smoldering fire at the end of the world. He felt as if they had found themselves in a passageway, in a narrow, immensely long corridor between two storms.

Tanvir turned and raised his head above the side of the boat. "I fear we're moving into the next front," he shouted into the wind, which was almost as strong as before.

"Where are we really going?"

"Only the gods can say!" Tanvir bent down, filled the bowl and dumped the water from the boat. "Anchor yourself better against the floor!"

227

The waves were suddenly up again, the wind blew spray from their crests. It was dark. Tobey crawled under the bench and lay down, blindly bailing the water out.

"There is still a third one," shouted Tanvir.

"What?" Tobey felt the wind rip the word from his lips and hurl it into the sea.

"I didn't want you to die!"

"I can't understand you," Tobey shouted.

The storm abolished the boundary between sea and sky. All light had suddenly disappeared; darkness fell over the boat like a blanket. Noise crashed down, the reverberation of exploding planets, fading worlds. The waves were no longer mounds or hills or mountains, but collapsing, massive continents, crashing against each other; the universe itself; colliding galaxies; and the boat was a speck of dust inside them. Tanvir yelled something, but Tobey heard nothing except the infernal din. He clung to a fastened oar and felt as a hand grabbed his foot, wound around it like a rope. Then everything was spinning; Tobey was flung around and immersed in silence, dragged out and flung back into the noise, then carried away. He screamed for his life, swallowed water. He saw nothing more, no boat and no wave, except the one that carried him on its back like an angry animal in a raging herd.

News from Megan

One year, Tobey. That's how long it's been since I have written to you. A winter storm blew the roof off the house by the sea, and the owners don't have the money to have it repaired. And neither do I. I have moved twenty-seven coastal towns to the east (I counted them on the map!) and I live in a rented house on the outskirts of the city. It's five kilometers to the sea, but I have only been there once or twice. The beach is flat, as if someone had leveled it (maybe someone really did), and everywhere there are cars and houses and restaurants and takeaway shops and flower pots and public toilets and benches and monkey bars for children. The sea is slate gray, even in summer. I can see it from my bathroom window; I live on the seventh floor. I'm considering going back to London to study English literature. Or I'll take a course in creative writing. I have read hundreds of books, but I don't know how to write one. Five days a week I work in a supermarket, clear things from the shelves and sweep the floor. In the summer, I helped out in a restaurant on Saturdays. My apartment has two rooms. In one there is a mattress on the floor, the other one is empty. I like to sit at my kitchen table and read. (Did you know there is an animal called the gray-faced sengi that weighs about 700 grams and is related to the elephant?) I would like to apply for a job in London, as a waitress in this new vegetarian restaurant I read about in the newspaper. It's called 'Meat Less People', and it was formerly a nightclub and before that a church. I would look for a small, light apartment, perhaps with a balcony. At the supermarket they asked me if I want to train to be a cashier, but I said I don't know. At night when I lie awake, I hear the sounds in the house, the hum of the elevator, the water in the pipes, footsteps, distant voices. Sometimes I imagine that I knock on one of the doors and ask the people who they are, what they dream about and whether they are afraid of dying. Do you dream of the past, Tobey? In my recurring dream I drive away in the car with Cait; the sun is shining and father stands on the porch and waves at us and holds you in his arms. Maybe I should take this training and become a cashier, and then I would have a real job for the first time in my life. I would sit at the register and see everything people buy, and I would scan their roasts and steaks twice. At some point I would give my notice and take the train to London, with people who are all younger than me, to learn how to write a book from an old man. Do you know how to write a book, Toto?

Who loves you?
Megan!

15

It was light when Tobey woke up, somewhere between a state of consciousness and sleep. The sea was calm, almost smooth. A light wind was blowing. Clouds cast shadow islands on the water's surface. Tobey had rested his arms over his suitcase, clamped his hands under the ropes. The life jacket kept his shoulders and his head, which was resting on the suitcase, above water. He blinked and saw a green expanse, grass-covered hills. The water was warm. He felt his legs, could not move them or did not want to, he wasn't sure. Once, perhaps just now, perhaps some time ago, something brushed against his bare foot, soft and swift. A seagull flew away silently above him. He closed his eyes; his tongue and throat were burning. He knew that there were two bottles of water in the suitcase, but he could not loosen the ropes; his hands felt numb. The suitcase would fill with water and sink as soon as he opened it. Megan's letters were in it.

He dozed off again and woke up minutes or hours later. The water around him was still warm and green. He thought of sharks, but he was too exhausted to panic. His brain produced images, a rusty projector in an abandoned cinema. The idea of being torn to pieces was an ice cold point in his head, which warmed in the sun and formed into something abstract. He prayed, a confused collection of statements from the Bible which he had read as a child. He laid his cheek on the suitcase; he no longer felt the wet rope. The leather skin and the underlying cardboard of the suitcase would become saturated at some point with water and dissolve. If he was still conscious then, he could bind both the bottles and the plastic bag with the letters to the rope that was wrapped around his belly. Perhaps he could also save his shirt before going down and place it as protection from the sun on his head. He pulled a hand out from under the rope and moved his fingers, scratched at the skin of the suitcase.

Then he remembered the knife. Jay Jay had forgotten to search his trouser pockets. Perhaps it had fallen out with the capsizing of the boat, he thought, and was now lying on the bottom of the sea. He breathed in and out a few times, and then he dipped his right hand into the water, groped for the pocket with the Velcro fastener and felt the handle with his finger tips. A sound escaped his throat, hoarse and strange. He pulled his hand out of the water. The sun was now burning in a clear sky. There would be no third phase of the storm, Tobey was convinced of it. He could survive, at least one more day, if he could get to the water bottles. He took his left hand out from under the rope and wrapped the bandages on the right one, made a fist, opened and closed it several times until he was sure he would be able to hold something properly. Then he let it slip into the water, pushed it into his pocket, clasped the handle and pulled the knife out slowly with bated breath. As he laid it on the suitcase, he let out a scream.

He waited a few moments, and then cut an opening in the top of the suitcase next to the ropes. The shirt was on top; he wrapped it around his head and tied the sleeves at the neck. At first he wanted to throw the insulating pad into the sea, but then he pushed it between the back of his shirt and the life jacket, let the top stick out a little and rested his head on it. Although the fact that the two flashlights still worked calmed him, the thought of spending another night in the open sea took his breath away. Finally he held a water bottle in his hand, unscrewed the top and

232

drank. He knew that he must drink in small portions and that the water had to be rationed, so he took another sip, closed the bottle and put it back in the suitcase.

He spent the next few hours alternately dozing and half awake. The sun had passed its highest point; Tobey estimated that is was about two clock in the afternoon. The first water bottle was half empty. He hoped he would be less thirsty in the cool of the night, and he resolved to drink the last sip remaining in the half liter no earlier than sunrise. The second bottle had enough for the whole next day. He would not think about what would happen after that.

He would never be able to remember whether he had first seen the fin or heard the engine noise. The visual and the acoustic events were so simultaneous that his brain supplied the information that the shark fin floating toward him was causing the faint hum. A scream exploded in his lungs but his throat was closed, and he simply gasped and noticed how everything in his body grew hard and cold, as if his heart beat for the last time and his bowels and his bladder emptied themselves. Then his mind stopped working; the world grew bright and swam before his eyes. A final reflex, the memory of a thought, made him reach for a knife, but his fingers did not move. Without knowing that he did it, he waited, hovering.

The path in the afterlife was uneven, the ride bumpy. Bright light pressed through his closed eyelids, he did not feel the weight of his body. He heard a distant hum, voices, the laughter of his fellow passengers, who were looking forward to meeting their relatives. Everything was white and light and beautiful. He saw a sea of clouds, from which protruded a fin, and opened his eyes.

Men's faces hovered above him, swinging like lanterns in the wind. He closed his eyes again. In heaven, there was a smell of fish and diesel. If he could have felt anything, it would have been a feeling of greater disappointment.

233

Murky light shone through the opening. Tobey lay on his back and blinked at the bright rectangle. He wanted to rub his eyes, but noticed that his hands were bound. From far away voices and snatches of music drifted; dogs were barking. Trying to remember was like climbing up the stairs from the darkness into the dawn. One step was the boat in a storm, the next the sea, the next the shark. He sat up. His ankles were tied together. A folded blanket was spread over the wooden bench. The room measured maybe three by three meters, the walls made of raw stone, the floor and ceiling made with planks. In one corner there was a chair, beneath it a plastic bottle. Tobey was not thirsty, which astonished him. He sat there and waited for the fog in his head to clear. Just when he had persuaded himself that he was able to think clearly, the door was unlocked and opened. A man entered the room, dressed in white, tall, a surprisingly well-groomed figure in this hole. He had to duck his head to keep from bumping it into the door frame. A second man shut the door; the balmy flow of air ebbed away, along with the torrent of noise, the voices, the clucking of chickens, the crying of children, the distant rattle of a motorcycle.

"How are you?" the man asked.

Tobey said nothing. He looked the man in the face for a few seconds—a narrow, dark face with black eyes, a black beard and black hair—then lowered his eyes. Ants were running across the floor, emerged from the cracks and disappeared into them.

"Do you understand me?"

Tobey nodded, without lifting his head.

"Can you tell me who you are?" The man spoke English without an accent.

Tobey watched an ant that was dragging a dead fly.

"Barry Spillane. Is that your name?"

Tobey looked up, glanced at the man briefly and then stared at the floor. "Yes," he said.

"Who, then, is this Tobey, to whom the letters are addressed?"

Tobey looked at the man. He was tired of strangers constantly reading his letters. And he was tired of being tied up and having to think about how long he had to live and in what way they would probably kill him.

"You're Tobey, aren't you? Why else would you carry these letters with you?" The man turned and opened the door and said something, two or three words in calm, commanding tone. A little later he closed the door, went to the chair, laid a cushion on it and sat down.

"You had no right to read the letters," Tobey said, and heard the ridiculously defiant tone in his voice.

The man took a pack of cigarettes from the pocket of his knee-length shirt and held it out to Tobey. "Do you smoke?"

Tobey shook his head.

"Well, I had that right," the man said quietly. He lit a cigarette and put the pack back in his pocket. "You were unresponsive, and I wanted to know who we pulled out of the sea and brought to our island."

"Why did you pull me out?"

"We're committed to helping people in need. And you were in need."

"Why am I tied up?"

"A precautionary measure."

"What are you going to do to me?"

"What do you think?"

"You're going to kill me."

"Why should we?"

"I know about the drugs."

"What are you going to do with your knowledge?"

"Nothing! I don't care about all that shit!"

"Do I have your word for it, Tobey? Or is it Barry?"

"Tobey. You have my word."

"Why did you lie to me?"

"When?"

"When you said your name was Barry."

"I don't know. Maybe I thought it would help me."

"It didn't help."

"That's clear to me. I'm sorry."

"Where's Tanvir?"

"Our boat capsized. If he hasn't drowned, he's floating somewhere in the sea."

"You sailed off together in a boat?"

"Yes."

"What kind of boat?"

"A lifeboat. Tanvir found it months ago, on the beach."

"Found it?"

"Yes. After a storm. It looked like new. It was named *Helena*, like the Greek legend. Troy was destroyed because of her."

"How pointless, isn't it?" the man said. He sucked smoke into his lungs, looked at the ceiling and let out the smoke. "Where were you going, you and Tanvir?"

"To an island. Tanvir said that for a fee the fishermen there would take us to the mainland."

"What kind of island?"

"I don't know."

The man looked thoughtfully at the smoke, which rose like a straight thin strip from the tip of the cigarette and it wasn't until it reached the height of the window opening that it was apprehended by the breeze and blurred. Finally, he let the cigarette fall to the floor and ground it out carefully. Then he got up, took the red cushion decorated with fringe from the chair, wiped it clean and went to the door.

"What happens now?" Tobey called.

"We'll see," the man said, opened the door and stepped out. The door was closed and locked.

"Let me go," Tobey cried. He jumped up and fell down.

"Let me out!" He crawled to the door and kicked it with his feet.

"Please!"

It was dark outside. A man had brought pita bread and a chair and placed a kerosene lamp in the window opening. Tobey lay on the cot. He had eaten and drunk and even slept a while, until loud voices had awakened him. They had come from a building nearby, and Tobey had identified one of them as that of the man who had interrogated him. The men (Tobey had distinguished three voices), had fought fiercely, and eventually a glass or a bottle had been smashed.

For about half an hour it was quiet, apart from the usual noise. Insects chirped, diesel engines hummed, people shouted to each other. From far away, Tobey thought he could hear music and voices from a television. He stared at the ceiling and tried not to think of the video in which masked jihadists slashed a young man's head from his neck with a sword. He sat up and looked for a sharp edge he could use to sever the rope, but found nothing suitable. He could not reach the kerosene lamp; the man had to climb on the chair to put it in the window opening.

The lock was unlocked, and then the door opened. The man came in, a chair in one hand, the cushion in the other. Outside there were two men. One was the bearded child. He stared blankly at Tobey. The second companion of the man in white, a scrawny guy in a floor-length, black cape, with a gun hanging from a leather belt on his shoulder, closed the door, but left it open just a gap wide. The man put the cushion on the chair and sat down. He looked tired, his eyes nervously moving past Tobey to the wall of rough concrete blocks. Outside, a match was struck; the men were talking quietly.

"I'm against killing people," the man finally said. His back was straight, his palms resting on his thighs.

"In my opinion, neither religious nor political motives justify murder. I grew up in Canada; people there adopted me. Good people, Christians, who made a lot of things possible for me. I grew up without a day of hunger; I was able to study, to take trips. I have seen and experienced many beautiful things in this country. But also a lot of ugly, disgusting things. I was in America and everything there was even more abundant, even more overwhelming. I was confronted with extravagance and licentiousness; people seemed anchorless, empty, lost." He looked at Tobey. "Have you been to America, Tobey?"

"No," said Tobey. "Why are you telling me all this?"

"Because I want you to know why I act the way I act."

Tobey lowered his head. He would have liked to have been one of the ants, running across the floorboards, half blind, without any knowledge of yesterday and tomorrow, life and death.

"I have devoted myself to all kinds of things," the man continued in a calm tone. "Sports, cars, alcohol. And then, at my professional peak but at the same time at my emotional and moral low point, I ended up with religion. I read the Bible; I went to church; I found Jesus Christ. —Have you found Jesus Christ, Tobey?" Tobey lowered his head.

"Answer me, Tobey."

"What does it matter?"

"It matters because I asked you."

"If I say no, are you going to throw me back into the sea?" Tobey cried. "If I say yes, will you chop off my head in front of a camera? And if I say I'm a Muslim? Will you let me live then? Well then, I'm a Muslim! Tell me where to sign!"

The man got up, stood in front of Tobey and hit him in the face with the back of his hand, once, and not very hard. The thin one with the pistol opened the door a bit, stuck his head in and said something. The man replied calmly, whereupon the thin one retreated but left the door ajar.

"You're a man without character, Tobey," the man said and sat down again.

Tobey laughed. His cheeks burned. The blow had finally awoken

238

him. Anger and hatred rose up in him, and he also noticed how a strange sense of serenity concerning his fate spread through him.

"What's so funny?"

"Character." Tobey groaned and shook his head. "I've been tied up and beaten so often lately that I've gradually started to feel like an animal."

"Faith in God distinguishes man from animals."

"Yesterday, in the sea, I prayed."

"Otherwise you don't pray?"

"It was a reflex. I was afraid of death."

"You're alive. Your God heard you."

"Yes, he makes a joke out of it, to save me from one precipice and then place me on the edge of the next one."

"He is testing you."

Tobey laughed again. "You see these ants? I would like to be one of them. That one there, for example." He raised his shackled feet and trampled the insect.

"You don't seem to be a Buddhist," the man said. He took out the cigarettes and lit one.

Tobey lay on the cot.

The man smoked for a while, his arms folded, his head slightly back. The guard at the door looked in, wondered about the silence. "Your tattoo—this cross with the barbed wire," the man finally said. "It could be the symbol for how I felt as a Christian back then. I was a lawyer; I lived in Vancouver, and later in Chicago. I made a lot of money; I had a great apartment; I drove a big car; I went to the movies; I went to church. I was one of them." He took one last drag, dropped the cigarette and put it out with his foot, which was in a shoe of black, shiny leather. "Are you familiar with the phrase by the German philosopher Adorno, 'There is no real life in the false one'?"

Tobey stared at the ceiling. The calm that had flowed through him like ecstasy after the blow began to give way gradually to disillusionment, which paralyzed him.

"I read it on the page of a tear-off calendar in my office. Something so ordinary can be the trigger for an epiphany. I stood at the window and looked out over the city, and I realized that for many years I had lived a seemingly real life, but everything that surrounded me was false: the people, the system, the civilization. I stood in a tower that was part of a fortress, and this fortress defended greed, exploitation, pornography, injustice. For a long time I had felt that my heart fundamentally abhorred these things, but who really looks at the bottom of his heart when his head is busy amassing wealth?" He got up and walked around. The light of the kerosene lamp flowed in yellow over his clothing. "On that day I decided to change my life, to take a new path. It led me back to my childhood, to Mindanao, where I had been taken from an orphanage. I found no one from my family. As I drove by one spot, I saw an old man who had fallen and hurt his head. I took him to the doctor and then to his house. He was a shoemaker, and because I showed an interest in his craft, he taught me how to make a shoe." He stood in front of the cot and raised his right foot. "These shoes are five years old. They are the product of my own labor. Look at them, Tobey."

Tobey turned his head and glanced at the shoe, then he looked at the ceiling again.

The man sat down. "One day I went to the workshop earlier than usual and saw the old man kneeling on a carpet and muttering words which I had never before heard from his mouth. He wasn't happy about my arrival and he sent me away. Only days later, he confided to me that he had been praying, and I had to promise him I would not tell anyone. When he read to me weeks later from the Koran, I knew my search was over."

Again there was silence for a while, interrupted only by the squeaking of the hinges when the thin one cast a glance into the room. The man gave him two cigarettes and said something, whereupon the bearded child went away. Then he sat down on the chair again. Outside a moped drove past, a horn bleated. For a few seconds music boomed from a radio and then ebbed. A dog barked; children laughed.

"I asked if you have found Jesus Christ, Tobey, and you owe me an answer."

Tobey did not want to talk anymore.

"Sit down and look at me."

Tobey sat up and looked the man in the face.

"I'm waiting for your response."

"We have all found him, even Brendan Murray, the cat smashed against the wall. Finding Jesus was part of religious instruction."

"What did you do to find him?"

"Answer questions: who his disciples were, which sea he walked on."

"That means 'find' to you?"

"That's what it meant to the school."

"And yesterday, in the sea?"

"Like I said, a reflex."

The man stretched out his legs and folded his arms. "I feel sorry for you, Tobey."

"Sorry enough to take these damn chains off me and let me go?"

"You're very lonely in your cynical atheism."

"Atheist? I'm not an atheist! I was raised Catholic! I received Holy Communion! I never left the church!"

"You would also describe yourself as a devout Christian."

"I'm in the club, at least as a passive member."

"Just now you even claimed to be Muslim."

Tobey laughed, a short, barking laugh. "Man, I would argue that I was a fucking Mormon, if it would save my life!"

"What did you want on the island, Tobey?"

"I was looking for my sister."

"Megan."

"I found her; she's dead. Now I want to go home. Away; anywhere."

"How did she die?"

"Tanvir said she drowned, but maybe he was lying."

"Why should he?"

"I don't know."

"People have drowned again and again in these waters."

Tobey closed his eyes, leaned against the wall.

The man lit a cigarette. "What do you know about us, Tobey?"

"Nothing."

"Tanvir didn't tell you?"

"Just that you sell drugs. And you can't agree on a name."

"Oh, the name. A vexing issue. Some of my colleagues rely on violence. They want a revolution, a coup, the faster and bloodier the better. I'm for action, for change and patience. As I said, I oppose killing people, regardless of the goal that is being pursued."

"Why not just let me go then?"

"I'm trying to save your life; I can't do any more than that."

Tobey opened his eyes. The door opened and the thin one with the gun shouted something. The man got up and went to him. When he turned around, he held Tobey's right shoe in his hand.

"This belongs to you," said the man, stood in front of Tobey and laid the shoe on the cot.

"I don't need it."

"Everyone needs a pair of shoes. Thanks to the MMP, no child goes barefoot on this island anymore."

"What does that mean, you're trying to save my life?"

The man sighed. "The hotheads say you're a risk and we have to do away with you." He sat down. "I say we take you to the island and wait to see what happens. Tanvir is gone, the drug trade discontinued, at least temporarily. Everything will calm down."

"Tanvir's island? Why should I go there?"

"You're worried about that? You'd be alive!"

Tobey looked down. His foot was no longer swollen.

"Should I bring you something to eat?"

Tobey shook his head.

The man looked at Tobey as if he had to memorize his face for a time when there was no more Tobey, only the memory of him. After a while he got up, took the cushion in one hand and the chair and in the other, and went to the door.

"Please help me," said Tobey. The man turned around. "I will," he said, then left the room. The door was pushed shut and the lock was locked.

Tobey sat there and looked at the shoe that was lying next to him on the cot. He took out the insole and was not surprised that the passport was gone. He moved his sprained foot; the pain was tolerable. The inside of the shoe still felt damp. Tobey thought about checking for the bills, but then let it alone. Suddenly he had the idea to buy his release with the money, and he called for the guards and threw the shoe against the door, but nobody seemed to hear. He lay down and closed his eyes, his ear listening to the piercingly high, regular warble of a bird from afar, until he realized that it was the ringing of a phone that abruptly stopped. The man would not be able to help him or intend to, so he would die, he was convinced of it. He thought about Jason Dwyer, who was dead and had left everything behind him. To die from an overdose of heroin no longer seemed so terrible to him as it had when the thought of his own death have been nothing more than the weak flash of an idea, the vague notion of an event that was so remote that its horror could not be measured. He had never shot up; alcohol, marijuana, cocaine and synthetic drugs had been enough for him to experience creative flights of fancy, to feel immortal, or at least alive, to endure the shabbiness of the narrow rooms, the cold in the practice room, the rejections from the music studios. Now he would have given anything to inject the warm poison, to doze off and not come back.

Tobey was tired, but he couldn't sleep. At regular intervals he nodded off and fell into bottomless depths, enveloped in scraps of dream, only to jolt awake seconds later and stare at the walls of the cell, which seemed to have grown even smaller since the petroleum lamp had gone out. Once he dreamed that Montgomery was with him, and when he woke up the bonobo was sitting on foot of the cot, looking at him. Tobey stretched out his hand and Montgomery touched it with a fingertip. He sat up and was about to say something, but Montgomery put his finger to his lips, loosened the chains, and helped him put on his left shoe. Then he turned to the wall so Tobey could climb on his shoulders and squeeze himself outside through the window opening. Montgomery held him by the feet, and Tobey slid slowly upside down from the outer wall down to the ground. After he got up, he wanted to help Montgomery, but the bonobo had already landed there beside him, took his hand and pulled him over dry grass to a fence, where he disappeared into a gap. Tobey crawled after him on his belly, followed Montgomery through an empty street lined with wooden huts and simple stone houses, ran limping and crouching past abandoned market stalls, hand carts and rickety truck through a clearing and only noticed, when they were resting in the protection of a narrow, unlit alley, that he was bathed in sweat and the beating of his heart almost broke his rib cage. His foot hurt, but he paid no attention to the pain. Gasping for air, he crouched next to a metal barrel filled with garbage and listened to the silence, mingled with the distant hum of diesel generators and the barking of a lonely dog. There was no house or window lit; there were no street lights. Tobey noticed that the sky was like a black cloth, the moon like a fine, curved crevice through which the pale light fell.

He estimated the time was three or four o'clock. The inhabitants of the place would get up soon, at least the fishermen whose boats he had seen. If it had not already happened, by dawn at the latest they would discover his flight and look for him. He did not know how big this island was, but he doubted that it offered many hiding places. The SMP or MPP called the shots here and certainly had numerous supporters; in a few hours every one of them would be searching for him and Montgomery. If they found him, Tobey was sure they would make short work of him.

When he was bumped lightly against the arm, Tobey winced. When Montgomery got up and ran down the street his hands, dangling from his long arms, touched the loamy soil of the ground and his head disappeared behind his curved back, which made him look like an animal for the first time, even though he wore the dark blue uniform. Tobey followed him, limping, and then they ran side by side across an intersection and a dusty field, a canal filled with brown water, and through a palm forest where pigs and cows were tied to stakes and raised their sleepy heads. A dog came dangerously close to them and barked furiously. Tobey threw stones at him, while Montgomery climbed a palm tree and waited until the dog disappeared into one of the backyards enclosed with bamboo fences, part of a squalid settlement composed of wooden shacks and corrugated iron huts. Other dogs began to bark, and Tobey and Montgomery made their getaway.

Half an hour later they were at sea. The first light of day drew a thin, dim line between the water and the sky. The beach was deserted; it smelled of rotting seaweed and a fire whose smoke wafted from a shanty town hidden behind the trees. Far away a pair of long wooden boats was anchored, barely moving in the gently rolling surf. Tobey and Montgomery sat down.

"Where is Chester?" Tobey asked softly.

Montgomery, his lower lip pushed forward slightly and his eyelids lowered halfway, sat and stared at his hands. His pants were dirty; his shirt had a tear.

"What about Chester?" Tobey whispered. "Where's Rosalinda?"

Montgomery looked at Tobey. In the dawning light it was difficult to say whether the look in his eyes was despondency or simply fatigue. His hands were resting on the earth like something that did not belong to him, but his fingers moved as if he was dreaming.

"How can we get away from here?" Tobey drew a sail boat in the sand. "In a boat?"

Montgomery looked at the drawing, and Tobey wondered if the bonobo understood him. The light strip on the horizon had grown wider; soon the sun would rise. It was clear to Tobey that they could not run around any longer without being discovered, and since Montgomery did not seem to have a plan, he thought it best to follow the beach for a bit, to hide somewhere and wait for the night. Near the beach would be the most likely place to search for them, he thought, and a forest or coconut grove in a remote part of the island would probably be the safest place, if remote parts of this island even existed. Without food and water, they could hold out for a day and a night. Coconuts contain a nutritious liquid, he recalled, but it was also difficult, almost impossible, to open a coconut without the right tool. He raised his head and looked out to sea, saw the shimmer, where the sun waited in hiding like a stunningly beautiful actress preparing for her entrance. He thought about Tanvir, who in all probability had been resting on the bottom of the sea a long time, and the suitcases, surging out there on the waves, filled with memories and dreams and money.

A few birds flew over them, but Tobey was too exhausted to envy them. Montgomery touched him on the arm and rose, and Tobey did the same. They walked through the grass that grew tough and thin out of the dry soil, and avoided the sandy patches in order to leave no footprints behind. In the distance Tobey saw a handful of wooden houses on stilts and when yellow light flashed in one of them, he ducked and ran crouching up to a group of bare trees, whose trunks curved inland, as if lashed by a wind that is resting in another time. Montgomery crouched down beside him and put a hand on his knee. They heard the rattle of a bucket and the voice of a child who called something out, a name perhaps. Far away a stammering diesel generator started up, dogs barked, at first two or three, and then a whole pack. It was the end of the night and possibly the beginning of the last day of his life, Tobey thought. When he looked at Montgomery's face, he believed he recognized the same thought in his expression. He grabbed the bonobo's hand and held it for a while, then he let go of it and crawled to the edge of the puny little forest, which by day would be about as suitable for hiding as the market place they had crossed a while ago.

Not twenty yards away, a rock rose up out of the dawning light, no bigger than a resting cow, surrounded by scrubby grass and some bushes. Tobey made sure that no one was nearby, ran off and threw himself on the ground in front of the rock. He hastily broke a few branches off and quickly saw that between the boulders and the undergrowth, which had yellowish leaves the size of a thumbnail, there was not enough room for him and Montgomery. He got up and ran on, the noise from the nearby settlement in his ears, where people climbed out of bed, washed themselves, cooked, looked after the cattle. The idea that every child would probably be looking for them soon made him run faster, despite the pain in his foot, although he had no idea where. Far ahead he saw a hut, a mast fastened with ropes towering from its roof. As they grew nearer the hut turned out to be a solid, upright building on stone pillars, with blue-painted boards and a roof of coarse corrugated iron. A tattered scrap of black fabric hung from the mast; the roof was dotted with bird droppings or the remains of white paint. The windows were open, torn curtains waved in the breeze. Next to the hut lay a boat, a long row boat painted yellow and green, full of ropes and buoys and crates made of gray plastic.

Tobey crept away from the sea to the opposite side of the hut, in front of it there were two chairs hewn from wood remnants and an overturned metal barrel, which had apparently been converted into a table. He

247

climbed carefully on a chair and looked into the room through a window. Three beds almost entirely filled the small, dark room. In each was a man, half naked and snoring, their limbs contorted in a way only drunks can manage. Beer bottles, newspapers, clothing and shoes lay in a heap between the beds, as if everything should be set on fire. Montgomery tugged at the leg of his pants and Tobey climbed down from the chair and walked around the hut with him to the boat. Paint buckets were in wooden crates; on the rudder banks lay brushes and palette knives and sandpaper. Two thirds of the boat, which stood on wooden rollers, had been repainted. Three pairs of oars leaned against the wall of the hut; the rusty anchor lay on a coiled rope. Nets hung from bamboo scaffolding, which gave off a foul smell. Fish as short as an index finger were strung on a line that stretched from a post to the roof of the hut. Although he could not imagine ever being hungry enough to eat dried fish, Tobey gathered a few and put them in his pockets. Montgomery scoured buckets and bags and dug a can of Coke out of a tool box, opened it and handed it to him.

"Thanks," Tobey whispered and took a sip.

After they had emptied the can they looked for more food, and found instead an old outboard motor wrapped in blankets. It was still dark, but the gap between the sea and the sky was wider and filled with a glow that was colorless and weak and nevertheless imbued with energy. Tobey estimated that not even half an hour remained for them to lift the engine into the boat and somehow get the boat into the water, before either the sun came up or the men in the hut awakened. They knelt down side by side and peeled the engine from the dirty sheets. It was a Tohatsu, a bulky, blue painted component that despite the many scrapes and dents looked like it would work. When Tobey shook it he heard fuel sloshing in the tank. He looked around for a can, but did not find one.

"What do you think?" he asked Montgomery quietly, pointing to the sea.

248

Montgomery sat cross-legged, with his head hanging. The fingers of his right hand were holding a corner of the sheet, the way Chester had always clung to Rosalinda's skirt. He raised his head and looked at Tobey. His eyes were empty, as if he had just opened them and would have to get along now in a strange world.

"Should we venture out to the sea by boat?" Tobey whispered.

Montgomery let go of the sheets, ran his fingers through the sand and sighed. The air seemed charged with granular blue light and the face of the orangutan appeared clearly for a moment. It seemed to Tobey as though he saw for the first time how old the ape was, how meagerly the hair covered the puckered, spotted skin in some places, how his ears stuck out from his head, wrinkled and leathery, as flabby as the flesh that hung from his thin arms. An old man, he thought, and regretted never having asked Tanvir about Montgomery's age.

Just when Tobey was about to touch him, gently, like someone sleeping or mourning, Montgomery got up and grabbed the sheet at two corners. Tobey did the same thing, and together they carried the engine to the boat and hoisted it into the interior, always careful not to make any noise. On the horizon more and more light surged upward and created a shimmering in the frayed band of clouds. The blue of the dawn, in which everything was indistinct and weightless, changed almost imperceptibly in the degrees of its brightness. Soon the cool gloom would turn into a dirty, colorless, transitional glow, then, for just a few minutes, into a warm yellow and finally into a hard, bright white, from which every object would emerge as if it had been die cut.

Tobey went to the stern of the boat and leaned against it. The boat was moving, sliding over the roots a few meters toward the sea, still peaceful, flat and still. Montgomery raised the weatherworn piles behind Tobey, carried them to the bow and put them under the hull. Fifteen minutes, Tobey thought, perhaps only ten. That was the time they needed to push the boat into the water and row out to the point where they could start the engine without being heard on shore.

Then he saw the man; it was the large, thin fellow who had stood watch at the cell door. He was pointing a gun at Tobey, and his face was illuminated by triumph and pride. Tobey and Montgomery remained standing where they were, twenty meters from the sea, the gentle lapping of the surf in their ears. All the blood seemed to drain from Tobey's head, all the air from his lungs. He wanted to grab on to the edge of the boat, but he did not raise his arm. The man called out and waved the gun. Tobey heard the voice; it was far away, in his head, in a dream. The thin fellow stopped a few steps away from Tobey, turned his head slightly to one side and called something out again, this time louder, a name: Jussif. He was panting; his turban-like headgear sat askew on his shaven head.

When the bearded child emerged beside the hut with a wooden stick in his hand, Tobey began to cry. His legs grew weak; he buckled and landed on his knees. He watched as Montgomery sat in the sand at the stern of the boat and closed his eyes. He listened to the way the thin fellow talked to the bearded child, felt a hand grab his arm and force him to his feet. When he opened his eyes again, he saw the bearded child step behind the thin fellow and strike him down with a stick. The man collapsed, and the bearded child stared at him, shocked and panting. Montgomery was still standing there, motionless, his back stooped and his head bowed, hands clasped over his face, and exhausted from something that had to be more real and more terrible than Tobey's fear of death.

Seconds later Jussif dropped the stick, raised his gun and hung it over his shoulder. Then he went to the stern and leaned against it, pushing the boat forward.

Tobey did not move. He looked down at the thin man; blood seeped from the back of his head. He was queasy, he was thirsty, and he felt an overwhelming desire to lie down. When the bearded child grabbed him by the shoulder, he winced. He watched as Montgomery stood up and swayed for a moment before he picked up a wooden pile and carried it to

250

the bow, where he placed it in the sand, slowly and seemingly unaware of the absurdity of the events. The bearded child used gestures to show him what to do, and Tobey braced himself against the hull of the boat. His feet dug into the sand, he heard the faint rumble of the wooden belly over the logs Montgomery had placed in the sand in front of the bow.

Then he sank and felt water on his ankles. Montgomery grabbed him by the arms and dragged him into the boat. Jussif heaved the motor into the mount at the rear and pulled on the starter rope with a violent tug. The engine made a grinding noise. A wave, too low to break around them, lifted the boat almost imperceptibly. Jussif pulled on the rope once more and the engine started, only to go out again immediately. Tobey gradually came to his senses. Montgomery crouched an arm's length away from him on the ground between the coiled ropes and stared at him. Tobey tried to smile, but he did not know whether he succeeded. He reached out and touched Montgomery's leg. Montgomery closed his eyes. A little later he tipped his head back as if someone had slapped him, and he opened his eyes again and clasped the cross thwart with both hands. Tobey turned away, leaned out of the boat and dipped his hand into the water, moving it like a paddle. He did not want to think about how pointless it was. He saw a man who staggered out of the hut, focused his eyes on the sea, turned around and disappeared, tumbling into the black rectangle of the door opening.

On his third attempt, Jussif managed to start the engine. A black cloud escaped from the blue block, which now began to shake violently and degenerated into a deep loud hum which grew worse as Jussif turned the gas tap. The boat took off and Tobey pulled his hand out of the water. The man rushed out of the hut and stumbled over the beach. He wore a white cloth which he had wrapped around his waist, and shouted something that was lost in the engine noise. When he was standing knee-deep in the water, he raised both arms. Then the first shot rang out. Tobey ducked his head and thought he heard the whizzing of the

251

bullet which flew past him. He lay flat on the floor and pulled Montgomery down with him. A moment later there were four more shots in quick succession.

The phase during which the light was yellow and warm lasted only a few minutes. It flowed beyond the horizon into the sky, floated on the water and enveloped every object. It made everything soft and indistinct and revealed the world one last time in a gentle, dull copper luster. It filled the boat and covered Tobey and Montgomery, who lay on the floor on their backs and looked into the cloudless distance, which unfurled more brightly each time they blinked, until eventually the whiteness so blinded them that they had to close their eyes.

They sailed along the coast rather than away from it, and when Tobey peered over the edge of the boat and saw the beach and trees, he shouted something to the bearded child, pointing to horizon. Jussif sat there, bent forward, as if he was still ducking from the bullets. His thin face was gray and contained no sign of relief that they had escaped the shots.

"Why aren't you sailing out to sea?" Tobey shouted.

Jussif did not answer. He bent even further into the head wind, his eyes narrowed to thin slits and his free arm wrapped around his belly.

Tobey thought that perhaps he would not liberate him and Montgomery after all, but wanted to return them instead to the band of rebels. The fellow possibly intended to hand them over to his leaders as personal prisoners and reap the praise and the reward for himself. That he had struck down the thin fellow was indeed strange, but under the rough jihadists certainly nothing unusual. Or the bearded child was actually crazy and did not want to give up killing the infidels by hand.

"Where are you taking us?" he cried, but then it occurred to him that the bearded child spoke no English. He looked around in the boat for something he could use as a weapon, but all he found was a screwdriver and a paint brush with a pointed handle.

On the shore palms, small forests, and fenced pastures moved by. Where a few wooden huts stood in a clearing, smoke rose. Telephone poles without wires lined an empty street. Fishermen loaded their boats, children waved.

As Tobey stretched out his hand for the screwdriver, Jussif fell forward. The boat slowed, and Montgomery awoke from his stupor. He uttered a long drawn out sound of distress and pressed himself against hull of the boat. Jussif lay there, face down. A plate-sized blood stain had spread across the fabric of the shirt on his back. The back of his pants were covered in blood, as well as the bench. Tobey crumpled the sheet that the motor had been wrapped in hastily into a bundle and put it under Jussif's head. The idling engine chugged in front of him. The boat had turned around and swung across the waves that gently rocked it. Montgomery crawled to the bow, where he rolled over and stopped moving. Jussif coughed up bright blood interspersed with bubbles that ran down his cheek and dripped onto the sheet. Tobey turned him onto his side and put a hand on his shoulder.

"Why did you do that?" he asked softly.

Jussif opened his mouth. His tongue was missing, as if he had bitten it off a long time ago, or as it had been cut off. He opened his eyes and coughed; blood splashed onto the sheet and onto Tobey's T-shirt.

"Where shall we go? Where is the hospital?"

Jussif's breathing rattled in and out, his eyes closed. Tobey left his hand on his shoulder for a while, then sat on the bench and steered the boat toward the shore. Behind the beach grew stunted trees that barely concealed the view of flat, grassless fields. Far away a range of hills rose up, blurring the harsh morning light.

Jussif drew up his legs and now lay there curled up like Montgomery. The fingers of the hand that was not covered by his body moved. When the engine stopped and the bow of the boat dug into the sand, Jussif sighed loudly and stopped breathing.

News from Megan

Do you recollect, Tobey, chubby little Maude Sheridan in the ditch, the yellow boots, that kept walking without her, the white leaves on the black asphalt, the silver-gray car, the sky in the puddles? Do you remember Frank Hennessy, who was hit by lightning as he polished the cross on the steeple? Can you still say what color the dress was of the missing woman on the posters who was found dead on the beach a week later, her pockets full of stones? (Light brown, with a dark brown collar and black buttons.) Do you dream sometimes of old Duncan Kerrigan, who they pulled from the septic tank right in front of our eyes? Do Patty and Rachel Bartlett also appear to you from time to time, as they lie in their beds in the burning trailer and hold hands? What do you think happens when we die? Is there a heaven where we will go on, along with all those who have gone before us? What is Seamus working on up there, without Sam, without a tractor, without us? (Most likely he is fixing the leaky clouds.) I wasn't at his funeral, because it didn't work. Someday, when we meet again, I will tell you everything. What do you remember, Tobey? What do you want to remember? The day that you gave Matt Coulter a black eye on the playground? The four minutes behind the fire station, when Louise Nesbitt didn't resist your kiss? (I pierced her voodoo doll with needles!) Your first ride on a motorcycle? (You looked like Jell-O on an anvil.) The moment when you almost hit Seamus and kicked a hole in the door instead? The evening when you went away? Your first appearance with the band? Us, on the hill, by the sea, in your room? (I'm leaving shortly to buy candles, and I will write more later. The place where I have ended up is strange; in nice weather the power fails; at night crabs come up from the beach and scratch on the front doors with their pincers; women visit you and show you photos of their dead children; millions of butterflies cover the lawn within seconds . . .) I'm back. It's three o'clock in the morning, and I've just decided not to throw away this letter. Do you believe you can tell if you're going crazy? Do you think Cait was in the process of going crazy? I would like to know whether it was easy for her to leave then. And I still don't know what the bear dreams about in the winter. (Right now a heavy rain is coming down. You would have predicted it, Toto, but you would still be amazed at how dark it is in broad daylight, how gigantic the noise of the drops that beat on the roof!) I think about spring, about warmth and colorful meadows and honey. Yes, of warmth and honey.

Who loves you?
Megan!

16

They sailed for an hour without seeing land and without encountering another boat. No tanker or freighter appeared on the horizon, not even a piece of wood floated in the water. Tobey had carried the bearded child's body to land. He had carried it to a mound overgrown with bushes and put it down. Columns of smoke rose from a forest; blows of an axe could be heard. There had to be houses, Tobey thought, and people that would take care of Jussif's funeral. He had placed leaves on his eyes and weighted the leaves with stones. Then he had said a few sentences, but not a prayer, and returned to the boat.

Montgomery slept, his head nestled in the shadow of a cross thwart, on a ball of rope. Tobey had soaked the sheet in water and tied it like a turban around his head, despite the blood. The sun was burning, but as long as they glided over the water the headwind cooled them. He had no idea where he was steering the boat. The sea was calm; they made good progress. Once Tobey believed he had seen the back of a dolphin, and his heart leaped. He thought of the dolphin in Dingle Bay, and tried to remember the name that the people had given him, but he failed. He thought of Briona Fanning, who had told Megan and him that after you die you come back to the world as an animal. He remembered how angry he had grown and that he had called the woman a liar, and how ardently

Megan had listed each creature, from the ant to the zebra, in whose forms she wanted to spend her next life. He still did not believe in reincarnation, but the idea that his sister had just swum by and shown him the way pleased him and distracted him for a while from the thought that the gasoline would soon be exhausted.

When the engine went out minutes later, Montgomery woke up. He raised his head slightly and squinted into the brightness. Now the heat was intolerable where they had stopped. It was quiet; only the sound of water could be heard, rubbing on the belly of the boat.

"We're a long way from the island," Tobey said. It didn't matter to him that the bonobo didn't understand. He decided to say something every few minutes, so he would not fall asleep or lose his mind from the increasing dehydration. He should have looked for coconuts when he brought Jussif ashore, he thought. With the screwdriver he might have been able to remove the outer fiber cover and pierced a hole in the shell. He reached into his pocket, pulled out a fish and smelled it.

"Hungry?" He held the fish out to Montgomery. Montgomery let his head sink back on the tangle of ropes and stared into space.

Tobey bit off a piece of fish and chewed in disgust. "Now we can simply float," he said, trying to make his voice sound firm and clear. "We'll land somewhere." He took the dry sheet from his head and dipped it into the water. Under the seat was a reservoir that was noticeable to him only now. He pushed a plastic buoy aside and passed into the darkness, unearthed oily rags, a tangled ball of fishing line, spark plugs and a few nails. At the far end were two bottles filled with yellow liquid. He opened one and smelled it. "Gasoline," he muttered. Montgomery looked at him for a few seconds, a dull film over his pupils. Tobey wrapped the wet cloth wrapped around his head, poured the contents of both bottles into the tank and started the engine. High above his head a gull flew, and because it made no difference which direction he took, he decided to follow her.

Megan sat on a chair by his bed. With his eyes closed, he listened to her voice. *Spiders and snakes come out at night, with fangs and pincers drawn, they will find you and bite, so you must not yawn.* Summer heat flowed through the open window. In the pond, a fish jumped through the luminous circle the moon cast on the water and then splashed back into his dark prison. *Bedbugs and ticks, are after your blood, they're up to their tricks, but try to sleep good.* Megan stroked his hair, then she stood up and walked to the door, a ghost in a white nightgown that was much too large, one she had found in a trunk in the attic and put on whenever she wanted to scare her brother.

"Don't go!" Tobey cried and opened his eyes. The moon hung so low above him that he had only to stretch out his hand to touch its scarred belly. The sea was still an enormous, motionless pond; each wave an endless, flat hill. Under the dome of the universe there was perfect silence. Tobey pushed away the sheet which he had spread over himself and Montgomery hours before to protect them from the sun, and sat up.

The boat was empty. Tobey called for Montgomery, shouted the name out into the night until he was so exhausted that no sound came from his throat.

Part Two

SONGS

1

The farm lay between the hills at the end of a dirt road. The sea was twenty miles away, as far away as the next town. Beside the house, a whitewashed cottage with two fireplaces, stood a wooden barn and two stables built of stone. The barn roof was covered with corrugated iron, the other buildings with slate. Fenced pastures continued up high on the hillsides; sheep mingled with the low clouds. Cows grazed on the flat fields, a horse stood under a tree, old and brown and patiently waiting to pull the cart or drag a tree trunk to the sawhorse to be cut. In the winter smoke rose from the chimneys, in summer clothes hung on the lines between the house and the fir tree, colorful streamers in the greens and browns and grays of the landscape.

Time had no meaning here; it was the period between the sunrise and the vanishing of light, between the morning milking and the evening feeding, between the fatigue that you shook from your bed-warm body and the exhaustion that occupied the body again countless hours later. Time was the span it took a cow to deliver her calf, that the corn needed to grow and the peat to dry. Time was the day a sheep was born or a pig was slaughtered, the cool eternity of winter, the breath of a summer.

Hours, minutes, seconds were something for the city dweller, that was how Seamus O'Flynn saw it, and he shook his head every morning when his daughter wound up the grandfather clock in the living room, as if each day would not inevitably begin without it, that even before the cock crows you woke up and got out of bed in order to get to work. As if you needed hands and numbers to know when the furnace was lighted, or the manure had to be brought to the field. Seamus O'Flynn's life did not run by the cycle of minutes, not between dates and time limits; it depended on the whims of nature, the weather, the mood of his cows, the occurrence of pests, on the maturity of the grain, the size of the potatoes, the weight of the pigs.

Fluctuating prices for milk, meat and cereals were, in the large, rough course of a year, insignificant eddies, nothing that worried Seamus O'Flynn. His father had never given a damn about the rest of the world, and he, too, saw no sense in it. He hated officials and politicians; when a candidate for the independents ended up on the farm during an election campaign, he chased him with a loaded shotgun from his field. When he fell from the hayloft and broke two fingers, he splinted them with pieces of wood and strips of cloth; he pulled out an abscessed molar by hand. Only a gaping wound persuaded him that is was necessary to visit the doctor in Killorglin, because even though he was a gifted artisan, Seamus could not sew. For a few years after his eyesight began to fail, he constantly lost his glasses in furrows and in the pastures, and at some point he tied the frames around his head with a piece of string.

Every day he got up before the first sunlight and trudged to the barn, wearing the long underwear he slept in, a jacket and rubber boots, and woke the cock and the cows, because he knew nothing else. And because he escaped the fact, out of sheer pigheaded zeal, that he was swimming against the tide without getting anywhere, that his farm was at a loss, an island, forgotten in time, which he so persistently ignored.

Tobey spent all day with his father; he helped feed the animals, muck out the barn, mow the fields. He watched when a cow gave birth to a calf and lambs got their ears tagged; he was present when a pig was slaughtered and a chicken's head was cut off with the axe. He loved to go along to a field with his father on a summer morning and check the size of the corn cob or to stand on a ladder and pick apples in the fog of an autumn day. For him the farm was the world; what might be around them did not interest him, and he could not imagine ever living anywhere else or doing something different from his father.

Tobey had no friends; he did not need any. If he wanted to talk, his sister listened to him; that was enough. Once a month his father, Megan, and he travelled into the city with the tractor or on the public bus, because they had no car. Then he watched other children, studied their gestures and tried to decipher their language, and each time came to the conclusion that they were incomprehensible beings with whom he had little in common and who would complicate his life rather than enrich it.

But he was not completely alone with his father and his sister on the farm. A neighbor came by every day, took care of the children, cooked, did the laundry and cleaned. Briona was the sister of Robert Fanning, a farmer whose farm was a few miles away. As a young girl she had killed her child and served a term in prison, and now she was over forty and didn't go after men any more. Everyone in the neighborhood knew her story, and although all shook their heads with pity when they saw the large, pale Briona, nobody wanted to have anything to do with her. Sometimes, while she was preparing breakfast in the kitchen, she was shaken by a fit of coughing that was so violent that it woke Tobey up. Then he lay there thinking about what Feargal Walsh had told him, that at the time Briona Fanning wanted to kill herself along with her baby. That she had gone out on a cold winter night in the rain and had stripped naked. That the next day she woke up in hospital in Tralee and a police officer was sitting on her bed and told her that her daughter was dead. Tobey had no sympathy for her. Because she was in the house, his mother did not come back. Because she cooked so well, his father did not miss his wife, whose realm had once been the kitchen, which was proved by a photograph that showed Cait O'Flynn in an apron, holding a loaf of freshly baked bread in both hands, smiling. Briona never smiled, at least not in the presence of Tobey. She walked bent over a little, and Feargal Walsh claimed she dragged her dead child around on her shoulders with her. Despite everything, she was so nice that it was almost hard for Tobey to hate her.

Every other weekend Uncle Aidan came to visit. He was years older than his brother and had never married. At sixteen he took an apprenticeship with a boat builder and then went on a world tour, from which he returned three years later. For a time he lived with his parents and Seamus on the farm again, helped with the farm work and repaired everything that was made of wood. But he knew that he did not want to spend his days in cow pastures and potato fields and mending foot stools and pig troughs, and only stayed because his mother was getting sicker and would not let him go. When Maeve O'Flynn died he was sitting by her bed and holding her hand, while his father and his brother brought in the hay, and when she was buried, he was the one who went up front and said something about her. After his mother's things had been given away or packed in boxes and brought to the attic, Aidan went away. He flew to British Columbia, where he worked for a cement company and learned in his free time how to build a log house, and then to Pennsylvania, to see how the Amish people made their wooden furniture. Two years later he was standing in a telephone booth in Norfolk, Nebraska, and learned from his brother that their father had died of a stroke. He flew home, where he met his future sister-in-law, Cait Millholland, young and beautiful and four months pregnant. He built a cradle for the child and stood with Seamus and Cait at the grave of his parents and then in the bar at Donovan

Inn and assured them that he was still not interested in becoming a farmer. With a bank loan and the little money Seamus could pay him as compensation for the farm he bought a remote, dilapidated house on the coast near Clonakilty, restored it, and started to build furniture in the barn. For a time a woman named Carol lived with him, but she soon tired of the isolation, the rough sea breeze and Aidan's unpretentious contentment, which she interpreted as a lack of ambition, and took off again. Aidan let her go without having to complain. Months later a dog turned up and wanted to stay. He named it Lorca, an anagram of Carol and the name of a poet who Aidan appreciated. He sold the chairs, chests of drawers and the cabinets that he manufactured in the barn to a furniture shop in Cork, which ordered more than he could deliver.

When the weather was good Aidan drove with Megan and Tobey to the sea; if rain fell or the wind was too violent, they went to eat and afterwards sat down at a quiet table in a pub and played cards, Lorca at their feet. Sometimes Aidan took them with him to a horse race or to the junior hurling games, sometimes to his house, where they ran around with the dog or crafted things in the barn from leftover wood. Tobey built small models of tractors, ships and airplanes, Megan little birds houses and coffins for mice, hedgehogs and squirrels. Once they made a trip to Valencia Iceland, another time to Dingle, where they and hundreds of other spectators admired Fungi, the trusting dolphin. When his car, an aged, moss green Volvo, was in the shop, Aidan came by bus and taxi. Then they stayed at the farm, playing cards in the house and hide-and-seek outside or whatever came to mind.

If they urged him, Seamus sat with them at the kitchen table for a game of gin rummy, but most of the time he worked in the field or in the barn and would not be seen again until dinner. From the moment Cait had gone away, Seamus O'Flynn watched his good luck, which he had perceived in his marriage and the birth of the children to be vast, growing constantly smaller. After Cait's flight he had grown from a hard-working man with plans for the future into an embittered loner who no longer worked from dawn to dusk because it gave him joy, but because it numbed him. He had never bothered to find out where his wife had gone. In a mixture of stubbornness and pride, he took care of the children and the farm. He bought books so he could learn how to bathe and change a baby, how to cook porridge and sterilize a bottle, what to do about childhood diseases and at what age to switch them from diapers to the potty. When he realized after a week that he hardly slept and forgot about such everyday tasks as clearing out the barn or feeding the pigs, he got some help. After the young woman, who left at the end of the summer to work as a nurse in Galway, Briona Fanning came to the farm. Seamus did not like the big, quiet woman, but she demanded little money and she was a good cook. Feargal Walsh said it was irresponsible to trust a killer, but Seamus did not listen to him. His wife had left him and made him the laughing stock of the area; in his opinion nothing worse could happen to him.

Briona enjoyed working on the farm. During her imprisonment she had begun to draw— first from memory, perhaps her dog, long dead; or the garden shed, where they had played as a child; things she saw in her cell: the bed, the vase, the window. Later she brought illustrated books from the prison library and tried sailing ships, flowers, animals, the Eiffel Tower, the Statue of Liberty. Briona soon noticed that Megan hardly did anything but draw, and that the girl had talent. She hung the pictures on the kitchen cabinets and the blank wall above the washing machine so Seamus could see how gifted his daughter was. When she did the weekly shopping, she sometimes bought a box of crayons or a drawing pad instead of dried soups and canned beans. With her wages she bought small gifts for Megan: a pen with four different color inks, a sable brush, a box of watercolors. Sometimes, at night, when she was in bed at her brother's house, she missed Megan. Then she turned the light on again, looked at one of the child's drawing and smiled.

When they were small, Tobey and Megan spent a great deal of time together. When her father was in the field and Briona was not there yet or had already gone, Megan took care of her brother. She taught him how to tie his shoes, clean his teeth, and smear butter on bread, took him along on her excursions and showed him birds' nests, badger's burrows and anthills, initiated him into the secrets of the beehive and explained to him how a butterfly came from a caterpillar and a frog came from a tadpole. When she saw that he had crushed a spider she took him to task, and when he tore the wings off three beetles she pulled his ear until he howled and Briona came to see if everything was okay. She could not understand why he insisted on being there when a pig was slaughtered, and what fascinated him about taking the still warm intestines out of a headless chicken. She had not eaten meat since she was four, and when she saw him greedily wolfing down half a dozen cutlets from sheep that had been standing in the pasture on the previous day she left the kitchen, went into her room and took a photo out that showed Tobey as a three-year-old with a young cat in his arm, which helped her forgive him a little.

Megan could hardly wait to be old enough to go to school. With Briona's help she had figured out reading and writing, and she could count to one thousand. By six she was devouring all sorts of reading material, whatever she got her fingers on, no matter whether it was a seed catalog or the Bible. When they drove into the city, Seamus had to buy her an old issue of *Reader's Digest* or *National Geographic* from Sheehan's, and for her birthday she always wanted a nature atlas or an illustrated book about animals. If Aidan or Briona asked her what she wanted to be when she grew up, she replied: a veterinarian, the director of an animal shelter, someone who made films about nature, or the director of a zoo. She struck the last career choice off the list after her fifteenth birthday when she went to the Dublin Zoo with Uncle Aidan and saw the caged animals.

267

Sometimes, when Seamus was watching his daughter, when she told Sam about her experiences at the pond or read out loud to a sow from a children's book, he wondered if she had become this strange creature because she had grown up without a mother, and if so, how much he was to blame. Perhaps, he thought then, he should have tried at least once to find his wife, to whom he was still married, and persuade her to return home. Maybe she was sitting somewhere, lonely and regretful, and waiting for him to take her back to the farm where she had been so happy the first two years. But then he remembered the day when he had come home from working in the field and found Megan tied to the porch railing with a rope and Tobey screaming in his crib, and knew once more why he did nothing to track Cait down. Feargal Walsh had equipment back then to contact the police, and Aidan offered to ask a friend who worked at the social services department for help, but Seamus did not want to spread the shame of being abandoned to anyone, especially not in front of unfamiliar officials who certainly had better things to do than search for a woman who did not want to be found. He was also the only person who knew the contents of the letter that Cait had left under the pillow for him, and it should stay that way.

Tobey envied his sister for her talent, to be able to draw something that was recognizable on first glance, and to describe something in such a way that you immediately knew what she meant. She patiently taught him the alphabet and the multiplication tables, and although Tobey struggled and could write simple sentences by seven, read children's books and add eleven and sixteen, at times he felt like a dummy beside her. Once she explained a difficult word to him and he jumped up and ran away, screaming around the farm so loud that the chickens scattered.

He loved Megan, but there was always an undercurrent of rivalry with her, as if it was about gaining just a little more of their father's attention, sparse in their house, than he gave her. Or as if it was about being in a constant struggle to distinguish himself from her and to prove that they were in fact as different as night and day. When she started school, he enjoyed having his father, Briona and the farm all to his own, but after a few weeks he missed her terribly. In the beginning she was still excited and told him about everything new she experienced: the school building, which smelled of damp clothes, floor wax and books, about teachers, about the other children, the subject matter and the strange rules of the schoolyard which she was slowly beginning to understand. Later, her reports were briefer and more prosaic, and she often remained silent throughout dinner, and answered only when her father wanted to know something. Once she came home completely distraught and closed herself in her room. When she didn't show up for dinner, Seamus asked her to open the door, and then she told him in tears that a few boys on the playground had thrown stones at a cat, and she beat up one of the boys and was called into the principal's office and punished with three hours of detention. Another time she left the school in the morning after she had rescued a bird that had flown into a windowpane and was left lying there wounded. In addition, there were repeated clashes with classmates which were often physical, and Megan's opponents ended up with scratches and bruises. A letter from the principal to Seamus O'Flynn said that Megan was a highly intelligent child, who unfortunately lacked the ability to fit into a system. At the end of the first half of the year, her teacher came to the farm to find out whether the girl's idiosyncrasies were connected to the environment in which she was growing up. In her report it was said that the family situation, affected by isolation and the absence of the mother, while not optimal, did not require the involvement of the welfare agency for the time being.

After each incident Seamus took his daughter to pray, and each time she promised to improve. She did not go so far as making friends at school, but she did nothing to increase the number of her enemies. In the second year she even took part in the swim team and wrote articles for

269

the school newspaper, and although she still occasionally disturbed the classroom by releasing the toads for the biology lesson, for example, or carrying a marten in need of care to school with her, soon she was only noticed because of her good grades, and because of her habit, during breaks, of humming self-composed songs to herself, hidden behind large sunglasses and something that everyone called her kookiness; all but the fat first-graders, who secretly sat near her and listened.

2

Tobey was convinced that all the school knew about the disappearance of his mother and considered his sister to be a gifted madwoman in a costume. He hated the teachers, the children and even the simple-minded janitor who constantly hung up notes with scribbled messages like FRESH WAXED FLOOR! And ENTRY PROHIBITED! For two years he had no friends except Barry Spillane, who greeted him and sometimes gave him half his lunch, then walked beside him, silent and chewing something that was larger and heavier than any bread that his mother sent along with him. Then one day Michael Kavanagh, whom everyone that did not simply ignore him called Mick, asked him if he played an instrument, and said that he and Jason Dwyer were about to start a band and needed a guitarist. Tobey hesitated briefly and then claimed that he played guitar, although he had never in his life held an instrument in his hands, and Mick asked him to audition with him as soon as possible. The next day, Tobey bought an acoustic guitar from Cormac Sheehan's shop for four pounds fifty and a songbook from Christy Moore for seventy cents. He had saved three pounds; he took the rest of the money from his father's wallet. The guitar looked like fretwork for a child who didn't have much talent for tinkering. Front and back were made of plywood stained dark brown, the neck and sides were painted, the pegs and the bridge made of black plastic. A logo was glued to the neck, the letters golden with red shadows: LA MAGICA. The song book turned out to be useless because Tobey could not read sheet music, so he got himself a practice cassette and an exercise book for beginners at Music Dempsey. When he learned the first chords with the help of a chart, he constantly feared that the instrument, which weighed less than an eviscerated chicken, would break in his rough, work-calloused hands. For months he struggled with half-steps, time signatures, quarter notes and rests, repaired the guitar with string and duct tape, and invented new excuses each time Mick Kavanagh asked him when he was finally going to come to a rehearsal. At the end of August, on the evening of his tenth birthday, Tobey smashed the guitar behind the house and burned it. The next morning he bought a used Sherwood acoustic guitar at Music Dempsey for thirty-five pounds, which he had borrowed from Uncle Aidan, practiced on it for two weeks and then let Mick know he now had time.

Mick's parents ran a pharmacy on the ground floor of a house that belonged to them. His sister Claire was twenty and married; his brother Mark studied Business Administration in Cork. After Claire moved in with her husband in Ennis, Mick transformed her room into a rehearsal space, despite protests by Mark, who came home on weekends and holidays and worried about his privacy. As a late arrival, Mick had always been the darling of his parents. When he was five he took piano lessons because he had insisted on it. When he was eight the elderly Miss Horgan could no longer teach him anything, and so he took accordion lessons with George Fowler, a retired postal clerk, who for forty years had performed with his brothers as The Fowler Five. After a year he lost interest and tried the saxophone before he began to be interested in stringed instruments, and within a few months could play the ukulele. That was when he got the idea to start a band.

Mick Kavanagh was thin and too small for his age; he wore glasses and stuttered slightly when he was excited. At school he was considered a nerd and a teacher's pet, even though his grades were average and he generally tried not to attract unnecessary attention. He did not harm anyone, did not participate in bullying or brawls, let others show off in physical education and thought only in dreams of addressing one of the girls, who, according to an unwritten law, were reserved for the good-looking, athletic and unscrupulous guys. Despite his success in the school orchestra he felt himself a failure, and the band seemed to be an excellent way to win friends and finally to become famous—if not worldwide, at least for a start in Killorglin and the surrounding areas. That Jason Dwyer was an eccentric, boastful fool and Tobey O'Flynn was the brother of Megan O'Flynn, secretly disturbed him, but in his situation he could not be picky. The limited choice of candidates was also the reason why he generously overlooked Tobey's mistakes on "Amazing Grace" and "Smoke on the Water" and welcomed Tobey as the third man on board.

They had grown up with folk music, like their fathers and grandfathers. They considered Rock and Roll to be pure background noise, heard it from a passing car, through an open window; when turning the dial of a radio. In the pub, they tapped their feet to the popular Irish songs about lover's grief and desire, homelessness and patriotism, things that they somehow knew, but for which they had not yet found their own words. They lived with the traditional music, the way they lived with the Gaelic Games, the church, and the weather. Tobey practiced scales and chords in his room and forgot all about the time until Megan knocked on the wall or began to sing loudly. Jason, who by nine had already looked over the fence and discovered rebels like Rory Gallagher, Van Morrison and Elvis Costello, flailed on his drums half the night in the garage, until a drum skin ripped or a stick broke. Mick played at home with his parents and neighbors, and performed in varying configurations at weddings, birthdays and the dedication of a new fire station. The melodies of their ancestors were their hymns, their holiday songs, their lullabies.

And then, when they were eleven, they first heard "Smells Like Teen Spirit" by Nirvana, and it was as if they had been in contact with a distant planet, with an alien species. They lay on the ground in Jason's room, sluggish from too much cake and soft drinks and from talking about such important issues as whether Lynn Colfer wore a bra, while Jason surfed channels from one station to the next. He was not only the only one of them who had his own television, but he also had the talent to talk his mother out of money for the most incredible purchases. Evidence of his recent triumph over her weak will was a satellite dish that received signals from outer space, messages from other worlds. Outside it was raining, the curtains were closed, and only the warm glow of the television lit up the room a little. Jason landed on MTV, where a long-haired guy shouted phrases like "I feel stupid and contagious. Here we are now, entertain us," and the three boys, yesterday still children isolated from the world and brave representatives of a musical tradition, became renegades.

They continued to make music with their classmates and cousins and neighbors, appeared with the youth orchestra on Saint Patrick's Day and on the opening day of the Puck Fair and performed a Christmas serenade for the residents of the nursing home. They didn't let on about anything, practiced scales and new songs daily and played what they had always played as if nothing had happened. Only when they were alone, in Mick's practice room, in the garage next to Jason's mother's house, in a basement, in the bathroom of an empty house, in the woods, in a rowing boat on Caragh Lake, in the vast and immeasurable loneliness of their heads, did they secretly practice other riffs, learn other lyrics, strike other attitudes.

Barry Spillane wanted to be in the band, which was called Eighties Best Breed, but Mick was against it. Barry, who was about a year older, did not fit into the picture, he said, and the accordion was completely inappropriate for rock music. He saw himself as the founder and head of the band

and claimed the sole right to determine who did and who did not join in. In his eyes they were complete as a trio and on the way to finding what he called their unique sound, something that was just approaching maturity and would be destroyed by the squawking, trapped-in-folk-music sounds of an accordion. For weeks Tobey had let Barry talk him into putting in a good word for him with Mick, and thought they should at least let him audition. He liked Barry, who, because of his obesity, was harassed even more brutally than him and Mick and Denis Kilduff with his crippled hand. While they were shunned by most of their classmates and left alone, Barry could not just disappear into obscurity as if under a cloak of invisibility. Despite the fact that his height was above-average for a twelve year old, he weighed twenty kilos too much, which did not surprise anyone who knew he had spent his life so far almost exclusively in his parents' butcher shop. The blonde hair on his round head was cut short and his face porous and slightly red, as if it were flooded continuously with waves of shame. He had a bulging, moist lower lip, a double chin and breasts some of the girls from the upper classes would have envied. Everyone, even the insignificant first-graders who could barely carry their own books, made fun of fat Barry, and none of them assumed the giant would defend himself. They relied on Barry's tolerance, although some of them suspected that hidden behind the soft mass of shyness and inferiority complexes there was not gentleness, but a core of dark despair, and that it was better not to disturb this core.

Barry failed the audition in Mick's room. He was nervous and sweating through his vest, which said THE CRANBERRIES and which he had bought the day before, without the knowledge of his mother, who decided what he wore. First, he played "Alive" because he knew that Eddie Vedder, the lead singer of Pearl Jam, was one of Mick's idols, then "Zombie" by the Cranberries. Mick appeared to listen with interest and even made notes, but Tobey saw that he only pretended, as if he would give Barry a fair chance. After the two songs Mick said Barry was undoubtedly good, but the accordion didn't fit into the musical concept. When he took him to the door, he said it was unfortunate that Barry was not a bass player, because that was what they needed. Barry thought for a second and then replied that he played the bass as a second instrument. It was not really true, but it was not quite a lie, because at the age of nine he had banjo lessons for few months before his teacher moved to Sligo with his son and his wife and there was no one who was able to take Barry as a student. Barry's grandfather Duncan played the accordion and offered to teach his grandson. Barry was not impressed either by the accordion or the prospect of spending an hour or more every day with his grandfather, who was rough and loud, and constantly teased him about the fact that Barry, as the scion of a meat cutting dynasty and future business owner, couldn't stand the sight of blood and could not use his hands during the slaughter. Barry was industrious and by the time he was twelve he was better than his grandfather. They still made music at least twice every week as a family orchestra, his father playing metal flute, his mother the violin and his older sister Antonia the concert flute, but with the hours elapsing painfully slowly in his grandfather's stuffy room, it came to an end.

The day after his audition for Mick, Barry bought a black Fender Precision electric bass and a Fender 400 Pro Combo - 500 Watt amplifier with the money he had earned and had saved from the holidays of years past, both second-hand, as well as music books for beginners and advanced students and CDs of The Who, Black Sabbath, Queen, U2 and Pearl Jam, so he could study how John Entwistle, Geezer Butler, John Deacon, Adam Clayton and Jeff Ament played. He worked in the shop only when it was absolutely necessarily, locked himself in his room and practiced. That he had played the banjo for a year benefited him, and although the bass felt very different and at the beginning he had problems with the strings, he made rapid progress. In the first weeks his hands clambered up and down the scales nonstop, he repeated chord positions

276

and tried various finger techniques. While his parents sat in the living room below him, he listened to CDs of the Dubliners, the Chieftains and other bands, traditional Irish music interpreted with modern instruments, and, in spite of conservative people like Niamh and Deirdre Spillane, he was not scared off. When he was alone at home or with Antonia, who he had let in on his plans to become a rock musician, he turned up the volume, tried out new techniques, emulated his idols and stood in front of the mirror, where each month he saw not only a better bass player, but also a thinner boy with a face that appeared from under the dwindling fat and grinned at him at the end of a long winter like a lost twin brother.

3

When Tobey watched his father as he repaired the old wheelbarrow or wrapped the broken handle of a pitchfork with wire, he felt sorry for this hardworking, stubborn man who was too proud to complain and too simple to despair. On some days his sympathy changed to contempt; then he threw away the tin bucket, whose holes Seamus had filled with tar-soaked jute, or made firewood from a rotten ladder. As he grew older and the time for a decision drew near, he argued with his father, often beginning at breakfast, reproached him for his naiveté and stubbornness, and the fact that he had failed for years to modernize the farm; if not for the future, which promised nothing for Seamus, then at least for the present. At the end of this conflict which, over the course of time had turned into angry monologues, reeling tirades containing accusations and justifications, Seamus locked himself in the tool shed with a broken tool, while Tobey rode away on a motorcycle, a BSA Bantam that was twice as old as he was, and stayed away until the morning.

Tobey was not the only boy in the area who fled his desolate home all night. He and the other three members of the band, who were now called Agents of Anger, met in a shed next to the old rope factory which had not been used for years, where they got drunk on beer and talked about music and girls and their glorious future. They had found discarded upholstered furniture, folding chairs and a table with sawed-off legs and had papered the walls with concert posters and pages from music magazines. In one corner there were two mattresses, in case they were drunk and no longer able to make it home, and in the middle of the room, framed by the bulky furniture, there was a stuffed otter perched on a tower of beer crates, holding a traffic sign in its paws that said DEAD END.

Mick had lined up a coal stove, but when it was too cold in the shed they met elsewhere, for example at Jason's, whose mother let them have the empty garage next to the house for hanging out. Her husband had been a policeman and three days before Jason's twelfth birthday he had been run down by a drunk, in broad daylight, on the road to Milltown, just thirty-eight years old.

In front of the shed there was a flat, uncultivated field, which became a swamp when it rained. At one of the long sides grew trees that blocked the shed off from a rarely traveled road; the other sides bordered similar desolate fields, separated from each other by nothing but a few crooked poles and wires. Crows perched on the poles, which the boys threw stones and empty beer bottles at them when they were bored. One of the properties was owned by a local construction company, which stored material and machinery there. Under corrugated iron roofs were stacked planks and beams and stones and bricks. To see the nearest inhabited house you had to climb onto the crane, which stood beside the office shed; it was five kilometers to the city.

The only females who had ever entered the shed were Katherine Dwyer and Megan O'Flynn. Jason's mother showed up the first summer after their occupation, satisfied that the boys did not share their kingdom with rats and that there was no immediate danger of collapse, and had left again with the promise to bring a rug over the next day. She seemed unaware or indifferent to the fact that she caused her son the utmost embarrassment. Jason boasted to his friends that he had more power over his mother than vice versa, and although they were reluctant to believe him, they were not surprised that Katherine Dwyer never showed up near the hut again.

Megan visited the boys' secret meeting place without their knowledge, on a summer evening when the quartet was rehearsing in Jason's garage. A week earlier Tobey had attacked Megan's pet cemetery, after Seamus had decided to invest the first bank credit of his life into his daughter's studies instead of the modernization of the farm and the future of his son. Megan thought about taking part of the savings her brother had been hoarding for years under the floorboards of his room in order to purchase a used motorcycle and donate it to the local SPCA in his name, but then she decided that a simple fine was not the appropriate punishment for his vandalism. She tore up one of his comic books to make him believe this was how she had avenged herself. A week later she took the bus to Tralee and bought a ten gallon bucket of pink paint and the most tasteless things she could find at Oxfam. On that particular evening she used a bike and a trailer to carry everything to the shed. There, she painted the walls bright pink, soaked the chairs and sofas with perfume from a half-liter bottle, picked up the empty beer cans and stolen road signs, the plastic skull and the rugby ball from the shelf, and replaced them with candleholders, romance novels and stuffed animals. Before she left, she hung religious pictures on the still wet walls and put a vase with a bouquet of artificial flowers on the table.

It never occurred to any of the boys that Megan might have had something to do with it. They suspected everyone around them, but not Tobey's sister. Because they did not want everyone in town talking about their hideout, they decided not to investigate. Each of them had his own theory and vehemently argued for it, no matter how absurd it was. Mick claimed that two singers from the church choir, whose gospel band he had declined to play piano in, were responsible for the deed. Barry suspected a couple of guys from school, tough guys and athletes who derided him as a weakling at every available opportunity. Jason could not be dissuaded from the idea that his mother was behind the affair, and punished her methodically with silence and rebellion. Tobey believed in this case that the motive was not revenge or humiliation. In his opinion, it was impossible that someone would take such an effort only to play a dirty trick on them, and reassured, or rather consoled himself with the story of the little girl who had arranged the shed this way because she thought he was leaving.

For weeks after they had entered the pink doll's house for the first time, they talked about nothing else but the crime and the possible perpetrators. The walls had long since been painted white and the upholstery aired out, and still the four habitually poured fresh oil onto the fire of their flaming imagination. They served each other new arguments and alleged evidence, and increasingly entangled themselves in speculation and contradictions. Eventually so exhausted by their obsession to solve the unsolvable and suddenly disillusioned, they clasped hands and solemnly swore never again to mention a single word of the story.

In the shed music was heard and music was talked about, but there was no music made. They practiced three or four times a week at Mick's or Jason's and played in the school orchestra; that was enough. The shed was their bunker, surrounded by enemy territory, their palace amid shabby normality. Here they turned up the volume on the CD player all the way, cried their sullen hearts out and puked out the window when they had too much to drink. Mostly they lay around, tired of the machinery of the school and the speeches of their parents, frustrated by the life they led, and growing euphoric for the time they were anticipating. When it was raining and they were in the mood, or just drunk, they pulled off their pants and ran to the field, threw themselves into the mud and disappeared in it, became invisible.

Mick told the others that they were a band who played in pubs and later in clubs and at festivals, to eventually fill concert halls and stadiums. He said that the beginnings would be hard, but at the same time promised them free beer and girls from such exotic countries as France and Germany. They had the reputation of not being very good and therefore loud, but because they didn't charge much and could only handle alcohol in moderation, they still managed to get a gig now and then in a pub, a gym, or on the outdoor stage of a village festival. Their repertoire included ten songs, four originals and six covers. At their first gig, after their opening number, a frenzied version of "Blowin' in the Wind," they were booed, and they decided on short notice to push back the punk oriented titles and to do their quieter songs first, hoping that after the first few bars of "Walking on Hills" people would be in a more friendly mood and later, with the ballad "Lake of Solitude," realize that they were witnessing an act of genius. But the audience in Murphy's Tavern did not see why their Friday evening spirits should be spoiled by four snotty-nosed brats that the four-colored posters claimed were a band, just because they dared to go on stage in torn trousers and lumberjack shirts instead of staying in their rehearsal room for a few more years. The people booed until the stage was cleared. They had been working all week, wanted to drink a few beers and listen to music, and they were not as generous and forgiving as Ron Fogarty, the business manager of the pub, who, as the former drummer of the only well known rock band within the county line, knew how difficult it was to get the first gig. Fogarty had listened to the boys and knew after two songs that they were not ready. But the four had pleaded with him and lowered their asking price even more, and besides, Fogarty was a friend of Niamh Spillane and patronized the butcher shop. Eventually he agreed, under the condition that the band did not use their own amp, but the one that belonged to the pub, which sounded good instead of rattling the windows.

After this experience Barry wanted to leave the band. He had confessed to his parents a week before the concert that he not only wanted to play Irish folk music, but also something called rock, punk, and grunge. The two had been surprised at how long their son had been able to deceive them, but also pleased to see him happy and filled with feverish pride. It relieved them that Barry had found friends he played music with, even if he used expressions like punk or grunge that meant nothing to them and the band's name confused them deeply. Barry told them about the concert at Murphy's Tavern and asked them not to come because it was his first appearance and he was nervous enough already, but they came anyway and were witnesses to his humiliation, which they tried to drown out with their solitary applause. The next day the band met at Jason's, and Barry claimed the public had only stared at him because he was still so big and still so fat. Tobey defended him and took the blame, explained plausibly that the reason for their failure was his new, unfamiliar electric guitar, a twenty-year-old amber-yellow Fender that Mick had squeezed out of an uncle for little money. But Barry stuck to his version, said that the band was better off without him and went home to work behind the store counter.

It was Mick, of all people, who persuaded Barry not to leave the Agents of Anger. Although as composer and arranger he was the hardest hit by the rejection of the public and had laid awake the whole night, he tried to cheer Barry up, appealed to his competitive spirit and told him stories about famous bands that, at the beginning of their careers, also had to accept criticism and setbacks. U2 had not always been so successful and, when they were still called Feedback and The Hype, they were often booed, he said. They sat behind the butcher shop on the wall that surrounded the place where the animals were delivered on slaughtering day. It was Sunday, the clouds had cleared, and a faint light shone on the roofs, the asphalt and the bent backs of the two boys.

For an hour Mick talked to Barry, explained to him how important the bass was, lectured him about the legendary sound, how everyone had vowed to find it, and explained in detail why the audience in Murphy's Tavern, with the exception of Barry's parents, had no idea of good music. Barry, still amazed that Mick had come to him, to win him back for the band, listened to everything, nodded from time to time or mumbled something, but it was only a word at the end of Mick's speech, hidden in a subordinate clause and quietly and quickly spoken, that persuaded him to change his decision and to stay in the Agents of Anger. The word was friendship.

In their neck of the woods there were not many opportunities to perform, and in Cork, Dublin or even Limerick they were neither good enough nor familiar enough. Once, they took part in a competition for young bands in Tipperary. Aidan, who now ran a small furniture company in Clonakilty, drove them down in his van. They played three of their own songs, but did not make it into the second round. Afterwards everyone took blame for the failure except Jason, and they had only rehearsed for two weeks, no more. Mick doubted in his abilities as a songwriter for the first time and threw reams of sheet music into the fire. Barry put his bass in the trunk and ended his diet. Tobey spent his time in the barn, where he screwed around with his motorcycle. They were seventeen and heard from all sides that the time was coming to think seriously about the future. Mick's parents had specific ideas about how their son should spend the next few years, and he made them believe that he would follow their plans. Barry was supposed to train at the butcher shop and take over one day. He would get used to killing the animals and the blood, said his father. Jason assured everyone that he alone determined what happened in his life, and academic studies were out of the question for him. Tobey tried to deal with the fact that his father would not modernize the farm, and because he was neither about to slide into ruin with him or wait until Seamus was too old to work someday, he prepared to leave for Kerry soon, just like Jason. The two no longer held onto the vanishing realm of their childhood. It was just a matter of killing time until they were of legal age and then taking off, preferably to Dublin. Jason could hardly wait for the day of his eighteenth birthday, the moment of the final victory over his mother, and he never tired of conjuring it up.

Outwardly, Tobey pretended to feel the same burning impatience as Jason. With him, he reveled in the colors of his new existence and celebrated deeds in the distant future. But secretly he still hoped for a miracle, an epiphany, that his father would come to his senses and would reveal to him at last that he must turn the farm over to his son, he did not want to lose both and end up like Feargal Walsh, who did not speak to the cows anymore and often slept in the kitchen in the winter, the only heated room in the house. For a time he believed that Megan would take over the farm because she had delayed her move to England and the beginning of her studies, and suddenly turned to things she had not been interested in before: how to couple the hay tedder to the tractor, for example, or how much profit a hundred pounds of potatoes would yield.

Eventually he confronted her. He had just gotten out of bed with a hangover and did not expect to encounter his sister in the house. She made him coffee and he asked her why she was still here and not in London and studying biology, why she was suddenly going to the field with Seamus, and wanted to know if the grain was rotting. "Because you don't do it anymore," Megan said calmly and quietly, but so emphatically that Tobey could not look her in the eyes. For the first time in days they had exchanged more than a few words. Tobey missed breakfast, which his father and sister ate at eight clock, after Seamus already had three hours of work behind him, because he was still in bed, and when it was time for dinner he was long gone, with Mick or Jason or in the shed, where they drank the beer that Barry purchased from the supermarket, showing his

ID with a flushed face, as if it was a permit for recognition and happiness.

Tobey should stop preaching to Seamus about modern agriculture and confusing him with loans and subsidies, Megan said. When she asked him to be patient and make gradual changes, so Seamus wasn't taken by surprise, he got up and left. From a hill he looked down over the land that he was not prepared to share with his father, not with this crazy, stubborn fellow who was not yet fifty years old and shuffled down there in his rubber boots full of holes, across the ground between the barn and the house, weighed down by a concern that had nothing to do with the farm, but a snapped fan belt, a loose roof tile, a broken shovel handle. Tobey closed his eyes and wished on him an accident or illness, nothing really bad, just something that made it unmistakably clear to this stubborn fellow it was time to give up.

4

The day Tobey decided to leave the farm and his father and his sister, was an ordinary Wednesday in October, two months after his eighteenth birthday. He saw his father less and less, so they hardly ever argued anymore, but this morning they had come to blows because of a coffee jug that broke during the dishwashing. Tobey had thrown the pieces in the trash, and Seamus had taken them out again and put them on the buffet in order to glue them back together sometime. This resulted in an obstinately conducted game of throwing away and retrieving, that ended when Seamus had disappeared into his shed with the remains of the teapot and Tobey had driven his motorcycle over Laharan and Curraheen to Glenbeigh, shouting with fury against the wind and the noise of the engine.

During this time of year there were hardly any tourists in the area. The few locals who had time in the middle of the day for a walk lost themselves between the dunes and the sea. There, by the curve of the bay, someone was flying a kite. It was autumn and the air was unusually mild. Deep in the sand the heat of summer was trapped between smooth polished pebbles and shell fragments. Tobey lay on his back, and because there wasn't much to see in the sky, after a while he shut his eyes. A week ago he had made one final attempt to convince his father to obtain a loan or an application for subsidies. But still Seamus did not want to know anything about all this, claiming to be a farmer, not a slave to the banks, and certainly no beggar or pauper. Tobey' stomach still clenched with anger when he thought about that evening. Because there was meat, Megan had gone to her room with sandwiches and tea, and Tobey and Seamus were left alone in the kitchen, drinking cold cider and chewing a chicken that Tobey had slaughtered by hand, plucked, gutted and roasted in the oven in order to bring his father out of his lethargy for an hour. Shortly before the end of the meal Tobey had placed a brochure from the bank on the table and tried to explain the principle of credit to his father, the way the physician explains the need for an inoculation to a child, and Seamus had responded as always.

Farmer, Tobey thought, and a laugh caught in his throat. Thirty sheep, two dozen chickens, eight cows, five pigs and an old nag that did nothing to earn his food, this nutcase called livestock. A year ago, Tobey had regularly read the trade journals displayed in the sales room of the feed mill in Killorglin, had studied newspaper articles in which the Farmers' Association and the Ministry of Agriculture advised farmers about how they could modernize their operations and increase their income. Now he was no longer interested in all that. Actually, he had known it for years, but this morning he had finally given up the idea of continuing the farm. He did not want to be a farmer anymore, especially not one like his father. He would rather work for a pittance in a factory in Dublin, as the stubborn idiot who helped drive the truck even deeper into the mud. He remembered Megan's solemn plea for understanding and patience, but he no longer had anything left of either. He had long ago accepted his mother's decision not to want to live with them, and found no understanding for this weak, cowardly fellow who had crept around like a ghost every day, as if she had only left him recently. Since he was not a little boy anymore and understood things that had previously seemed like unsolvable mysteries, he refused to see Seamus' brokenness as a consequence of a traumatic injury. And he also refused to forgive his father for making

288

him and Megan unwilling witnesses to his miserable loss.

Tobey leaned on his elbows and squinted into the brightness that had gathered on the horizon. In the distance a woman was moving; a pair of gulls circled over her head like thoughts. Radio music wafted across the parking lot and then, with a dull sound of car doors closing and the rapidly fading noise of an engine and the barely audible sound of the waves, everything grew quiet again. Tobey lit a joint, smoked half, put out the fire with spit and put it back in his jacket pocket. He fell on his back and put an arm over his eyes. His body was heavy. After a while he hummed the song they had rehearsed the night before. He reminded himself that he had been an adult for fifty-four days, but his joy about it gave way to sadness and an emptiness that he could not understand. Along with Jason, who would celebrate his magic eighteenth birthday in December, he eagerly awaited at every opportunity the day when they disappeared to Dublin, the location of future triumphs. When he was alone, he felt discouraged and still hoped something might happen that would keep him from going away.

A few days before he had watched as his father climbed up a ladder to replace a number of loose tiles on the barn roof, and imagined that the clumsy man lost his balance and fell. He remembered newspaper stories in which accidents on farms were reported, electric shock, kicking cows and collapsing haylofts. As he watched his father he fought against the wish to see him dead, but did not consider it wrong to expect something that should have long ago occurred, in his opinion would occur, and indeed must: that Seamus O'Flynn, through his unworldliness, his stubbornness and greed, would perish.

It was dark when Tobey parked the motorcycle against the wall next to the Spillane's house. The next building, an ugly yellow bungalow, was almost a hundred yards away at the end of a field where a few sheep and horses grazed in the summer. The land belonged to Barry's grandfather, who would not permit anything to be built on it as long as he lived. Behind trees and lights could be seen the flashing of a stoplight.

Barry heard the motorcycle and came out of the house. He waved and walked across the courtyard, where there was a Ford station wagon and a van, both bearing the logo of the butcher shop. He had on huge white sneakers, dark green cargo pants and a gray T-shirt. To the dismay of his parents, who still saw him as their successor, he wore his light, thin, hair shoulder-length. In the last two years he had managed to maintain his ideal weight, and because he had finally stopped growing at eighteen, his size appeared only imposing instead of grotesque. Tobey told him that he wanted to go away to Dublin, this very night. They sat in the courtyard, on the plastic chairs that had been located in the Spillane's garden until Deirdre could no longer bear the sight of them. "Do you have a place to stay?" Barry asked. "I'll find something," Tobey said.

They were both silent for a while. Someone rode by on a bicycle; at every pothole the bright sound of the bell rang out. From further up the road came the barely audible rustle of traffic. Wind swept over the field and swirled up straw and balls of sheep's' wool. "Have you already told the others?" Barry asked at some point. "No." Barry nodded, proud to be the first one Tobey let in on his plan. Tobey picked up a few pebbles. Barry did not need to know that he had rung the bell at Mick's for half an hour in vain and wanted Jason to be the first one he called from Dublin. "Can you lend me something?" He asked. "Sure." Barry got up, climbed on a chair and climbed over the wall.

Tobey threw the stones at the pipe that led down from the gutter of the slaughterhouse and disappeared into the tar base. Then he took the joint from his coat pocket, lit it and smoked the whole thing. A woman called out a name in the darkness several times, a shutter rattled, and in one of the backyards a dog barked. Tobey could sense the rain that would fall within a few hours, yet it made the notion of leaving that night even easier. His empty stomach seemed to float in his body. He stood up and

290

walked around. It felt as if he was moving on sand. In the tar lining he saw cracks and scratches, a maze of curves and squiggles and endless lines, the plan of his life.

Barry brought him three hundred Euros. "My parents say you should come in and eat something." Tobey counted the money. "I'm not hungry." He put the bills in the breast pocket of his leather jacket. "Thanks, man. I'll pay it back to you as soon as I can." Barry nodded. "No rush," he said. Although it was cool, they remained seated and looked at the windowless walls of the slaughterhouse.

"How's Megan?" Barry asked as casually as possible. "Good," Tobey said. "When is she beginning her studies?" – "No idea. In a month. A year. Never." – "If you go away, will she stay here?" Tobey shrugged, picked up more stones and threw them against the pipe. Megan had long ago stopped giving the animals on the farm names, but she was still extremely upset when one of them was killed. She had seen the plucked chicken in the kitchen and silently left the house, and he had become aware once again that he understood less and less what was going on in her head and what, apart from the fact that they were siblings, still bound him to her.

"I don't eat meat anymore," Barry said. "For the past two weeks." He grinned as Tobey turned to him. "And what do your parents say about that?" Barry picked up some stones and shook them in the hollow of his hand. "I don't care," he said. "Are you taking over the shop?" – "I don't know. No." Barry let the stones fall between his shoes, one by one, his head bowed. In the last school year, he was asked by the rugby team if he wanted to join them, but he had told them no. He found that he had fought enough, for years, without being noticed by anyone. "Now I'm helping out. Dad's rheumatism is acting up."

Tobey said nothing. A few days ago he had seen Barry behind the meat counter. At work, he wore a white apron and a silly hat, under which he had tied his hair into a knot. Tobey by-passed the shop so he would not embarrass Barry.

"Can you mention it to her," said Barry. "That I don't eat meat any-more, I mean." – "Sure," Tobey said. He knew that Barry had been in love with Megan for years, although his friend had never revealed it to him or his sister. He was convinced that the reason Barry was so tor-mented and had starved himself down to a normal weight was because he hoped Megan would finally appreciate him, now that he was an adult and not a fat sack anymore and a member of a band. Tobey could have told him that he would remain no more interesting to her than all the other young men in the area, but left it alone. He did not know much about his sister's love life, and although a morbid curiosity and jealousy robbed him of his sleep when Megan stayed away all night, he entrenched himself in his ignorance like a dark, uncomfortable cell. What he had learned from the dubious sources who were fed with lies and rumors, was enough for him to suspect that Megan went to Limerick or Galway rather than get involved with a guy from the neighborhood. A few years earlier Declan Boyle, who was then two classes ahead of Tobey, declared that he had overcome Megan O'Flynn's final barricade.

"I'd better get going." Tobey saw the cloud of breath in the light that fell on the wall from the street lamp and lost itself in the yard. He wiped his hands on his pants and stood up. The cold had settled under his skin; he shook his legs. "We'll see each other in Dublin." Barry also got up. "Maybe." He lowered his eyes for a few seconds. Then he looked at To-bey and nodded. "Yes. We'll see each other."

After they had embraced each other awkwardly, Tobey walked to his motorcycle and drove away. Barry remained on the street for a while and looked after him. When the rattling of the BSA finally died away, he could hear his father's voice and the music that came from the open kitchen window. In the garden behind the house Antonia called for the dog, which the family had bought days earlier, after lengthy discussion and against the veto of his grandfather. Kieron Spillane argued that dogs that didn't guard either a farm or a flock of sheep were useless parasites and did not belong in the house, and he acknowledged that he had been overruled with the oblivion of the puppy that seemed to be crazy about him, of all people.

The wind picked up, and Barry pulled the hood over his head. A few weeks earlier he had seen a note on the supermarket bulletin board on which someone had offered a Norton *Commando*. He had long considered photography and imagined himself buying the gadget and driving around through the country with Tobey, but then he had lost the scrap of paper with the telephone number, and when days later he stood in front of the bulletin board, the note was gone.

An old yellow Toyota drove past him without its lights on. The driver, a loyal customer of the butcher shop, waved to Barry, and he waved back. Someone else who saw him standing behind the counter in a plastic apron for the rest of his life, he thought. For a while he remained in the cold evening air, then went through the back door into the house and into his room, lay down on the bed and imagined how Megan would re-act to the news that he had become a vegetarian. He closed his eyes and listened to her humming, like she did back then in the schoolyard.

Tobey parked the motorcycle in front of the barn and looked at the house. It was shortly after nine, and there were no lights on either in the kitchen or in his father's room. Seamus O'Flynn went to bed early, and they often heard him long before midnight moaning and groaning in his sad dreams. Tobey could not see whether Megan was there; her room was around the back. He took off his helmet and drew in the air, which was damp from the coming rain and smelled of earth. For a while he stood at the open stable door and listened to the sounds. The cows were moving in the dark; Sam shuffled his hooves; the pigs grunted in their sleep.

In the kitchen, he drank a glass of milk and turned on the radio. On the table were a dirty plate and an empty teacup. Seamus just left everything where it was, because he knew that Megan would take care of it. Unlike Tobey, who had not been in his father's room for years, every other week Megan carried a basket full of dirty clothes and sheets out of the gloomy room, empty except for a narrow bed and a cupboard which smelled of sweat and cattle and bitterness. Weather permitting, the laundry hung on the lines behind the house, and Tobey pictured his father's shirts and pants, moving in the wind as if they were dancing from relief at being free for a while from that leaden body.

After the last sip of milk he turned off the radio, took a roll of trash bags from a cupboard and went upstairs to his room. Then he pulled out all the bureau drawers and stuffed two pairs of pants, two shirts, and a sweater, T-shirts, underwear, and socks in a garbage bag, which he tied together with string. He put the guitar in the artificial leather case, packed CDs, sheet music, books and odds and ends in the drawers and the closet and put a pair of boots and a pile of music magazines under the bed.

Megan entered the room without knocking. She looked around and sat on the chair in front of the desk.

"Sam is limping," she said after a while. She wore black pajama pants and a white T-shirt. Outside, the trees rustled in the driving wind. Tobey was silent. Soon it would rain, he thought. "Do you even care?" – "Yes." Megan hit her bare foot against the bag. "What's in there?" – "Nothing," Megan looked at her brother. Tobey held her gaze for several seconds, then he rose and took his passport, a pocket knife, a lighter and a handful of change out of his desk drawer, and stowed everything in the pockets of the leather jacket that was lying on the bed. "Are you going away?" When Tobey didn't answer, Megan knelt down, pulled on the garbage bag with both hands and pulled a shirt out of it. "Don't!" Tobey cried. He took the shirt from Megan's hands and crouched down to stuff it back into the bag. "You can't just disappear!" Megan pulled at the garbage bag until it was finally ripped to shreds and the clothes were scattered on the floor. "Stop it, damn it!" Tobey pushed Megan away and gathered up the clothes.

Megan stood there for a few seconds and watched Tobey. When she reached for a sweater, Tobey grabbed hold of her wrist. She squirmed and broke free, jumped to her feet and kicked at the pile of clothes and at Tobey. He grabbed her leg, cursing, and she fell and hit him in the mouth with her elbow. He screamed in pain and anger and rolled over her, pressed down on her with the weight of his body and tried to seize the arms she struck him with. Snorting, she threw her head back and forth and rammed a knee in his back.

After a while Tobey noticed that she had grown tired, as the violence of her rebellion diminished and her breathing grew calmer. Her face, covered by strands of hair, was turned away; she had closed her eyes, still flashing with anger; her eyelids quivered. He lowered his head and felt the sweat from her neck on his cheek, smelled the sleep on her T-shirt. She was breathing normally, the tension in her muscles relaxed. He still held her arms, felt her pulse, the beating of her heart. He lifted his upper body and looked down at her. She relented and turned her head, opened her eyes and looked at him. The notion of hitting her in the face exhausted him so much that he released her wrists. She pulled him down to her, and he gave in and sank, a heavy animal in a warm mire. He found himself in a dream, not in reality. Megan panted softly, her lips were dry. His blood mingled with her saliva. Megan whispered. Heat flowed from her hand. Tobey closed his eyes, forgot his power. Their old life had ended. Outside, the first raindrops fell.

5

Tobey woke up and did not know where he was. He lay in a bed, his head felt heavy. He turned around, waited until his eyes adjusted to the darkness. Then he saw the chair, on which hung his clothes, the cardboard box with his things, the guitar. Light penetrated through a crack in the curtain. Tobey remembered the house in Ranelagh, the dirty white façade, the staircase with the worn steps, the large, cool room.

He rolled onto his back and closed his eyes. Down in the street a car alarm clamored like a startled electric bird. Yesterday they had moved in, Tobey recalled. Jason knew the owner of the house, an old man for whom he sold Moon Boots at the market, hats and gloves, cheap goods from China and Taiwan. Albert Crotty occupied the four rooms on the first floor. Tobey had met him only a few days earlier when they visited the apartment, which had been standing vacant for years. Crotty was eighty-two, and small and narrow, like a child who does not want to eat. He wore gray suits and black ties and shoes, and when he listened, he narrowed his eyes. Tobey had put on his best clothes to make a good impression on the old man, but Crotty seemed not to notice the coffee stains and pen ink on his own shirt, let alone the new jacket Tobey kept for special occasions. The four-room apartment was in a sorry state and really uninhabitable. In the kitchen neither the stove nor the refrigerator worked, in the bathroom the tiles had come loose from the walls, and in all the rooms the cupboard doors, dismantled furniture and wallpaper rolls were scattered on the floor. Like an occupant who visited his destroyed home after a fire, Crotty had broken out in front of every room in low, murmuring lamentations, while Jason had assured him incessantly that his and Tobey's requirements were modest, and they could straighten up the room without much effort. After much persuasion, Crotty had finally agreed to let them rent the apartment for an absurdly low price.

Tobey fumbled for the water bottle beside the bed. He could still feel the last two weeks of work in his bones. He and Jason had carried the broken furniture down to the street, cleaned the floors, painted walls, glued tiles, repaired windows, replaced the old, broken refrigerator with a good used one, and mounted the cabinet doors. Using boards from the hardware store, they constructed bed frames and purchased the cheapest mattresses they could find. Tobey's chair came from the dump, Jason's bed from a renovated hotel. The bed linen, some crockery and cutlery, towels, a kettle and a toaster, they had obtained cheaply at Woolworth's and Oxfam, and even a few books.

The water was warm and still tasted like rust. The angry warble of the alarm stopped, but the siren of a fire truck pierced through the streets, distorted and droning like the howl of a wounded cartoon monster. Today was Sunday, Tobey remembered. On Saturday he had played guitar on Grafton Street and earned a few Euros, just enough to buy beer, eggs and milk and bread and set aside something for the rent. Until a week ago he had worked filling a huge dishwasher in a hotel kitchen with dirty dishes and cutlery. Before that, he dressed up as a sandwich and walked back and forth in front of a branch of Subway and had sorted empty bottles in the basement of a pub from the evening until the early morning hours and connected the hose to a full beer keg when the bartender shouted through the hatch. In the summer he had helped a woman sell fruit and vegetables in Moore Street.

297

Tobey could hear Daphney Maloney rattle a pot lid in the kitchen below him, shut the cutlery drawer, run water into the sink or open the refrigerator door, jangling the jam and pickle jars. The rhythmic beating of a whisk, interrupted by short pauses, penetrated through the floor, then the sound of a knife chopping onions and parsley on a wooden board. Tobey sometimes believed that he could hear the creaky grinding of the pepper mill, the muffled bubbling of boiling water, the movement of the rolling pin over the dough. The smorgasbord of sounds reassured him, gave him the feeling of being witness to a perfect world, which had escaped miraculously from the madness that prevailed outside the house walls.

The room where he had lived until two days ago had been a silent chamber, a sealed box which almost nothing penetrated, neither air nor noise from one of the other apartments or the sunless courtyard. Sometimes the water had rumbled in the pipes or the wind whispered in the kitchen flue, but mostly it remained dead silent. Under him lived a family from India who operated a restaurant in Gardiner Street, and of them Tobey had only seen the grandfather and a little girl who sat in the yard and drew in good weather. The tenant above him had been a young woman from Poland, who he had met occasionally in the stairwell and who had never returned his greeting, whether from shyness or aversion, Tobey could not say. Her name was Jana Panufnik, at least that was what it said on her doorbell, and when she was in her apartment she didn't do anything audible, neither listening to music nor watching TV. It seemed that she always came home at dawn, often when Tobey set off on an early shift, and he imagined how she took off her clothes in her darkened apartment, slipped on a white nightgown embellished with lace, lay down in a coffin lined with velvet and slept all day.

The first five weeks he had lived over a gambling hall in Ringsend, in a square hole with a grilled opening in the wall through which the warm air blew, carrying the scent of burnt bread. He found a job in a Centra supermarket ten days after he arrived in Dublin. On Wednesdays, when he had the day off, he helped out in the gambling hall and sat behind the counter and operated the cash register or went around and gathered up empty bottles and trash. Martin, the owner of the hall, bred zebra finches. If there wasn't much going on, he brought the cage down from his apartment on the first floor and explained to Tobey, what he had to do to care for the animals. The minute customers came—mostly young men in jogging suits and old men with pockets full of cash—and the squawking noise of the machines broke out, Martin carried the cage back to the apartment. Hise living room walls, as Tobey had seen on a short visit, were covered with jungle wallpaper.

Tobey straightened up, pushed aside the curtain a little and looked out. The air, a fine, cloudy fog, stirred outside the window. Below, pigeons perched on the ledges, their bellies tinted yellow by the neon signs of the betting offices. He threw back the covers and sat down. As a child he had been an early riser, but now he did not get out of bed before eleven. He banged out a few chords on the Fender, practiced a tune that he couldn't get out of his head. His fingertips were filled with warmth. He liked the sound of the guitar when it was not connected to the amplifier, which was in the basement where he practiced, wrapped in a blanket. He tried not to think of the farm, or his father, or Megan. For a while he practiced the fingering pattern of a solo that he had not been able to get right for weeks, mumbled a simple-minded text that rhymed without making sense. Finally, he got dressed and went to the bathroom.

Jason sat at the kitchen table. He was wearing plaid slippers lined with lambs-wool, socks, a red track suit and the dark blue winter coat he had taken out of his mother's closet before setting out in the direction of Dublin. The radio was playing so softly that it was drowned out by the muffled noise rising from the street. Jason's head was resting diagonally across his left hand, his right holding a pencil which he used to scribble in a notebook, drowsily and without pausing. His lips moved while writing,

299

and occasionally he gasped for air, as if he had forgotten to breathe.

This was the life that he had wanted all along. This was the kitchen where Jim Morrison ate warmed pasta, where Johnny Rotten washed dishes, humming to himself, where Kurt Cobain watched while the tea was brewing. His room was the room where song lyrics were written on the crumbling plaster of the walls, phrases full of radiant power. This was the apartment where he wrote music history, slowly and drowsily into a tattered, lined notebook, labeled with the word NOTHING.

Jason had arrived in Dublin five weeks after Tobey. His mother had thrown a birthday party for him at Murphy's Tavern, the location of the band's first public failure, her helpless attempt to tell her son one last time that she did not consider making music a suitable lifestyle. She had invited all of his friends that she knew, and made them take a pledge not to tell Jason anything about the party or the place where it was being held. Besides Mick and Barry, none of the boys adhered to the vow of silence, and by the day of the big event Jason had been in on the secret for quite some time. While Katherine Dwyer was at the bakery picking up the cake, decorated with the bittersweet sentiment FINALLY 18! in dark chocolate, Jason gathered up the gifts that were lying around and went to the bus stop. The party had taken place anyway, even without him. Mick and Barry had come, and a few of the boys that Katherine mistook for her son's buddies, and who only showed up because there was free beer. Mick, who had only received the assignment from Katherine a few days earlier to call Jason on the cell phone one hour before the party and persuade him to come to Murphy's Tavern for a beer, played a couple of happy songs on the out of tune piano, while Barry was hopelessly over-burdened with the task of comforting his friend's mother, and drank more than he could handle. While Jason was riding the bus through Limerick, Katherine was reading Barry the message that Jason had left for her on a slip of paper: I AM GONE AND I AM NOT COMING BACK. HAVE FUN AT THE PARTY. When she began to cry, Barry took her outside, accompanied by whispers and giggles.

He had sold the drum set to a boy whose face was covered with bad acne and who had taken away the drums, cymbals and stands in a trailer attached to his moped. The new drums, a black Pearl set with Paiste cymbals, were in a basement room under the hall, where Albert Crotty stored his lackluster treasures. Jason bought it with the money he had been saving for years: pocket money stolen from his mother's wallet, proceeds from the sale of things that he had wrested from Katherine and which he had tired of at some point. To make a rehearsal room out of the basement hole, they taped Styrofoam on the walls and the ceiling and installed a floor of particle board, which they covered with carpet remnants. In the garbage they found two armchairs and bought a gas furnace to heat the room a little before rehearsal. They ran a power cable up the stairs into the storeroom, where Crotty had set up his office. When everything was ready, they inaugurated the space by getting drunk and playing some of their songs. But without a keyboard and bass it didn't sound right, somehow.

A week later Jason brought home a fellow who, with his short hair and excess weight, reminded them of their previous friend Barry, and who was also a bass player. His name was Dermot MacAllister; he was twenty-eight, recently arrived from Glasgow, and his way through Dublin's chaotic music scene was just as uncertain as Jason's and Tobey's. Despite his age, Dermot was not a very good bass player. But he could go all out and mistreated his instrument devotedly, pounding the strings with his paws, sweating and panting. In between, he jumped into the air and lashed out with his legs. At his weight, this was tantamount to a show of strength that Jason, in his childlike enthusiasm and the elation from being permanently inebriated, found brilliant, but Tobey thought was just embarrassing. Because Dermot could not read notes, he recorded the songs in the rehearsal room, to learn them chord by chord in the laundry room of the

301

house where he lived with his Irish wife. They called themselves the Post No Bills and rehearsed three, sometimes four times a week. After two months, their repertoire consisted of six songs. Four of them were punk numbers from Jason's flourishing output, fast and loud and full of rage at everything. One song was called "Burning Flags," another, "Mighty Mother." To ensure that the musical field was not left entirely to Jason, Tobey had written two grunge songs, the first compositions of his life, ambitious experiments with guitar solos, whose implementation demonstrated the limits of his abilities. When writing, he realized that he could easily think up new tunes, but not the lyrics. His attempts at rhyme were miserable, his metaphors hackneyed, and when he imitated other bands, Jason and Dermot recognized the original song after just a few lines. He bought volumes of classical and modern poetry, just to see how untalented he was. He listened to Bob Dylan and Tom Waits and Leonard Cohen and knew he would never get close to them. When he sat on his bed, wrapped in a blanket and struggling for words, it made him think of Megan, who came up with poetry just like that. Then he tore up his sheet of paper and cursed his sister's talent, almost grateful to have another reason to hate her.

The solution to Tobey's problem was named Mick Kavanagh, who wrote lyrics with the same ease with which he had previously written essays. Unlike Jason, who threw around words and phrases and paid no attention to either rhythm or rhyme, Mick told a story in each song that had a beginning and an end. His theme, love, was simple and inexhaustible, and recurred in countless variations. He, who had never been with a girl in school, but was constantly walking around with a broken heart, availed himself when writing the lyrics of the longings and the torments which had constituted his youth. To recall these feelings and to put them into words came to him as easily as putting together notes and mixing sounds and voices. In the lyrics he became an impostor, a sailor, who bragged about storms and islands and whales, without ever having seen

302

the sea.

When a piece was finished, Tobey hummed the tune, accompanying himself on guitar, and recorded it. He sent the CD to Cork, where Mick, accompanied by his mother's concealed pride and the caring skepticism of his father, was studying piano and composition at a private music school. In his abundant spare time, Mick wrote not only the lyrics to Tobey's songs, but also the bass parts for Dermot. The academic program lasted two years and was a compromise which Mick had agreed to with his parents. Although their son had already indicated to them early on that music was his purpose in life, they had prescribed the profession of pharmacist for him. They regarded his piano playing as a hobby, his spending time with the band as a phase which Michael was going to grow out of like other boys grew out of their enthusiasm for souped-up mopeds or horror movies. By paying his way through school, they were assuming the risk of losing their son completely to the unprofitable art of making music, but they secretly held fast to the certainty that he would abandon his youthful exuberance at some point, come to his senses, and take the path they had predetermined, indeed delayed, but all the more insightful and repentant. Condescendingly they saw him through his first semester, sat in the front row at the Christmas concert and applauded, full of sincere love for their unmistakably talented son, and mutually assured themselves of the increasingly remote chance that Michael, of all people, would be one of the three or four who, among the less than two hundred and fifty graduates, would later be able to live their passion.

During Tobey's and Jason's first summer in Dublin Mick visited them. He had grown thinner and taller, but maybe it only seemed that way to Tobey because Mick was dressed entirely in black, his hair was short and he had simply become an adult. He had a travel bag with him and his portable keyboard, and when he got off the train at the Heuston Station, he waved the DEAD END sign that he had taken from the stuffed otter. They ended up in the first pub they saw, where they continued to sit until late at night, drinking whiskey and Coke and talking, breathless and excited just like they had years ago in Jason's room. Mick talked about his studies, of the new musical spheres he had entered, and the world-shaking events of Killorglin. Tobey and Jason praised their exciting new life in Dublin, without mentioning the lousy jobs, the winters in rooms that were difficult to heat, or the countless bands that fought for opportunities to perform around the city. They showed Mick photos of the basement where they practiced and the band, which was no longer called Post no Bills, but Ministry of Fraud instead.

Mick spent the first night on an air mattress beside Tobey's bed. At the time Tobey still lived in his quiet room between the Indian family and the Polish vampire, and Jason with a waitress he had met in a pub in Temple Bar. For the remainder of his three-week stay Mick rented a room in a dormitory at Trinity College. He had written some new songs, listened to Jason's compositions and lectured about the death of punk and the immortality of jazz, which he had just begun to discover. In the rehearsal room, he patiently pointed out errors to Dermot and looked away when the sweating giant performed a leap that was laughable and yet the highpoint of a lousy session. Because they could not agree even after a week on a style, Mick lost interest and spent his days in museums and galleries and taking excursions.

When Mick left, he promised to come back in the fall, but all three of them knew that would not happen. While Mick walked to the train platform Tobey looked him over and suddenly felt infinitely tired and empty. It seemed to him in this instant that it was not only the prospect of a future in a reasonably acceptable band that was disappearing, but also an important part of his past. The rain, which had been occupying his mind for hours, finally struck the roof of the train station concourse. When Mick turned around one last time before he boarded the train, he waved to Tobey. Maybe that was the moment when something seemingly

304

significant ended, he thought, when you recognized that the attempt to carry a piece of your childhood with you into adult life was idiotic and doomed to failure. He stood there until the train left the concourse and then walked over to Jason, who was sitting with a can of beer on a bench and writing in his notebook.

It appeared there was nothing that could have thrown Jason off track, not even the fact that Mick would probably soon turn his back on the band, if he had not done so already, as he travelled back to Cork, to sit in bright classrooms instead of a dark basement, to be with teachers and affluent children instead of his friends. He didn't like Mick's eulogy about the death of punk and the hymns to jazz and fusion, and even though he could play anything on the drums, whatever anybody requested, he found Mick's last compositions too difficult and snobbish, and he doubted that anyone in Dublin wanted to hear this kind of music, with the possible exception of a few stock brokers and tourists; arrogant, white wine sippers, with no sense of what was genuine, spirited, unreasonable. He was constantly dragging new candidates to the basement, more and more wannabe guitar heroes who were always too drunk or too stoned to carry a tune, and were only allowed to come back because they brought drugs: grass, speed, sometimes a little cut cocaine. Every week he put together a new band and gave them names that he forgot or changed the next day. Once he managed to land a gig at an open-air festival whose organizers could not afford the big names. In the sleepless night before the gig, which was taking place on a field in Saggart outside of Dublin, he had the idea to have the band, which was simply called Judge Jason and the Guilty Victims, perform dressed as judges and convicts. Although Tobey and the second guitarist, Owen Kane, a student of political science with a penchant for amphetamines, were against costumes, they appeared on stage the next night in black and white striped pants and vests, while Jason, dressed in a white wig and a black robe, sat behind his drums and announced every song like a courtroom sentence. The festival-goers, at least those who still had a thing for punk and weird costumes or were just simply drunk, were quickly fascinated. Some danced and cheered between numbers, clapped and whistled, whereupon Jason stood up, beat the drumsticks against the microphone stand, and threatened to vacate the premises. Tobey got tangled up in almost every guitar solo and stepped around the sponsor's inflatable, man-sized bottles with rage and shame, but the people seemed to regard it as a component of the show, just like Dermot's leaps into the air.

If there hadn't been a cable fire that caused a power outage, ending the event five hours early, that September evening would have gone down in music history, and if the reporter from the scene page for *Totally Dublin* had written less about the inglorious end of the festival and more about the band, standing the dark, interrupted by the whistles of the public, Judge Jason and the Guilty Victims would have become famous. They would have suddenly gotten offers for gigs, first on the island, then in England and on the continent, would have bought themselves iron balls with leg irons and had background singers dressed as prison guards on stage. They would have proved to Mick and to the world that punk was not dead. At least that was how it seemed to Jason, who had disappeared for days after the fiasco, and then emerged out of nowhere again, with a small stray cat in his arms and new songs in a notebook, that were more bitter and blacker than anything he had ever written.

A month later Tobey landed a gig. He had met a woman who attended the same course in Literary Writing that he did, and whose brother was the manager of a club in Temple Bar, where live concerts were sometimes held. On the quiet Monday nights Simon wanted to try a kind of talent show, where unknown bands would play to win the favor of the audience. He heard a demo CD of the band, which had once again changed their name and was now called *The Spectators*, and found the material unusual enough to give the four guys a chance. After four lectures on con-

306

temporary poetry, which had not made him a better songwriter, he dropped the course and Tobey never saw Janet Devlin again, but the agreement with her brother remained unchanged. Although Jason did not think much of talent competitions, he had no arguments against an appearance at a club in the trendy Temple Bar. They rehearsed more often now and put together two sets of five songs that, at Tobey's and Owen's insistence, relied less on punk. And they would no longer put on costumes.

Then Dermot's wife kicked him out, a day after her thirtieth birthday and five years too late, as she called to him out the living room window, tearful, yet full of rage. She had packed his belongings in the dilapidated Datsun, which was now where he lived. He spent the first two days after the separation in the car, in a parking lot in Clontarf, where he could see the lights of the ferries and freighters in Dublin Bay at night. He imagined that the passengers on board the ships were happy men, souls inspired by confidence, their desires fulfilled under the sparkle of the stars. He found one of Helen's hair clips in the glove compartment and cried. He listened to the radio until the car battery died. When a police officer shined a flashlight into his den of misery and asked him to get out, he called Raymond, the son of his mother's only sister. Because the car would no longer start, they had to leave it behind and ride Raymond's scooter to Drumcondra, where Raymond lived in a two-room apartment.

During the day he lay in Raymond's former study on a folding bed and wallowed in self-blame and self-pity. By late afternoon, before Raymond came home, he left the apartment and sat in a bar where he ordered a beer every hour and hoped the fat waitress would sit at his table and listen to him. When the bar closed, he went to one that was still open, then to Griffith Park. In the first light of day that slowly spread over the city along the edges, he made his way back, stood near the house and waited until Raymond drove up on a scooter, went to his room and fell at last into a sleep fraught with dreams, from which he woke after a few hours, battered and thirsty.

One night he stumbled drunk from a bar onto the street, right in front of a taxi. The car struck his left leg, broke his tibia and shattered his knee-cap. The taxi had just started off, so the force of the impact was respectively low. Nevertheless, Dermot was flung onto the sidewalk two meters away, at the feet of a woman who suffered such a shock that the paramedics who arrived shortly thereafter also had to tend to her. Dermot lay on the wet asphalt and looked at the night sky. He felt nothing. It was pleasant to be lifted up and driven off, immersed in fragments of swirling yellow light and wailing sirens, swaying and lurching, a sweet substance in his veins that let him slip away.

The band visited him in hospital. He smiled as they entered the room he shared with five other men. Magazines, books, fruit baskets and plates of sweets were stacked on all the bedside tables; his alone was empty except for a water jug and a glass. Tobey put the latest issue of *Rolling Stone* on the blanket, Jason a flyer for the club where they would be appearing in three weeks, and Owen a bar of chocolate from the shop beside the clinic. They stood around the bed and listened to the story about the accident, which began with the crash and ended with the awakening after the operation. They could imagine that Dermot had been drunk, and why. After he failed to show up for their rehearsal on Monday, Tobey and Jason had searched for him and learned from a neighbor that Helen had moved in with her parents in County Wicklow. Two days later, when Dermot didn't turn up at their rehearsal room in the basement again, Tobey went to the police, but it wasn't until the accident happened that the missing person was found.

Although the attending physician had advised him against it, a week after his release Dermot appeared on the stage of the Silver Skull, a second-rate club in Temple Bar, and flailed, woozy from pain medication, on the strings of his bass. His left leg was bandaged from ankle to hip and kept stable by a construction of rods and cuffs. He played poorly. He was out of practice and his thoughts seemed far away, and he suffered because his healthy leg was tired and he couldn't perform any jumps. After three numbers he had to sit down on a bar stool; during the second set he stayed in the dressing room. The people didn't want an encore, but only a few of them booed. The Spectators cleared the stage and disappeared forever.

The next day they were called Plastic Surgery Unit, but Owen Kane was no longer a member. He said he wanted to concentrate on his studies. They sat in a pub in Anners Lane, drank coffee and smoked. Dermot wasn't there; the gig hadn't done his leg any good. When Jason saw that he couldn't stop Owen, he threw all the money he found in his pockets on the table and walked out. In front of the pub, he struck his palms against the window and then crossed the street, without paying attention to cars, which had to slow down because of him.

Tobey, too, thought about putting away his guitar for a while and looking for another job, maybe a different apartment. He realized that he had been flailing around for a year in this huge, scary city, which he endured just to the point that he did not flee from it. He had been playing guitar because that was something familiar, something that reminded him of former times, the best part of his past. He had attached himself to Jason, whose equally creative and destructive energy was enough for two, had closed his eyes and let himself drift in a river of music and illusions and drugs. But now Jason's promises of success tired him. He did not want to memorize the ever-changing band names anymore, did not want to approve the next parade of stoned guitarist or watch Dermot's leg heal. He longed to slow down, for daylight, for a kind of pattern. He wished Owen all the best and resolved to talk to Jason.

But then Mick came. Unannounced, he appeared at the door one day in February, even more serious and thinner and dressed in even more black. He had dropped out of his classes, seven months before receiving his diploma, which, he said, wasn't worth the paper it was printed on. His parents had told him they considered his time in Cork as an interlude, which would end with his return to Killorglin, where he would train to be a pharmacist. His refusal was followed by their threat to end his allowance, and before it came to that he grabbed his suitcases, took a bus to Tralee and then the train to Dublin. David and Margot Kavanagh no longer understood their simple world, found emotional support from Father MacMahon, and talked with Katherine Dwyer, all of whose letters to Jason had remained unanswered and who considered it almost luck to meet fellow sufferers.

Mick brought back the old spirit of the band. The fire of jazz burned in him, but he was willing to reduce it to an ember, and, together with Tobey and Jason, to search for a style in which none of them had to compromise too much. He found a room in public housing in Ranelagh, just two miles away from Tobey and Jason, and a job as a pianist in a hotel. At the same time he gave piano lessons for children of wealthy families. He earned enough money to pay the rent, to eat, and to put away something toward a used keyboard, a forty-year-old *Roland*, that had been waiting for him since time immemorial in the basement of a music store, because he was the only man in Dublin who appreciated the instrument's repertoire of old-fashioned sounds. He made the trio pledge to stay away from coke and speed and to limit alcohol and cannabis, like the old days. As of now they rehearsed four times a week, more or less sober, and wasted no time fooling around. Each of them contributed a few songs, except Dermot, who was happy if Mick's arrangements did not completely overwhelm him. Although they were anxious for gigs and needed money, they did not make the mistake of leaving the rehearsal room too soon. They tried many new things, afforded themselves the luxury to be picky, argued and made up again and felt that they were on to something that was worth the effort. At the beginning of spring, they had reinvented themselves as a band and even agreed on a name.

310

Jason's current girlfriend, an unemployed fashion designer with a *Prada* pocket full of pills, took pictures of them standing in front of a factory building and looking earnestly into the camera. In the rehearsal room, they made a demo CD and sent it to all the important people in the Dublin music scene. The owner of a nightclub on Parliament Street let them perform. He wrote in the program notes that The Loyal Treaters sounded like a mixture of the early Police and Talking Heads, which Mick and Tobey felt was high praise, and Jason regarded as at least not an insult. The audience liked them, generously overlooked several slip ups, and demanded an encore. The performance was followed by others, all in small clubs. They played at a Newcomer's Festival in Limerick and an Open Air Festival in Wexford, and one gig led to another. Because Tobey was the only guitarist left after Owens's departure, he practiced every day and grew better and more confident. After a gig in a pub in Sandyford, he spent the night with a woman who had come behind the stage for his autograph, and although she was gone the next morning, he felt for the first time in his life like a real rock star. Dermot was still suffering over his separation from Helen, drank too much and limited his bass playing to a few variations, simple chord progressions that any beginner could handle after a month. When the weather changed he noticed his bad leg, drank even more and played even worse. Mick wanted to get rid of him, but Tobey and Jason always put in a good word for him, though they saw for themselves how much he hurt the band.

During the second week of May Tobey's father died. Barry called and said Megan had found him in his shed. Seamus O'Flynn's battered heart had stopped beating while he was busy trying to repair the broken handle of a sickle. Tobey went to Killorglin, and when he got to the farm by taxi, Megan was no longer there. In the kitchen there was a letter in which she told him she had done everything necessary for the funeral and relinquished all claims on the farm to him. She wrote nothing about where she was and what she was doing. At first Tobey took it for a bad joke, but when he saw the bare rooms and the empty stable, he knew she was actually gone and would not be coming back any time soon. He tried to reach his uncle in Clonakilty, but the line was dead, and when he called the furniture factory, they told him Aidan was somewhere on the road in the wilderness of Canada. He met with Father McMahon to discuss the progress of the funeral, and with Barry, who told him that he had helped Megan sell the sheep, pigs and cows. Sam had died of old age, a year after Tobey went away, and was buried near the tree in whose shade he had stood on sunny days. Feargal Walsh, who, thanks to Father MacMahon's regular visits had regained God and speech, had talked about it in the store, and about the fact that she had given all the neighbors chickens, but not him. Barry was still very excited because Megan had turned to him, and when Tobey told him she had left for an unknown destination, he was stunned. He promised to come to the funeral, but Tobey didn't want to have anyone around him on that day. His sister was missing, his uncle had left town without notice, and his mother did not respond to the letter from the authorities, a copy of which had been dispatched to Tobey, with the comment that he should get in touch with the agency to review questions about the inheritance. None of them would be there when Seamus O'Flynn's remains were placed in the earth, and Tobey intended to let the brilliance of their absence shine forth. His behavior puzzled Barry, and he had to promise to report to him the day after the funeral. Gareth Dunne, whose harvester Seamus had borrowed from time to time, came into the church to render his last respects to his neighbor, as well as Jim Maher, the seed seller with button eyes and transparent ears. Bridie O'Hara was there, who never missed a funeral, and John Hanlon, the sullen, always freezing sexton, who was waiting in the last row of pews until the crowd of mourners passed and he was able to lock the church door. Feargal Walsh sat next to Tobey and sobbed during the priest's entire speech. He smelled of peat fires and barn and brandy, and when he blew his nose into his handkerchief it sounded like someone in sheer agony put a curse on this place, which no longer offered him any consolation. Before the ceremony started, Father MacMahon had asked Tobey whether he intended to say a few words, but Tobey had declined; he did not want to send a conciliatory lie along behind his father, and spared everyone present his reckoning.

He spent the night in a B & B outside Killorglin and took a taxi to the farm again the next day. In his room, he stuffed a few things in a travel bag, closed all the doors and put the keys in the hiding place which Megan knew. When he sat in the garden next to the fire pit by the apple tree and found a charred page from an old sketchbook of his sister's, an infinite sadness seized him, and he went back into the house, wrote Megan a letter and put it on her bed. Then he found that what he had written was foolish and full of errors, stuck the page in his pocket and left the house.

He went on foot to the place that, through the vast world of childhood, had grown small and wonderless. In the dilapidated barn on Fintan Kilduff's property was the grave stone that Megan had set up for a run-over cat. She had scratched SALLY in the sandstone with a nail, and below that: MURDERED. He could well remember the day when he and Megan had found the animal by the side of the road. Megan had dug a hole with her bare hands and a piece of wood and buried the corpse with dignified gravity, but without the religious mumbo-jumbo she so loathed. She claimed to know the man who had the animal on his conscience, and a week later it got around the village that Terry Lawlor's BMW had been so badly vandalized that the young racer broke down crying at the sight of his one-and-all and had not been responsive for days. Almost reverently, the men described to each other how scarcely a square centimeter of the midnight-blue metallic paint was left without a scratch, how the perpetrator had cut the rubber seals around the windows out of their frames, skillfully bent the windshield wipers and slashed the tires. And in a mixture of indignation, pity, and joy, they jabbered on about poor Terry, who had been absent from his job at the hardware store and had grown pale and thin ever since that terrible Sunday, on which a fanatical car hater had torn out a piece of his heart. Rumors and speculation about the possible perpetrator made the rounds, but unlike the case of the desecrated shed, Tobey knew this time that his sister was responsible for this act of revenge, even if she had never admitted it to him.

In the early afternoon they drove to Glenbeigh in Barry's car. His parents had paid for Barry's driving lessons under the condition that he helped in the shop for at least two more years. His father's rheumatism nagged him even more and Antonia had moved to Galway, where she was training as a kindergarten teacher. He did not have to go to the slaughterhouse; the meat grinder and the sausage machine were set up in the room behind the shop. Once he had the license in his pocket he bought an eleven year old Nissan, which he battered and scratched so badly while still on the premises of the car dealer, who stared in disbelief, that his parents didn't even request that he display the butcher shop logo on the doors.

They lay down in the sand a few steps from the parking lot and looked into the sky; the sun filled the spring with pale white light. Except for the constant sound of the surf and the occasional cry of gulls, it was quiet. Tobey talked about Dublin, about the lousy rooms in the early days, old Crotty, about the stoned guys Jason had brought to the rehearsal room, about the unsuccessful performances and the turnaround brought about by Mick's appearance. Barry had heard it all already on the phone, but he urged Tobey to repeat the stories. He kept on asking, insisted on a description of the smallest details, and could not get enough of the images of the city, which seemed to him to be, despite its pervasive sadness and inhospitality, a place of boundless vitality, as far away from Killorglin as the nearest inhabited planet.

Tobey had to spend the evening with Barry's parents and his grandfather. Deirdre had invited him to dinner and brooked no opposition. There were plenty of meat and potatoes and fried eggs for Barry. Niamh and the grandfather took every opportunity to comment on Barry's vegetarianism. Niamh was affectionately teasing, while Kieron Spillane displayed his lack of understanding with scorn and an expression of ridicule. Both believed Tobey, who was hungry and polishing off more schnitzel, was on their side, and tried to draw a conclusion from him which would confirm their opinion that Barry was a misguided dreamer, embarrassing for the family and their tradition. To put Barry in the shop behind the counter was about the same as if you had placed a Muslim preacher in the pulpit of a Catholic church, Kieron said. But Tobey let their taunts and attacks fall on deaf ears and responded that everyone should live as they thought fit, and besides, he knew a deaf record seller in Dublin. That didn't help Niamh and Kieron and they wanted an explanation from Tobey, but then Deirdre brought in the dessert and coffee and forbade the men from any further discussion on the subject, that their argument had disturbed the family peace for far too long. She asked Tobey to tell them about Dublin, which he did in dazzling colors. Kieron listened to this a while in silence and skepticism, then he went outside with the dog, who had been lying under the table the entire time. A breeze came up and stirred the green and yellow checkered flag of Kerry, which was stretched on a rope between the house and the property wall. The dog was barking in the garden; Kieron whistled through his fingers.

After dinner Tobey and Barry walked to the shed next to the ruins of the former rope factory. They paused at the sight of the interior, now totally different, and exchanged a few words with three drunk boys who were just about to turn a chair into kindling to fire the furnace. Barry knew all three, Tobey one by sight. Rory was the little brother of Louise Nesbitt, the girl who had not resisted being kissed by Tobey five years earlier. He also knew who Tobey was, and asked whether the stories they told about him and Jason Dwyer and Mick Kavanagh were true, but Tobey did not want to provide them with any additional material for gossip. They left the boys with their beer and their fantasies, went to the field and sat on the top platform of the crane, where they could see the lights of the suburbs, and further away, could imagine the blackness of the sea. Barry had said very little during dinner, and even now he was silent. Tobey tried to cheer him, by calling his father and his grandfather Spillane stupid windbags. Because Barry's mood did not improve, he stood up and imitated Dermot MacAllister's awkward leaps for a while, until his friend laughed. Clouds were pushing in from the coast and covered the few stars above their heads. From the shed, the boys' jeers rang out. Tobey said that it would rain in less than ten minutes. They climbed down, walked to the car and drove off, while the first drops began to bounce against the windshield.

They sat in a pub which they had only rarely visited before. The Red Fox Inn was a few miles outside Killorglin, not far from Caragh Lake. At one table sat a family with four children, at another an old married couple. A radio was playing, Irish folk music mixed with the voices of the guests. Tobey drank beer, Barry cola, because he was driving. Sheepishly Barry explained that Megan had hugged him when he told her he had become a vegetarian. He said she would definitely come back soon, and Tobey let him believe it. Then they talked about music and instruments, and Tobey talked about Mick's forty-year-old keyboard, the rehearsals, which proceeded with much more discipline than before, and how hard it was to convince Dermot that he had to work hard and improve if he wanted to stay on as the Loyal Treaters' bassist. He asked Barry if he was still playing, and Barry was almost embarrassed to admit that he still practiced on the bass every day, even though he was not in a band anymore.

When they walked to the car hours later, Tobey looked into an open garage illuminated by white light, where he saw a man repairing the handle of a metal bucket, and he began to cry. He was standing in the nearly empty parking lot, shaken by violent sobs that exploded from within him like the sudden fever of long-suppressed disease. It had stopped raining. A dog trotted past the deserted tables and chairs of the beer garden, hanging his head, tired or lost in thought. Barry did not know what to do; he continued to stand a few meters away from Tobey and went over to him only after a while, to lay a hand on his shoulder. He wanted to say something, but there was nothing he could think of that made any sense or offered any consolation. Tobey, his hands over his face and his upper body bent forward, struggled for air, trembling and groaning, turned and walked quickly across the asphalt lot to a tree beside the road, leaned with his eyes closed against the trunk, pressed both hands against the damp bark and took a deep breath in and out, until the pressure had eased in his chest and he opened his eyes and looked at the garage, where there was no longer a light and no man. He kicked the trash can that was standing beside a wooden table, the surface coarse, as if it had been hewn with an axe. Bottles and cans rolled across the ground; the wind was too weak to blow away the newspapers and potato chip bags. Barry said something, so quietly that Tobey did not understand him. The dog stopped and looked over at him, an old animal, thick and bulky like a sheep in winter wool. Tobey picked up a beer bottle and hurled it against the tree, but it didn't shatter. He threw it a second time, and even then it didn't break. For a while he just stood there and stared at the tree, as tired as the dog. Eventually Barry touched him on the arm, and together they went to the car, got in and drove away.

The next morning Barry picked Tobey up from the B & B, but instead of going to the station in Tralee he drove past Farranfore and Castleisland toward N 21, which led to Limerick. Tobey said nothing. He leaned back in his seat, and although his head still hurt, and a heaviness pressed in on his chest and stomach, he smiled. The street was empty and shiny from the rain; it looked as if it had been built just for Barry and him and would dissolve into the dull gray nothingness behind them like a bridge that existed only in dreams.

Tobey stood in front of the bathroom mirror and shaved. Warm air rose from the electric stove beside him. Laundry hung on lines above the bathtub, whose walls of rusty water had been painted with sepia-colored patterns. It smelled of paint and the glue under the freshly laid tiles, which sparkled dark blue in between the old ones which had turned dull from the chalk. A ladder leaned against one wall; its rungs, covered with plaster and splashes of paint, led to a hopper window. Jason had replaced the broken pane with a new one the day before. Instead of putty or silicone he used electrical tape and then declared that the renovation work was over, even though the items on the list that he and Tobey had created were all nowhere near checked off.

After Tobey had finished dressing, he went into the kitchen. Jason was still sitting at the table and scribbling in his notebook. The cat was lying on his lap and raised its sleepy head when Tobey entered the room, blinked at him and curled up again. Jason had given him the name *Rotten*, because the animal had been neglected and sick when he found it in the front garden of a condemned house in Kilmainham. He had spent the previous night in the emergency room of St. Jame's Hospital, where he had waited for a doctor to tell him that his chance acquaintance, who had collapsed during her alcohol delirium, was doing well under the circumstances. After he had left a fancy name and a false address and phone number at the reception desk, he had aimlessly walked through the streets of a neighborhood at dawn and landed at a construction site where the thin, filthy animal was sleeping in an overturned bucket.

Weak sunlight pierced through the window. It was lunch time; most people sat eating their meal; hardly any noise intruded from the street. Although the heater was running Tobey shivered and he went to the stove, put water on for coffee and put two slices of bread in the toaster. While he waited, he heard the sound of Jason's pencil on paper. "The weather is getting better," he said. Jason stopped writing and looked at him as if he had not noticed his presence until now. "What?" He asked. "The weather," said Tobey. "It will be good." He poured boiling water over the coffee powder. "Should we go out? It will be raining again at five." The cup warmed his hands. "Sunday," Jason said softly. "Elves and fairies." Tobey nodded, smeared butter on the toast. "Elves and fairies," muttered Jason, and his hand slid with the pen across the paper.

Tobey ate and drank while standing, then he went to his room and put on shoes and a coat. Rotten slipped through the door and looked around, and before he could crawl under the bed, Tobey lifted him and took him outside. Jason was waiting in the hallway. He was wearing red sneakers, black leather trousers and a dark blue winter jacket on which his mother had sewn hundreds of shiny silver buttons, which made the fabric look in places like the scales of a lizard. Tobey poured some dry food on a plate and sat it in front of Rotten. While the cat hastily ate, Tobey and Jason left the apartment. In front of the door they found a pot with a piece of paper attached that said WARM UP! Tobey carried Daphney Maloney's Irish stew into the kitchen and stashed it in the fridge. In the evening they would eat until the pot was empty, rinse it, and put it in front of Daphne's door with a note inside that said THANK YOU! The neighbor had started the Sunday ritual when Tobey and Jason were renovating the apartment and fed on bread, cheese and sardines, and it looked like she wanted to continue it for a while. Rotten, who had not left a single crumb on the plate, rubbed Tobey's legs and made complaining, demanding sounds. Tobey picked him up and set him in the hallway, closed the kitchen door and left the apartment. Jason was standing in the stairwell. The buttons on his back glistened metallically in the light that fell from the upper window.

Half an hour later Tobey and Jason sat on a bench in Mount Pleasant Tennis Club and watched two girls, fourteen-years old at the most, training. The sun was somewhere above them, an enormous pool of spilled light. There was no wind, just the sound of balls being struck could be heard, and occasionally birds chirping in the trees that surrounded the club grounds. Sometimes one of the girls groaned when she flailed at the ball, or let out a loud groan on impact. Then Jason tilted his head back slightly and smiled. "We should write a song about them," he whispered. "Yes, we should," Tobey said. He felt good, almost happy. They had placed a folded blanket over their legs like old men in the park. A blackbird was singing. No instrument can sound like that, Tobey thought, and closed his eyes.

In the afternoon they met in the rehearsal room. Barry was already there and was screwing around on his amplifier. He had grown a beard and tied his hair in a pony tail. The first two weeks he had stayed with Jason and Tobey; now he shared an apartment in an old building with four students in Dundrum. On that evening he had arrived in Dublin with Tobey, he had called his parents and told them he wanted to stay a while and think about his future, which left Niamh and Deirdre Spillane speechless and plummeting into a deep depression.

Barry was the new bassist for the Loyal Treaters. Dermot had tried in vain to win back Helen, giving her the car that he never used. He had left it at the door and promised to stop making music and to find a real job. He had borrowed money from Tobey and Mick, bought a suit and invited Helen to a restaurant in Fleet Street, but she wasn't taken in by him a second time. She sold the car and settled a part of the lawyer's fees with the pathetic proceeds. When Dermot got the divorce papers he drank even more and began to gobble up pills. He arrived late to rehearsals or not at all. Once he was indeed in the rehearsal room on time, but had forgotten his bass. At first Barry only filled in for him, but it was clear that Dermot would forfeit his place in the band. One month after Barry's arrival in Dublin, Dermot overslept during an appearance and did not answer the phone. Mick and Tobey went to his apartment, where a neighbor told them that Dermot had moved out weeks ago. Tobey once again filed a missing person's report with the police, and again Dermot Paul MacAllister was found in a hospital. He had gulped down painkillers and sleeping pills, and only survived because he had fallen asleep at the YMCA with a lit cigarette in his mouth. The cigarette had set his mattress on fire and tripped the fire alarm. He did not smile anymore when his friends entered the room, and he did not speak a word. He seemed not to recognize the visitors, staring through them, his eyes puffy, his face bloated. Tobey had brought along the new issue of *Rolling Stone* but took it back, just like Mick did with the box of chocolates.

They were rehearsing two new songs, one by Mick and one by Jason. In an elegiacal ballad Barry played accordion instead of bass, and all four of them beamed. They thought about the old times and dredged up episodes, euphoric and nostalgic like veterans at a victorious battle. They brought entire summers to the dim light of the basement, larger-than-life scenes and fleeting images, distant, vanishing sounds, immature emotions. They tossed out phrases the way they used to throw the rugby ball, laughed and fell silent and shook their heads in disbelief at the sight of their own history. They didn't see Dermot until he was standing in the room. He had grown thin; in his faded green parka he actually looked skinny. His wet hair stuck to his skull; the pale, freshly shaved skin of his face shone. The door closed behind him; he blinked. The amplifier hummed like an electric hive; rain water rushed in the gutters behind the walls. Dermot was holding something black in his right hand and lifted it with a slow, flowing movement to his temple. The crack of the weapon exploded between the walls, penetrated the Styrofoam and encountered stone, backfired in the form of a shock wave, exploded a second time in the heads of the four boys and left trembling air that smelled like sulfur, like something sweet and heavy, and silence.

Part Three

RAIN

1

In the light of dawn she crept out of the sleeping bag and went to the water. From the interior of the island the first birds called, sporadically, drowsily. The sea washed slowly and almost silently over her feet. Cool air blew over her body. The thought of being abandoned touched her with sudden intensity, and she shuddered. She felt the sand flow around her ankles as she sank down into it. While falling asleep there had been a song in her head; now she took the melody up again, humming to the rhythm of the waves, which were no higher than a cat's back and broke a few steps in front of her—a crackling murmur, paper being crumpled, one sheet after another, softly, slowly. The sunlight was a pale yellow that rose slowly upward like liquid on fabric. Megan crouched down and washed her face.

Minutes later she made her way onto the path with her bag on her back. Dazzling brightness spread over the beach and fell on the surface of the water and on the leaves of the palm trees that loomed into the sky like paper silhouettes, unmoved by any breeze. The birds had awakened each other and affirmed their presence and were now silent again. The sand was warm under Megan's feet, and she put on the sneakers that she had been carrying in her hand. Behind a bend she saw a ship that seemed to lie at anchor, fifty, perhaps a hundred meters away. She stopped, then went up the embankment and moved in the shadows of the trees on a partial boardwalk that ran in a crooked line between the sea and the forest. The ship was not very big, but made of metal. It reminded Megan of the fishing vessels in Dingle Bay, which she had seen as a child. She sat down and waited, and when she was sure that nobody was on board, she got up and followed a well-worn path that led into the dark silence between the tree trunks. Here the air was palpable, warm and humid and smelled like mildew, like something slowly decomposing. A persistent noise came from the ground, a prickling and scraping, quietly, work performed in secret. Above it hovered the endless hum of insects like the sound from the inside of a huge electrical system.

Megan saw the woman at the same second she herself was discovered, and she stopped. The woman also paused in her steps. She wore a white T-shirt, a blue scarf wrapped around the waist and sandals on her feet. Her short hair was blond, her skin tanned. Megan raised her hand. The woman looked around, but continued to press a rolled red bath towel against her stomach with both hands.

"Hello," Megan said, just loud enough to overcome the distance.

"Who are you?" the woman cried.

"I thought I might find a job here." Megan took a few steps toward the woman, who again looked around in all directions. "I'm a veterinarian."

"Who sent you?"

"Nobody." Megan stopped about ten meters away from the woman. "I worked for Jeffrey Salter."

The woman thought for a moment, but did not seem to recognize the name. "How did you get here?"

"In a powerboat. Three men brought me. Fishermen." The woman looked over Megan's shoulder, as if the men might appear from the trees behind her. "You shouldn't be here."

"Why?" Megan stretched out her arms, as if to show that she was unarmed, a harmless visitor.

"You have to leave."

"I can't. The men are long gone."

Nearby a bird cried, and the woman jumped.

"Can I talk to someone?" Megan asked. "Maybe with the director of the research station?"

The woman said nothing. She continued to look at Megan but her eyes were expressionless, tired like those of a mother who has given up even the attempt of trying to teach her child something.

Megan walked the final steps toward the woman. "My name is Megan O'Flynn." She reached out her right hand.

The woman lowered her eyes. It seemed as if she would press the towel even more tightly against her stomach. Megan guessed she was probably in her mid to late twenties. They were the same size, but the woman had a powerful physique and a round, soft face. Jeffrey Salter had shown her a photo of five women and eight men. They stood in front of a building that had the letters IPREC painted above the entrance in blue on the white façade. Megan could not remember the face of the woman who was standing in front of her. Certainly the staff changed constantly on the island, she thought, and people changed their appearance over time.

Megan dropped her arm. "I'll see you later," she said, and walked past the woman along the path in the direction where she suspected she would find the research station. When she turned around the woman was still standing there, motionless, face turned toward her.

After the twilight of the forest the clearing appeared in front of her like a reservoir filled with brightness. In the meantime the air had warmed up; a few inches above the ground it began to quiver. At the edges of the rectangular field, between two rows of white painted stones, cut grasses and shrubs grew knee-high. Shoe prints and the tracks of a rake and a wheelbarrow covered the road. The building Megan approached was perhaps ten meters long and built of bricks. It stood on columns of concrete piles and had a red corrugated iron roof, on which solar panels were mounted. On the once-white façade five dark blue letters were emblazoned: IPREC. To the left, on the short end of the clearing, Megan saw a wooden house on stone pillars, the floor boards painted white and the window frames blue. A fishing rod leaned against the railing of the staircase that led up to the door.

A man appeared from behind the wooden building and headed for the clearing. He was wearing a white T-shirt, dark blue trousers and a baseball cap of the same color. He had a shovel over his shoulder, and he stopped when he saw Megan.

After a few steps Megan also stopped. "Hello," she called, raising her hand.

The man did not return the greeting. He spoke into a walkie-talkie and then seemed to wait. Although the last rain had obviously fallen some time ago, he was wearing rubber boots. Nothing about him was threatening. He rested the shovel blade on the ground and grasped the handle with both hands. His gaze turned to Megan.

Megan took one of the two water bottles out of her bag and drank until it was empty. She thought about the straw hat that had flown from her head on the boat trip and which she would have now gladly put on.

A few minutes later another man came along the road. He was bald and slightly larger than the one with the shovel, but fatter. He was wearing sneakers, sand-colored knee-length pants and a bright yellow shirt with short sleeves. When he got closer, he took off his sunglasses and looked at Megan.

"Hello," said Megan, without stretching out her hand this time.

"Who are you?" the man asked. He narrowed his eyes, which distorted his face into a grimace, expressing the greatest discomfort. "What are you doing here?" His voice was a bit too high; his accent sounded French.

"My name is Megan O'Flynn. I heard about this island and I'd like to work here."

"Work?" The man's mouth puckered.

"I'm a veterinarian."

"That's not possible," the man said quickly and then ran his hand through the air, as if he was shooing away an insect. "It's impossible." He put on his sunglasses. "Impossible."

"Are you the head of the research station?"

It seemed as if the man had to think about the question. "Well," he said finally and without looking Megan in the eyes more than a fraction of a second, "I can assure at least that we . . . that we aren't hiring anybody. Nope."

"I can do any kind of work," Megan said. "Cleaning. Cooking. Whatever our want."

"We have a cook," the man said quickly, again with a dismissive gesture. "How did you get here? Who sent you?"

The question, who had sent her, asked for the second time, made Megan laugh. "Nobody. Professor Salter told me about the research station. I'm looking for . . . "

"Jeffrey Salter?" the man interrupted.

"Yes."

The man's expression changed from strained to thoughtful. His skin was light brown. Thousands of freckles, only slightly darker than his skin, covered his arms and hands, neck, face and bald head. His eyelashes were almost translucent, his lips pink and brittle.

"You know him?"

The man looked at Megan, slightly confused. "An acquaintance," he said. "How did you get on the island?"

"Fishermen brought me in their boat."

"Fishermen," the man repeated. He rested his chin on his chest and looked at his sneakers, which were tied with frayed cords. After a while he raised his head. "How do they know . . . ? We're not so easy to find."

"I searched for a long time. Jeffrey could only tell me . . . " Megan fell

329

silent when she heard the engine noise.

The two men turned their heads. A vehicle that looked like an army jeep, painted white, with a flat, worn fabric roof mounted on poles, appeared at the other end of the clearing and stopped in front of the brick building. A larger, thinner man in a light suit rose from his seat, climbed the stairs and disappeared into the house.

"Come along," said the bald man and started walking.

Megan followed him. The Filipino with the shovel walked a few steps behind her. The sky was a gray metallic blue and cloudless; the sun was indistinguishable from this vast brightness. There was still no wind; not a single breath of air moved the dust raised by the man's shoes.

In the room Megan entered, it was dark. Only the light that fell behind her through the open door kept her from stumbling as she walked behind the man. A carpet cushioned their steps. Music wafted toward them, so quiet that Megan perceived only the high notes. She felt the cool air in the building, even though the ceiling fans in the corridor were not turning. Framed pictures hung on the walls, but she could not figure out what they represented.

The music ended seconds after the man knocked on the door where he had stopped.

"Yes!" The voice was loud, the sound irritated and bored at the same time. A drawer rumbled as it was pushed shut.

The bald man opened the door and leaned halfway into the room. "You have to take care of something," he said, opened the door wide and took a step aside so the man at the desk could see Megan.

If the man was surprised he did not show it. He folded his hands over his stomach and looked at Megan. His suit jacket was hanging over the chair. The hat he had worn outside lay on the table next to a bottle, a half -full glass and the anatomical model of a head with an open skull. Behind him was a window; light penetrated through the cracks in the lowered

330

blinds.

"She just appeared," said the man with the bald head. "Claims that she came with fishermen in a boat; nobody sent her."

The man behind the desk did not take his eyes off Megan. "Is that right?" He asked quietly.

"Yes. Last night," Megan said. "I heard about the research project and would like to work here."

The man closed the skull, and then he laughed.

"She knows Jeffrey Salter," said the bald man.

"I worked for him." Megan took a step forward and now stood on the threshold between the hallway and office. "I'm a veterinarian."

The man shook his head in amusement, emptied his glass and stood up. "Come in," he said, pointing with a sweeping movement of his arm to the chair that stood in front of the desk. Then he pulled the bamboo blind up halfway.

Megan entered the room, put the backpack on the floor and sat down.

"She can't stay," the bald man said in a low voice, as if Megan would not be able to hear him then.

"All right, Malpass, I'll take care of it." The blond man nodded his chin toward the door. Malpass understood immediately, left the room and closed the door behind him. The blond man stopped and stared at the wall, as if he was trying to see through it. "You can go!" he cried and listened to the steps departing down the corridor before he held out his hand to Megan. "Torben Raske."

Megan grabbed his hand. "Megan O'Flynn."

Raske sat down. Megan guessed him to be forty-five, fifty at most. He had a long, angular face, a narrow mouth and blue eyes. His hair was straw-blond and just long enough that one combed-back strand fell again and again over his forehead. Tanned, with perfect white teeth, he fulfilled almost every condition for good looks, and yet there was something that prevented Megan from finding him attractive.

331

"Then let me hear what you have to say," Raske said and leaned back in his chair.

"I worked for Jeffrey Salter. He told me about the island."

Raske rubbed his chin. "Jeffrey Salter. I think he was a member of the Board for many years. How is he?"

"Good, I think. He's in Australia for a month."

"What exactly did he tell you?"

"That you're working with primates here. Behavioral research and communication. All very unorthodox."

A grin passed over Raske's face. "Yes, we don't do the usual science stuff here, that's for certain. We're not interested in quick successes or spectacular discoveries. Since its beginning, IPREC has provided the rarest and most valuable resource available to those of us who do research." He paused. "Time," he said then and smiled, as if he wanted to take away the weight of his words. "And we have plenty of that here." He moved his chair closer to the table. "On the island it passes more slowly than elsewhere." He leaned back and spread his arms. "How old am I? Guess."

Megan acted as if she had not already assessed her opponent long ago. "Forty?" She said.

Raske beamed. "Fifty-two," he said. "In Europe, I would probably look sixty, and I'd feel seventy." He crossed his arms over his chest and smiled dreamily. "But back to the question of how you found us. I mean, we're not exactly in the phone book."

"Jeffrey could only tell me which region I should search. He came here once. By helicopter."

"I think I remember. That was some years ago."

"When I started out, I didn't think I'd find the island. But I can be stubborn."

"True." Raske grinned.

"I hope I didn't break any rules by coming here."

332

"No, that's not it. Don't worry. It's just . . . Since we work with apes, it's important to observe certain precautions. Visitors can bring diseases to the island."

"I'm healthy."

"Obviously." Raske let his gaze rest on Megan for a while. "Who did you say brought you here?"

"Fishermen."

Raske nodded. "And how did they know where the island was?"

"They didn't know. We sailed around for a long time before we landed here."

Raske folded his hands and rested his chin on them. "Where did you set off from?"

"I don't remember. It was a tiny, backwater town. A few huts on the coast. Sopang. Bulong. Something like that. After I left Manila, I spent a week traveling." Megan let her voice sound casual. She held Raske's gaze. She lied, and it was clear to her that he knew it.

"I understand." Raske nodded again. Then he got up with a jolt. "A drink? I have cognac, whiskey and beer."

"Thank you. It's too early for me."

Raske looked confused for a moment. "Don't think that I'm an alcoholic. I've been on my feet since four o'clock in the morning." He pointed to the bottle and the empty glass. 'This was my aperitif before dinner." He looked at Megan. "Are you hungry?"

Megan had eaten a cereal bar for breakfast. "To be honest, yes."

"Well then, come along." Raske took his jacket from the back of the chair, put on his hat and went to the door to open it for Megan.

Megan stepped into the hall.

"You must excuse the lack of light," Raske said as he locked the door. "Currently only two of our generators are working. The one for the kitchen and the one for the laboratory." He went ahead, his jacket over his arm. "Although we barely age here, devices and machines have a very low life expectancy."

Outside a wave of bright light swept over Megan, and her body encountered the heat as if in resistance to it. A handful of birds flew by, fuzzy dots that seemed to dissolve in the sky.

"It's right over there." Raske pointed his hand at a building on their left and started walking.

Megan hung the backpack over her shoulder and followed him. In the shade of the trees the Filipino was wrapping a piece of wire around the shovel handle, and for the length of a breath Megan felt her heart clench. The leaves of the bushes along their path were covered with dust. A beetle, big and dark as a chestnut, flew up beside her. Megan watched it and imagined how she would draw the insect sitting on her palm. In addition to the water bottle in her backpack there were five notebooks, a drawing pad, colored pencils, a box of watercolor paints and brushes. Two of the notebooks, each with a hundred lined pages, were full of writing, and Megan believed she could feel their weight.

From the building, built of brick, but not resting on columns, wafted voices, the clatter of cutlery and the smell of food. Raske was waiting for Megan at the door, so they could enter the room together. At a long wooden table sat the young woman from the beach, Malpass and an older woman. When the three of them noticed Raske and Megan, they fell silent.

"We have a guest," Raske announced and laid a hand on Megan's shoulder. "Megan . . . " He looked inquiringly at Megan.

"O'Flynn."

"Megan O'Flynn. Right. She has applied for a job with us." Malpass mumbled something unintelligible.

"Megan, this is Carla Sarmiento." Raske pointed to the older woman and Megan nodded to her with a deadpan face. Where her skin was not covered by fabric, it shone brightly in the dim light of the dining room; in front of the room's four windows, curtains that looked like bed sheets

334

were stirred by the breeze of ceiling fans. Her faded teal shirt was clean but wrinkled, her black hair shoulder length and pulled back from her forehead by a red scarf. "Carla is our expert in the broad area of communications. What did you say the title of your PhD thesis was?"

"It was a hundred years ago. I've forgotten." Carla skewered a piece of chicken on a fork, shoved it into her mouth and chewed listlessly. She had long since turned her gaze away from Raske and Megan, staring pointedly at her plate, filled with rice, peas and a chicken leg.

"Well, something about prepositional thinking in apes, anyway." Raske pointed to the young woman. "This is Esther Bialskis, our long-time intern. Esther comes from Lithuania."

Megan and Esther nodded to each other. Esther was wearing a blue T-shirt instead of the white one, with IPREC printed on the front in white letters. Stiff strands of her hair stuck out in all directions, and Megan imagined touching it and felt the salt on her finger tips.

"You know this gentleman already. Guillaume Malpass. If you want to know about genes and stem cells and genetic material, ask him, he's a walking reference book. A quite voluminous one, as you can see."

Malpass smiled sourly, and continued to push the peas back and forth on his plate with the fork.

"Sit down." Raske pushed an empty chair away from the table.

Megan hung the backpack on the back and sat down, while Raske went to a door opening at the narrow end of the room, pushed apart the curtain strung on a cord of colored wooden beads with both hands and shouted something into the dim light behind it. Water flowed into the sink, a pot lid rattled, and the clear voice of a woman rang out, an almost musical roar which drowned out the barely audible violin sounds from the radio.

"The food is coming in a moment," Raske said, and took two forks and two knives from a plastic container that stood on a table near the wall.

"Only rice and vegetables for me," said Megan.

"Don't you like chicken?" Raske put the silverware on the table. "There is still some beef stew leftover from yesterday."

"I don't eat meat."

Raske seemed irritated for a second, and then said only: "Good. No problem. Rice and vegetables." He went back to the wooden beaded curtain, and shouted a new command into the kitchen. Then he opened two bottles of the beer on the table, sat down opposite Megan and pushed a bottle toward her. "But you drink beer, right?"

"Usually not at this time of the day," Megan said, reached for her bottle and knocked it against Raske's.

"Welcome to Monkey Island," Raske said, showing his wide grin.

Later, Raske showed Megan around. Carla and Esther had hardly spoken during the meal, and eventually Malpass went out to smoke. The cook, a young, buxom Filipina, had briefly shown her face, and Raske had introduced her as Rosalinda.

"As you can see, our best years are behind us," Raske said, pointing to a wooden house, painted blue, whose damaged roof was covered with makeshift sheets of plastic and in front of whose door lay a ladder. "That was once our visitors center." He laughed as if he had made a joke. "When guests came, members of the Board or local politicians, for instance, that is where we explained to them what we do here. They were also allowed to see our research subjects, but only choice specimens, and only behind thick glass."

You mean the primates?"

"Exactly."

"Can I see any?"

"One or two. We can do that." Raske pointed to two corrugated iron buildings, as big as naves, which stood at a distance between puny, withered-looking trees. "Until recently the one over there was a workshop. There, in the hangar, where the tractor is. Which, of course, is broken. And the other one was a storage shed."

They followed the path a piece and left the clearing behind them, came to a small pond and crossed over a field overgrown with dry grass where the insects rose in clouds, only to sink down immediately afterwards and then float up again. The chirping of insects swelled up and down like smoothly undulating waves. Megan saw a lizard on a tree trunk and black ants that swarmed from a hole in the ground. It was early afternoon, and the ground was baking.

The wooden houses were all white and had blue window frames and door frames. Beside each door there was a number painted, from one to ten. Seven of the houses looked empty and neglected; in one the window panes were missing. A little farther away a wooden tower rose in the air, perched on the top of a water tank. There were a half dozen solar panels leaning against the tower, a few boards and a sign the size of a movie screen with an inscription that was so weathered Megan could not read it.

"In the past, ten custodians and their protégés lived here," Raske said. "Now there are two." He went to the house with the number three, knocked on the door and opened it a crack. "Jay Jay?" When no one answered, he closed the door and turned to Megan.

"I can imagine where they are." He went back to the footpath on which they had come. "It's not far."

Megan followed him. Behind the second house, in a fenced square of bare earth, there was a toy backhoe made of yellow plastic. Only now did she see the three letters on the water tank, painted broad and black on the gray metal: MPP.

What Raske called the lab was a brick building, twenty meters long, with a corrugated iron roof and few windows, each no bigger than a darkened television screen. The façade was covered with brown, sun-bleached synthetic cells, the roof painted green where it was not covered by the panels of a photovoltaic system. On one wall hung a white sign with a red cross. The hum of a diesel generator could be heard, and over that, like ugly-sounding wind chimes, the clanging of metallic blades.

As the door slammed shut behind Megan, she embraced cool air. She could smell the cold, as if they were walking into a clear autumn night. It was quiet in the building, the noise of the generator only a distant hum, a fly in a jam jar.

"Here are the uncomfortable rooms," Raske said, "and at the same time the most pleasant." He was walking down the short hallway and opened a door, which was as thick as a mattress.

Megan saw a piece of wall and floor, half a table. Through a window covered with blue film a little light penetrated. A man was sprawled on the floor, eyes closed, a pillow under his head. He wore dark trousers and a light shirt; his feet were bare. The silver shells of headphones covered his ears; a cable wound over his belly into an MP3 player.

Only when Megan crossed the threshold did she see the animal. The orangutan sat on a stool and looked at her. On his legs lay a book, a picture book with photos of ships. He wore shorts and a colorful Hawaiian shirt, and a hair brush hung on a string around his neck. He was barefoot, moving his toes. On a small wooden table beside him was a lamp that spread diffused light, an empty bowl, and a glass half full of pink liquid that had a drinking straw sticking out of it. Except in zoos, separated by bars or glass panes, Megan had never seen an orangutan that size. During her short time in Borneo, she had had no direct contact with the injured or feeble mothers who were sometimes brought into the ward with their young.

"That's Nelson," Raske said. "He was one of the first to be brought to the island. Say hello to Megan, Nelson."

The orangutan, his thick lips pursed, showed a few yellow teeth and then devoted himself to the book.

"Nelson is not exactly a showpiece. He would rather goof off than work. Just like that one there." He turned around and lightly pushed the resting man in the side with his foot.

The man did not even flinch. With one smooth motion he took off his headphones, opened his eyes and looked at Raske.

Megan, may I introduce you to Jay Jay? He should actually be working with Nelson, but he is equally determined to explain to me why he is sleeping instead."

The young Filipino put the headphones on the floor and stood up. "We learned words," he said, "then Nelson tired."

"Oh, Nelson was tired." Raske seemed to think. "And so you laid down for him there, right?" He looked at Megan and smiled.

"Four hours learned. Both tired."

"Yes, yes, all right," Raske said, and went to the door. "No wonder Nelson is getting fatter and dumber." He turned on the overhead light and opened the door. "Are you coming?"

Megan smiled at Jay Jay and left the room behind Raske.

The sun sank here so quickly that you could see the nails in the fence at the end of the road at one moment and not even the road itself in the next. In the blink of an eye the sky changed colors from blue to yellow, from red to gray, and finally black. For a short time the birds and insects were at rest.

The croaking of the frogs was the first thing heard Megan when she woke up. The sounds rolled through the darkness, rose up like bubbles and burst. Megan needed a moment to remember where she was. She had lain down after Miguel, the man with the shovel, had repaired the toilet tank in her bathroom and screwed a new bulb in the ceiling lamp, which was also a fan, and Rosalinda had made the bed. Now she lay there and looked at the window; behind it night had fallen. Raske had arranged the room. It was too late to return to the mainland, he had said, and that they would talk further over dinner about her continued presence on the island.

Megan sat up. Her throat was dry. She took the water bottle from the bag and drank. Then she looked at the clock, which read half past seven. She could not remember when and where Raske expected her. For a while she looked at the framed photograph on the wall above the bureau, a river delta from a bird's eye view, branching streams and sandbanks, speckled with thousands of white dots, the bodies of herons. Finally she got up and went into the bathroom, where there was a towel and a bar of soap. Her face was so tanned that her eyes seemed larger. Her hair was too long, and she decided to cut it as soon as she found a pair of scissors. When she thought about how hair grew back and had to be cut again, she was overcome by a great tiredness and a feeling of despair. She turned the ring on her finger a few times, but it didn't help.

After her shower she put on fresh underwear, a colorful wrap-around skirt and a white, long-sleeved man's shirt, all things she had bought at the market in Manila. She should not have given away the sandals, she thought as she slipped her bare feet into the sneakers. Annika was wearing the sandals now. Megan closed her eyes. She heard Felipe, Jeremy and Annika talking; they lay behind her on some pillows, drinking ice cold beer and laughing about the dog who was snapping at the moths. She would not even sit down with them, had no desire to smoke their joints and listen to their stories and their same old jokes. She saw the boards over the swimming pool where someone had drowned: a boy from San Francisco, an old Dutch woman, the former owner of the hotel, a drunken guest.

Megan opened her eyes, got up and left the room. The house she was staying in was about the size of a trailer home, like those Megan had seen in American movies, and was next to two others adjacent to the laboratory and the former visitors center. There were a few trees with thin, smooth trunks growing around the wooden houses. Solar-powered lamps cast their dim light on the first meters of the road that lead to the clearing. A garden hose was curled up on the ground next to a rusty rake. Megan realized she did not live here alone. Outside the window of one house there was laundry hanging on a line, at the door of the other was a pair of boots.

In the building where Megan had eaten lunch with Raske and the others, a light was burning. Hundreds of mosquitoes and moths buzzed around the two fluorescent tubes which were protected from rain by a piece of sheet metal mounted above the door. A small animal, a cat or a rat, ran away and disappeared into the darkness as Megan approached. The light gained and lost power to the rhythm of the generator, whose fluctuating noise level reminded Megan of the engine of the boat which had brought her to the island. When she reached the door and put her hand on the knob, she heard voices. She put an ear to the warm wood and listened.

". . . anyway out of here. The sooner the better." It was Carla. She sounded drunk.

Malpass mumbled something, and then he shouted: "Maybe you could let me in on it?"

"I'll find a way. I don't intend to stay here until I rot."

Malpass muttered something unintelligible to himself again.

"The kid—this Irish girl—she can replace me."

Malpass laughed, and then coughed. A bottle fell over. "Merde!"

"You're an idiot."

"Oh yeah? And you're suffering from delusions again! Replace you!" Malpass laughed even louder.

Carla let out a loud torrent of words in Spanish, of which Megan thought she understood only the curses and the insults intended for Malpass. Then there was silence behind the door. Megan waited a while, but other than the generator, the faint tinkle of glass and Malpass' occasional murmur, there was nothing more to hear. She crept to the window and

341

looked into the room. Carla sat at one end of the long table, Malpass at the other. He smoked; she drank. Megan thought they looked like a bickering couple in a play. Raske was not there, or Esther, either. In the middle of the table there was a pot, from which protruded the handle of a ladle. The ceiling fan turned and mixed the cigarette smoke with the dingy light that fell from the neon lamps. Behind the wooden beaded curtain, it was dark.

Megan crossed the clearing and walked past the visitors center in the direction of the laboratory. Even from a distance she saw a light behind the windows. A bat swept through the sky in front of her, and she looked up and saw the black cupola above, and the boundless beauty of the stars within it, and for a brief moment the heaviness dropped away from her and she smiled. She touched the ring and breathed in the air, which was warm and filled with the chirping of insects and salt. Under a tree she sat down on the ground and put her head between her legs, which she clasped with both arms. She did not want to cry, she told herself, she had no reason to. She was humming with a different voice.

They sat on the porch. The calendar said it was summer. Rain fell, but it was not cold. They were rocking back and forth. Her mother's dress was a meadow full of flowers. They sailed on a ship, just the two of them; they had left the squaller at home. Mother's face hovered over the bright sea. Her voice was a dolphin. Little Megan, a big world, a thousand questions. One can hardly say any more what holds the world together. Little Megan, a big world, one thousand and one stars. It is not gold and it is not money that holds the world together. It is the phrase: I care about you. They were rocking back and forth. Mother's face was the sun. The wind was blowing, but Megan was not cold.

She opened her eyes. A bonobo sat on the ground in front of her and inspected her. He had stretched out his arm; his finger touched her foot. She was not frightened. The bonobo was wearing blue, knee-length trousers, a blue shirt with short sleeves and a blue cap with a black visor. He let out a sound, a quiet, upward rising sound like a question, and moved his hands.

"He asks if you're okay."

Megan looked up and saw a man standing a few meters away. In his white, floor-length robe, embroidered along the hem and over the chest, and with his dark skin and the grey hair trimmed around his bald head, he looked like Manprasad, an Indian regular at Lilly and Nandor's Golden Dragon in London.

"You needn't be afraid of him," the man said.

"I'm not." Megan wiped the tears from her face and clasped the bonobo's fingers, which were again rested on the instep of her left foot. She looked the animal in the eye and said, "I'm doing very well."

The bonobo puckered his lips, as if he doubted her words, and uttered a short, deep sound. His eyes were large and black; Megan thought she could see herself within them.

"His name is Montgomery."

"Hello, Montgomery. My name is Megan."

Montgomery took off his cap, and Megan smiled. Then she rose, and Montgomery put the cap back on.

"Megan O'Flynn."

The man stepped closer. "Tanvir Raihan."

They shook hands. If Megan had not been wearing sneakers with thick soles and Tanvir only sandals, they would have both been the same height.

I just arrived today."

"Yes, Jay Jay mentioned it to me. May I ask what the purpose of your visit is?"

"I would like to work here," Megan said. "I'm a veterinarian." She was still firmly holding Montgomery's index finger with her left hand. The bonobo had sat down beside her and was engrossed in observing her hand.

"Did IPREC bring you?"

"Oh, no. I'm here on my own initiative. I don't even know if the research station needs a veterinarian."

"IPREC hasn't employed anybody in over a year." Tanvir raised his hands apologetically. "Of course that doesn't mean you don't get the job."

"Do you need a vet?"

"Have you talked to Torben Raske?"

"Only briefly. Actually, I was supposed to eat dinner with him, but I fell asleep. And I've forgotten when and where we agreed to meet."

Tanvir looked at the sky. "It's about quarter past eight now. Surely Torben has invited you to his place. Should I take you there?"

"If it wouldn't inconvenience you."

"Not in the slightest." Tanvir pointed his arm in one direction. "This way," he said, and walked away.

Montgomery and Megan followed him, hand in hand like a pair of lovers. Megan glanced at her watch and was not surprised to see that it said twenty minutes after eight.

Torben Raske lived in a plastered and whitewashed stone building surrounded by palm trees, with a flat roof and windows set deep within the walls. When you walked through the grass up the slightly rising plain toward it, you could hear the faint sound of the surf on the left, while on the right the dark silence of a small forest reverberated.

Tanvir had led Megan up to the point where the nature trail turned into a path paved with curbstones and coarse gravel, and had turned back with Montgomery. At their leave-taking the bonobo had once again removed his cap before he shook Megan's hand. Montgomery, Tanvir declared, attached great importance to good manners.

Raske had waited to eat. They had agreed on seven o'clock, but the delay was not worth mentioning. Rosalinda had cooked something that

344

only needed to be warmed up in the oven. He showed her the house, including the bedroom, and he mentioned the names of the photographers whose large-format pictures dominated the walls of all the rooms. He said he had wanted to be a war reporter and that his parents had other plans for him, more ambitious, more acceptable. To please his mother he had studied Economics in Trondheim and in defiance of his father he undertook a three-year world tour after graduation. While the vegetable casserole heated in the oven, Megan heard the stories about vermin-infested hotels in Managua and corrupt police in Mexico City, about a bus accident in Greece and a school of stranded pilot whales in Lofoten. Raske said that he had boxes of black and white photos of these travels, but he did not want to spoil Megan's appetite. Then he showed her a photo which he claimed was the only one with a beautiful subject that he had made in his life. The picture showed a moose, drowned at the bottom of a frozen lake in Alaska. The layer of ice and the water below were so clear that the animal appeared to be cast in formaldehyde. Megan said that she found it beautiful but Raske did not believe her, even though it was the truth.

Now they sat in upholstered rattan chairs in the courtyard, a square enclosed by three stone walls and a house wall and filled with lantern light. Norwegian jazz cooled the air: piano, trumpet, bass, drums. A gecko clung to a wall; a red line formed from the proximity of an ant trail.

"Too bad that you have only now arrived," Raske said as she ate warm banana bread and drank coffee that tasted like cinnamon and chocolate. "A few years ago, we were looking for people like you."

"A few years ago I had a practice in Yorkshire."

"Hard to imagine." Raske smiled. "How did you end up in the Philippines?"

"On a detour to Borneo."

"You've worked with orangutans?"

Megan nodded. "I was the head of a veterinary rehabilitation station."

Raske looked Megan in the eyes, and when she did not evade his gaze, he leaned back and stretched out his legs. "Why did you leave?"

"For personal reasons."

Raske raised his hands like someone who has surrendered. "No more questions." He grinned.

For a while they listened to the music that made its way from the living room into the outdoor air, a clear, lazy river.

"Why is the station so . . . " Megan was looking for the right word.

"Run down?" said Raske. "Shabby? In ruins?"

Megan nodded.

"It's a long story." Raske offered Megan more banana bread, but she refused. "That boils down to one thing: we have too little money."

"And how do you finance all of this?"

"Well, every year we still get a large sum from a foundation. But out of that we pay for employees' salaries, the maintenance of the station, food, fuel. We pay the local authorities—rather, we grease their palms so they will leave us alone and we can do our work. All this costs a lot of money. For larger repairs we simply lack the resources right now."

Megan drank the last sip of coffee. "How many primates do you work with in your program?"

"Program." Raske laughed. "Of the original twenty laboratory animals, only four are left."

"I just met Montgomery."

"Oh yeah? And his custodian? Tanvir Raihan?"

"Yes. He brought me here."

Raske, who had finished his coffee long ago, pulled a bottle of beer out of the bucket filled with ice water that stood beside his chair.

"And did he tell you any stories?" He opened the bottle and filled both of the glasses on the table.

"Stories? No. He didn't say much. The walk exerted him quite a bit, I

346

think."

"Tanvir is getting on a bit." Raske made a face, as if that statement troubled him. "And he is, how shall I say, a somewhat strange man, a loner. He doesn't eat with us; he stays away from most meetings; he does what he wants. And he has told everyone here a different adventure story about where he came from and what he did before." He reached for his glass and drank half of it down. "An opaque character. You should stay away from him." He put the glass back and smiled.

Megan looked into the light of a lantern that was made of metal and yellow glass, placed on a coral boulder the size of a refrigerator. Yellow light attracted fewer insects, Raske had told her before eating, and actually there were few butterflies or moths in the courtyard. She smiled back, just enough to show Raske that she had heard him, and at the same time so ephemeral that he could see how little she thought of such advice. "Four primates, you say?"

"Right. In addition to Montgomery and Nelson there is an old chimpanzee named Chester, and Wesley, a five-year-old bonobo." Raske rose. "Excuse me one second." He went into the house to put on another CD. When he returned he was carrying a metal box in his hands. He sat down, put the box on the table and opened it. "Do you want to know a secret about me?"

"A dark one?"

"I'll let you be the judge of that."

Suddenly Megan knew exactly what it was about Raske's appearance that she did not like. It was his skin, free of faults like wrinkles, scars, spider veins and age spots, this smooth, milky coffee brown layer which enveloped the rounded edges of his skull like velvet lining the recesses of a jewelry case. She was glad to know now what bothered her about his features, could hide it and concentrate entirely on being disgusted by his self-indulgent, arrogant nature. "Why not," she said, and slipped forward on the chair to the first black and white photograph Raske handed across

347

the table to her. The image showed a dog lying on the ground. Raske waited a few seconds, and then offered Megan the next photograph. There was also a recumbent dog in this one, but with one difference: his fur was dirty and one spot on his neck was dark and matted. Megan took the third picture in her hand and looked at it.

"He's dead," she said after a while.

"Yes." Raske gave Megan the next photo, then another, until there was a small pile in front of her.

"Dead dogs," Megan said.

"Nineteen," said Raske.

"Did you kill them?"

"No."

"How does anybody find such things?"

"By chance." Raske took the top photograph from the deck. "It started with this one. In Cadiz, Spain." He reached for another picture. "Then I found this one here. Garrison, North Dakota."

Megan sat back and drank her beer.

"Lublin, Poland. Winnipeg, Canada. Salima, Malawi. Lagos, Nigeria. Guaymas, Mexico. Medellin, Kolurnbien. Manaus, Brazil. El Pilar, Venezuela. Port-au-Prince, Haiti. Bonneville, Utah. Karasburg, Namibia. Adrar, Algeria. Tigre, Argentina. Khon Kaen, Thailand. Brest, France. Kassala, Sudan. Kumasi, Ghana."

While Raske put the photos back in the box, Megan emptied her glass. Then she got up.

"Oh, you want to go already?" Raske also stood up.

Yes. I'm tired." Megan thought about yawning, but then changed her mind.

"Are you sure?" Raske glanced at his clock. "Its not even midnight."

"I need some rest. It was a long day." Megan went to the open sliding door which led into the living room.

"I hope I didn't drive you away. With the photos, I mean." Raske passed her and went ahead to turn on the hall light.

"I'm a vet. I've seen worse things than dead dogs."

"Of course." Raske took her jacket from the coat rack.

"You don't have to come with me."

"I insist." Raske put on his jacket and took a flashlight from a shelf.

"Really. I can find my way alone."

"It's dark," Raske said, and opened the door. "You'll get lost." He turned the flashlight on and off again.

"I found this island." Megan went outside where it was slightly cooler than in the inner courtyard and a light wind was blowing. "Right?" She stretched her right arm out, turning her palm up.

Raske hesitated, and then gave Megan the flashlight. "Please." He did not take the trouble to hide his disapproval at Megan's hasty departure, and her stubbornness. With his velvety chin he pointed to the plain. "Straight ahead, right past the woods, left at the clearing."

Megan nodded. "Thank you for the meal." Because she was not keen to end the evening on a negative note, she forced a smile.

That seemed to appease Raske a little. "Don't mention it," he said, and also donned a smile. He walked beside Megan; the gravel crunched beneath their shoes. "So far, we haven't even talked about your future here."

"I guess there isn't one."

"Well, we already have a doctor. Tanvir. But he's a physician. That's what the papers he showed me claim, anyway." Raske stopped, brushed a lock of hair away from his forehead and pretended to be thinking. "Wesley broke his foot a week ago. And the elevated values from Chester's liver function tests need to be investigated immediately. Is that challenging enough for you?"

Megan had walked ahead and now stopped. "Does that mean you're offering me a job?"

"I'm offering you a boring position on a boring island, free food and poor accommodations. And a little money."

"Without wanting to see my credentials?"

"If you're an impostor, we'll throw you into the sea." Raske looked at Megan for a few seconds, and then grinned.

"Maybe I should go for a swim on a regular basis, starting tomorrow." Raske, still grinning, stretched out his right arm, and Megan walked over to him, grabbed his hand and shook it. Then she turned on the flashlight and walked away. Where the gravel road ended and the path through the field began, she stopped and looked back. Raske was still standing there, a black silhouette in front of the bright background of the house. Megan shut off the flashlight, turned around and ran into the darkness.

2

She had slept badly. The turning of the ceiling fan created a grinding noise, but no sooner had she turned it off then the heat under the mosquito net had grown unbearable. Early in the morning she stretched out with the sheets on the thin carpet in front of the bed and eventually nodded off.

Now she sat alone at the long table in the kitchen hut, a cup of coffee with milk and a plate of scrambled eggs and tomatoes in front of her. It was nearly nine o'clock, but other than Rosalinda, Megan had not seen anyone. Rosalinda had told her in awkward English that everyone here slept late and rarely came to breakfast before ten o'clock, sometimes not until twelve or one. When Megan asked where Raske was, Rosalinda answered that he went off every other day by boat and did not return until late in the evening. Where Raske went, she did not know or did not want to say.

After Megan got a second cup of coffee from the kitchen and sat back down at the table, Carla came in. She wore wide, sand-colored pants, a black T-shirt and white canvas slippers on her feet. She sat down across from Megan, took off her sunglasses and smiled. "Good morning," she said. Her hair was still damp from the shower and combed straight back. The skin on the slope of her big, long nose was peeling.

"Good morning." Megan smiled slightly.

Rosalinda emerged from behind the wooden beaded curtain and went straight back to the oven.

"You're up early." Carla leaned her elbows on the table, laid her head on her hands and looked at Megan.

"I couldn't sleep anymore."

Carla nodded, as if she was acquainted with the problem. She puffed out her cheeks and drummed her fingers against the stretched skin. When Rosalinda brought her coffee, she scooped four spoonfuls of sugar into the cup and began to stir. "I hardly do anything else but sleep." She yawned. "This here," she said, looking down and puckering her lips, "keeps you awake for a while. Three or four hours." Now she stirred counterclockwise.

"Not more than that." Once again, she increased the speed of rotation, and then she finally took the spoon from the cup, licked it and put it on the table. "Are you going to stay?"

Megan watched as the liquid turned slower and slower and finally came to a standstill. "It seems so," she said.

Carla nodded slowly, clasped the cup with both hands, lifted it up, blew on it several times and carefully took the first slurping sip. "Good," she said, leaving it unclear whether she was referring to the coffee or Megan's decision.

Rosalinda brought Carla's breakfast, a plate piled with potatoes, fried eggs, sausages, bacon and bread. Carla sighed, sprinkled salt on everything and began to eat. Between bites she looked at Megan. "I hope you don't mind."

"What?"

"The meat."

"Don't worry."

"I mean, as a vegetarian."

"In the past, I would have condemned you. Not anymore."

"Why not?"

"With time people become more moderate. More compassionate."

"To hell with moderation and compassion."

Megan did not know whether she should laugh. "People also get tired."

"To hell with being tired," Carla muttered.

The door opened and Malpass came. in With his baseball cap, a rumpled polo shirt, frayed shorts and sandals, he looked like a tourist fallen from the cruise ship and stranded on the island. He took off his cap, mumbled a greeting and disappeared into the kitchen.

"Do you know where I can find Chester and Wesley?" Megan had finished eating and took the last sip of her coffee.

Carla looked at Megan with a blank stare, chewing. Then she gulped and asked, "Do you want to start getting to work already?"

"I should look at Wesley's foot."

"Oh." Carla puffed her cheeks and pressed air through pursed lips. "Orders from Thor?"

"From whom?"

"Nordic god. Four down." Carla wiped the grease and egg yolk from her plate with a piece of bread. "Raske. We call him Thor." She pushed the bread into her mouth.

"Yes," Megan said, "he said I should look after the two of them."

"I'll take you there."

"Thanks." Megan stood up.

"Not so fast." Carla signaled for Megan to sit down again, banged the spoon against the cup a few times and shouted. "Hey, Malpass! If you'd take your paws off the cook for a minute, she could bring me some coffee!" She looked at Megan and rolled her eyes.

An hour later, Megan and Carla walked past the pond, took the path that branched off to the right, followed it up to a palm grove where a sow with her piglets was prowling around, and then crossed a field; at the end of it there was an impressive wooden house. With its two floors, the garret windows, the veranda enclosed with balustrades, the wide tapering stairs, the hanging flower pots and the mighty tree whose branches touched the ridge of the roof, it looked like a colonial villa in the Caribbean or a mansion in the South, and at the sight of it Megan thought that the only thing missing was the Hollywood swing, to make the house look like the houses in the pictures that her mother had cut from magazines and collected in a shoe box.

They stopped at a clearing, ten meters away from the stairs leading up to the entrance door in the shade of the veranda. Under their feet there was limestone, white as snow. In a circular flower bed framed by smooth stones the size of loaves of bread, grew flowers that Megan had never seen before.

"One more thing before we go inside." Carla lowered her voice, as if the people in the house could otherwise hear her. "Nancy Preston likes to see herself as the head of IPREC. Let her maintain that illusion." With that she walked across the landing, climbed the stairs and pulled a cord attached to the door, whereupon four muffled notes from a glockenspiel rang out inside.

Megan was barely standing beside Carla when a wing of the double door was opened. The boy, who Megan guessed to be fifteen, was combed and dressed in clean, ironed clothes. Under one eye he had a large, dark birthmark. His right hand was on the doorknob; in his left had he held a knife. "Yes?"

"We want to see Nancy," Carla said.

"Are you expected?" The boy's English was perfect. His black shoes, white socks, short gray pants and dark blue shirt were reminiscent of a school uniform. He had white, but crooked teeth, and he opened his mouth while speaking only as far as necessary. He seemed to forbid himself from smiling.

"No, we are not." Carla sounded irritated. "But I'm sure she'll have time for us."

"Whom shall I say is calling?"

"Good God, just tell her that Carla and a new employee are here." Carla leaned on the door frame with her right hand, pulled off a shoe with the left, shook it and pulled it back over the foot. "For God's sake!" she murmured.

"Please wait here." The boy pushed the door shut.

"Ruben is a little asshole," Carla said after the boy's steps had died away.

"What's he doing here?" Megan asked. "Is he some kind of domestic servant?"

Carla pushed air through her teeth contemptuously. "Yes. But he thinks he's the supreme master of ceremonies for the Queen of England."

The door opened again, and Ruben let Carla and Megan enter. "Miss Preston awaits you in the salon."

With a sigh Carla entered the house, and Megan followed her through the corridor, cluttered with furniture, umbrellas, planters, vases, and regional arts and crafts and crammed with pictures. Past the stairs that led to the upper floor, they came into a large light-filled room with a table, two chairs and a blackboard in the middle. There were books and magazines on the table next to pens, a tape recorder and a stuffed rabbit. The walls were empty, except for a stack of multicolored cushions. Large wooden boxes, painted white, had been placed in a row.

Megan picked a sheet of paper up from the floor that was scrawled with clumsy numbers and letters. The boy hurried past her, also passed Carla, and through a wide open door entered the room that was apparently the salon. There, in a massive armchair of worn, brown leather, a woman sat and smoked. She had to be about seventy, Megan guessed. The paleness of her skin was intensified by the long black and undoubtedly expensive dress she wore, and which seemed almost grotesquely out of place here. The blonde of her hair was dull from age and from the hairspray she used to hold her towering hairdo together, supported by apparently indiscriminately distributed bracelets, pins and clips.

The two apes sat on a carpet on the floor beside her. Chester, the chimpanzee, held a building block in each hand, but stared as if transfixed at a bowl on a chair that was filled with pieces of apple and carrot. He wore long dark blue pants and a light blue polo shirt. Wesley, whose plaster cast was covered with colorful ornaments, leafed through a picture book, but stopped when he saw Megan. The bonobo wore long red trousers and a green, long-sleeve shirt.

In one corner, half under a table, there was a dog, a light brown Labrador. Apparently asleep, he had not even raised his head when Megan and Carla entered. Perhaps he was deaf, Megan thought.

"The visitors, ma'am," the boy said formally, presenting almost a parody of a butler.

"Carla," Nancy exclaimed in a broad Texas accent, "how charming of you stop by!" She stretched out her arms, and ash fell from the cigarette onto the newspaper in her lap.

"Please excuse me for simply barging in, but I would like to introduce you to someone." Carla signaled for Megan to come to her. "This is Megan O'Flynn. She's a veterinarian."

Megan walked over to Carla. "Nice to meet you." She smiled at the woman and allowed herself to be examined from the shoes to the crown of her head.

"Veterinarian, you say?"

Megan nodded. Through a large floor-to-ceiling window on her right light fell into the room. Two walls were dominated by shelves with books, old editions to judge from the leather bindings, classics, perhaps scientific works. In addition to a sofa, atop a chest of drawers made of black, glossy wood, carved at the corners with leaves, flowers and berries draped from entwined branches, there stood a mantel clock and an empty vase; next to those there was a mirror, a hair brush and a single white glove.

Megan thought how bizarre it would be if the woman in front of her was Cait O'Flynn; if this strange old woman was her mother, who went away in order to be happy, or less miserable, and had landed here on this island with all the eccentrics; a prematurely aged, desperately dressed up woman concerned about her position, a has-been who let herself be treated like a queen by a little boy and whose royal household consisted of two apes. She detected sadness, an unexpected gust of wind, and she wavered slightly and stopped smiling.

In the meanwhile, Ruben had taken a seat on the chair with the knife and cut a carrot into pieces, which he dropped in the bowl on his knees. Chester watched his every move, while Wesley continued to focus on Megan.

"Megan has come all the way from Ireland to work with us," Carla said, and she sounded as if she was talking to a child.

"Hard-working people, the Irish," Nancy said, belching a cloud of smoke. "But also proud and rebellious. Are you rebellious?"

Megan took a quick look at Carla, who was still wearing her mask-like smile, and then turned back to Nancy.

"I don't know," she said. "Sometimes."

Nancy drew on her cigarette and inhaled the smoke, by concentrating and taking a breath through her mouth with pursed lips. "I think Sean Connery was the best James Bond ever. What do you think?"

For a moment, Megan wondered whether the information—that she had never seen a James Bond film and that Sean Connery was not Irish but Scottish—would add any significance to the conversation. Then she smiled and said, "I like him very much."

"At that time, nobody smoked in the movies yet," Nancy said. "In the American ones, I mean. Do you smoke?"

"Not anymore."

Nancy, enveloped in smoke, nodded thoughtfully and touched her tower of hair with her free hand, and it seemed justifiable for her to worry about its stability.

"Megan is actually a vegetarian," Carla said, ignoring Megan's sidelong glance.

"Oh, gosh," Nancy sighed. "Don't tell me you're a health nut. And therefore an abstainer." She put the finished cigarette, smeared with lipstick almost up to the filter, in the ashtray on the round table beside her.

"I am not," Megan said.

"Well yes, it's your thing." Nancy moved her hands with her yellow fingers in a kind of wave. "You still get the job, sweetheart."

Pushed lightly in the side by Carla, Megan stepped forward. "Thank you," she said, and did not know whether she should reach out her hand or make a curtsy. Finally, she simply took one step back.

"Ruben? Get us fresh lemonade and two glasses." Nancy intricately folded up the newspaper. "We must make a toast."

"Yes, ma'am." Ruben handed Chester and Wesley each a plastic bowl full of carrots and apple pieces, pushed Nancy's cigarette butt into the ashtray and went into the next room. While Chester tackled his portion, as if he was starving, Wesley put his bowl on the picture book and would not take his eyes off of Megan.

"Megan wanted to see Wesley's foot," said Carla.

"Tanvir was here yesterday. He said everything was fine."

"Just to be sure." Carla pushed Megan gently in the direction of the bonobo.

Megan walked toward Wesley in a crouch. "Well, let me see," she said, gently raising his cast foot. Wesley, his eyes still directed at Megan, let out a softly wailing sound.

"You fake," Carla said, and stroked Wesley's head.

Ruben brought a carafe of lemonade: water swimming with lemon slices and ice cubes, sepia-colored from the brown sugar, which had settled in a thin layer on the bottom.

Megan knocked against the plaster with the knuckle of her index finger on her right hand. She had never treated an ape before. During her studies she had visited the clinic of a zoo and watched as a female gorilla had a tooth pulled under general anesthesia. "How long has it been in a cast?" she asked.

"A week," said Carla. "Ten days, perhaps."

Wesley whined a little, as Megan pressed against the cast in a few places.

"Is he getting much exercise?"

"Hardly any, since the accident," Nancy said. "When he's not sleeping, he sits and looks at picture books."

"How did it happen?"

"He fell out of a tree."

"Is something wrong?" Nancy wanted to know.

"I'm not sure," Megan said. "I'd like to remove the cast and take a look."

"Oh, gosh," Nancy said.

"It would be best to do that in the infirmary." Carla gave Megan one of the glasses that she had received from Ruben. "Salud." She drank a toast to Megan and Nancy.

"It's nothing serious, right?" Nancy held her full glass in one hand and lit a cigarette in the other.

"No," Megan said. The lemonade tasted sour; the cold crept up to her temples. The sweetness came only later, in the sediment of sugar crystals. "Nothing serious."

In the evening the four of them sat at the table and ate bean stew with rice. Malpass, who never seemed to make the effort to hide his bad mood, said that from now on they would probably only have a meat-free diet. Esther smiled self-consciously, the way someone smiles over an embarrassing or failed joke, and Carla asked him to keep quiet. Megan was unperturbed; to her Malpass was nothing more than the shadow of a cloud, something dark that lay over things for a while and then disappeared.

Carla made sure that a lot of beer was drunk. Before the dessert, consisting of papaya pudding and rice cookies, she toasted Megan informally. Then, for no apparent reason, she told a story about a car accident that, through a miracle, she had survived unharmed. Malpass, who only drank Sprite, said the story was fictitious, and stuck a few cookies in his pockets.

After dinner Carla suggested that they take a few bottles of beer to the beach and, as she put it, stare at the fucking ocean. Malpass found the idea absurd, preferring to stay in the hut, a decision that surprised no one. Esther packed the beer in a cooler and Megan helped her carry it. Carla, a blanket over her shoulder and a flashlight in hand, walked ahead of them. At each root she stumbled over, she swore loudly in Spanish. She was a poet of rage. Sometimes she stumbled and gave a sermon of curses so long that it seamlessly faded into the next one, when an obstacle almost brought her down again. It was not mindless rage or uncontrolled obscenity that formed the sound of her savage songs; it was anger and amusement at her own awkwardness, a litany of adjuration, blame and pleas. Father MacMahon had claimed that everyone prayed in their own way.

On the beach they spread the blanket and sat down. It was cloudy; there were no stars to be seen. A light wind came from the sea and trailed away over the sand, which still exuded the heat of the day.

"Look at that," Carla muttered. "All the water."

Esther swung open the lid of the cooler.

"How long would I have to swim before I got home?"

"Where is it?"

"Buenos Aires."

"A long time."

Esther opened three bottles of beer and handed them around.

"What are you doing here?" Megan asked, after they had each taken a sip. "I mean, what is there still to do on the island?"

Groaning, Carla kicked off her shoes. "Nothing," she said.

"Almost nothing," Esther said.

"We're waiting."

"For what?"

"For something that will take us away from here." Carla drank half the bottle and wiped her mouth with the back of her hand.

Esther rose and walked a few steps to the sea. She picked up something, looked at it and dropped it. The waves were not breaking; they simply collapsed, leaving foam bubbles back in the sand, soundlessly collapsing.

"And why are you here?" Carla asked after a while. "What brought you to this godforsaken island?"

"The usual," said Megan. "A broken marriage, the words of an old man, love of adventure."

"Two of those themes are familiar to me. Who is the old man?"

"Jeffrey Salter."

"Never heard of him."

"He writes."

"What?"

"Everything possible. Mainly philosophical texts. But not only that. One of his books is called *The Turkey: a Tragedy*. Published by a small university press in Vermont."

"Turkey?"

"Yes. How a baby chick becomes a five pound roast. And the ecological, social and ethical aspects of meat production in America. In the final chapter, he discusses the question of whether animals have feelings."

"Of course they do."

"I think so too, but that view is very controversial."

"Idiots, anybody who doubts it. I had two cats, a black one and a gray one. Brothers. Inseparable. If one woke up after a nap and the other one wasn't there, he would begin to run through the house and cry. He was only reassured when he had found his brother. When the black one died, the grey one didn't eat for days. At some point he disappeared. Forever." Carla rolled onto her back. "I'm sure they're both up there now. In a tight embrace. Happy ever after."

Megan emptied her bottle and stuck it in the sand between her feet, neck first. The surf sounded like a freight train in the far distance, rolling by very slowly, and loaded with Christmas trees.

"And can it be fixed?"

"What?"

"Your broken marriage."

Megan laughed and shook her head. "I hope I was divorced a long time ago."

"You don't know?"

"No." Megan lay down and closed her eyes.

For a while the two women were silent. They heard Esther toss driftwood onto a pile.

"Did Thor, that's to say Raske, tell you that things at IPREC are pretty bad?"

"Yes. And that it can't be ignored."

Carla rolled to the side and groaned as she reached for the cooler to take out two bottles. She opened the bottles, gave one to Megan, took a long sip and lay down on her back again. "Actually, everything here is a joke."

"Is it true there was once an experimental program here with twenty primates?"

"It's been a while. Back then, the money flowed more generously."

"What money?" Megan sat up and took a sip of beer.

"No idea. Thor controlled the finances. Anyway, we had everything we needed back then."

"And why not now?"

"Times are bad."

"Who pays you?"

"Nancy's foundation." Carla looked over at the fire, from which hardly any smoke was rising. Incandescent sparks flew out of it, whirled through the air and went out.

"What are you doing with the money?" Megan asked. "You can't spend anything here."

"All of it goes into an account. In two or three years I'll use it to buy myself a house in Boca. That's a district in Buenos Aires. Where I grew up."

"What exactly is your job here?"

Carla laughed. "I eat and drink. I sleep. And I write reports about studies that I've never done."

"For whom?"

"The Board of Trustees. Loud do-gooders. They think they're immensely important. They decide each year whether IPREC gets money."

Megan looked out to sea. "There's a ship," she said, pointing to a few lights that moved on the dark surface.

"That's Thor," Carla said, without taking her eyes off the fire. "He's running late today."

In the room the bedside lamp was burning. In front of the open door hung a lantern, where butterflies fluttered along with moths and mosquitoes with long legs and transparent wings. Megan stood on a chair, pushed up the metal hood of the ceiling fan where the wires were hidden, climbed from the chair and turned the switch. After a few turns, the hood slipped down the rod and there was a scraping sound. Megan got toilet paper, turned off the fan, climbed on the chair again and stuffed the paper into the hood.

"You have to take apart the wiring."

Megan jerked and almost lost her balance when she turned around.

Tanvir stretched out his hands protectively. "I'm sorry. I scared you, didn't I?" He wore wide white trousers and a blue and white checked shirt that was stretched over his stomach.

"Well, a little bit." Megan jumped from her chair and wiped her hands on her pants.

Montgomery was standing in the dark behind Tanvir. The blue uniform and hat made him look like a chauffeur.

"I saw the light and thought I'd drop by for a minute."

"Hello," Megan said. "Hello, Montgomery."

The bonobo took off his cap, pointed at the fan and the chair and made a few quick hand signs.

"He says you should be careful."

Megan looked at Montgomery. "Thanks, I'll be careful." Then she turned to Tanvir. "Come inside. Both of you."

Tanvir entered the room, but Montgomery remained outside. "He doesn't like fans."

"Why not?"

"They turn too quickly. Everything that moves fast makes him uneasy."

"Me, too, actually," Megan said. She turned on the fan and the rotor blades began to spin. When the maximum speed was reached, the rod vibrated so violently that the hood slid down little by little, until it rested against the engine block, causing the grinding noise.

"Cheap junk from China. Montgomery is right not to trust the thing." Tanvir looked around the room. "Do you have any wire? Or string?"

Megan turned the switch off. "I don't think so."

"Wait." Tanvir went out and disappeared into the darkness. Montgomery was still standing in front of the door, his cap in both hands in front of his abdomen.

"Would you like something to drink? I only have water." Megan took

364

the water bottle from the bedside table. "Drink?"

Montgomery shook his head and moved his hands, which Megan interpreted as a "no" and maybe a "thank you."

"Come inside. Look, the fan isn't spinning."

Montgomery's eyes followed Megan's outstretched arm to the ceiling and he finally entered the room, but stayed by the door.

"I don't like very many fast-moving things either. Cars, for example. Or people who are in a hurry." Megan sat on the bed. "Images in commercials. Flashing blue lights."

Montgomery looked at Megan. He had not moved since coming into the room.

"You don't really understand what I'm saying, do you?"

The bonobo reached a hand into his pocket and pulled something out of it. Then he walked over to Megan and opened his hand, which held a seahorse.

"Is this for me?" Megan pointed to herself.

Montgomery nodded.

Megan took the seahorse gently and looked at it. The head of the weightless, thumb-long creature was bent forward, as if in sleep or a devotional pose. The tapered tail curled up in front of the abdomen, a perfect spiral, smaller than a roll of licorice. At the end of the long nose curved tiny nostrils, and out of its side grew a fin like the stump of a wing. Megan ran her fingertip over the dry skin, light brown and almost transparent in some places, followed the grooves on the neck that were thin as hairs and the sharp points that ran down the back.

Tanvir came back and climbed on the chair.

"How do you say "thank you" in Montgomery's language?"

"Thank you. He understands more than two hundred words and simple sentences. *Thank you. Good. Hot. Cold. Go home. Throw a ball in the basket.* It's best if you look at him when you talk to him."

Megan looked into Montgomery's face. "Thanks."

Montgomery pursed his lips and blinked, and then he sat down and put a hand on Megan's knee. He looked at the ring on her finger and touched it tentatively.

"That's from my brother," Megan said.

"That will make Monty happy. He thought you were married."

Megan laughed.

"He likes you." Tanvir bent a piece of wire to the right, hung it under the faceplate, moved it up a little and wrapped the end of the wire around the rod.

"And I like him, too. How do I tell him that?"

"Oh, don't worry, he knows." Tanvir stepped down from the chair and turned on the fan. "You see, that will hold," he said, after the blades had rotated a few times at high speed in a circle and the hood stayed in place.

"Thank you," Megan said. "Unfortunately, all I can offer you is water."

"We drank a little just now. And we don't want to disturb you any longer; it's obvious that you're tired." Tanvir carried the chair to the little table, which stood against the wall next to one of two windows, and turned the fan to the lowest level. "Monty, let's go!"

The bonobo turned his head to Tanvir.

"What are you waiting for? Megan wants to go to bed."

Montgomery looked at Megan for the length of two breaths, then took his hand from her knee, got up and went to Tanvir.

"I wish I could talk to him," Megan said, rising.

"You can." Tanvir took Montgomery's hand and went outside. "Good night."

"Good night." Megan went to the door and looked after the two of them. When Montgomery turned to her, she waved.

Two hours later Megan was still awake. She was lying on her back, her arms and legs spread, and let the cool air from the fan blow over her body. Before she had gone to bed, she tried to write in her book, but soon gave it up. She had spent ten minutes shadow boxing, then showered and sat down again at the table to draw the seahorse, but couldn't even manage that. She had meditated and eventually lay down and watched the circling of the fan for a long time until she dozed off, only to wake up minutes later, wide awake and still worn out.

The clock on the bedside table said half past one. Megan slipped through the gap in the mosquito net, got dressed and left the room. For a while she stood in front of the building and breathed in the night air. Most of the solar lamps along the paths were broken or had consumed all of their stored energy. Above those that stilled glowed, insects danced. In one of the trees sat a bird the size of a pigeon, that Megan only noticed as it flew away.

The neighboring rooms lay in darkness and silence. Under the window of one were the taut ropes still hung with laundry; outside the door of the other were a pair of boots and a box full of fishing tackle. Megan knew that Esther lived next to her, but she had not seen or heard her. The boots and the box belonged to Miguel, who seemed to go to bed early and get up at dawn.

She went back to her room to put the two notebooks under the mattress and pocketed the flashlight, then locked the door, followed the path to the right and crossed the clearing. She sought the moon in vain; it was concealed somewhere behind the thick layer of clouds that was low over the island and emitted just enough brightness that Megan did not need the flashlight. She thought of going to the beach. Perhaps there were enough embers left from Esther's fire to ignite a new one, she thought. Then she was suddenly hungry and had a desire for a beer and decided to look around in the kitchen hut. Carla had shown her where the key was and how the gas stove worked. She had also warned Megan and enjoined her to clean up everything behind her, so she wouldn't spoil things with Rosalinda.

Even from a distance she saw the light. It did not come from the dining

367

room, however, but from two windows in the adjacent part of the building, in which Carla and Malpass lived. The prospect of drinking a late, or as the case may be, an early beer with Carla, pleased her. When she was about twenty paces from the building, she heard a male voice. She stopped and recognized Malpass's French accent, the rolled R's in the palate and the soft consonants which were stretched in places where you least expected it. Malpass was loud and angry, and he spoke without interruption. Megan walked past the building, where in a barred shelter gas bottles, crates, cans and chairs, were stored, then crept to one of the two windows fitted with wire mesh and listened.

". . . For the future! And anyway! This shipment from Mindoro! I can't approve that at all! What we need are the spare parts for the desalination plant! And the engines! And we need three new refrigerators! No new laboratory animals or whatever you have sent for! No wild creatures from some jungle! No new dolls to play with!"

It was quiet for ten or twenty seconds. Then Raske's voice, quiet and calm, made its way outside.

"I wish you wouldn't upset yourself so much."

"Upset myself so much? Upset myself so much?" Malpass let out a laugh. "You'll be glad that I'm only upset! And that I don't just pack it all in! And piss off! I think about it every day! Every damn day, believe me!"

Raske said nothing.

"Nothing of what I've ordered has arrived! Nothing!"

"Today I was at Delgado's. He says there are delivery problems. Bottlenecks. I assure you."

For a while neither said anything. Glass clinked against glass; a floor board creaked. Megan held her breath.

"So there's really no more money coming? None at all?" Malpass sounded calmer.

"Not from the old source."

A chair creaked. Megan imagined how Malpass pressed his weight against the backrest, tilted his head back and stared at the ceiling.

"We're shutting everything down. Are we shutting everything down? Is that it—we're going to stop?"

"You're an idiot, Malpass."

"Oh! Yes? Really? An idiot? An idiot, huh?" Malpass' voice almost cracked.

"Could you be a little quieter? Lord God."

"Carla is sleeping on the beach! She can't hear me on the beach, can she? Carla?" Malpass shouted: "Caaaarlaaaaaa!"

Megan ducked instinctively.

"Stop it." Raske remained calm.

"Okay. Yes, yes. So I'm an idiot, huh? Because I call a spade a spade? Because I see when the shit . . . as they say, hits the fan?"

"You're an idiot if you think that we're going to stop."

"And if nothing else comes? No money? No material? No nothing?"

"There is enough money there."

"Enough? There's enough? And why haven't I received any? For three months?"

"I wish you'd drink, Malpass. Damn it, at least beer. Beer calms you down."

"I don't drink."

"That's the problem."

"Three months. I don't do this for free."

"Nobody does it for free. You'll get your money. If you want to have it in your account every month, you'll have to find another job."

With a hiss a cap was unscrewed from a bottle and fell on the table. Megan was so thirsty that her throat hurt. She shifted the weight of her body to her left leg. Out of fear that the timber paneling might creak, she did not lean against the wall.

"The day after tomorrow we shoot the film."

"The day after tomorrow? That wasn't what we planned."

"Now it *is* planned. If we send the film next week, in two months the money will be in the account."

"I hope so. I hope so. What if this fellow comes back? Then we're screwed."

"He won't come. You worry too much, Malpass."

"Oh yeah? And this girl? This Irish girl? She just appeared like that. What is she doing here? Why did you give her a job?"

"Megan. This Irish girl is called Megan. And she showed up right on cue. She's a new face—just what we need."

Malpass seemed to be thinking. "Ah," he finally said. "All the same. I think she should disappear." A match was struck. Seconds later Malpass coughed.

Megan sat down; the soil was sandy and soft.

"Besides, she's a good vet. Wesley's foot got inflamed under the cast, and she noticed it. Would you rather be treated by Tanvir or her if you get sick?"

"By a veterinarian?"

"We're separated from apes by three genes."

The two men appeared to reflect on that fact for a time. A bottle was placed on the table.

"Tanvir, that miserable incompetent," muttered Malpass.

"I'm not going to talk about him. Actually, I want to go to bed. It was a long day." Chair legs slid over boards.

Megan jumped up and went as quickly and as quietly as possible to the end of the hut.

A little later the door opened.

"See you tomorrow."

"Yes."

Raske walked away. Megan saw his back, the bright shirt that disappeared into the darkness. Malpass coughed and spat, then he closed the door.

Two bottles of beer still floated in the water left by the now melted ice in the cooler. On the beach, covered along the outer edge with driftwood and strands of seaweed and illuminated by feeble moonlight, the white plastic chest with the red lid looked like a foreign object, as if it had washed to shore or dropped from an airplane. The glow of the dying fire lay under a layer of sand, a few charred branches sticking out of it. The blanket was gone, as were the empty bottles.

Megan opened a bottle on the rim of the cooler and drank it in one gulp until there was nothing left but a small residue. She sat down in the sand, clasped her arms around her bent legs and looked out at the sea. When she turned her head to the left and waited until her eyes adjusted to the darkness, she recognized the thin, curved line, broken in some places, of the boardwalk and, a little further out, the gray metal hull. She drank the last sip of San Miguel and opened the second bottle. She thought about what she had just heard, trying to interpret individual sentences, but it didn't work.

When she got up and walked a few steps to the water, there, where two rocks rose, gray, smooth humps, she saw the body lying in the sand. At first it frightened her so violently that the bottle almost fell out of her hand, but then she noticed the dark rectangle of the spread blanket, the pages of the open book, the peaceful movements of Carla's breathing under the thin checkered cloth. She went so close to the sleeping woman that she could see her face, the slightly parted lips, the small gold earrings, the limp hand, whose inner surface was much lighter than the forearm. Two meters away she sat down, drank beer and watched the woman, secretly hoping she would wake up and talk to her. Sometimes Carla's finger moved or she turned on her side, quietly whispering in a dream.

When the beer bottle was empty, Megan stood up and walked away.

3

Megan woke up because she thought there was a knock. She looked at the clock, which showed half past ten, put the mosquito net back and clambered out of bed, but when she was halfway dressed and opened the door, no one was there. She told herself she must have dreamed it, pulled her pants and the shirt off again and went to shower. Then she stood under the running fan and dried herself off.

Fifteen minutes later she entered the empty dining room. There was no one in the kitchen and, because she was hungry, she gathered together bread and butter and a glass of honey, poured a cup of coffee from a thermos next to the stove, and sat down at the table. She had barely buttered a slice of bread when Rosalinda came in. The cook was wearing a colorful skirt and a yellow blouse and in each hand she was holding a rope sling from which a number of fish were hanging.

"Good morning," said Megan, strangely happy to see a human soul.

"Good morning." Rosalinda could not seem to decide whether she should return Megan's smile, and spread her mouth, with full, deep red lips, a little wider. "You found food." She breathed heavily, as if she had been running to protect the fish from the heat or from the flies, some of which were still crawling on the silver-gray bodies streaked with yellow lines.

"Yes," Megan said, although she was not sure whether the woman had asked a question or made a statement.

"You want eggs? Tomatoes? It's quick."

"No thanks, no need for that." Megan pointed to the three slices of bread on her plate.

"I'll make. You wait," Rosalinda said and disappeared into the kitchen. The clicking of the wooden beads, which she had set in motion with her corpulence, rapidly trailed away in the sounds of flowing water, the clatter of cutlery and the rhythmic pounding of a knife blade on a wooden board.

Megan stopped eating and waited, as Rosalinda had instructed. The mirror image of one of the ceiling fans turned on the surface of the coffee in her cup. Outside a small colorless bird flew by, drawing a wavy line in the light-filled background. At the spot where the cook had been standing with the fish, a few drops of blood glistened on the linoleum. On the very bottom of the jar of honey, as if trapped in amber, there was an ant.

Esther came in and sat down across from Megan. "Hi." Her eyes were still puffy from sleep, her hair unkempt. She had on the gray sweatpants that she had worn the night before, and the blue IPREC shirt.

"Hi."

"Hot today, huh?"

"Yes."

Esther leaned her elbows on the table and rested her chin in her hands. "Are you able to sleep?"

"Not so good."

Rosalinda came out of the kitchen and brought Megan a plate with scrambled eggs and fried tomato slices, served with half an avocado. She asked Esther if she wanted the same thing she always had. Esther nodded, but as Rosalinda walked away she called after her: she really wasn't hungry, coffee and a slice of toast would be enough.

Megan burned her tongue on the tomatoes and took a sip of coffee, now as good as cold.

"Where in Ireland are you from?"

"The southwest."

Esther stuck out her lower lip and blew air across her face. Megan really wanted to know what the specific color of her eyes was, but she didn't want to stare at Esther. Green, she thought, with flecks of yellow in them, maybe gold.

"Do you miss it?"

"Sometimes."

Esther let her arms hang down and her upper body fall against the back of the chair.

"I miss my parents. I miss Palanga; the cold sea." She let out a long breath of air. "And I miss my language."

"Say something in Lithuanian."

Esther laughed. "No."

"Come on. Just one sentence."

With closed eyes Esther said something that sounded beautiful and strange and sad, and then she looked at Megan, smiling self-consciously.

"How long have you been here?"

"Almost three years."

"Three years as an intern?"

Esther lowered her eyes, running her fingernail along a groove in the table top. "There isn't anything else to do."

Rosalinda brought Esther's coffee and toast. On her forearm a silver crystal glittered—the scale of a fish. She filled Megan's cup and went back to the kitchen.

"Why do you stay?"

"We're paid," Esther said. She picked up a piece of toast, looked at it and put it back. "There's no work at home."

Megan ate everything on her plate and then pushed it away. "How did you get the job?"

"It's complicated." Esther poured milk into her coffee and stirred it. Then she looked into the cup, where the black and white liquid turned brown, and made a face as if she no longer had any desire for it. "I studied biology. In Vilnius. Last semester I had a thing with one of the professors. He took me with him to a congress in Madrid." She began to pick out the soft section of a slice of bread. "On the second day we had a huge fight, and I ran away. When I came back to the hotel in the evening, he was gone. I sat in the lobby crying, with no money. And then Torben appeared."

"He was also at the Congress?"

Esther nodded. She put what was left of the slice of bread on the plate. "He offered me a job. All of a sudden. I couldn't even go home to say goodbye to my family. I called my parents and told them I had a great job overseas. The next day we flew to London. Torben had something to do in England. Two weeks later I was here."

"Then you didn't finish your studies?"

Esther shook her head. She played with the pieces of bread, formed them into balls, pushed them back and forth, lined them up. "I can earn money here. In Lithuania, I would be unemployed. Or I'd be sitting at a supermarket checkout."

"Where does Torben go with the boat?"

Esther raised her head and looked at Megan. "Why?"

Megan was quick to smile. "No reason."

"I don't know." Esther took a sip of coffee. "To the mainland. Shopping."

"Three times a week?"

Esther shrugged her shoulders. "Maybe he has a girlfriend somewhere." She got up, wiped her palms on her pants. "I have to go."

"Me too. To see how Wesley is doing."

"Well then." Esther smiled, but the look in her eyes when she glanced at Megan was empty. "We'll see each other later."

"Okay."

Esther stood there for a moment, indecisive, and then she walked to the door and left the hut.

Megan drank her coffee. In the kitchen, a radio was playing. Over the clinking of a piano and a cheerful childlike singsong she could hear the steady ratcheting of the knife, which Rosalinda was using to clean the fish.

The windows were open; a barely perceptible breeze streamed into the room. Chester sat in a chair, separating the kernels from a boiled corn on the cob with his fingers and putting them in his mouth. His eyes were glued to the screen of a television that was standing, along with a video recorder, on a table in front of him. As far as Megan could tell, there was a film about coal mining playing. Excavators and trucks, as large as single-family homes, pushed black clouds of exhaust into the empty sky above a moonlit landscape. The sound was turned down; the motors of the machine sounded like distant coughing.

"You really don't want anything to drink, dear?" Nancy sat enthroned in her chair, smoking. She wore white sandals, white trousers, a white blouse and a blue blazer, which had a golden coat of arms sewn on the breast.

"No, thanks," Megan said and wondered if it was necessary to repeat that she had just come from breakfast. She had treated the inflamed site of Wesley's foot and was now about to put on a new bandage.

"Most people drink too little, you know." As if to confirm this statement, Nancy took a swig from her glass. There was a jug of lemonade on the table beside her.

Megan wrapped the top of the bandage with tape so that the bonobo could not undo that end, then she strapped the padded support around his foot, which she used to replace the plaster cast. When she finished, she put an antibiotic tablet in Wesley's mouth and held a glass of orange juice to his lips.

"Do you drink alcohol, my child?" Nancy asked.

"From time to time."

"Very unhealthy," Nancy said and blew out a cloud of smoke that rose to the ceiling like the diesel fumes from the machines which Chester was still watching with fascination.

Megan picked up Wesley's glass and stroked his head. The bonobo was lying on a towel, which was spread over the carpet. Again and again he reached out a hand and touched Megan's face or hair.

"Especially in this climate." Nancy put the cigarette butt in the ashtray where it continued to burn, because Ruben was not there to put it out. A wisp of smoke curled up toward the ceiling.

Megan had seen the boy. He was walking with the dog across a field, slowly and apparently deep in thought, like an old man with his long-time loyal companion.

Nancy got up, groaning. "And how does it look?"

"Very good. Everything's fine."

"Won't you stay a little while? We're going to do a few lessons." Nancy looked at the television. "The movie is almost over."

"Lessons?"

"Well, I try to keep these two here on the go. Brainwise."

"Won't I be in the way?"

"Not at all." Nancy picked up the highest book from a stack on the bookshelf, placed it behind Chester and waited until the credits ran, then turned off the television and the VCR. "So, lazy bones, now you show our Miss Doctor what you can do." She took Chester's hand and led him into the adjoining room. "Would you please bring Wesley?"

Megan lifted the bonobo and carried him in, where she sat him on the chair next to Chester. Only now did she notice that both wore dark blue trousers and a gray short-sleeved shirt, which made them look like boys

377

in school uniforms. On Chester's shirt there were several dark spots, presumably the remains of a hearty breakfast. He put his forearms on the heavy wooden table which was empty except for two pens and Nancy's book, and Wesley copied him.

"Children, pay attention!" Nancy stood in front of the blackboard, where someone had drawn a tree, a flower, a house, clouds and a sun. "Chester, please come to me."

Chester glanced at Megan, and then he rose from his chair and walked to the front.

"So, Chester. Where are you? Where's Chester?"

Chester turned his head and looked at Megan.

"Yes, Chester, we have a visitor today. So you have to work especially hard. So where is Chester? Is Chester ... in the tree?"

Chester shook his head.

"Is Chester on the cloud?"

Chester shook his head again.

"Is Chester in the house?"

Chester nodded vigorously.

"Right. And where is the house? Show it to me."

Chester went closer to the blackboard and tapped his finger against the picture of the house.

"Very good. And where is the cloud?"

Chester pointed to the blue chalk cloud.

"Right. And the sun? Where is the sun, Chester?"

Chester pointed at the sun, a yellow sphere radiating perfectly straight beams on the house, the tree, and the flower.

"Well done, Chester." Nancy patted Chester's head. "You can sit back down."

The chimp went to the table and sat down.

"That was easy," Nancy said, and pushed the blackboard to the side. Then she went to the boxes, five of which stood against the wall,

378

and lifted up one of the lids. "Well, now it's your turn, Wesley." She took a sheet of paper out of a clear plastic binder which was attached to the inside of the trunk lid. "Oh, you can't come over here. Megan, would you be so kind?"

Megan helped her carry the box to Wesley's table.

"Thank you, darling." Nancy held the sheet of paper in front of him at arm's length and squinted. "Let's see. Here." She dropped the paper and looked the orangutan in the face. "Wesley, please give me the tennis ball. The tennis ball."

Wesley turned to Megan and pursed his lips.

"Say it to him."

"Give me the tennis ball, Wesley."

Wesley gripped the desk with one hand, leaned over the box and searched among the other items for the desired object. He took out a model airplane, a plastic bucket, a children's shoe, a spoon, a bird feather and a book, and finally held the yellow tennis ball out to Megan.

"Hey, thank you." Megan took the ball. "Bravo."

"Well done, Wesley," Nancy said. "And now give us the whistle."

Wesley looked at Nancy, and then Megan.

"The whistle, Wesley," Megan said.

Wesley began to rummage through the box again, which contained at least fifty items. A little later he held a toy trumpet in his hand and looked at it.

"Whistle," Nancy said.

Wesley put the trumpet back in the box and continued to look. When he had found the fife, an oversized model made of red plastic, he gave it to Megan.

"Very good, Wesley."

"And what can you do with the whistle, Wesley?" Nancy asked. She put a hand on Wesley's shoulder, and Wesley turned to her. "What - do - with the – fife."

Wesley took the fife from Megan's hand, put it between his lips and blew. The sound that emerged was so high and shrill that Chester covered his ears. Megan laughed, and Nancy wrote something in the notebook.

After the lesson, which lasted an hour, Nancy and Megan sat down on the porch, drank lemonade and ate peanut butter cookies, which Rosalinda had baked using a recipe from Nancy's mother. Chester practiced gymnastics on a web of ropes that were stretched between three trees, while Wesley watched him with his stuffed rabbit in his arms. The chimpanzee performed a few daring maneuvers, as if to show the young bonobo that he could do everything without falling and breaking his foot. In the forest behind the house birds called from time to time, and when it was completely still, Megan thought she could hear the surf breaking against the rocks in the distance, a barely noticeable noise carried by the wind into the interior of the island.

"Shall I guess what you're thinking?"

Megan looked at Nancy. "What?"

"You're thinking: I could stay here forever."

Megan laughed. "Oh, well. Forever."

"Let's say, a long time."

"For a while, yes."

"Isn't there anybody waiting at home for you?"

"Actually, there isn't even a home anymore."

Nancy lit a cigarette. "And no family?"

"I have a brother." Megan looked at Chester, who was hanging upside down from a rope and began to rock back and forth.

"No parents?"

Megan shook her head.

"Oh . . . " For a while Nancy puffed absent-mindedly. "I'm an only child," she finally said. "Unfortunately. What's your brother called?"

"Tobey." Megan closed her eyes for a moment.

"Do you have contact with him?" Nancy put a hand on Megan's knee when she didn't answer. "Dear, a brother. As a child I would have given anything for a brother."

"Back then everything was alright."

"And then?" Nancy took her hand away. "Oh, that's none of my business. Excuse me."

Megan leaned against the wall and stretched out her legs until her toes touched the railing. "In a marriage, you'd say that we drifted apart."

Nancy took a sip of lemonade. "I know about that," she said, after she had put the glass back on the tray that was on the bench beside her. "I was married for forty years. No, wait . . . thirty. Robert, my husband, and I met in school. He studied economics and politics, and I studied law. Bobby was five years older. When he finished, we got married. My parents were very rich and not unhappy that I was a wife instead of a lawyer. For a year Bobby and I traveled around the world, an endless honeymoon; a wonderful time. Then we bought a house in Fort Worth. I wanted children, but he did not. He always postponed it. And then when we tried, it didn't work. Something with his—you know—sperm. Well, he began to work more and more; we saw each other less and less, and I was bored in our huge house. So we established a foundation, something for me to care about."

"Are you still married?"

"No, no. Bobby died a few years ago."

"I'm sorry."

"His heart. Too much work." Nancy sighed.

"I'm divorced."

Nancy looked at Megan with wide eyes. "Oh, you don't say!"

Megan nodded, smiling.

They watched Chester for a while, who in the meantime had lay down in a hammock and continued to swing. Wesley was still sitting under the tree, engrossed in picking at his stuffed bunny.

"It was really forty years!" Nancy suddenly said out loud. "Not just thirty! My God, sometimes I think the lessons are for me, and not for those two there!"

Megan laughed. She rose and put her hands on the warm wood of the porch railing. The sky lit up. It was blue and so deep that it seemed almost to touch the palm trees. She saw Ruben and the Labrador approaching the house with slow steps and with bowed heads, an elderly night watchman and his dog, both tired from bearing the light.

In the afternoon Megan went to the lab, but there was no one there and the front door was closed. In the kitchen hut she drank a glass of orange juice and ate a banana, and then she stood in front of Carla's window for a while and listened in vain for noise. The first person she met was Miguel, who was repairing the roof of the welcome center. He stood on a ladder, attaching a section of rain gutter.

Megan waved as he turned to her. "Hello."

Miguel waved back.

"You're repairing the roof." The statement was so clumsy that Megan regretted the sentence the second she uttered it.

"Yes."

Megan stood there, one hand held to her forehead as a sunscreen, and wondered what she might say next, while Miguel looked at her, as if he was waiting for permission to continue working. Two pieces of corrugated iron leaned against the wall next to the ladder; on the floor there were wooden slats and boxes of nails and screws.

"Don't fall down!" Megan finally shouted.

"Yes. No."

Megan nodded again and followed the path up to the small houses along the water tower. She heard the music from afar, broken fragments of unmelodious sound, as if it was being played by all stations at

382

once. Through the excited melody there was a dissonance attached that sounded more like a sawing noise as she drew closer. The first thing she saw was Carla with a cloth wrapped around her waist and a yellow T-shirt full of splashes of color, using a large roller to paint a wall white. Esther seemed absorbed in painting a door blue. She was wearing jeans cut above the knees, a bikini top, and, on her head, a hat made of newspaper. Jay Jay was causing the noise, cutting wooden slats with a hand saw. Nelson sat next to him and picked up every slat that fell on the floor and examined it thoroughly, as if to check its suitability.

When they saw Megan, everyone stopped working and sat in the shade of the wooden board that was leaning against the water tower. In the cooler there were cans of Coke and Sprite, and large water bottles and melon slices wrapped in plastic film. Nelson was sitting next to Jay Jay and plucked the wood shavings from his fur before he had anything to eat and drink. He had his own bottle of orange juice and a Tupperware box filled with apple slices.

"Why didn't anybody tell me that today you were doing renovations?" Megan did not drink anything; she had the ridiculous feeling that she had not earned it. She wanted to sit next to the orangutan, wanted to touch his hand, his fur, the skin on his soles.

"A spontaneous idea from Thor," Carla said.

"You were with Wesley." Esther took off the paper hat and poured cold water on her head. Her fingers were blue.

"And why are you doing all of this?"

Carla opened a can of Coca Cola. "Tomorrow is Capricorn Day." She lifted the can, as if making a toast, and took a long sip. "Jay Jay, explain it to her."

Jay Jay was self-conscious and shook his lowered head.

"Come on. It was your idea—your favorite film." Carla poked him lightly on the shoulder.

Jay Jay cleared his throat. "The title of the movie is *Capricorn One*. Three astronauts are going to fly into space, but before they start they're taken out of the rocket and brought to the desert. There, in a large hall, a moon has been constructed. It looks real. On the television, they tell people the astronauts are on the moon, but it's not true at all. Everything is a deception, like here."

"I don't understand."

"We're only painting the façades," Esther said. "So the houses look as if they're inhabited."

"Movie sets." Carla took a piece of watermelon, unwrapped the plastic film and took a bite. Juice ran down her chin and neck.

Megan remembered what Raske and Malpass had discussed. "A movie?"

Carla nodded and spit watermelon seeds between her feet.

"Yes," Jay Jay said. "I'm filming." He beamed.

"And who is it for?"

"The Board of Trustees," Esther said. "A few people in Texas who want to see what goes on here before they release the money."

Megan paused for a moment. "Why? It's Nancy Preston's money, isn't it? Can't she just arrange it?"

"Apparently not. It has something to do with the foundation and taxes and God knows what." Carla threw the watermelon rind in a bush, wiped her hands on her T-shirt and stood up. "And so each year we make a small film." She stretched and walked back to the house where she had been working.

Jay Jay also stood up. "Come on, Nelson," he said. "Back to work." He took the orangutan by the hand, and together they picked up the wooden slats from the floor and carried them to the meadow behind the houses.

"How much money are we talking about?"

"No idea," Esther said. "I just know that's how our wages are paid." She got up and stretched her lower back. A blue patch of color glittered on her left foot. She drank from the can and put on her paper hat. When

384

she went back to work, Megan followed her.

"Can I help?"

"You're a veterinarian," Carla said. "You have a steady hand. You can paint the house numbers."

"That's fine with me." Megan grabbed paint and brushes and outlined the contours of the "2" that was visible under the white paint.

In the late afternoon they stopped working. All ten houses had a white façade, a blue door and a blue number beside it. Most of the weeds in the vicinity had been removed, and the dry grass cut. In the field behind the second row of houses they put up posts in a shape that implied the proposed construction of five more houses. Raske had paid them a visit and expressed satisfaction with the results and with Megan's volunteer work. To avoid giving the impression that he and Malpass were not doing anything, he talked a little about some of the preparations in the laboratory building and assembling the props. Then he unloaded a crate with fruit and beverages and drove away in his jeep.

They brought the remaining materials and the tools to the corrugated metal shed which had once housed the workshop and now contained a tractor without tires, more trailers of various sizes, lawn mowers and wheelbarrows. Along one wall there were work benches and on another cabinets, some of which were missing doors. Above the steel cross beams that supported the roof, there were ladders, boards and rolls of wire mesh. In one corner Megan saw a half disassembled diesel generator next to the individual parts of a huge engine; in another, solar panels and a tank made of black plastic, the size of a VW bus. The floor, a thin coat of cement crisscrossed by cracks and broken in many places, was covered by a finger-thick layer of dry soil as fine as dust. Small birds fluttered back and forth between the metal beams under the roof, as if they practiced flying in here. The air smelled of diesel fuel and rotting leaves and Megan could feel how her pores began to open and her T-shirt stuck to her skin.

"My neck is killing me," Carla said. She washed the paint roller in the sink and rotated her head. When she and Megan turned on the faucet, at first there was only a faint moan from the line, the regurgitation of a sick little animal, warm air. Then a trickle of brownish liquid flowed out and eventually something like water.

"I'm going for a swim now." Megan had cleaned the brush and was now washing her hands. She had repainted all ten numbers and then helped Jay Jay set up the posts for the fictional houses. She was tired, but the thought of cooling water, slow motion and silence made her alert enough to take a walk to the beach.

"I'm going to shower and lie down for a while," Carla said.

Esther scrubbed the blue paint off her hands. "I'm coming with you," she said.

Half an hour later Megan and Esther were swimming in the calm sea, its depths infused with the dim light of evening sun. They swam in parallel to the beach, because Esther did not trust being out in the deep water. From time to time Megan submerged, touched the sand and picked up a stone or a shell and slipped back up to show Esther her find, like she had in the past, ages ago, when she brought treasures up from the bottom of the pond to show Tobey.

Esther was not a good swimmer. She lifted her chin so far out of the water that her eyes turned to the sky instead of the gentle landscape of waves and the dazzling light film on the surface. She hardly moved her legs at all, which meant that her position was more upright than horizontal and she devoted all of her energy to the work of her arms, hectically and without any rhythm. Sometimes, after she had not taken a breath for a while out of sheer fear of swallowing water, she struggled for breath, throwing her head back, gasping for air. After a few minutes she was so exhausted that she paddled back to the shallow water in order to rest herself.

Eventually they lay down in the sand, there where it was damp and the waves reached their feet. Megan looked into the sky-blue void for a while, and then closed her eyes. She heard Esther breathing next to her and she willed herself not to be sad, and she succeeded. She could feel the way the salt dried on her face. A single bird gave a short cry, then another, again and again, until it stopped, because no one answered.

"Megan?"

"Yes?"

"How did you get here?"

"Fishermen brought me. In a boat." Megan sat up. Esther was wearing the same clothes she had worn for painting and Megan felt funny in her bikini, which she had bought in a shop in London's airport, two hours before her flight to Borneo.

Esther raised her legs, clasped them with her arms and laid her forehead on her knees. She looked like someone preparing for a collision or a crash. "Did Torben bring you?"

"I saw him for the first time here."

Esther pawed the sand with one foot.

"Why do you ask?"

"Just making conversation."

Now, shortly before it vanished behind the horizon, the sun appeared like a sulfur-yellow ball, not quite round, as if it was compressed by the weight of the darkness that thrust it aside. At the point where it seemed they would meet in a moment, shone the sea, clouds towering above it, azure blue on the inside and their blurred edges a pale yellow.

Megan's forearms and the backs of her hands were full of blue paint splashes. With a bit of wet sand she rubbed her skin. "Do you love him?"

Esther spun her head around and her eyes flashed. "No," she exclaimed and sprang to her feet. "Why do you think that?"

"I don't know. It was just a guess. A hunch."

"But how did you get that idea?" Esther was so agitated that her Baltic

387

accent came out. She stood there with clenched fists; behind her head the sun died away and for a few seconds traced a shimmering line around her body.

"Well, you were a student; he brought you here." Megan stood up. "You're beautiful."

For a moment Esther stared at Megan. Her face was made of glass, a mirror that could break at the lightest impact. She was breathing as heavily as she had after swimming. Suddenly she turned and ran away, first along the water's edge, then up to the bushes and trees that held back the sand and were in turn held in place by the sand, a crooked, incomplete fence between one nothing and another.

Megan ran after her, ran across the beach and fell on her as Esther stumbled and collapsed.

"Go away!" Esther shouted and put her arms over her head as if she expected to be hit or kissed.

Megan sat astride her, grasped one arm and then the second, held them tight, and waited. "I'm sorry," she said when Esther finally stopped squirming and, with her head turned to one side, lay there with her eyes closed, panting, her face distorted into a grimace.

The last light between day and night spread over the beach and with it a calmness into which even Esther's wheezing sank. Then darkness came. Megan bent down and when a strand of her hair touched Esther's cheek, Esther turned her head and looked at her. Her face was still reminiscent of glass, but now soft and liquid. Her stomach rose and fell under Megan, her fists were already open, her fingers slightly curved, as if ready to reach for something. Her breath met Megan's lips. Two seconds passed like an eternity.

"I'm sorry," Megan whispered, loosened her grip on Esther arms, got up and went to the rocks where their clothes and the towel were, put on her cargo pants and looked for her T-shirt, didn't find it and put the towel around her shoulders. Then she went up to the trees and along the path, which flowed like a bright river between the banks and the low-lands.

Eventually Megan noticed that she had no idea where she was. Nevertheless, she continued in the direction she had taken and that she knew was wrong. Once she was startled when a pig broke out of the thicket in front of her and disappeared among the roots of a sparse grove. She thought of Emma and Holly and called after him, still breathing heavily, but the animal did not appear again. The sky above her was more clear than in any previous evening. That part of the moonlight not lost in the vastness of the universe fell on the world and lay as a thin gloss over everything. Between the sound of crickets and cicadas she heard frogs croaking, but she knew that it could not be coming from the pond near the station that she must have left far behind. She went through thick, waist-high grass and imagined she was a bug in the fur of an animal.

Suddenly there was nothing surrounding her, no trees, no bushes, only sandy soil with ankle high undergrowth and boulders. Lowlands opened before her; at its end was the sea. Megan sat down. Her stomach growled, but the thought of food was repulsive to her. She let herself fall on her back and began to count the stars. As a child she could recite all the planets in the solar system, alphabetically or by size. Tobey only had an interest in the moon and used binoculars to look for the flag that had been left behind by American astronauts. She had invented stories for him, wild fairy tales about space: The ring of Saturn belonged to God's wife; chocolate came from huge mines on Mars; Pluto was inhabited by talking dogs. Later, when he was older, he had never questioned her about her lies, probably because he was ashamed that he had believed her back then. Perhaps, she thought, she also saw her brother somewhere in the sky and remembered the summer nights on the farm, and how they had climbed the ladder to the roof of the barn and on to the Milky Way, where there were flying tractors and all the dead cows lived on happily forever.

She was not crying; it was the salt that was burning in her eyes. She got up and wiped the earth off her bare arms. An almost imperceptible breeze blew over her. Without thinking, she walked left and soon left the barren plain behind her and unexpectedly entered the vast dome formed by the leaves of a palm grove. This time she was not startled when a pig appeared beside her. She talked with the animal, and it looked at her carefully, as if it was simply surprised by the language in which it was addressed. Two or three other pigs wandered around the trees, sniffing and grunting, brown, slender bodies on thin, almost delicate legs. Megan heard chickens and smelled the compost pile long before she reached it.

The house was built of wood and bamboo and covered with the usual corrugated iron found around the island. It was so far away from the nearest palm tree that a falling coconut could not hit it. There was a light burning behind the windows, but there was not a sound. An old bicycle with a trailer, a block of wood that had an axe stuck in it, two barrels of rain water, a folding chair and a shovel were the only things that Megan could see as she stood on the cleanly swept porch and wondered whether she should knock on the door or continue walking.

"Come on in, it's open!"

Megan winced and took a step backwards. The voice seemed familiar.

"I know it's you, Megan!"

Megan went to the door, pushed it open and entered the house. Yellow light from several lamps illuminated a room that seemed twice as big as the building around it. Raw boards, painted translucent white, formed the walls that were covered from floor to ceiling with pictures, maps, posters, newspaper clippings, photos, scribbled notes and countless other things, found objects from the beach, debris thrown into the ocean and spit out again, bleached by the sun and removed by someone who recognized their bizarre beauty.

"Good evening." Tanvir was sitting at a square wooden table that seemed to be constructed of the same boards as the walls, and he was peeling a potato. Above him a fan turned, just so fast that the loose edges of the paper on the walls lifted like the individual feathers of a plumage.

"Hello," said Megan. A butterfly fluttered past her into the lighted room, and she closed the door.

"Won't you sit down?" Tanvir pointed to the second chair. Megan pulled the chair a bit away from the table, but remained standing. "Where's Montgomery?"

"He had lessons with Nancy today and he's sleeping there."

Megan sat down and tightened the bath towel around her chest. From somewhere there was the smell of fire. On the table, next to a pot with water where peeled potatoes floated, there was a radio with a crank on the back.

Tanvir saw Megan's gaze. "If you want to hear music, you have to wind that thing."

Megan shook her head and looked around further. In one corner there was a bed with a faded brown woolen blanket spread over it. There was a book on the pillow, on the book a pair of wire glasses. Three stacked boxes were used as a bedside table where one of the lanterns stood. On the wall above the bed hung a huge map of the world, the ocean surface covered with hand-written notes and doodles. On shelves over a bureau there were books, along with carved figures, like the ones you could buy at Asian markets.

"Are you hungry?"

"What? Oh, no. Thank you," Megan read a sentence that was written with black brush strokes on a sheet of paper and pinned to the wall: EVERYBODY'S GOT SOMETHING TO HIDE EXCEPT FOR ME AND MY MONKEY.

"When was the last time you had something to eat?"

"I don't know. At eleven."

"That was at least . . . eight hours ago. I'll cook and you'll eat." Tanvir dropped the last potato into the pot and got up. "Take a look around. I'll be right back." He took the pot and the lantern from the table and went to the door. "If you're thirsty there's water, and there's a glass. He pushed the door with his foot and went out. A moment later the door closed from the outside.

Megan stood up and filled a glass with water from a plastic canister. She drank it in one gulp and filled it again. On one wall there were newspaper clippings, yellowed, curled originals and some better preserved copies, some of them in color. Megan glanced at the headlines: the Landing on Mars, Massacre at Columbine, Invasion in Iraq, Billy Wilder Dead, Missile Tests in North Korea, Attack in Madrid. She saw blurred images of Bill and Hillary Clinton, an oil tanker that had broken apart, an African woman in a desert landscape, an aircraft carrier pilot in a uniform with shields and batons. Beside a poster which explained in both Tagalog and English how to protect against malaria, hung the cover of the single "Que Sera" by Doris Day, along with a postcard that showed a barn where a small propeller plane had crashed. A Frisbee made of black plastic that had grown dull and brittle, printed with the word ETERNITY, hung next to the head of a doll that had no hair or eyes and a broken wooden paddle whose red paint had almost completely peeled off. Megan saw a crumpled pocket map of New York, a postcard with van Gogh's *Sunflowers*, a Tarot card with the three swords that had been torn and glued back together, a page from the Manila phone book, a stamped and signed drug prescription, a flyer for a night club in Boston, between them a completely deformed Halloween mask that represented Saddam Hussein or Groucho Marx, five pacifiers, sunglasses without frames, half a life preserver with the inscription MEL, a rose, the stem made of plastic and the petals of pale red cloth. Between the bureau and the first shelf hung photos of Montgomery, Chester, Wesley, Nelson and other primates, all with a tinge of yellow and overexposed backgrounds, as if at the moment of shooting an explosion had illuminated the scene. Montgomery looked sternly into the camera, like an old man who does not want to understand the meaning of being photographed. Another picture showed Carla laughing and Esther posed in front of a table with a cake full of burning candles. Megan read a poem by Robert Frost that someone had typed with a typewriter, and then a sentence cut from a newspaper that said THE WINTER OF DISAPPOINTMENT LEAVES US ALL FREEZ-ING, followed by an exclamation mark that had been added with a red felt-tip pen. Gray sheets of paper, criss-crossed by numerous horizontal and vertical fold lines, covered half the wall beside the table, hand-drawn blueprints for a house that appeared to be identical to the one in which Megan was now standing. A new layer of paper and relics hanging from the edges covered the plans, covered the pen lines, notes and coffee stains and pencil sketches of beam structures, window frames and door handles.

Megan put the half-full glass on the table and walked out. She found Tanvir behind the house where he stood at a brick oven with a knife and chopped something on a wooden board. A few chickens with their duck-lings were running around; pigs rustled in the dark.

Tanvir looked at Megan. There were tiny beads of sweat on his fore-head.

"That towel looks like a mink stole on you." He put the knife away. "Were you swimming?"

"Yes, just now."

"I can't swim. Not really, anyway."

"When I came out of the water my T-shirt was gone."

"Lost?"

"Well, it was gone; not there anymore."

"You see over there?" Tanvir pointed to a rope that was strung be-tween two palm trees, where clothes were hanging. "Take what you need—a T-shirt, a shirt; help yourself."

Megan went to the clothesline, chose a black T-shirt with the white IPREC logo and put it on.

"I don't even know how many of those there are," Tanvir said when Megan was standing beside him. "Nancy Preston had them made. White with black lettering, black with white lettering, white with blue lettering, blue with white letters, short sleeves, long sleeves; you could dress half the Philippines with them. We use them as cleaning rags."

"Thanks anyway."

Tanvir waved. "I hope you like fish." He pointed to a circle of stones on the ground which contained glowing coals. Above the coals, on a metal grating, were two fish.

"I'm not hungry."

"Appetite comes with eating; you'll see." Tanvir took the lid off the pot and stabbed the knife blade into a potato.

"Perfect," he said. He poured the hot water into a metal bowl and put it on the stove. "I'll rinse the dishes in this later." He went to the hearth to take the fish off the grill with what appeared to be self-made wire-cutters, and put them on a plate. "Would you please take the pot with the potatoes?"

Megan carried the pot into the house and placed it on the table. Tanvir took the plate with the fish and the wooden board which contained something that looked like chopped parsley. Then he took two plates and cutlery from the cupboard beside the door and signaled for Megan to sit down. He took his own place only after she was seated, and passed her down a plate, a fork, and a knife.

"You're pretty stubborn, huh?"

"You have to eat," Tanvir said. "Believe me. I'm a doctor." He began to fillet one of the grilled fish and remove the bones.

"I'm a vegetarian."

Tanvir looked at Megan in amazement. His raised eyebrows were jet black and the short hair encircling his head from ear to ear was gray, almost white. "Really?" He nodded. "My mother was a vegetarian." He continued trying to dissect the fish. "And an ardent follower of Mahatma Gandhi." He got up, took Megan's plate and put three potatoes on it, which he crushed with a fork and drizzled with oil from a dark glass bottle. Last, he sprinkled parsley over them. "My mother liked them like this the most." He pushed the plate toward Megan. Then he sat down again, separated the fish from the skin and put it on his plate.

Megan ate a bite.

"And? A poem, right?" Tanvir took three potatoes from the pot. "One by William Carlos Williams."

Megan smiled. "I'm not familiar with him."

"He wrote poems about apples and plums in the refrigerator."

Within minutes Megan had cleaned the plate, but when Tanvir wanted to fill it again, she protested. "Maybe later," she said. "You eat first."

"Are you also an ardent follower of Gandhi?"

"Well, I admire what he has done. Very few people know that he was a vegetarian." Megan took a sip of water. "If they even know who Gandhi was."

"My mother believed in reincarnation," Tanvir said. "She wouldn't eat a chicken, which was probably her great-aunt born again." He looked at Megan, chewing, lips shiny from the oil he had poured over his potatoes. "Why don't you eat animals?"

"Because it's my opinion that it is wrong to kill them."

Tanvir nodded thoughtfully. "Do you believe that animals have a soul?" He pushed a piece of fish onto his fork with the knife, but did not raise it to his mouth.

"Do we humans have one?"

"Bingo! Already we're in the midst of a fundamental debate," Tanvir cried happily and pushed the bite of fish into his mouth.

Then they were both silent for a time, as if they wanted to assure each other that they were not interested in being immersed in such a conversation or considered the time for it too early; too early this evening, too early at all.

"How did you know that it was me?" Megan finally asked. "Earlier, when I was standing in front of the house."

"That's simple: because no one visits me here. Apart from Torben Raske, who comes from time to time, to show me that he is still here and still lord of the island."

"You don't like him?"

"No. As little as he likes me."

Megan started to say that she did not particularly like Raske either, but then let it alone. She looked at the world map behind Tanvir's head, which was blocking England and Ireland.

"He was here today, to reproach me for my negligence in the case of Wesley's plastered foot."

"It was just a small area that got infected."

"That could have led to a serious complication." Tanvir got up and fetched the water container. After he had filled both glasses, he sat back down in his place. "The fact that I'm not a vet doesn't excuse my negligence."

"He's much better now."

Tanvir shook his head. "It's carelessness that has become the norm on this island," he said and sighed, his eyes fixed on the plate that was empty except for the bones and skin of the two fish. "Everything is going to rack and ruin. You probably have to be stronger than I am to resist this gravitational pull." He raised his head and looked at Megan, smiling with a pinched mouth.

"How long have you been the doctor here?"

"But I'm absolutely not," Tanvir cried, and sounded almost happy again. "I can put a cast on an ape's foot! But Torben Raske wouldn't even take an aspirin from me!"

Megan leaned back; the bamboo chair, held together by straps, was surprisingly comfortable. "Why? Is it because you . . . " She broke off the sentence.

Tanvir smiled. "Because I'm not white? Perhaps." He leaned back as well. "But I think it has more to do with arrogance, with hierarchies, academic strongholds of vanity that are impregnable for people like me."

"People like you," Megan repeated. "You're a doctor!"

Tanvir smiled again. "What makes you so sure?"

Megan looked at Tanvir, speechless for several seconds. "I assumed it," she said, "because you treated Wesley."

"I plastered his foot and . . . "

"The cast was perfect," Megan interrupted Tanvir.

". . . and didn't notice a festering wound."

"That can happen to any veterinarian. Any doctor."

"Torben Raske disagrees. He has forbidden me to continue the primates' medical care." Before Megan could counter with something, Tanvir rose with a jerk and said, "But I better not anyway, because now we have a real veterinarian here! Dessert? There are oranges in honey and baked bananas."

Megan shook her head.

"Oh, come on. There are few things sadder than eating a dessert alone. So?"

"Then just the oranges," Megan said, because she realized that Tanvir wouldn't give in.

"Two orders of oranges in honey, coming up right away." Tanvir hurried out and came back shortly afterwards with a plastic bowl full of oranges. "Take two," he said and sat down at the table.

Megan began to peel the first orange. "I don't quite know what I should do here," she said after a while.

"Well, you're young. You're drifting and you want to discover something new. You're entitled to."

Megan shrugged. "Why are you here?"

"I wanted to work with primates. That was my dream. A long time ago."

"And? What happened to the dream?"

Tanvir spread his arms. "Look around." He took a plate from the cupboard and placed it in the middle of the table.

"How long have you been here?"

It seemed as though Tanvir was thinking it over, but then he said only: "Half of an eternity and three years."

Megan put the orange wedges on the plate. "Tell me about the three years."

"You're pretty stubborn, huh?"

Megan laughed and nodded. "It looks that way."

Tanvir puffed out his cheeks and blew air through his pursed mouth. He was still in the process of removing thin white layers of skin from the first orange. "Three years ago, the last doctor for the research station, an overweight, homesick Greek, left the island with flying colors. So I thought my time had come. I thought, now at least they would give me this job, even after I was not allowed to participate in the primate programs and was treated like an unwanted intruder, only tolerated because he was a friend of Nancy Preston, the Texas cow, who they wanted to keep milking for a while. I imagined that over the course of time I could earn respect as a doctor and ensure that they would let me work with the primates." He looked at Megan. "I'm a good doctor, you know. In any case, I was one before . . . " He lowered his head and concentrated again on the orange in his hand. "Well, at any rate, I was wrong again. The lords and ladies of science refused to accept me into their exalted company. They said a doctor was not needed at the research station, and preferred to medicate themselves from the richly-stocked pharmacy. Last year Raske stitched a cut on his foot himself, simply so he would not have to ask me." He laughed dryly.

"Why couldn't Nancy Preston insist that you get the job you wanted?"

"Oh, Nancy . . . " Tanvir cut the orange into eight wedges and put them on the plate. "Her influence here is . . . very limited, to put it mildly. She serves on the whole here as a kind of, how should I say it . . . figurehead, if you know what I mean. With her, one keeps up appearances, to a certain extent; she stands for stability and confidence. These are important factors when it comes to applying for money from the foundation."

"Capricorn Day."

"You've heard of it?"

"Today I helped paint the huts."

"This is by now the only occasion when Torben Raske needs my help. A spectacle as magnificent as it is pitiful."

"What exactly happens?"

"Oh, we enact an idyllic IPREC world. We walk around in freshly pressed coats and pretend we are just about to overcome the final hurdles in the communication between humans and primates. All very impressive."

"And people from the foundation believe it?"

"It seems so."

"Why a movie? Why doesn't anyone come here, to see everything on site?"

"A few years ago when the company still operated to some extent normally, a representative of the foundation visited us. Raske had tried everything conceivable beforehand to stop him: invented malaria cases, storm damage to the guest house, problems with the ship's engine, quarantine regulations. But nothing helped; the man came. Well, what passed for a man. A neophyte, perhaps thirty or thirty-five, green in the face from the stormy passage and still completely exhausted from jet lag. You should have seen him." Tanvir laughed and shook his head. "He was wearing a khaki-colored safari suit, a cowboy hat, and giant walking shoes. Around

399

his neck hung a compass, binoculars, and a camera. He looked like a cross between a Boy Scout, Indiana Jones, and the American tourist he actually was."

Megan had peeled and divided the second orange and took a third out of the bowl. "Were there more people here at the time?"

"Four or five. But Raske told the young lad from the foundation that ten other employees were at meetings or on vacation. Prior to the visit he had also arranged everything so that it looked as if the station was well maintained."

"Wasn't he disappointed to see so few primates?"

"In addition to Montgomery, Chester and Nelson, he also got a look at a chimpanzee, Maxwell, who wore glasses and was very intelligent. Oh, and Gwendolyn, a delightful older female bonobo. We didn't have Wesley then; he came later. He couldn't have contact with the others, because of quarantine regulations. In reality, there were no other primates on the island."

"And? Was he impressed?"

"Well, after he had recovered from the long trip, he suffered from food poisoning and was in bed for three days. When he was halfway back on his feet, his living quarters were infested with ants. And the day before his departure a spider bit him, and his hand swelled to twice its size." Tanvir stood up and scanned the wall above the bureau. "Somewhere I have a picture of the poor guy." He put on his glasses and stood with his face close to the wall so he was able to recognize things. "Here." He took down the photograph, which was attached to the wall with a pin, and gave it to Megan.

"He doesn't look like Indiana Jones here anymore," Megan said, looking into the pale face and deep-set eyes of a small man who seemed to have escaped death at the last second.

"The fish poisoning and the ants had something to do with Raske, without a doubt," Tanvir said, then sat down again and began to peel the second orange. "And even the spider—I wouldn't put it past him. It bit the unlucky boy while he was taking underwear out of his bureau."

"But why? He was already there."

"So he wouldn't come back a second time. And so he would advise everyone at home against visiting the island." Tanvir took a knife from the cupboard drawer and cut the orange into small pieces. "You can wash your hands if you want." He pointed to a spot near the door, where there was a round metal tank with a protruding faucet mounted above a plastic container.

Megan got up and ran water over her sticky fingers. "Does IPREC receive much money from this foundation?"

"A lot. In any case, enough to justify Capricorn Day."

Megan turned off the faucet, wiped her hands off on her pants and looked at the cupboard doors plastered with layers of paper and photographs and postcards. One piece of paper said MONKEY DOES WHAT MONKEY SEES and on another: NOBODY KNOWS ANYTHING. One photo showed the Titanic at the time of departure from the port of Belfast, one of a rhino lying on a road in front of a battered car, and a third of Laurel and Hardy wearing pointed hats on their heads. Megan lifted one of the postcards, which was only fastened with a piece of tape, and saw that the back was empty; there was not any text or a stamp. The themes of the cards were completely different and apparently collected at random, like the texts and quotations on the notepads and newspaper clippings: a Buddhist temple, Che Guevara, the burning Zeppelin at Lakehurst, a donkey with all four legs plunged into rubber boots, the Eiffel Tower at night, Orson Welles, Monet's water lilies, a beach at sunset.

"You must think I'm crazy," Tanvir said in the stillness.

Megan turned to him. "Not at all."

"Like one of those psychopaths in the movies. Eventually the police come to track him down and enter his room, which looks like this, and everyone is speechless."

"The ones in the movies are always obsessed with a particular thing or person. You're not. You are not a psychopath. Although you now seem obsessed with removing the seeds from every orange."

Tanvir paused in his work, as if he only now realized what he was doing. "Oh this. The seeds have to be taken out, believe me." He pointed to a picture hanging beside the cupboard, the only one that was framed. "Do you know Walton Ford?"

Megan looked at the picture. "No." The art print showed a chimpanzee with an iron collar around his neck, from which a heavy chain stretched to a ring embedded in a wall. On the checkerboard of the marble floor in front of the animal there was an open book with the leather cover facing up, along with a pen. The chimpanzee looked at Megan. His eyes seemed apathetic, indifferent, even though in the background, beyond a stone balcony parapet and a sea, a city was in flames. *A Monster from Guiny*, Megan read on a piece of tape stuck to the frame.

"A great painter," said Tanvir. "Unfortunately, I don't have his illustrated books here."

"Not here? But where?"

"At my brother's. In Boston."

"Is that where you're from …from Boston?"

"Well, I was born in India. In 1986 I went to America with my brother."

"What about your parents?"

"They're both dead. My father died in a mining accident when I was fifteen."

"My father is also dead," Megan said quickly, as if one death could take a little of the horror away from the other.

"My condolences. Had he been dead long?"

"Yes." Megan pushed the orange peel to the side. "What about dessert?"

"Didn't I tell you? Appetite comes with eating!" Tanvir got up, took two half coconut shells from among a number of them that were on a shelf of the cupboard, two spoons and a glass wrapped in paper, and sat down again. Then he filled the coconut halves with orange pieces, served some honey from the jar and pushed the bowl and a spoon toward Megan.

They ate for a while in silence. The oranges were so sweet and the honey of such intense flavor that Megan thought it was unnecessary to say anything. When they were done, they both lifted their bowls to their lips and drank the juice that had collected and mixed with the honey. Tanvir grinned with satisfaction, and Megan could not help but smile.

"And now you must tell me something about yourself," said Tanvir.

"Must I?"

"I have given you something to eat; now it's time for you to present your gift to me. Words. A story."

"Can't I just wash the dishes?"

Tanvir shook his head, leaned back and folded his arms over his chest.

Megan thought it over. She wanted a beer, but she did not want to ask Tanvir for it and perhaps embarrass him. "In Borneo, in the sanctuary for orangutans, there was a baby who had come by the name Nunu," she finally said, put her palms on the table and bowed her head, saw the grain of the wood, the cracks and stains. "Nunu was found by game wardens, who periodically brought orphaned pups to us. The unusual thing about Nunu's case was that she was brought in with her dead mother. Someone had found both of them in a palm oil plantation. Orangutans often wind up there in search of food, because they're driven out of the few forests that still remain, and there is no place where they can escape. Perhaps Nunu's mother was born there, where the plantation is now. She had been shot, and we knew by whom, and all we could do was house this emaciated, terrified and completely filthy creature and try to save her life. The mother had been dead for two or three days, the process of decay had begun, her body was bloated, the smell unbearable. The game warden had tried to take Nunu away from the corpse, but the little one clung so desperately to the fur that they would have had to break her fingers to loosen the grip. She was dehydrated and had a wound on her back, and we attached an intravenous drip and disinfected the wound, but she was half dead and we couldn't give her any sedatives to make her open her hands, and so there was no other choice but to wait until she finally fell asleep and we could separate her from her mother. When the babies die, they do so in the first three or four days after their admission, and everyone was sure it would not be any different with Nunu. But she didn't die. She was totally listless and never uttered a sound, not when they cleaned the wound and not when they gave her injections. She wouldn't drink, and we had to nourish her through a feeding tube to prevent her from starving. One of the local nurses took care of her, carried her around everywhere and gave her more time to finally get around to eating the porridge that all the babies were given. Nunu grew, but she wasn't really living. She didn't respond to anything, did nothing, except to breathe and swallow and defecate. When she was old enough she came to the nursery, an enclosure where the little ones who had miraculously survived could play and test their energy and their courage to climb scaffolds. In the first weeks Nunu sat there, staring into space, but eventually she moved a little, raised her head, and looked around. The next day she walked a few steps, and on the next and so on—a terrible effort. Just watching her as she dragged herself from one end of the enclosure to the other was agony." Megan's right hand was moving slowly back and forth across the table. When she realized after a while what she was doing and that she had forgotten to continue telling the story, she sat up straight and, with her eyes closed, took a deep breath. "When she was two, Nunu was allowed into the first outer enclosure. There were trees, comparatively small trees, the largest about five meters. Some of the adolescents tried their hand at rock climbing; performed gymnastics on the lower branches; there weren't any ropes and swings anymore. One day Nunu also started to take an interest in the trees. At first she just sat there and looked up at them, but eventually she touched one of the roots. She placed her hand on the bark for several minutes, as if she wanted to see whether or not the tree would do anything to her. It was a long time before she had enough confidence in herself and in the tree to try to climb it a short distance. You have to imagine small Nunu, small with long, thin arms. As she stretched these arms out to one of the lowest branches, covered it with her hands and was just about to pull herself up like all the others were doing around her, she realized that she lacked the strength. She spent the next day reaching her arms out to the branch, trying to clasp it in her hands and pull herself up. But she couldn't even get her feet off the ground. —Well, at some point she managed, two weeks later, maybe three. And again a few weeks later she was able to climb a short way up the trunk. When she was four years old, she came into the second outer enclosure where the really big trees were. I really saw Nunu for the first time here." Megan raised her head. "Everything I've told you so far comes from a film. One of the staff filmed Nunu every day; they met for hundreds of hours. I was stuck in the quarantine station and had some time to look at the tapes. Everyone at the camp was very excited and happy to see Nunu's development, to witness how out of this picture of misery, slowly and with incredible effort, a being emerged that more and more resembled an orangutan girl, although not very cheerful, but after all, one that was not dead and would one day return home to the jungle. —I stood in the tower that had been built for paying tourists, watching Nunu through binoculars. At the station there was no work for me to do except stand with the guests in this tower and race through the text that the intern from New Zealand had raced through a week earlier. Whenever I was in the tower I looked for Nunu, and most of the time I found her sitting on the lower branches of a tree. She had grown a little by now and her arms had gotten stronger. When she climbed, she still looked very uncertain, but she made progress every day. —The day that I will never forget was a Monday. On Sunday it was raining heavily, and now the sun was shining. In the afternoon it was very hot, even under the roof of the tower. Nunu sat on a branch and just seemed to wait for evening to come and to be taken back to the sleeping quarters with the others. But then she suddenly began to climb. She grabbed the branch above her head and pulled herself up, stretched her arm out to the next and again to the next. She did it slowly, and obviously it still took her a lot of effort to pull herself up. On each branch that she reached, she had to rest briefly before she climbed further. Soon she seemed to be exhausted, but she could not stop climbing higher and higher. The tree was a giant; its crown soared high above the tower. When Nunu was about fifteen or twenty meters high, she sat down. She sat and rested, and her eyes were just as empty as the day and the week and the month before. The spark of life, which everyone at the station yearned for and talked about, was not shining in her eyes even now, despite this apparent triumph over her fear and her frailty. She sat there a long time without moving. Maybe she was afraid of the climb down, I thought, and wanted to tell someone. I put down the binoculars, and then she let go. I saw her as a small point below, and even believed I heard the impact of her body on the ground."

Tanvir was silent for a long time, perhaps because he was waiting to see if Megan would continue the story, or because he was thinking about what he had heard. Megan didn't say anything and was glad for the silence. She drained her glass and looked at the table. Tanvir let his arms, which he had until now held folded across his chest, hang down, as if exhausted by what he had heard.

"She let go, you say?" he asked. "Isn't it also possible that she lost her footing? Slipped?"

"She tilted forward," Megan said, without looking up. "Slowly and de-

406

liberately, like a child on the edge of a swimming pool."

"You had put away the binoculars."

"She wanted to fall," Megan said, softly but firmly.

"She wanted to die . . . " Tanvir seemed to weigh this possibility. He put his hands on the table, picked up his spoon and looked at it with a wrinkled brow, as if there was a message stamped in the metal, an answer. "She was dead, right?" he suddenly asked.

"She lived for a night and a half a day." Tanvir got up, took the plates and coconut shells and the cutlery from the table and walked out. He was gone for a while; Megan could hear him. When he returned, he held a steaming coffee pot in his hand. He placed two cups and a jelly jar with sugar on the table. After he had filled both cups, he took a spoon, unscrewed the lid from the jelly jar and put the spoon in the sugar.

"Thanks." Megan pulled a cup toward her.

"I envy you. Despite this experience."

Megan looked at Tanvir.

"You were in Borneo. You did something for the orangutans there."

"I answered questions for people who came to a tower."

"Carla said you were the director of the veterinary department."

"Carla spoke to you?"

Tanvir could not hide his embarrassment. He scooped three spoons of sugar into his coffee and stirred it. "She's the only one."

Megan nodded. "Carla is okay."

"That she is."

"Esther, too."

"Yes. But much too young." Tanvir put the spoon on the table. "For me." He chuckled, and then cleared his throat.

Megan smiled. She picked up the radio set and turned the crank. Then she pushed a switch to ON. The reception was poor or the station was not set correctly, and the music was distorted and superimposed with a spherical noise over the loudspeakers. A woman's voice could be heard, a

407

trumpet, distant and vague, in addition to the gentle sound of the grinding crank. That was the way it had sounded when Tobey turned on the radio in the kitchen, while a storm was approaching from the sea.

"I lied to Raske," Megan said, when after a few minutes the crank on the back of the apparatus came to a standstill and the music broke off. "So he would give me a job here."

Tanvir grinned. When he drank, he sipped.

"I'm not a real veterinarian. I had to do my practicum in a slaughterhouse and chucked it all."

"I am truly indeed a doctor, but I cheated on an important exam."

"At least you have a license to practice medicine."

"A piece of paper."

"Without it we're not allowed to practice."

"You practice."

Megan laughed dryly. "Oh yeah, right, that is until now the highlight of my career."

"You imagined it would be very different here, didn't you?"

Megan took a sip of coffee, which was still very hot. "Admittedly, I'm a little disappointed. On the other hand, I should be glad that things at IPREC are so bad and the station is dependent on people like me."

"I really don't want to dispute the fact that you are needed here in a certain way, but I think the main reason Raske let you stay is because you are going to appear in his film tomorrow."

"You mean he'll send me away when the film is finished?"

"Not necessarily, no. But there won't be much for you to do. No one here has much to do."

"I can live with that. It may surprise you, but I like it on the island."

"Oh that doesn't surprise me at all. The place has its charm, no doubt." Tanvir blew into his cup and took a sip. "However, there is a danger that after a certain period of relative inactivity one will fall into a state that I would describe as a carefree game of hide-and-seek from reality. Or, if I

408

were to express it in less flattering words, as an irresponsible vegging out under the palm trees."

"Irresponsible to whom?" Megan asked. "One's self? Society?"

"One's self, of course. The term 'society' inevitably loses any relevance here. Even the thought of re-entry into the human collective, into a social structure, becomes more absurd here with each passing year. Look at me, look around." Tanvir spread his arms. "Can you imagine me in civilization? Among housewives, accountants, children?" He dropped his arms suddenly, as if it was not necessary.

"Yes," Megan said, a little too quickly. Then she nodded. "Yes, I can. Maybe not accountants and housewives, but among children."

Tanvir smiled. "I'll take that as a compliment." He lowered his eyes and looked at his hands for a while, which he had placed around the cup in order to warm them. After a while he raised his head and looked at Megan.

"You shouldn't stay here, Megan," he said gravely.

"Why not?"

"Please don't get me wrong, I think it's wonderful that you have appeared, and I am sure Montgomery feels the same way. I enjoy your company very much . . . But the island is not a place for you. All of us here are no company for you."

Megan laughed uncomfortably, even though she knew that Tanvir was not making a joke. "Are you afraid that the sweetly-doing-nothing virus could skip me?"

Tanvir turned the cup in his hands. He was obviously having a hard time finding the right words. He took a deep breath, as if he was about to launch into a speech, but then remained silent.

"Will it ease your mind if I promise you that I'll work every day I spend on the island?"

"At what? There is nothing to do; you've seen that yourself."

"That's not true. There are Nelson and Montgomery and Chester and

409

Wesley."

"Oh, the primates . . . " Tanvir said, as if Megan had mentioned a tiresome subject.

"Yes. As I see it, Nancy can well use a little help."

Tanvir raised his hands and let them fall back on the table surface. "Your decision seems to be definite." Resignation and anger resonated in his voice.

"Yes," Megan said, "I'm staying." The certainty with which she had spoken these three words surprised her; a few hours ago she would have never imagined seriously thinking about such a decision, let alone making it. Now that this step was done, she felt a little better, less lost in this strange place that had neither received nor rejected her, and where she would try to live for a while as someone else.

Tanvir breathed noisily in and out and it sounded like a sigh that was missing something, something irreparable. He closed his eyes for a moment. Then he opened them and looked at Megan. "Promise not to follow my example, and at least reconsider leaving the island soon."

"I promise," Megan said, and to drown out the silence that followed, she moved the crank on the radio and turned it on.

Midnight was long gone when Megan walked up to her living quarters. As expected, there were no lights burning in Miguel's windows, but Esther seemed to be awake. For a second, Megan was tempted to knock on the door, in front of which stood a pair of white sneakers, but then she let it go and went into her room. On the floor there was a sheet of paper, and she turned on the light to read two sentences written in meticulous capital letters: MORNING BREAKFAST AT 11 O'CLOCK. CAN I COUNT ON YOU? Below them were two letters, T and R: Torben Raske. Megan took off her clothes, cleaned her teeth and stood under the shower. As always, very little water came out of the shower head, and it was warm and brown and smelled like mildew and slightly like chlorine. When there

410

was finally more water flowing, Megan lifted her face to meet it and shook the shampoo from the little bottle with the logo of the hotel, which already seemed to her like the memory of a distant world.

Suddenly too tired to comb her tangled hair, she lay on the bed. She had wanted to ask Tanvir about so much, but then remained silent like him and repeatedly charged the battery of the radio and listened to the almost imperceptibly dragging music, that sounded as if it was echoing from a gramophone, violas and oboes, a piano, the lasts signals of a dying culture. She had begun to cry and did not notice it, and Tanvir had moved to her side, totally confused, to put his hand on her shoulder, gently and for a very brief moment, and she had said everything was all right; it was the music that stirred her. Out of the cupboard, that pantry of comforting things, he had taken a can which contained four round biscuits covered with dark chocolate, each the size of the circle an adult can form with the thumb and index finger, and he asked her to take one, and then, while she wiped away her tears and ate the biscuit, he told her that the source of this delicacy had dried up months ago, and there was no room for hope, unless someone could track down the recipe and learn to bake them.

The fan turned and for a few blissful minutes her damp skin felt cool. She did not hear the door open, only when it closed. Through the veil of the mosquito net she saw a figure which slowly broke out of the darkness. The movement of Esther's arms as she parted the fabric seemed like a ritual gesture to Megan, like absolution for a crime yet to be committed.

4

When Megan woke up, Esther was no longer there. The slip of paper on the bed beside her proved that she had not been dreaming. DID NOT WANT TO WAKE YOU. SEE YOU AT 11. ESTHER. On the back was the message from Raske. Megan lifted the mosquito net and groped for the clock. When she saw that it was just a little before ten, she lay back down. The room was filled to the last corner with light that pierced through the thin curtains, the floor, the ceiling and every wall lined with brightness. The diesel engine fell silent and the fan stopped turning. When she closed her eyes, she felt the weight of Esther's body next to her. So she wouldn't fall asleep again, she got up and went into the bathroom. She looked at herself in the mirror for a while. Eventually, she realized she was looking for some transformation in her face, but except for a red spot on her neck she found nothing. She washed, dressed, and left the living quarters.

On the path to the kitchen hut she saw Miguel and Jay Jay, who were sweeping the square in front of the visitors center and mowing the grass along the fence. She waved to them, and the two swung their hats, as if they were standing on the deck of an outbound ship. Behind one of the windows Nelson sat on a chair and seemed fully focused on waiting for the first visitors.

The only one in the kitchen hut was Carla, who had put on makeup and coiffed her hair and was rummaging around in a travel bag. The table surface was littered with clothes, sunglasses, and cheap jewelry.

"Buenos Dias!" Carla shouted, took out a yellow blouse and unfolded it.

"Good morning." Megan sat down, and not two seconds later Rosalinda came through the wooden beaded curtain and brought her a cup of coffee.

"Big breakfast for you," said the cook, and it did not sound like a question, but a command.

"Only a few scrambled eggs and toast, please."

"I know," said Rosalinda and disappeared.

"Thor was looking for you yesterday." Carla pulled a pair of white pants open at the waist and tossed them on the pile of laundry.

"I was with Tanvir."

Carla looked at Megan, but then took another pair of pants from the bag, this time brown with light stripes.

"I came across his hut by chance while I was walking."

"How is his tooth?" Carla carefully folded the pants and put them together in a pile, which she seemed to have some purpose for later.

"He didn't mention anything. Did he have a toothache?"

"Apparently not anymore."

Rosalinda brought in a huge serving of scrambled eggs with steamed tomatoes and four slices of buttered toast. In a bowl there were banana and pieces of apple. She put everything in front of Megan, took Carla's empty plate and walked back to her kingdom.

"He says you're the only one who talks to him." Megan loaded scrambled eggs onto a slice of toast and took a bite.

"Talk to him? Did he say that?"

"Yes."

Carla lifted her chin. "Hm." She put on sunglasses and looked at her-

413

self in a mirror that was lying beside her coffee cup.

"How discreet."

"He had just started cooking and invited me to dinner."

"Did he tell you his life story?"

"No."

Carla put away her sunglasses and began to stuff the clothes on her left back into her travel bag.

"Why don't the two of them get along with one another, he and Raske?"

"Ask them." Carla pointed outside with a nod. Megan turned and saw Raske and Tanvir coming along the road toward them. Raske was wearing a bright suit, a matching straw hat and mirrored sunglasses, Tanvir wide black pants and a white doctor's coat. Raske, about half a head taller, progressed rapidly, while Tanvir, a few meters behind him, did not even try to keep up the pace. When Raske opened the door, Tanvir waved to Megan and Carla briefly and moved on.

"Good morning, ladies!" Raske shouted, even before the door closed behind him. The fact that Megan and Carla only muttered a greeting, seemed not to tarnish his good humor. "A perfect day for a movie!" He took off his sunglasses, grabbed a red suit jacket, threw it right back on the pile and turned to Megan. "I see that my message reached you. Very good." He looked at his watch and clapped his palms together. "Then I would say let's go!" He went to the door and opened it.

Megan quickly finished eating, while Carla stowed the rest of her things in the bag. Then they stood up and pushed their way past Raske into the fresh air. Carla seemed to want to escape the blazing sun, and ran across the clearing to the trees that lined part of the path to the laboratory building.

"Spending your nights on the beach now, like Carla?" asked Raske, who did not seem to mind the glare and the heat.

"I went out for a walk." Megan tried to follow Carla, but Raske prevented her by taking the path that ran along the long side of the clearing.

"That's not completely safe at night."

"Why?"

"You could fall and . . . I don't know ... sprain your ankle. Ask Carla."

"I had your flashlight with me."

"The batteries don't last forever."

"I sat down somewhere and looked at the sea. And turned off the flashlight."

"I went by your place shortly before midnight."

"I like to look at the sea."

For a while Raske fell into a brooding silence, and Megan realized that he would have preferred to question her outright, where she had been and what exactly she had done. When she stopped and slipped off a shoe to shake out a nonexistent stone, he waited for her.

"I wanted to talk to you about your salary," Raske said, when they finally reached the shade of the trees.

"That can wait." Megan saw Carla enter the laboratory building, imagined the cool air inside, and quickened her pace.

"What do you think of five thousand?"

"Five thousand what?"

"Dollars. Per month."

Megan stopped and looked at Raske. "You're kidding?"

Raske shook his head. "Plus a Christmas bonus." He grinned.

Megan was speechless for a moment. "That's a lot of money for so little work," she said.

"May I conclude that you accept the offer?" Raske held out his right hand to Megan.

Megan hesitated for two seconds, without quite knowing why, and then she took his hand and shook it.

"I have kept something from you," Raske said as they covered the last meters to the laboratory building. "There's no vacation." Without waiting

415

for Megan's reaction, he pulled open the door and entered the building.

"I knew there was a catch," Megan said. Raske laughed, and she followed him into the dark hallway.

In the first room Chester and Wesley were sitting on colored, air-filled plastic balls, watching spellbound as a film flickered on a small television. Snow-covered meadows turned green within a few seconds, then icicles rapidly melted and flowers broke through the earth and unfurled their petals with the speed of opening umbrellas. Tanvir and Carla were busy placing folders on a shelf, while Malpass lifted a computer screen from a crate and put it on one of the tables that Montgomery had covered with papers, pens, pencils and notepads.

Tanvir and Megan nodded to each other. When Megan put her hand on Montgomery's shoulder the bonobo grabbed at his head and seemed only now to notice that he was not wearing his cap. He wore long dark green trousers and a blue T-shirt that said IPREC in white letters on the front and the back, his name and the number 18. A short, high humming came out of his mouth, and for a moment he touched Megan's hand. Then he proceeded to distribute pens, notepads and transparent boxes of paper clips on the surface of the table.

Raske had taken off his hat and sunglasses, and set both on one of the filing cabinets. He looked around, flipped open a book and pushed a printer to the end of the table. "Mr. Raihan, you can tell Miguel he should leave now."

Tanvir put the last folder, which, as far as Megan could tell, was empty, on a shelf and then left the room.

"And Jay Jay should come and take care of the generators!" Malpass shouted into the hallway.

"Are there problems?" Raske took off his jacket and laid it over a chair. "We begin in an hour."

Malpass joined a cable to the monitor and to a keyboard.

416

"Fluctuations," he said before crawling under the table to untangle the cables.

As if to confirm Malpass' fears, the light on the ceiling flickered, but some seconds later burned as brightly as before.

"He should look at the transformers." Raske took a sheet of paper from the table, crumpled it and threw it into one of three empty bins standing against the wall. "Oh, Carla, could you please make sure that Chester and Wesley are kept busy for a while?"

Carla said something in Spanish that could be taken for either a friendly response or an impertinence.

"And do something with the trash cans."

"Si, Señor."

Raske entered the hall. "Do you speak Spanish?" he asked Megan, and requested with a gesture of his hand that she come with him.

"No."

"I can't either." Raske opened a door. "It's probably better that way."

In the second room there was a freshly covered examination table, a desk with a computer, two chairs and a number of technical devices that Megan thought she remembered from cardiology. On one wall hung colored wall charts which represented the bone and muscle structure, the course of the veins and arteries and the internal organs of a chimpanzee, and the cross section of a primate's skull. Tomographic images of a monkey's brain had been inserted into a light box, framed certificates and diplomas hung above a bookshelf, and on a stool with metal legs and a plastic seat there was a rolled up stethoscope.

Raske opened the drawer of a filing cabinet beside the desk, picked a few folders at random from the suspended files and distributed them on the table. "Better," he said after he had taken a few steps back to look at his work. He turned on the screen and waited until the blue desktop background appeared with the white IPREC lettering. Then he clicked on an icon that looked like a spreadsheet. "Those were the good old days," he muttered and left the room.

"Shouldn't I help the others?" asked Megan, gradually getting tired of running after Raske.

"I want you to see everything, just to get an impression."

The space behind the third door looked exactly like the first, with one difference: there were no computers on the tables, but refrigerators, metal boxes and microscopes, and the many shelves were filled with numbered boxes in different colors. One of the walls was dominated by a metal panel on which completed forms had been attached with magnets. In a glass cabinet Megan saw test tubes, and two white lab coats hanging from a hook by the door.

"Where are the chairs?" Raske turned on his own axis, raised his arms and dropped them again. He also let out a short sound that did not express his helplessness, but rising impatience and anger.

Megan shrugged her shoulders as she looked at Raske. It was not yet twelve, and she was already infinitely tired; the prospect of having to spend the rest of the day in Raske's presence weighed her down with a leaden cloak of exhaustion.

Raske stomped the floor and cried, "Malpass! There are no chairs in room three!"

"They're in here," Malpass shouted back. "Chairs are scarce! Have you forgotten already?"

Raske mumbled something, shut the door and opened the next one. The room was a slightly different copy of the previous one. On the tables there were appliances that looked like small televisions; the shelves were lined with black and white folders; from the walls hung clipboards containing sheets of paper that were inscribed with letters and numbers.

At the end of the hallway there was a room that was twice as big as the others. Through four windows, instead of two, light fell into the room and cast bright rectangles on the blue carpet, which substituted here for the gray marbleized linoleum. Except for a cabinet painted green and a

small table where several stacks of books were piled, there was no furniture. Colorful fabric bags filled with polystyrene spheres, inflatable plastic
balls and cushions were spread around on the floor. On one wall there
were large-format color prints, landscapes that depicted green hills,
brown plains, and snow-capped mountain peaks. Halogen lamps were
integrated into the white-painted ceiling and in some places speakers;
from the center a fire detector protruded. In a wall niche the dark monitor of a flat-screen television glinted.

"The classroom." Raske inhaled deeply and then exhaled. For a while
he stood with drooping shoulders between the colorful seats and looked
at the picture of a fjord, as if he was overcome with a miserable home-
sickness, then he stooped to pick up a book and placed it with the others
on the table.

"Lovely," Megan said, because she could think of nothing else. Raske
sighed and pressed the buttons of a remote control that he directed toward the screen. "It's been broken," he said, "for two years." He put
away the remote control. "An expensive piece of equipment, plasma." He
did not sound complaining, let alone distressed, more like someone who
sees the decline of things as inevitable, and therefore feels something a
little like satisfaction. He rolled a ball aside and went through a second
door that Megan had not noticed until now.

The narrow side room looked like it was being used as a storage
area. In one corner boxes were piled to the ceiling, in another appliances
that obviously no longer worked. On top of the lowest tower of boxes
there was a manual typewriter. Clothes, mainly white and light green tops
and pants like the ones worn by the medical staff in hospitals, covered a
folding table; on the floor underneath was Carla's travel bag, shining yellow. There was only one window; two neon lamps burned on the ceiling.

"You can change clothes in here," Raske said. He pushed a mop bucket
to the side with his foot and pulled down the shade on the window. When he saw the expression of uncertainty and skepticism on

419

Megan's face, he smiled. "I've planned three roles for you." He pulled a sheet of paper from his back pocket and unfolded it. Megan O'Flanagan, veterinarian from Ireland. Edwina Carmichael, neurologist from England. And Susan Falcone, a linguist from America."

"O'Flanagan?"

"We play roles. In case someone from the foundation should get the idea of tracking down one of the names, which we don't assume will happen, he is not supposed to find out immediately that you never got your doctorate."

Megan stared at Raske.

"Or that you left the EWSI station in Borneo after two months. Without ever having been in a managerial position." Raske folded the paper again and put it back in his pocket.

"You seem to have your sources," Megan said after she had pulled herself together.

Raske nodded.

"And you gave me the job anyway?"

"I'm giving you time on this island."

"And a lot of money."

"You can earn that today." Raske took a white coat from the table, held it up to himself with outstretched arms, dropped it again and turned to a woman who had entered the room behind Megan's back. "Vera, how nice to see you," he said.

Megan turned and saw a young dark-haired woman in a light green hospital gown, who was holding a cardboard box in front of her chest with both arms.

"Hello," the woman said with a heavy Russian accent. She wore large round earrings made of colored plastic, and her horn-rimmed glasses had slipped to the tip of her nose.

"Megan, may I introduce you to Vera Dimitrova? Vera is a speech therapist from Belarus. She was in Manila for a few days."

Vera sat the box on the table and stretched out her hand to Megan. "Very pleased to meet you."

Megan shook the hand mechanically. "Hello."

"I have to take care of a few things." Raske looked at the clock. "In half an hour?"

Vera nodded. "See you soon."

Raske gave Megan the coat. "This would suit you," he said, grinned and left the room.

Vera closed the door and leaned her back against it. She was as tall as Megan, her orthopedic shoes with the thick soles misleading. Her face was heavily made up, almost white. On her cheek, an inch away from the right corner of her mouth, was a dark, resplendent mole. Her long black hair was wound into a disorderly knot and rose-colored plastic hair pins with heads the size of cherries hung from the strands.

"I'm supposed to change clothes in here," Megan said. A strange feeling of unrest had come over her; she could not say whether the reason was Raske's revelation or the sight of this woman, who was bashful one moment and thrilling the next.

"I'll help you," Vera said and walked over to Megan. When she was standing close she took off her glasses, put both hands around Megan's neck, pulled her face toward her and kissed her.

Megan froze. Then, as the realization dawned on her with a violent beat of her heart and she suddenly grew weak and her lips opened slightly, Esther's laughter exploded into her mouth, a snorting explosion of warm air that tasted like coffee and cream. Writhing and holding her stomach, Esther stumbled backwards, dropped her glasses and sank to the ground, where her wig had half slipped off her head and she groaned and struggled for air with such a distorted face that Megan could not say whether she was laughing or crying.

"Oh, so you think that was funny?"

Esther sucked air into her gasping lungs and nodded vigorously. Be-

421

tween her forehead and her hairline there was a narrow strip of brown skin without make-up. One of the wooden sticks slipped out of her bun and fell to the floor.

Megan sat next to Esther, who tilted backwards and continued to lie on her back, quivering again and again under a new fit of suppressed laughter.

After a while, when her breathing had grown shallow, Esther touched Megan's hand with her fingertips. The generator cut off and the neon lights went out with a crackle. Two thin beams of light fell into the room on both sides of the blinds and ran like luminous lines across the floor. It was warm. The heat beat against the roof from the outside and caused it to crackle softly; otherwise there was absolute silence. Megan bent over Esther and traced the shape of her lips with a finger. Esther opened her eyes. Her lips were warm and brittle, her teeth white and small, like those of a child. She brushed a strand of hair from Megan's face, closed her eyes and waited. A sound emerged from within her, a low hum in her upper body, not louder, just more intense, a murmur, soft and supported by a growing impatience. Megan kissed her, and Esther sighed and fell silent. Then the generator started running and white light filled the fluorescent tubes and lit up the room. Esther covered her face with her hands and turned her head to the side. Megan suddenly felt strangely self-conscious and sat up. A beetle with shiny green armor ran across the floor, and she would have gladly picked it up and examined it closely, but she continued to sit and loosened the laces of her sneakers, just to have something to do. Esther took her hands from her face and put an arm over her eyes. Megan did not understand what she softly said.

When steps could be heard coming from the corridor they both jumped up. Megan rummaged through the clothes on the table; Esther took the lid off the box that was filled with wigs. There was a knock, and Esther shouted that the door was open. Miguel entered the room bashfully, said hello, placed a heavy mirror against the free wall beside the table and hurried away. Megan put on a wig with shoulder length blond hair and sunglasses and looked at herself in the mirror. The resemblance to her mother, the way she had looked in the parking lot of the supermarket in Dublin, was so amazing that she pulled the wig off her head and threw it on the table.

"What is it?" Esther stepped behind Megan and hugged her.

Megan took off her sunglasses. "Nothing."

Esther kissed Megan's neck, but Megan broke away and took one of the bright green lab coats from the pile of clothing. "We should get ready," she said and pulled the lab coat over her T-shirt.

"What's wrong?"

"Nothing," said Megan, more indignant than she had intended. "I'm just not a blonde; that's all."

Esther stood there for a moment perplexed, and then marched in front of the mirror and adjusted the wig, put on her glasses and left the room.

It was late afternoon when Miguel brought the extras back to their island with the boat. They had played domestic workers, gardeners, cleaners, and laboratory aids. Women dressed like nurses with chimpanzees and bonobos in hand walked through the picture; one even sat at a table and stared at an empty glass plate through a microscope. An old man who radiated the dignity of a professor stood dressed in a white coat next to the laboratory building and acted as if he and Malpass were deep in conversation, while in the foreground Raske addressed a few questions to Carla, who was playing herself. Finally, five men were put into suits and guided as local politicians to the visitors center, which was, however, never to be seen from the inside, and on into the laboratory building where Megan, Esther, Carla, Malpass and Tanvir simulated a high level of activity. Instead of money, all the extras received four T-shirts with the IPREC logo and a souvenir photo with Nelson, who put on a straw hat and sunglasses for the occasion.

Megan played her three roles as best she could. She had taken great pains to look like three completely different people, had made herself up with light and sun-tanned skin, with wrinkles around her eye and the freckles of her childhood. Among the wigs, in a jewel case, there were various colored contact lenses, false eyelashes and even teeth. In the disguises she had seemed in a strange way familiar to herself rather than foreign, had regarded herself in the mirror with amazement. Raske had given her a sheet of paper with the typewritten questions and answers, and an hour to memorize them. As Megan O'Flanagan, she needed to make several attempts before she could speak her lines without mistakes into the camera that Jay Jay aimed at her, but after that it was better, and for the role of Edwina Carmichael she even spoke with a slightly haughty accent, which she remembered from her life back in London. She examined Wesley's leg and put the splint back on again; she shined a light in Nelson's eyes and in Chester's throat and she listened to Montgomery's heart, which beat loud and fast for her. She looked at Carla, who was wearing a black, curly wig and huge sunglasses and had enlarged her breasts with tissue, and she listened to Esther, who was sounding out something in English like a child, with earnest diligence, an imperfect perfection that touched her.

Now she went, without makeup and in her own clothes, to Nancy Preston's house. Everyone was present except Miguel, who was rowing the extras home, and Tanvir, who, at Raske's behest, was supervising Chester and Wesley in the laboratory building. They looked like the tired crew of a low-budget film. Jay Jay, still cheerful and shouldering the camera, went ahead. Carla, Esther and Megan followed him at a distance. The evening light was mild, the heat almost gone. Carla and Esther carried a cardboard box with hospital gowns and wigs, Megan held Montgomery by one hand and Nelson by the other. Raske and Malpass had fallen behind. Malpass was tired; he was sweating and had placed a wet towel around his neck. He was chatting during his walk with Raske, quietly and sibilantly, punctuated by brief pauses in which he took a breath.

Raske said nothing. In the past seven hours he had said enough, had given instructions and had spoken into the camera as the host of a documentary, serious and confident and with the sparingly used smile of a man who is certain of the positive effect of his words; who knows that text and tone of voice and image selection had functioned exactly the same way in the years before and would change nothing about it; who knows that he is hiding decay and dissolution, and can transform the rest into something presentable that the Board of Trustees in Texas would glorify as romantic simplicity, as a Spartan, scientific zeal fueled by bliss, in which the pure, the good, and the useful thrived. It was difficult to say whether he was ignoring Malpass, was lost in thought, or tired of listening. His face was as smooth and unruffled as ever, except for his mouth, which was growing narrower by the hour, as if he had to press his lips together to keep from bellowing. During the afternoon he had changed his shirt three times; he was carrying the fourth on a coat hanger made of wire, while the jacket was slung over his back on his index finger. He held up his chin, as if in anticipation of the wind that pulled apart the purple clouds high above him and would at some point touch down on the island.

There, where the path was covered with coarse gravel from a bay on the other side of the island, he stopped. Malpass, absorbed in his monologue, walked several steps further, until he noticed the absence of Raske at his side and also stopped. Raske made no effort to keep from being noticed by Jay Jay and the three women when he spread out his arms with the shirt and jacket and finally asked Malpass to shut his mouth. Jay Jay was already on the porch and was filming the new arrivals. After Raske glanced at him once, he lowered the camera and sat down in one of the four wicker chairs that were lined up next to the door. Malpass murmured something unintelligible, but then decided it was obviously better to leave Raske in peace. He drank water from a plastic bottle that

425

he had been carrying around all day, and stood, head bowed, to the side, as Raske walked past him and the round bed planted with flowers over to the house, went up the five steps and pulled the cord on the door bell.

Nancy Preston was waiting for them with a little refreshment, which she had brought from the kitchen. She insisted that everyone eat something before they began work. Ruben had carried chairs into the living room and walked around with a tray of tuna, egg, and cheese sandwiches, while Nancy managed the lemonade pitchers. With a cigarette in her mouth, she sat in her chair and filled every empty glass held out to her. She wore white sandals, a sand-colored pantsuit, a loosely knotted Hermes scarf around her neck and discreet pearl jewelry, consisting of a brooch and earrings. The most striking thing about her was her dark red painted fingernails and matching lipstick. Megan was already accustomed to seeing her shape her hair in a tower with lots of hairspray. When Raske sat down beside her and tried to explain the process of filming, Nancy waved and said she knew what she had to say.

After everyone, including Nelson and Montgomery, had something to eat and drink, Carla, Esther, and Megan dressed in fresh hospital uniforms, put on wigs and quickly applied make-up. They spent the next hour trying to act like Nelson and Montgomery's teachers, taking objects out of the chests, drawing things on the blackboard and acting as if they were pointing out important information in large bound notebooks. The recordings were intended as filler, as short video clips with voice-over recordings provided by Raske between the scenes with Nancy, who went into raptures for the viewers about how rewarding it was to work with the primates and how peaceful life on the island was, while the world was in a perpetual cycle of war, hatred, and destruction. For an example of the horrors from which the IPREC station was spared, and to also discreetly allude to the date of recording, she held a three-day-old *New York Times* up to the camera and commented on a bomb attack in Iraq and a rampage at an American school.

Raske stood next to Jay Jay with a glass of lemonade in hand and let Nancy go on. It was obvious that her idea to jump back and forth wildly between complacent lectures and endless chatter drove him up the wall, but he remained calm and used each of her breaks, while she puffed on a cigarette, to stop recording, praise Nancy and steer her skillfully where he wanted her to go. In this way he managed to elicit a few coherent sentences from her that would prove to the members of the foundation that everything was going well, work with the primates was as successful as it had been in past years, and that she would not oppose renewed financial support from IPREC. Finally he sat down beside her, asked her some questions and asked her to send a greeting to Texas.

Four hours after the troop had entered the villa, they left again. By now it was half past nine, the sky black and the air warm and noticeably stirred by a faint breeze. In front of the laboratory building they met Miguel, who came from the beach and took delivery of Nelson. Raske thanked them all briefly, and then retired with Malpass and Jay Jay to one of the rooms to view the digital video. Because Tanvir was still watching over Chester and Wesley, Megan offered to take Montgomery to her place for a while. Carla, tired and still in high spirits, announced she was going to the kitchen hut to tip back a few bottles of beer. She was still wearing the mint-green hospital uniform and a wig with long brown hair and was disappointed when no one followed her. Alone, she set out on the path, disappeared in the dark and sang a song in Spanish that sounded harsh and mocking.

Shortly after midnight Tanvir came to pick up Montgomery. Megan, Esther and the bonobo had eaten the fruit Rosalinda brought to fill the wooden bowls in the rooms every day, and then played several memory games. Esther had taken the cards out of her room after Montgomery asked her for them, first by touching her arm, and then turning over

427

imaginary cards. "Memory?" Esther had asked, and Montgomery nodded and clapped his hands.

Esther was asleep on the bed, surrounded by twin apples, bananas, coconuts, flowers, trees, shells, fish, starfish, cups, spoons, glasses, suns, houses, balls, trousers, vests, shoes, beetles, lizards, and butterflies. She held a card in her hand, moving her fingers now and then in a dream, slowly, not fluttering as they had during the game, when she hesitated over the second card, yet to be exposed, only to choose the wrong one again.

"I'll go along with you," Megan said quietly and pulled the door shut.

"Don't you want to stay with her?"

"No."

Tanvir walked to the path. Montgomery was waiting for Megan and reached for her hand as she stretched out her arm. They left the lights of the houses behind and crossed the bright moonlit field. Insects rose from the short scrubby grass along with the long-drawn sounds of crickets. In a hollow large quantities of withered blooms had collected that looked like folded paper in the twilight, and Montgomery stopped and pointed, to show Megan the beauty of this sight.

"How did he do with Memory?"

"He won. All ten games."

Tanvir lowered his voice. "Don't you know that he's cheating?"

"What? How?"

"He's a six-year-old child, dressed up like a bonobo." Tanvir was laughing. "You should see your face."

Megan was aware of the kind of silly face she made; she continued walking and pulled Montgomery along with her.

Tanvir giggled and followed her. Bats flew over their heads, sailing at a tilt back and forth to the end of the field and diving into the darkness of the grove. Megan and Tanvir were silent. Stars sparkled in the sky, just to remind them that this island floated in space and was doomed. On a trunk with bark as bright as yellow paper, ants traveled in the cool protection of the night. Megan liked the noise created by walking through the grass, a scratchy rubbing, a brush in Sam's hair. She told Tanvir because she wanted him to know that she was not sulking. He asked what animals she had on the farm and whether she had been happy as a child. Yes, she said, for a long time, a far too short eternity, she had been happy. They walked together through the darkness, and since Megan didn't say anything else, Tanvir asked nothing more. Before they entered the path between the trees and heard the pigs grunt, he turned on the flashlight.

In front of the house Tanvir made a new fire in the hearth and put on a pot of water. Inside, he cleared notebooks and several books from a bench by the wall and prepared a bed for Montgomery with a pad, a pillow and a blanket. He apologized for the heat and said something about a broken generator and the lack of spare parts.

The bonobo sat down at the table and started to draw on a sheet of paper with a pen, as if he wanted to make it clear that he was not yet willing to go to sleep. He had taken off his hat and laid it beside him. Because Raske had also assigned different roles to the primates, during the course of the day Montgomery had to change three times and was once again wearing the long blue pants and blue short-sleeved shirt, a kind of uniform that was as typical for him as the colorful vest and short pants were for Chester. He pursed his lips and wrinkled his brow as he filled the page with squiggles and lines, a tangled network at first glance, that was slowly becoming an ornament-like floral pattern.

"You owe me a story," Tanvir said when he brought in the pot with hot water and prepared a mug of tea. "For dinner the other day," he added when Megan gave him a quizzical look.

"I told you a story."

"About an orangutan, not about you."

Megan placed the second chair next to Montgomery and sat down. Leaves were growing out of the stems, circles formed new flower

429

heads, the lines overlapped, forming an increasingly dense web. Tanvir placed two full cups on the table, brought in an empty wooden box from outside and then took a seat on it. He pushed a cup to Megan, put sugar in his, and stirred it.

"It has to be about me?"

Tanvir nodded.

Megan pulled the cup toward her. Her mirror image floated in the brown tea. On the paper lines flowed next to lines, until there was no more space left. Montgomery put down his pen and gave her the paper. There were countless flowers, a whole field spread out before her, an organic maze in which the vista was lost.

"Thank you." Megan put her hand on Montgomery's arm.

Montgomery lowered his eyelids for two, maybe three seconds, like an old man who is uncomfortable with the words "Thank you." A sound came from his throat, something between a song and a sigh; he put on his cap, climbed from his chair and left the house.

"Where is he going?" Megan asked.

"He looks after the chickens. I think he knows how many there are, and he counts them. If one is missing, he searches for it."

"Does he eat them?"

"I haven't killed a chicken for over fifty years. They're my companions. And when they're in a good mood, they lay an egg for me."

"And the pigs?"

"Do I eat them? No. They adopted me. Raske said that they belong to IPREC, but I don't care."

"Do the chickens have names?"

"Only one. The oldest. Miss Ellie."

"Miss Ellie. Nice."

"From 'Dallas'. Do you know the TV series? Miss Ellie is the mother of the Ewing clan."

"When I was little, we didn't have a TV, and later I didn't want one."

Tanvir took a sip of tea. "What did you do in the evenings and on rainy Sundays?"

"Read. Draw. Write."

"Write? What?"

"Scientific papers on the musical perception of pigs. Speculation about the function of dust on moth wings. Stories."

"Tell me one."

"But they're not about me. None of them are about me."

"It doesn't matter." Tanvir folded his arms across his chest and leaned back.

Megan looked down at the drawing, engrossed in it. The wood around them expanded, crackled. She liked the idea that it performed, that is still lived.

"In a tree in a garden lived a woodpecker," she finally began. "When the weather was fine a young boy sat under the tree and carved on his wooden gun, or read a comic book. One day Morse code was explained in one of the issues, and the boy learned it. As the woodpecker tapped on the trunk, the boy wrote. What he read was so incredibly beautiful and, even for a little boy, of such overwhelming truth, that in comparison to this bird, he seemed stupid and ugly and insignificant. He took his sling-shot and killed the bird. The woodpecker fell down dead and pierced the boy's heart with its sharp beak. Their blood intermingled and covered the boy's writing and beauty disappeared from the world."

Tanvir sat there for a while staring at a point on the wall over Megan's left shoulder.

"The end," Megan said.

Tanvir, his arms still folded across his chest, did not budge. Once he gently stroked his hand over his bald head and groaned, seemed to take a deep breath in comment, but then said nothing, and made a face as if he was digesting heavy, indigestible food.

At some point Megan had to laugh. "Is everything okay?"

431

Tanvir raised his eyebrows, sat up straight and put his hands on the table. He breathed deeply in and out. "Are all of your stories so . . . " He moved his hands, as if to form the right word with them.

"Short?"

"Dismal."

"None of them have a happy ending, if that's what you mean."

Tanvir nodded, pressing his lips together.

"I wrote them for my little brother. I wanted to scare him. I wanted him to believe that animals have magical powers. That each beetle he crushed possessed the power to take revenge on him from beyond the grave."

"And? Did he believe it?"

"Yes, for a while."

"What is your brother's name?"

Megan drank her tea. "Paul."

"Does he live in Ireland?"

"On the farm. He takes care of animals, old dogs, donkeys and horses that nobody wants anymore."

"Then the stories had an effect somehow."

"Yes," Megan said, wincing when a large insect crashed into one of the window panes.

"But I still haven't found out anything about you."

"My life story isn't very exciting."

Tanvir poured himself a cup of tea. "I don't believe that. Every life is a wild sequence of world-shaking events and heartbreaking drama."

"Oh yeah? Yours, for example?"

"But certainly."

Megan leaned back and folded her arms across her stomach.

"I'm listening."

Tanvir grinned. He scratched his head, clasped his hands and bowed his head as if he was about to pray. But then he looked at Megan and his tired eyes twinkled. "The short version or the long one?"

"The reasonable one."

Tanvir's grin was even wider. He cleared his throat and put his hands, palms down, on the table. "Well, I will spare you with dates. Only this: The Great War was over when I was born. The British Empire had just separated my country into two halves, and, as fate would have it, the great dirty world welcomed me into that part which is known to you as India. Why and what I lived for had long been a mystery to me. I lay around sleeping, dozed away the years. A woman—I never knew who she was, because she died before I could ask her—appeared sometimes and took care of me, the way you take care of a pan of food on the fire, so nothing burns. When I was four years old, my parents took me to the fields for the first time. My bigger brother showed me what to do, and I spent the next four years lifting stones, digging ditches and plucking pests off the plants. I truly believed that this was my life, but they sent me to school, because the country needed engineers and architects and doctors and teachers, not more ill-educated farmers who could hardly feed themselves. School." Tanvir laughed and shook his head. "You should have seen it, our school. Four walls made of mud bricks and a corrugated iron roof, not much better than the hut where I ate and slept. And the teacher was a greenhorn from Calcutta, barely finished with school himself, tall and so thin that sometimes we gave him the piece of flat bread or the boiled egg that we had brought with us from home. He really wasn't born to teach; that you can believe. He was shy; his quiet voice got lost on the way to the back rows, and if he reprimanded us for anything we had to refrain ourselves from laughing. Nevertheless, he taught us the basic necessities, all right, and when I was ten I could read and write and knew I wanted to be a doctor. I wanted to earn a lot of money, live in a city, and drive a car. I wanted to save people from death and my parents from their miserable life to which they resigned themselves so humbly and silently. I hated them for it and myself too, because I was a child and could

433

do nothing except watch how they went to the fields every day at dawn and came back in the evening, their skin covered with dried mud and hungry and almost too tired to eat. —I was a good son, I may say so, yes. I helped wherever it was possible. I fed the two goats, cut the grass in the meadow that was off my route to school, gathered drift wood at the river for the stove. I stole vegetables from other gardens and sometimes an unattended shovel, an abandoned bucket, a piece of rope. It was clear to my parents that I had stolen these things, but they never said anything. They could use everything I brought home, so they never asked me questions. I knew that their poverty was embarrassing to them in front of my brother and me and we never talked about our position, never about the scarce food, the confined living space, the lack of money. When I think of the sounds of my childhood, I hear the bleating of goats, the scratching of the metal hook in the fireplace, the patter of rain on the roof of our house. And the silence that existed between us, our lack of words during daily chores, our mute coexistence during the meal, our silence on the long road to work in the field." Tanvir raised his head slightly and looked into the void, as if he was listening to the past. His face was soft, his dark skin undulating in the lantern light. Then he looked Megan in the eyes and smiled. "Silence is the true sound of childhood."

Megan also smiled. "Yes," she said, and with that, everything had been said about this subject.

"I was industrious, that I was. I learned as though my life depended on it, and that of my parents and my brother. When I was twelve, the teacher returned to where he had come from, and another one took his place, older, who told me after a month that I was something special, that I was smarter than the rest of the class and belonged in a high school. But the next high school was far away, and because we had no money, I stayed where I was. At the same time I wanted to go away, away, no matter where. I despised my parents for their poverty and I pitied them. Once, when the lessons were canceled because the teacher had eaten something spoiled, I went to the village instead of going home. You need to imagine a sleepy backwater, a few hundred shabby huts, a handful of handsome houses, a marketplace, a bus stop, from where a bus travelled into the big wide world, hawkers, food stalls, kiosks, shops filled with trinkets that my naive enthusiasm turned into precious treasures. I saw bullock carts, rickshaws, bicycles and even cars, a singular commotion, noisy and dusty and wonderful. And I saw men and women in clothes that were not dirty and torn, and children who stood around or walked along the street dawdling, as if they had nothing to do and all the time. And I hated my life so much more and I wished something would happen, something big, something powerful. I wanted a hurricane that would lift me and carry me off and settle me somewhere in the world where it didn't stink of goats and no one was so stupid and tore pages out of textbooks to make fire. —And my wish came true. There was a typhoon, and with it a never-ending rain that drowned the land in water. For three days and two nights we sat on the roof of our house, with nothing but bread to eat at first and later raw millet from a damp bag, and we drank the milk from goats; then a boat came and picked us up. We had to leave the two goats on the roof because there was no room in the boat, and when we came back a week later they were gone, stolen or run away, maybe eaten by stray dogs. The walls of the house had collapsed, the few pieces of furniture damaged or washed away, the fields covered with mud and debris and flotsam. My mother wept at the sight of the destruction; my father, my brother, and I searched for a few things from the meter-thick mud: clothes, dishes, an axe. We found a single shoe and a red plastic bucket that did not belong to us. The next day my father took us to the fields and we hauled away branches and tree trunks and pieces of houses that had once been somewhere, and the stench of rotting animals hung over everything, and when we had drunk the last drop of water my father said that it was impossible to clear the fields and cultivate them and then wait until the time came for the harvest. We would starve to death before then, he said, so he decided to go away to another place, away from the coast into the interior of the country, to Ranchi in Jharkhand, where there was allegedly work for him. One of his brothers lived there, he explained to us, and had told him many years ago that the coal mines were constantly looking for men who were not afraid to climb into the dark bowels of the earth, and he did not know this fear. How could he, I thought; he had never penetrated deeper into the soil than the plow he dragged across the field like a brainless ox. And now he stood and talked about leading us into a new life, as if he had remained silent all along to save up enough words for this speech. My mother cried the entire night, which we spent sleepless on rotting straw, but the next day she was the first one prepared to march away. Because my parents had only worked the land and did not own it, we left our old home with the little money that had survived the flood in a tin can in the niche by the fireplace. It was enough to take us, very slowly but alive, to our destination. Did I feel guilty? A little maybe, yes. But actually, I knew that was nonsense. Please don't get me wrong; I'm far from showing off, but I already had sufficient intelligence at that time to believe neither in the power of desire nor even in higher powers, and certainly not in a God who would answer the prayers of an embittered boy and flood half a country in a deluge." Tanvir drank the rest of his tea and filled both cups.

Outside the cicadas clamored, and in between Megan thought she could hear the occasional call of a bird.

"Do you believe in God, Megan?"

"No."

"Can I ask why?"

"There isn't one. Not for anybody."

Tanvir shoveled sugar into the cup and stirred it. He nodded. When he stopped stirring, he also stopped nodding. "My parents were Hindus," he finally said. "But they lacked, how should I say it, a connection to relig-

436

ion. They had inherited it from their parents and grandparents like a cast-iron pot or a blanket—a legacy, so to speak. They followed the rules, took part in the major celebrations, now and then made a sacrifice at home or at the temple, but mostly they were too tired even to pray. I think that this unpronounced attitude toward religion was the reason we left and did not stay like our neighbors, who continued their reliance on the gods, even when the situation was almost hopeless." Tanvir got up, fetched the pot of hot water and poured it into the teapot.

Megan also rose, walked to the window and looked into the darkness. "Montgomery has been outside a long time," she said.

"Ah, I forgot." Tanvir put down the pot, opened the door and stepped outside.

Megan followed him, locking the door behind her. "Maybe something has happened to him?"

"Don't worry," Tanvir said. "Sometimes he sits with the chickens or pigs for hours." She went to the chicken coop, a small, shoulder-high hut on stilts wrapped with barbed wire. On the roof, made of boards and tar paper and gently sloping toward the back, there was a ladder. Tanvir looked into the dark opening, behind which Megan believed she detected a pale body. They walked on, past the intertwined bodies of several pigs, and then Tanvir stopped. "Or he's asleep." He pointed to a hammock, stretched between two trees, where Montgomery was laying.

Megan took a few steps closer and observed the bonobo. He lay on his side, one arm hanging down, one leg bent, his knee touching his belly. When he breathed he made a gentle rattling sound, and one time his eyelid quivered as if he was winking at Megan in his sleep.

"And now?" Megan asked quietly. "Should we leave him here?"

"Yes," Tanvir whispered. "I'll pick him up later."

They went back. Except for the buzzing of cicadas it was quiet. Bright moths floated in the darkness; from the windows, cracks, and crevices yellow light shone. The door and the floorboards creaked; the whole house moaned like a being that is disturbed in its sleep. Tanvir and Megan sat down at the table; the tea was still hot.

"Where was I?" said Tanvir.

"On the journey."

"Of course, yes, on the way to Ranchi. Well, as I said, we went there to live, but we were at the end of our means; we had no money. And we never saw my uncle; he had died years ago. His children and grandchildren were as poor as us, landless peasants, miners, day laborers. My shame to be a member of this family grew immensely in the face of these ragged kinsfolk. We found accommodation with a man my father claimed was the eldest son of his brother, therefore my cousin. He lived alone and my mother, my brother and I were his slaves. Anantram bred chickens in a yard behind the shed he called home and he was willing to share with us, because he had such a big heart. My father found work in a coal mine, and we fed chickens and cleaned the yard; we placed the eggs in a sort of wooden chest where they hatched; we took care of the chicks and made sure that the older animals in the narrow farmyard didn't peck each other to death; we chopped off the heads of those who were ready for slaughter; we plucked them and collected the fine feathers in one bag and the coarse ones in another; we removed the livers, hearts and lungs and threw them into a bowl and threw the rest of the innards into a bucket; we drove away the cats that ran along the walls above our heads; we stood barefoot in the chicken shit; we trapped the animals Anantram chose; on hot days we inhaled the dust they kicked up, and at night we coughed it out; we dreamed about them; we moved like them; we ate their heads and became them. —I didn't go to school anymore. I didn't exist. Out of the fear of being as dumb as a chicken, I remembered the books I had read, the countries that the teacher had described to us. I solved arithmetic problems in my head, wrote essays, held silent lectures, quoted poems that no noise in the farmyard could drown out. Two years passed in that way, and when I was fifteen, several mine shafts collapsed and thirty-two workers were killed, including my father. The dead were left in the ground; a rescue would have been too complicated and expensive. My brother got my father's shoes and his only pants, I a shirt that was much too large. After that, there was no longer any reason for my mother to stay with my brother and me in Ranchi. One of my many cousins, a thin, shy girl with crooked teeth who could not find a husband, went to Madhya Pradesh, and we went with her. In Bhopal my mother took a job in a sewing factory, and my brother, then about twenty, worked as a kitchen hand. I delivered food. I brought hot meals to people who had no time to go to a restaurant, to their office, to their workshop, or wherever they worked. One of my regular customers was an old man who ran a small office on the ground floor of his house. He transcribed for people who could not read or write—letters, filled out forms, read official announcements to them, private mail and prescriptions. His name was Jahawar Bindra, and he liked me. In the afternoons, when I had finished my rounds, I went to see him; I could sit on a cushion in a corner and rummage through his books. He spoke several Indian dialects, English and some French, and his library was so extensive that the only room left for him and his wife was a tiny bedroom and an even smaller kitchen. In school I had learned Sanskrit and a little English, and I devoured everything which had been collected in this realm of knowledge and stories: Plato and Heraclitus, Schopenhauer and Rousseau, Austen and Dickens, Twain and Melville, Dostoyevsky, and Tolstoi. I wallowed in encyclopedias and medical books, atlases and multi-volume scholarly anthologies, learned everything about silk worms, a lot about the oceans and a little bit about human anatomy. I can now quote two sonnets by Shakespeare and a poem by William Butler Yeats; I know where the town of Nakhodka is and how high the Nanda Devi is and how many bones move when you nod your head."

"How many?"

"Twenty-two. —Jahawar taught me how to type letters on his type-

439

writer, an Underwood that weighed tons. Soon I was spending the entire afternoon and evening with him pounding on the keys, and used the breaks, when there was nothing to do, to read. He paid me a decent wage for my work and at some point I stopped delivering meals. My mother was not excited about my new job at first, but when I put my weekly wages on the table in front of her every Sunday, she changed her mind. We lived in a room above a workshop where tubs, buckets and pots were made from tin, and I was glad for every minute that I didn't have to spend there. Jahawar and his wife Rachna were admittedly old, but I had decided to treat them like my parents. I simply turned my world around, made the two of them my father and my mother, and made my mother and my brother two strangers with whom I shared my sleeping place. My mother didn't seem to mind. She worked in the sewing room fourteen hours a day, washed and mended clothes for me and my brother and tried with limited success to make a decent accommodation out of the hole in which we lived. Often she did not return until night, fingers and back stiff and eyes that needed glasses, red and swollen. Then she was happy, when we were there and my brother had brought a little food with him and we could sit together for an hour before she went to bed." Tanvir fell silent and looked for a while blankly at the table, as if he had lost the thread. He grabbed the teacup, blew in it and took one sip, then another. Suddenly he lifted his head and looked at Megan like someone who realizes that he has company. With a hasty gesture, he put down the cup. "Are you ready to go to sleep?" he asked. "I talk and talk, but perhaps you're tired. As tired as my mother after a thousand meters of yarn."

Megan smiled. "I'm wide awake."

"So shall I tell you more?"

"Yes."

Tanvir took a deep breath, held it for a moment in his lungs and then exhaled. "Five years passed." He snapped his fingers and folded his hands. "While I was growing up, my mother shrank. I grew into a young

440

man; she was stunted, an old woman at less than fifty. Her vision grew weaker and weaker, and I bought her a pair of glasses from my savings, but she had already lost her job at the sewing room. She didn't have to work anymore; I earned enough money, and my brother brought home something to eat every day. My mother slept a lot, despite the noise from the workshop. Sometimes, usually at night when it was cool, she sat on her wooden stool, in the light of a lantern, and sewed a button on my shirt or mended a tear in a piece of my brother's clothing. With the glasses she could see well, but because she had never learned to read and we didn't own a TV, her only pastime was sewing. —It shames me to this day that it was only shortly before she died that I got the idea to give her a book. One with lots of pictures, of course, and few words. The copy that I brought her back then, she loved more than anything else. It was a volume with colored drawings of trees and leaves, flowers and blossoms, fruits and berries. The entire afternoon she sat at the window, absorbed in contemplation of a pomegranate, which she had never heard of before, whose geometry and beauty she not only recognized, but also seemed to admire. —After her death I lived with Jahawar and his wife, even though the two of them had very little space for themselves among all the books. I slept on the roof under a fabric awning; in the rainy season I slept on a folded blanket in the office. A year passed, then a second, and a third. I wolfed my way through the books, crammed down knowledge the way my brother ate food. I took over the desk from Jahawar, who could not write anymore because the gout made his hands noticeably unusable. And because his eyes were getting worse, I gave him my mother's glasses, and he read to his customers, but he made many mistakes, skipped lines and had to constantly start over again. The man I had made my father had been old when I first brought him food, and now he was ancient. My head was growing heavier; his seemed to lose weight, as if the ballast he had gained by reading had to be dropped before the impending journey. He died in the summer, the same month as my mother four years earlier. Rachna, his wife, wanted me to stay with her, and I did. I shopped for her, I cooked, I cleaned, I read to her. In between, from eleven to four, I kept the office open. At night, when I could not sleep because of the heat and the noise of the city, I studied the professional medical literature. I still wanted to be a doctor; you need to know that I had not given up this dream, an audacious one for a yokel. —Less than half a year later Rachna died; she did not want to live anymore without her husband. She and Jahawar had no children, so she bequeathed her house to me. My brother was living in a tiny room above the restaurant where he worked, and I invited him to join me. He was now over thirty and weighed one hundred and ten kilos. He listened to music, Indian folk music, and soon the house was filled with it. He lived upstairs, where Jahawar and Rachna's bed still stood, and one day he asked me if I would teach him to read. —My brother could not read! All these years I was so busy becoming an intelligent man that I had not noticed this fact. I had never asked myself what he was doing in his spare time, what his dreams looked like, whether he was happy or not. It took almost a year before Syed could read. He also learned to write, but his hands were so huge and plump that the pen disappeared in his paw. I had secretly hoped that he would be able to help me one day in business, but he was too slow and his writing was illegible. But he devoured the books, which surrounded him in his wide bed. When he was through with all the Indian works, he asked me to teach him English, and after another year he had the courage to tackle the rest of the library. —Those were good years. Syed brought food in the evenings, and in good weather we sat on the roof, filled our bellies and talked about books. Syed preferred to read biographies of famous people: Diogenes, Marc Aurel, Da Vinci, Columbus, Napoleon. He not only dived happily into the lives of strangers, but also seemed to take cover, how should I say, behind these historical figures, to hide from a world that often demanded more courage from him than he could muster. He was very shy, you know. As a child he had been quiet, as silent as our parents, and when he grew up, suddenly he had to talk, had to answer questions and open his mouth when he wanted something. I don't know if he had started eating so much out of grief. Perhaps it was only because he loved it, as much as he loved music. Or because he worked in this restaurant where there was the smell of food all day. Once, when we dragged a mattress on the roof and he was completely out of breath, I asked him if he wanted to lose weight, and he said it wouldn't work, because then he would have to eat less. So he stayed fat, but did not seem to make much of it. One night when we had both grown talkative from too much beer, he entrusted me with the fact that he had never been with a woman. He said it was better that way; women would only bring trouble and strife and questionable recipes into the house. And he didn't feel alone, because he had the food and the music and the books and me. I agreed with him, because I did not want to hurt him and was completely inexperienced in matters of love myself and needed consolation. —Well, a few years passed by that way. The world was spinning, but it turned without me and my brother, and we told ourselves furthermore that it was better that way. Syed was the assistant to the cook, and I bought a new typewriter, a Royal Arrow with smoother, clockwork-like mechanics. When I had put enough money aside, I hit the books again, and at thirty-one I started studying medicine; I graduated six years later. I did my internship in a small hospital, which was only five blocks from our house. It was dilapidated and too small and the equipment antiquated, but it had a courtyard with a lawn and trees and a garden pond with colorful fish floating under lily pads. The work was hard and the pay lousy, but I lived modestly. My only possessions, except the house, were the typewriter and the used bike that I had bought to ride to the university. —Did I still dream of a car, a silver Mercedes with tinted windows that was quiet and cool inside and smelled like leather instead of feces and garbage? The answer is yes. But that dream had become a thought before falling asleep, a fleeting image, a gimmick. It no longer propelled me through the night, making me wake up with the feeling of painful emptiness. I no longer had to get my parents out of their miserable life; I did not have to leave some place to arrive somewhere else, where everything was better, cleaner and less humiliating. I had new interests. One of them was a nurse. Her name was Sita; she was young and beautiful. And married. Her husband drove the ambulance. He was ten years younger and a foot taller than me. If there was an accident anywhere, he sped off with screeching tires and sirens going and people jumped to the side, so they wouldn't get caught under the wheels. His name was Rahul and he loved the speed, the lurching around the curves and the howl of the engine. More than once I sat in the back of his car and feared for my life and that of the victim, and more than once I wished Rahul would crash into a wall and die. Not only did he drive very fast, but also very well, and he did not do me the favor of dying and leaving behind a grieving widow who needed comfort and a new husband. After about a year I was tired of waiting and wrote Sita a letter in which I confessed my love, and proposed that she run away with me somewhere else and start a new life. —Have I mentioned that I was almost forty years old at the time? And my great love was just twenty? Even now, after such a long time, I get a cramp in my stomach when I think of the moment when Sita made me realize how presumptuous and inappropriate my proposal was and how seriously she took the obligation she had entered into by her marriage, even though, or precisely because, this was an arranged marriage. She wanted to know whether, while writing my foolish lines, I had even thought for a moment about the suffering that we would create with our actions. She asked me whether I would be indifferent if her parents and in-laws sank into sorrow and shame at our dishonorable betrayal. And I … I said yes, I would be indifferent; I wanted to spend the rest of my life with her, starting now, at this moment; and then I kissed her, and she gave me a slap, not very violent, but rather that of a teacher who strikes a student who is actually her favorite. —Well, after this incident, I left the hospital forever. I went back to my office and read people messages from aunts and uncles and the trade office and new tax laws and newspaper articles and instruction manuals, and I typed letters for them, everything but love letters. And I advised them on health issues. One man, for whom I had translated something into English, had an open wound on his leg that was festering, and I washed it and bandaged it. I put a splint on the broken little finger of an old woman who had dictated a letter to me for her son in Australia. So one thing led to another, and eventually people came to me not only because they had something for me to read, write, or translate, but also because they were afflicted with an inflamed eye, a sprained foot, or an upset stomach. These people did not have much money, so I wasn't rich, but I was still satisfied, in a strange way almost happy. I was amazed at myself. As a little boy I wanted to be a doctor in a crisp white coat and snatch people from the jaws of death, wanted to live in Mumbai, drive a large German car and live at the top of a skyscraper, far away from the filth and stench, a safe distance from miserable life and death, whose witness I refused to be. —And there I was. I sat in street clothes behind a scratched desk, drove the rickety bicycle to the pharmacy and lived in the shadows between the houses instead of in the light of heaven. My patients weren't elegant, they didn't smell good, they didn't speak the same language as me, they could not afford a new heart when the old one gave out, they did not pay with a card but with jingling coins and small, greasy, unfurled bills, or reached like a magician into a basket and pulled out a plucked chicken, a pair of shoes, a towel." Tanvir smiled and shook his head a little. Then he rubbed his eyes, emptied his cup and put it down. "The rest of the story is absurd and terribly true, and requires many days of storytelling. But I can give you the last chapter in ten minutes. What do you say?"

"I'm sitting here," Megan said. "I'm listening."

"The city was called Bhopal and it still is. My brother and I were two among hundreds of thousands. We lived in a house; we belonged to the privileged class. All around us there were huts made of garbage, debris and plywood, cardboard and tires. People lived in them, incredible as it was. They cooked and ate in them; they slept under the roofs made of wooden planks and plastic sheeting; they made love in their beds of rags and thin blankets; they raised their children and held the hands of their parents, who lay in a corner on the only mattress and waited for their next lives. During the day the girls, themselves still children, took care of the little ones, played with them, told them stories. The boys hired themselves out for a few rupees, collected recyclables from the garbage dumps, marched through the streets looking for something, so they wouldn't have to go home in the evening empty-handed. The men and women worked in factories, of which there were many, some of them owned by foreigners, attracted by the promises of corrupt politicians, low land prices, tax breaks, lax laws, lack of safety requirements, cheap labor. — Then came the night from the second to the third of December, Nineteen Hundred Eighty-Four. Forty tons of a chemical whose name won't mean anything to you, leaked out of a Union Carbide tank. The substance was used to manufacture a pesticide. By human error, carelessness, sabotage, or a chain of tragic circumstances, it came into contact with water. The tank did not withstand the pressure, and a cloud began to spread and killed hundreds of people within minutes. Syed and I woke up because of the acrid stench and went to the roof. In the streets and alleys there were the bodies of humans, cows, dogs. Birds had fallen from the trees. We wrapped ourselves in wet sheets and lay on the floor; our eyes were burning; we could hardly breathe. We heard screaming women, the crying of children, the wailing of sirens. I wanted to help, wanted to call out to the dying to come upstairs, away from the corrosive gas, but I did not move. My body felt as if my skin had been removed; I couldn't see; in my lungs a fire blazed. —In the first three days ten thousand people died, probably more; over a hundred thousand were injured. Later, many suffered from cancer; deformed children were born, I myself gave birth to a few. Even today, tens of thousands suffer from the consequences of the disaster. And they are still waiting for compensation."

"And you?" asked Megan.

"Syed and I were lucky. We recovered quickly. Since then, my eyes are sensitive and I give out of breath quickly. Nothing important. A month after the accident, a Canadian aid organization invited me to talk about everything, to give lectures. Two of their representatives came to see me; they had seen me in a film report on television. But I didn't want to leave, I wanted to help. There were still people dying, every day. Eventually Syed .persuaded me. All his friends from the restaurant were dead: the three cooks, the two waiters, the two boys who cleaned the vegetables and washed the dishes, the dog, who had waited patiently in the back yard for a bone. He couldn't bear the misery; he barely slept; he didn't even find solace in eating. We flew to Toronto, and I spoke to politicians and intellectuals, scientists and doctors, chemistry students and environmental activists, to housewives, exiled Indians, students, trade unionists, and church groups. I even visited a nursing home, but the people were disappointed with my presentation. The director had mixed something up and announced me as a ventriloquist." Tanvir gave a short laugh. In his eyes there was a hard glint; his hands remained still for a moment. He got up and, seeming to have forgotten what he wanted, rubbed his head.

"What happened to Sita?"

Tanvir looked at Megan, as if he had not understood her. He put his hands on the chair. Finally he said, "She died on the first night. Rahul on the second."

For a while they were both silent. If she listened closely, Megan could hear the soft drumming of the moths beating their wings against the window panes.

Eventually Tanvir sat down again. "Well," he said, "during a trip to Boston Syed met a woman, Evelyn. She worked as a secretary for the

447

Dean who had invited me to lecture at his college. Syed accompanied me on all my trips; neither of us wanted to be alone. Three months later they married. I barnstormed for a while through the world with my misfortune in my suitcase, canvassed for donations and did my best to support the groups that had filed a lawsuit against Union Carbide. Star lawyers from America scrambled to represent the victims, in return for a large share of the expected compensation, of course. But before anyone was charged, Union Carbide negotiated a deal with the Indian government and paid two hundred and forty million dollars to the relevant people. I cannot begin to imagine how much money disappeared into the pockets of corrupt politicians and officials. In any case, Union Carbide was off the hook. A former neighbor of mine was given a one-time payment of ten thousand rupees, at that time around a hundred dollars. Most of those who lived on my former street got nothing at all. —After six months in Canada, I flew back to India. In Bhopal, I worked for three years in a hospital outside the contaminated zone. I lived with other doctors in a new building; my room was on the top, on the eighth floor; I could hardly bear the sunlight. At night we watched cricket matches and quiz shows on television together. We all drank quite a bit, but didn't talk about it. And we didn't talk about our work, either. After I held two dead infants in my hands in one day, I went home and wrote my notice. I was at my wit's end. I couldn't sleep. I took pills and dreamed it all over again, again and again. Those who were blinded. The burned skin, that shimmered at times like mother of pearl. The gasping of the children with eroding lungs. The faces of the expectant mothers who already knew what I would say before I opened my mouth. The stunted fetuses, washed out of the bellies by the poison and as little human as the puppies in the kennels. The faces of the politicians and the publicists." Tanvir stared at the table top. Then he took a deep breath, only to let it out a little later with a groan. "I went to Canada and later to America. For a while I tried to collect donations. That's how I met Nancy Preston. Her

448

foundation was very generous. At a presentation in Houston we got to know each other and we became friends. She told me about IPREC, and I was thrilled. I wanted to have as little to do with the world as possible for a while, and the island seemed to me to be a suitable place for that."

"And your brother?"

"Syed and Evelyn are still living in Boston. We haven't seen each other for over ten years." Tanvir nodded, sighed, then rose and took his cup to the sink.

Megan stood up as well. Her head felt heavy from listening. She drank the last sip of tea and went to Tanvir, who took the cup from her hand, in order to wash it. "Thank you," she said, touching his arm briefly. "For the story."

"Alas," Tanvir said quietly, without looking at Megan.

"I think I'll walk slowly."

Tanvir dried the cup and put it away. "And I'll go check on Montgomery." He opened the door and closed it after he and Megan were outside. Insects buzzed around the lamp above their heads.

They walked past the pigs, which stirred and panted but did not wake up. The bonobo was still sleeping in the hammock. He had turned over and was now lying on his back. His chest rose and fell slowly; now and then one of his toes twitched.

"Are you going to leave him here?" Megan whispered.

"Yes." Tanvir went back to the house, got a flashlight and gave it to Megan.

"I'm collecting extraneous flashlights."

"Consider them gifts. I still have a few left."

"Thanks."

"I thank *you*." Tanvir made a slight bow.

Megan smiled. Then she walked along the path between the trees in the darkness. When she turned on the flashlight, she turned around. "My brother's name is Tobey, not Paul. And he doesn't live on our farm, but

449

in Dublin. And we haven't seen each other for a long time."

Tanvir raised his hand. Behind him the lantern was burning, his face was in shadows.

Esther was not there when Megan walked into her room. There was no electricity; the fan wasn't turning. The diesel generators appeared to be giving up one after another. Megan lit the kerosene lamp and took off everything but her slip. The Memory flashcards were in a stack on the bedside table, but she didn't find a piece of paper with a message anywhere. Megan washed her face and brushed her teeth. She drank the rest of the lemonade from a bottle that was on the bureau. The heat was unbearable. A few flies circled the ceiling, silently, like particles in a vortex. Megan considered taking her bedclothes to the beach and lying down next to Carla, but then decided against it, turned off the lamp and opened the door and both windows, to allow the air in the room to circulate a little.

She could not sleep anyway. She lay on her back and stared at the ceiling. Through the silence, the ringing noise of cicadas retreated. Megan closed her eyes. Next door, Tobey played the guitar. For a while she hummed along. She knew how to make herself tired. There was only a little struggle between sleepiness and sleep. She pushed one hand under her panties and turned on her side. No sound escaped from her, just breathing.

When she opened her eyes, she saw the figure at the window. She raised her head and the silhouette disappeared. Megan jumped out of bed and rushed outside. A man ran away. A small man. A boy. Ruben. Megan panted. Above her was heaven, but no moon, no light. She went to the bathroom, turned on the water and sat on the floor. Rain, she thought.

5

Megan woke up with a tense neck and a headache. Two mosquitoes had bitten her. It was seven o'clock. She tried to remember when she had gone to sleep, but she couldn't. The windows and doors were still open, but the air didn't stir. Silence surrounded her; the generator still seemed to be broken. Her mouth and her throat felt dry, and she got up to look for a water bottle, even though she knew there wasn't one. She went to the bathroom, and then she got dressed and left the room.

The sky was illuminated, a silver-gray dome, the white bands of clouds passing through. A little egret was sitting in a tree and flew away when Megan walked across the clearing to the kitchen hut. The door was locked, but thanks to Carla, Megan knew where the key was, and she took it out of the gap between two boards.

In the kitchen she drank cold tea and ate an orange. The levers and hoses and gas cylinders of the black iron stove looked forbidding, so she didn't boil any water for coffee or fry an egg. She cut two slices of bread from a loaf, smeared them with butter and sprinkled sugar on top of it. With this and the teapot and a glass she went out, locked the door and put the key back into hiding. While she ate the bread, Miguel went by on a moped at the other end of the clearing, the bed of his trailer full of gas cylinders. She stood up and waved, but he didn't notice.

Later she went to the laboratory building, where she met Jay Jay and Nelson, who were watching a movie together about giant trees. The room was dark except for the screen and an indicator light on the VCR; the sound was turned off and only the distant hum of the generator could be heard. Nelson followed along with interest as a camera at the trunk of a redwood climbed to the crown, and at the same time ate nuts from a bowl which he pressed against his belly with a hand. Jay Jay complained about the elderly orangutan, who woke up in the morning at six o'clock and did not rest until he got his food. In the past, Nelson had never gotten out of bed before nine or ten o'clock, he said in his rough English, and wanted to know if there was anything that could be done about this trend. When Megan explained to him that primates, like humans, needed less sleep with age because they were not very active during the day, Jay Jay looked at her with narrow eyes and nodded in resignation. To cheer him up, Megan suggested that he should do something with Nelson in the evening, take him for a walk or play as long as possible and make him tired, but he said, after sunset Nelson wanted no part of anything; he wouldn't even watch television.

Because she felt sorry for Jay Jay, Megan promised him she would think of something. Then she left the two of them alone and went through the hall to the storeroom. There, she took the typewriter, a manual Olivetti, from the stack of boxes and put it on the table. The sheet metal cover had rusty spots where it was damaged by bumps and scratches, but the ribbon was still in good condition despite the humid air. The white letters, numbers and symbols on the black keys were partially rubbed away through use, which made them look like foreign symbols. In the belly of the machine lumps of dust had collected, and Megan blew and shook them out. Then she rolled a sheet of paper into the machine and pressed all the keys in succession, and soon the hard blows became a gentle clacking and the loud chatter of the gears a soft purr. When the page was full she looked for replacement ink ribbons, but found only lots of paper clips, tape, erasers, pens, notepads and index cards.

She had carried the Olivetti, a stack of paper and notebooks to the beach and built a table out of a few stones and a board. Now she sat leaning against a tree in the shade and read the text she had written in Manila. Under the mattress in her room were one hundred and seventy pages of a first draft, but really she still did not know exactly what she was doing. Maybe she was actually writing a book about her childhood. Maybe this was just a pathetic attempt to console herself over the passing of time. Still, she liked the sound of her words, the melody of their sentences, but she had no idea if the sum was going to turn into music, something that might be capable of moving someone, like a song by Ella Fitzgerald or a sonata by Chopin, and if it was really about that.

She squinted and looked out to sea. Her neck had relaxed, the headache was gone. She thought of writing a letter to Esther, and composed the first sentence over and over in her mind for so long that she forgot the reason for the letter. There were clouds on the horizon, heavy cows at the end of a pasture. She did not want to think about Tobey and how much she missed him, not about her dead father, and not about Cait, who had probably never noticed the white glove was missing. The sea was an endless surface and at the same time a dark cosmos full of beauty and garbage, life and death. How easy it was to be sad, she thought, and how easy it was for someone on this island to feel lost even without the corresponding sense of pain. She rolled a piece of paper into the machine. She had to return the long way, opening the door to the room of her childhood and collecting the images before they faded. The letters of the keys were inverse metal reliefs, beating against a cloth ribbon soaked with black ink. It was only on the white of the paper that they became words and took on meaning. Some glowed. The stack, weighted down by a stone, grew as slowly as a hair. When she thought about how many ways there were to tell a story, she was seized by despair. She decided to go for a swim, later. The water would carry her for a while. No one came to find her; no one bothered her. There was not even a bird attracted by the clicking of the typewriter. She scratched her leg where the mosquito bites had formed red marks. The sky changed color; wind brushed across the earth like the hem of an old woman's skirt. Megan followed the shade cast by the tree on the sand. Her head was a dark room, the page in front of her a canvas. What she remembered flowed out of a ray of light and dust and heat. A crab waved to her, but she did not have the strength to wave back.

Megan was lying on the bed when Carla knocked. Miguel had repaired the generator; the blades of the fan were turning and created the illusion of cooling. It was evening. The brightness vanished in the dusk like white primer under the first coat of thin blue paint. The heavy air, the same old sounds and the blessed assurance that nothing would happen, lulled everything. Megan rolled over on her side and raised her head.

Carla walked into the room. "Am I disturbing you?" she asked out loud, as if the answer did not matter to her. She was wearing rubber slippers, colorful shorts and a plain white T-shirt. A yellow kerchief held the hair back from her face.

"No." Megan sat up. She had been dozing. Her fingers were stiff and she massaged them until the joints cracked.

"Are you coming to dinner?"

"Where are the others?"

"No idea. I'm hungry."

Megan rubbed her eyes. "Me too." She stood up and took her pants from the chair, put them on and slipped into her shoes.

"Does it still work?" Carla ran her finger over the keys of the typewriter.

"Yes." Megan tied her laces.

"Are you writing something?"

"Yes."

"What?" Carla sat on the chair and looked at Megan, as if she was expecting a long answer.

Megan took the watch from the bedside table. "Oh, I don't know for sure." She adjusted the time on the watch, which had stopped. "Nothing great, anyway."

"My father writes. Poems. He's retired. At one time he was an official for the water company, but he has a soft spot for literature. He reads a lot. After dinner, he always retires to his chair with a book. Then, the living room is a forbidden zone for the rest of the family. Some of his poems have been published in magazines. They're not great, either."

"Can you recite one?"

"No," Carla said, and seemed only now to think about this failure. She leaned her forearms on her knees and looked at her feet, the long toes and peeling red paint on her nails.

"Is your father still alive?"

"Yes." Carla looked up. "Not yours?"

Megan tied a shirt around her hips, knotting the long sleeves at the front of her stomach, and went to the door. "My parents have been dead for a long time. A shipwreck. When I was three." She waited until Carla was outside, and then shut the door.

"Dios mio," Carla muttered as she caught up with Megan, who hurried toward the kitchen hut, as if she was starving.

Rosalinda had cooked rice and beans, fried thumb-long fish and corn and baked bread and peanut cake. There was beer and lemonade with ginger to drink. The radio in the kitchen was playing classical music, piano sounds bubbled across the room. The reception was poor; the music came and went, tides of sound, rolling closer and then ebbing. Rosalinda sat down for a while at the table, drank a glass of lemonade and told a wild story about distant relatives in Mindanao, Muslim rebels, and the kidnapping of a truck with two thousand chickens. When she had finished, she crossed herself and went back to her realm, tuned to a new channel, and hummed along in competition with a Filipina singer.

"Where are the others?" Megan asked. She put her gnawed corn cobs in a bowl and wiped the butter from her mouth and chin with a paper napkin.

"Thor and Malpass left this morning in the boat."

"Where?"

"Probably the mainland."

"What are they doing? Shopping?"

"That, too." Carla took fried fish from a bowl. The fish included the heads and the tails. "I think they have a few sexual exploits going on."

"Malpass?"

Carla laughed. "Well, he's a guy."

Megan took a sip of beer. "And Esther?"

"She probably went along."

"When did they go?"

Carla shrugged. "Nine. Ten. Didn't you see the ship? You were on the beach."

"Not at the rocks. On the other side."

"They probably took the CD with the movie to the post office."

"Can't they do that over the Internet?"

"There hasn't been Internet here for a year. Something to do with the satellite system."

Megan took another ear of corn and put a toothpick in each end to hold it. "But Raske and Thor have Internet access somewhere, right?"

"Sure. In the hick town where the police station is. He bribes the pigs there and he can use their computers."

"And you?"

"What for? I write letters."

"Don't you get some, too? From your parents, for example."

456

"Yes. I have a mailbox. The post office is right next to the police station."

The two ate in silence for a while. In the kitchen, a male voice blared a love song, a bizarre mixture of pompous opera and a snappy pop hit. Carla devoured a good dozen fish and two plates of rice and beans. She drank a third bottle of beer and Megan wondered how she tolerated the pace in this heat.

"Can I read it?" she asked suddenly.

"When it's done. Maybe."

"There used to be a library here. In the visitors center. Two hundred books, at least." Carla pushed her empty plate aside and took a piece of peanut cake. "Then this hurricane came along and tore the roof off. A week long rain. The books were just sludge."

It made Megan think about the flat in London, of the rooms filled from floor to ceiling with books. She remembered a time when a life without books would have been unimaginable to her. Now, she owned not a single one and felt empty and light in a pleasant way, like someone who had stuffed herself with candy for years and eventually stopped.

"Before the rainy season comes, I'm going to scram," Carla said. She looked at Megan for two or three seconds. "Forever." She lowered her eyes. With her long fingernails she picked nuts from the piece of cake on her plate and slipped them into her mouth one by one.

"What?" Megan put the ear of corn on her plate. She noticed how upset she sounded. "Why?" she asked, somewhat more composed.

"Six years is a long time."

"You've been here that long?"

Carla nodded and her whole upper body swung back and forth. "Half a dozen years in September."

"You said you wanted to buy a house in two or three years."

"I will. I have enough money to last a long time." Carla opened two bottles of beer and pushed one over to Megan. "You should come with

457

me."

Megan laughed. "What?"

"I want you to come with me," Carla said seriously.

"To Buenos Aires?"

"Away from this island."

Megan smiled uncertainly. "I don't want to leave here."

"But you should. Believe me."

To do something with her hands, Megan grabbed the beer bottle. "I just arrived. I like it here."

"There are other islands where you can take a vacation."

"I'm not here for vacation."

"But? What are you doing here, Megan?"

"I'm a vet."

Carla shook her head.

"Thor hired me."

"You turned up without being asked. He'll let you stay for a while."

"That's exactly what I want!" Megan pushed her plate away with so much force that it hit the rice bowl.

Carla said nothing for a time. She drank her beer and lined up the peanuts that she had picked out of the piece of cake in front of her.

Rosalinda came in, a bowl of fried bananas in her hands. "You're eating a lot. Good," she said, put down the bowl and carried the dishes with the rice and beans into the kitchen. The next time she brought in a pot of coffee and took the empty plates.

"Malpass wants to go, too," Carla said after they had eaten two of the fried bananas in brown sugar and drank a cup of coffee.

"He should. I won't miss him."

Carla exhaled noisily. "He and Thor just argue. Something is brewing there."

"Then it's a good thing if he leaves."

"Everything is falling apart here, Megan."

"We'll see." Megan forked a banana onto a plate and ate a piece. The sugar was almost caramelized, the fruit of the banana soaked with rum.

"I'm going to stay until the next payday. Three weeks. Think about it, okay?" Carla slipped her right hand across the table as if she was about to touch Megan, but then she grabbed a paper napkin and wiped her mouth.

Megan was silent. She listened to the music from the kitchen—high, long-drawn notes, a cello, an oboe, rising and falling like the songs of whales.

"Don't tell Thor anything about my plans."

Megan nodded.

Carla got up and dropped the crumpled napkin on her plate.

"I'm going to the beach. Are you coming?"

"Maybe later."

Carla took two bottles of beer from the table. "Till then," she said, and went out. The door slammed behind her and for a moment her head was wrapped in cool white light and a blizzard of whirling insects.

Megan ate the remaining bananas and drank two cups of coffee. For a while, she hoped Rosalinda would sit down with her, but the cook did not appear. She drank the last beer, which had grown warm. The mosquito bites had ceased to itch. Her body felt heavy and motionless, her head light from caffeine, a balloon tied to a mountain. It was as if the tips of her index fingers vibrated from hitting the typewriter keys. She thought of the sheets of paper under the mattress in her room. Two hundred pages. Part of her childhood, a fragment of her life, perhaps half a book. Everything and nothing. When she peered through the wooden beaded curtain, she saw Rosalinda kneeling on the floor and scrubbing the tiles with a brush and foamy, soapy water. The radio played opera; arias filled every corner of the room. Maybe one of her sentences was of less value than a single note of this music, she thought, one page less than a chord.

She did not want to think; she left the barracks and ran across the clearing. The slow change from evening to night took place, the last few flecks of brightness stained dark blue. The potency of colors disappeared from everything; there were no lights, no more sparkle and shimmer. Nevertheless, the air had not cooled.

When Megan saw the sea, she stopped. She could see Carla, sitting in the sand with her back turned toward her. The sky was brighter than the sea and stood out at the horizon pale yellow on the water. There were no clouds, just stratified layers of discolored air, one above the other, in which the last faint glow of the sunset visibly faded. The monotonous roll of the waves calmed Megan a little. After she had drawn enough breath, she turned around and went back. She left the buildings behind the research station and took the road to the villa.

With the wide staircase and lighted windows and the way it stood in its disconcerting size and beauty in the evening light, the house looked almost stately. Megan went to the back and crept up to the wooden steps leading to the porch. Now she heard the music, the slurred voice of a singer, scratchy violins, tin trumpets, and a rattling drum set. There was no other furniture in the room she was looking at except two chairs and a round table. A few mats and pillows lay on the floor, various sized balls, tennis rackets, and several colored ninepins. On the walls there were skipping ropes, hula-hoop-rings, rubber bands, and a target. An empty pitcher and three plastic cups took up the surface of the table.

Megan walked forward cautiously, stood beside the next window, waited a while and then peered into the room, which she recognized as the classroom. On the tables there were books and magazines; the blackboard was covered with children's scribbles; a plastic shovel stuck out of an open chest; a yellow T-shirt hung over the back of a chair.

Before Megan went to the last window, she heard Ruben's voice. She did not understand what the boy said, but suspected that he was calling Nancy Preston. She moved back and pressed herself against the wall. A little later the door opened and closed. Steps sounded on the veranda floor, the clicking sounds of dog paws on wood. Megan crouched behind the railing, hoping that Ruben and the Labrador would take the stairs and move away from the house. In fact, the two hit the path toward the meadow and soon disappeared among the trees.

In the second Megan put her hand on the door handle, the music inside grew silent, but began again after a short time. Megan waited a moment, then entered the house and closed the door quietly behind her. The music seemed to come from the room where Nancy Preston spent most of her time. After a few bars, Megan noticed that Nancy had not turned the record over; once again the man with the nasal voice sang about a day at sea, sailing boats, and sunshine. Megan climbed the stairs and opened the first available door. The scent of heavy perfume wafted toward her. Although the carpet covered the wooden floor and muted her steps, Megan did not enter the room. Next to a wide bed on a table there was a lamp with a floral shade burning. From a leather chair, rose a crooked tower of newspapers. There were carafes, powder boxes, porcelain figurines, spectacle cases, framed photos, a bowl full of jewelry on a bureau. On the wall above the bed hung a large picture that was so dark Megan could not make out anything. In the diffuse light of the adjacent room she saw clothes to be ironed and rows of shoes.

Behind the next door was the bathroom, with a tub and sink. A house coat made of dark blue silk was hanging beside a mirror. The room next door was empty; you could see a wicker chair and two rolled and tied carpets. The last room was Ruben's. Megan took off her shoes and went inside. The ceiling lamp, made of braided cane and a paper-covered ball, cast its light on a bed, a dresser, a chair, and a table. A folded wool blanket, covered with hair, lay on the floor, and on top was a chewed, stuffed animal. The walls were bare; just above the head of the bed a bulky crucifix of dark wood was displayed. Megan opened the wardrobe, where pants and shirts and two blue blazers hung, and on several shelves there were underwear, socks and T-shirts. On the floor near the wardrobe were highly polished black boots, and in front of the bed slippers in a checkered fabric. On the table were a notebook, several pens and scissors. Most of the pages had been cut out of the notebook and the remaining ones were empty. Megan placed the chair in front of the wardrobe, but there was nothing on top, not even dust. She raised up the mattress with both hands and found two flat packages, wrapped in plastic.

She sat on the floor, leaned her back against the bed and opened one of the packages. The first thing she held in her hands was the shirt which had been stolen from her at the beach a few days earlier, brown with white print. It had not been washed and smelled faintly of sweat and soap and the sea. She unfolded it and looked at the curved letters of the script on the front: BARNABY & PHELBS BOOKSHOP LONDON. Beneath that, in a smaller, unadorned typeface, it said: BUY & SELL. In the basement shop in the East End she had bought ten to twenty books every month for two years. The owner, who was named neither Barnaby nor Phelbs, but Lipshiz, loved his work and regarded it as a challenge and great fun to track down a rare or out of print work for a customer. Megan would have gladly learned more about the old man, who drank a lot of tea and scratched his back with a small, carved wooden hand fastened to a bamboo stick, but he had always been so immersed in his work, constantly absorbed in catalogs and newspapers and phone calls, that there was never a suitable moment to talk. Perhaps he had died in the meantime, she thought, and a hint of sadness and melancholy tightened her chest for a few seconds.

In the plastic bag there was also a stack of papers and a smaller transparent plastic bag with a flat garland of coiled hair, which Megan did not have to remove to know that it came from the drain of her shower. The papers were the missing pages from the notebook. On the top, written in large, carefully painted letters was her name: Megan O'Flynn. On the second, the empty package of a cereal bar was attached with tape. She had brought several of them with her to the island. On the third sheet Ruben had drawn in pencil the outline of her room. The fourth was filled with a single handwritten word he repeated countless times: REALITY. On the next sheet, in large red letters, were the numbers 15, 28 and 13, and on the last, three sentences: MEGAN DOES NOT EAT MEAT, MEGAN CAN SWIM, and MEGAN LOVES APES.

In the second plastic bag there were sheets of paper on which Ruben had pasted photos of actresses, singers and models that he had cut from newspapers. Megan recognized a few faces, but she couldn't remember their names. The pictures were black and white, giving them the technological bleakness of police files. The collection included twenty-three pages, a well-thumbed album of longing, heartbreakingly shabby and in its childlike seriousness more luminous than any glossy magazine.

Megan put the things back in their silly hiding place, but she hung the T -shirt on a hanger in the closet. Then she put on her shoes, walked out of the room and down the stairs. The gramophone was still playing the same song. She left the house, ran a little way across the meadow and followed the path to the research station.

In her room she took the typed pages and folders from under her mattress and went in search of a new, less naive hiding place. She wondered if Ruben would want to read something like this, and was amazed at how little it would bother her. One window seat was loose and Megan scratched the paint off the grout with a fingernail, struck against the board with her fist a few times from beneath and raised it just enough to be able to slide the notebooks covered in newspapers and the sheets of paper into the cavity.

Then she was thirsty, and made her way along the path to the kitchen hut. By now night had fallen. Gusts of wind swept over Megan weakly and got caught in the leaves of the trees, without causing them to rustle. When the building appeared in front of her, she saw Raske and Malpass through the window and wanted to continue to the beach without a beer, but Raske waved to her.

"How nice to see you," he shouted when Megan entered. He wore long light pants and a blue shirt with the sleeves rolled up. His hair was combed back from his forehead and looked stiff, as if it was reinforced with gel. He stooped to pick up a cardboard box and placed it on the table. "I brought you something. *We* brought you something."

Malpass simply grunted, as ill tempered as ever. He was eating fried fish and rice and drank water swimming with ice. His white cotton shirt had a tear at the collar and there were thin scratches covering his neck.

Megan lifted the lid of the box open and peered inside.

"Be my guest," Raske said.

First Megan lifted a stethoscope out of the box. It was new; she had to take off the collar with the manufacturer's logo and remove the plastic wrap on the ear plugs to try them out. Her heart beat was normal, just fast enough in the heat.

"There's more inside."

Megan unearthed a blood pressure monitor, then a penlight, like the ones nose and throat specialists used, various packaged calipers, scissors and scalpels, a box of tongue depressors and latex gloves, several sets of test strips for urine samples, a shrink-wrapped pack of disposable syringes, a plastic bag full of tape, gauze, bandage rolls, sterile cotton, clamps and safety pins. At the bottom there were drugs: ointments, drops and tablets.

"If there's anything missing, let me know." Raske sat down at his seat next to Malpass, who wiped his greasy hands on a napkin and lit a cigarette.

Megan nodded. "Thanks." She put the things back in the box. They were also going to stay on the island for a while, she thought, and was both relieved and depressed by the idea.

"Have you eaten?"

"Yes. I wanted to get a beer."

Raske got up, went into the kitchen and returned with two bottles of beer. He opened both and gave one of them to Megan. "Tomorrow we'll set up a treatment room." He smiled, knocked his bottle against Meagan's and took a sip.

Megan drank, too. The ceiling fan turned above her and spread the smoke from Malpass' cigarette.

"I hear you spent the day writing," Raske said after he had taken his seat again. He dipped a piece of bread into a dish with olive oil and laughed as he looked at Megan. "Miguel told me. He heard the typewriter and he saw you."

"I typed up a few notes."

"Good. You have to do something here, to kill time." Raske pulled the plate with the two fried bananas Malpass had left for him forward.

Rosalinda brought a pot of coffee and cleared away the dirty dishes. She was humming a song that was playing on the radio, and ignored Malpass, who, poorly hidden behind clouds of smoke, stared at her. After she had disappeared into the kitchen, Malpass got up, muttered something and left the hut. His shirt gleamed in the dark and the glow of his cigarette floated next to him like an affectionate firefly.

"Where's Esther?" Megan asked. Standing, she felt queasy and sat down, although she would have preferred to go to the beach and drink beer with Carla.

"She wanted to take a shower." Raske ate the last bite of banana, put the spoon on the plate and pushed it aside. "She said she wasn't hungry." He took a sip of beer and dabbed at his mouth with a napkin.

"Were you on the mainland? Shopping?"

"Should we bring you something back next time? Shampoo, chocolate, a newspaper?"

"Can I come?"

"The place isn't very attractive, to put it mildly."

"That doesn't matter."

Rosalinda came in to load the rest of the dishes on a tray and take them into the kitchen. Seconds later she let out a loud scream, and the plates and glasses scattered on the floor. Raske and Megan ran into the kitchen, where Rosalinda had climbed onto a stool like a cartoon character and with a trembling hand pointed to a corner of the room from where a grinding noise came, overlaid with sustained, shrill whistles. When Megan's eyes adjusted to the dim light, she saw the rat. The animal was caught by the front paw in a mousetrap and was turning circles in pain and panic and the trap, attached to a stone with a string, struck the tile floor again and again.

Raske went into the corner and stepped on the string. The rat froze and fell silent for a second, then she tried to flee again, but the shortened string prevented it once and for all. She rolled around and shook her front leg, from which the trap hung, and her high pitched whine mixed with Rosalinda's cries.

"Take that broom there and strike it dead," Raske said.

Megan stood and stared at the rat, which now laid on her side, breathing heavily, the wood of the trap like a shield in front of her body. The whistling died away, and as Rosalinda, sobbing, held both hands in front of her mouth and finally grew quiet, a quiet, frantic gasping sound could be heard from the exhausted animal.

"The broom, Megan!" Raske said loudly and calmly. He waited a moment, and when Megan did not move, he lifted one foot and stepped on the rat. Tiny ribs broke; a heart, no bigger than the piece of meat used for bait, exploded. One last note escaped the lean body, a bit of air and blood, perhaps a soul.

Megan broke her gaze from the dead animal and turned around. While Rosalinda climbed off the chair groaning and Raske wiped the bloody sole of his shoe on a scouring cloth, she took four bottles of beer from the refrigerator and left the kitchen and the hut. Finally a noticeable wind was blowing. The sky was clear of clouds, and every star was in its place. Megan walked quickly, almost running. The cold bottles struck against each other, clinking softly. She was sick; she filled her lungs with the night air.

"Megan? Wait!"

Megan turned and saw Raske coming along the path. She stopped and waited. The weight of the beer bottles tugged against her arms; water dripped on the sandy soil.

"Are you okay?" Raske asked when he reached Megan.

Megan nodded.

Raske wiped his hand across his forehead, which was gleaming with sweat. "That wasn't pretty, huh?" He tried to smile. His teeth gleamed, two immaculate rows.

"No."

"All the same, it was a rat."

"It was a living being. Why not put out poison?"

"Have you ever seen a rat that died of poison?"

Megan looked down and shook her head. There was a lump in her stomach. She wanted to lie down in the sand and drink a beer. And then another.

"You grew up on a farm. Weren't there any mice?"

"Yes. But my father didn't care. He thought the little bit of grain wasn't worth fighting over."

Raske laughed. "It seems to run in the family. The love of animals." Maybe there was a faint mocking undertone in his last words, maybe not.

Megan shrugged her shoulders. The necks of the beer bottles were hanging between her fingers, which started to hurt; the jagged crown caps cut into her flesh.

"Have you ever killed an animal, Megan?"

"I accidentally crush ants and swallow mosquitoes."

"You know what I mean. You went to school."

"We practiced on preserved specimens, if that's what you mean."

"On frogs?"

"They were no longer living."

"Could you kill an animal? If it would help your research. Say, a lab mouse. It would have to die so people could live."

"I wanted to be a veterinarian, not a scientist."

"You would have to euthanize animals. Hamsters. Dogs. Horses."

"I didn't become one."

"Can it be that you're naive, Megan? Possibly a bit of a coward?"

"Because I broke off my studies?"

"Because you refuse to accept facts."

"What do you want from me?"

Raske looked Megan in the eyes and seemed to think before answering: "I'm afraid I can't tell you that." He smiled and raised his arms in a feigned gesture of regret. Then he turned around and walked back to the hut, over which white light hung like mist.

Megan gazed after Raske for a while. Finally, she followed the path toward the sea. When she reached the narrow strip of vegetation that separated the beach from the grassy plain, she sat down. She opened a beer bottle by prying it off against the closed cap of another one. Tobey had shown her the trick, with Coke bottles back then. She finished the beer in a few gulps, got up and walked on.

There was no trace of Carla. Megan climbed onto one of the rocks and called to her, but the beach was empty. After a while, the feeling of loneliness has subsided in her and she jumped into the sand. On the edge of a rock she opened three beer bottles and lay down. The sight of the stars almost made her forget her anger at Raske. She wondered how he knew that she had grown up on a farm. She had mentioned something about her family background to only two people on the island: Tanvir and Esther. Raske couldn't have found out anything about her from the Internet. She had never entered her name into a search engine, but she was

468

sure there were no entries relating to her. Perhaps, she thought, Raske had called the administration in Killorglin and found out her former address. She imagined him gazing with the satellite eye of Google Earth on Ireland, on Kerry, how he saw the streets and paths as they emerged from the blur, endless hills and fields and meadows, and finally the farm, the three buildings, the pond, the tree whose shadow covered Sam's grave. Then she decided the idea was absurd. This huge effort just to find out something about her. Someone must have told him. Tanvir or Esther.

She drank until all the bottles were empty. Until the stars were moving. Until the sound of the breaking waves became the peaceful snoring of a huge animal. Until her eyes closed.

It was almost dark in the basement. Even in front of the windows, through which you could have been able to see the sidewalk, shoes and the bottom half of legs, there were books. Here and there a lamp was burning, a cave of light in the narrow canyons. Sometimes heavy leather-bound tomes fell from a stack, came loose like boulders from a cliff and crashed to the ground. Megan's job was to put these books back in their places, but for each copy she picked up, ten plummeted into the depths. Mr. Lipshitz was sitting behind his desk, drinking tea and talking on the telephone in a language that Megan was sure she had heard before, without remembering where and when. He wanted to scratch his back, but the bamboo stick with the little carved hand at the end was missing. He hung up the phone and called Megan. Books toppled off the shelves; dust mixed with the dim light. Megan stood in front of the towering table, whose legs were mighty trees. She reached into her pocket, pulled her hand out again and opened her fist, then her mouth.

"What?"

"I need you. For the rat."

"Megan."

Megan recognized her name and opened her eyes.

"Hello."

Megan sat up. Her head was heavy and she had a bitter taste in her mouth. She recognized Carla, who was smiling, and she made an effort to smile back.

"You were dreaming."

"Yes." Megan breathed deeply in and out a few times.

"About a rat?"

Megan moaned and buried her head between her knees. "The hand was for her."

"All right." Carla put a towel around Megan's shoulders.

"Tonight there was this rat in the kitchen. She had her paw in a trap." Megan fell back into the sand. "Raske trampled her to death."

Carla rolled out a blanket and sat next to Megan. "About three years ago we had a rat plague on the island. Pretty scary, believe me. Now we try to keep them in check, but the critters are smart."

"Sometimes I wished I could operate differently," Megan said softly. "Not to feel compassion for every vagabond beetle."

"La Santa Megan, Patrona de los Seres Inferior."

"What?"

"Holy Megan, Patron Saint of Inferior Beings."

Megan put an arm over her eyes. "I had too much to drink."

"Sleep here tonight."

Megan rolled over on her side, leaned on her elbow and looked at Carla. "Why are you leaving?"

"My mother's eyes. She can hardly see anything. My father is completely overwhelmed."

"Buenos Aires," Megan whispered.

Carla lay down and closed her eyes. "I'll buy a big house. We'll all live there. My father will read out loud to my mother from books."

Megan got up and stood there swaying for a time, as if gusts of wind were tugging at her. She turned her back on Carla, untied the knot in her sleeves and wiped her eyes. Then she put on the shirt. A gull sailed past.

"Are you coming back?"

"If I'm not too tired," Megan said, and walked across the sand to the gap in the bushes, which looked in the darkness like an open door in a garden wall.

Along the way she stopped every few minutes. It seemed to her as if she had to wait each time, until the alcohol-rich blood that was pumped into her head when she was walking started to flow again. She did not give in to the desire to lie down, but only because everything started spinning as soon as she closed her eyes. Once she sat down on the ground and cried, but then she pulled herself together and thought of the guidebook she had bought in London, wondered why she was crying, and stopped when she could think of no better reason than the fact that she was sad.

She stumbled over a root and imitated in make-believe Spanish Carla's deluge of wild curses. Among the trees she began to sing, but stopped when her singing woke the birds, who fluttered up drowsily into the night sky. She called after them to stay and in doing so shooed away even more animals. When she wandered off the path and fell down, she forced herself to laugh, continued to lie on her stomach for a while and inhaled the fragrance of the earth. She suddenly felt warm and she decided to go swimming. After she had picked herself up, she walked on, singing softly.

She was not frightened when she entered her room and saw Esther sitting on the bed. She turned on the light switch, but nothing happened. In the stifling air she felt drunk again. The fan was the propeller of a crashed airplane, the shaft a stranded ship. She opened both windows, took a match from the box and lit the kerosene lamp.

Esther stretched out her hand and Megan sat down beside her.

"Where were you?"

"On the beach."

471

Esther stroked Megan's forehead with two fingers and brushed a strand of hair behind her ear. "Your eyes are red. Were you crying?" She took Megan's hands in hers, as if they needed to be warmed.

"No."

"Where were you yesterday? I was waiting for you."

"With Tanvir."

"But why? He's an old liar."

"He's my friend." Megan shook off Esther's gentle grasp and stood up. She took off her shoes and then her pants and shirt.

"Did he tell you about his life?"

Megan did not answer and went into the bathroom.

"Where did he come from?" Esther called. "In the story he told me, from Bangladesh. During the famine he met George Harrison and Eric Clapton, and went with them to England. In Liverpool he brewed coffee for Apple Records. He brewed coffee for The Beatles!"

"It's a great story."

"He's a liar! And he's not right in the head!"

"Who is?" Megan stood in the shower and turned on the water. Esther continued to talk; she could hear it through the noise. One of Tanvir's life stories was true, and she was sure it was the one he had told her.

After the shower she dried off and went hastily to the bed. Esther had taken off the wrap around skirt and was lying under the mosquito net in a slip and a tank top.

"I need the sheets."

"What?"

"I want to go to the beach. I can't sleep in here."

"We certainly don't have to sleep." Esther rolled quickly to the edge of the bed, grabbed Megan's leg and pulled her down on the mattress.

Megan did not resist. She laughed when Esther sat on her and pressed down on her wrists.

"Do you love me?"

472

"Maybe."

"That's better than a no, right?"

"Yes."

Esther bent over Megan, touched her face with the tip of her hair.

"Would you die for me?"

"Don't ask such a thing."

"Would you?"

Megan turned her head away. "I'm drunk."

"Yes or no."

"Who turned off the lamp?"

"Don't you want to go to the beach anymore?"

"No."

Esther let go of Megan's wrists, raised her upper body and took off the ring she wore on her right hand. "Here." She put the ring in the hollow of Megan's breasts. "I want yours in return."

Megan took the ring in her hand and examined it. It was made of gold, or at least gold plated. In one setting, woven like a basket, there was a black stone, crisscrossed with bright veins.

"It belonged to my grandmother."

"I can't accept it," Megan said. She took Esther's hand and placed the ring inside.

"Why not?"

"I can't give you mine."

"Who is it from?"

"From my brother."

Esther lay down next to Megan. "What's his name?"

"Tobey."

"To-bi," Esther repeated. She ran a finger over Megan's belly and whispered something in her own language.

Megan closed her eyes. The world was spinning slowly.

6

Megan spent half the morning with the drawing pad on her knees under the narrow roof of her room and drew a half-wilted blossom which the wind had blown from one of the bushes. She did not know the name of the plant and decided to ask Tanvir. Maybe Rosalinda was familiar with the local flora, she considered, or Miguel. It was not yet noon and the air was relatively cool. When she washed the color from the watercolor brush or sharpened the pencil, she squinted out into the brightness that spread in front of her, otherwise her eyes rested on the paper, the paint strokes, the cloudy areas of color. On the same page, she had drawn a shell from three different perspectives that she had found on the beach and about which she knew as little as the flower with the large, wrinkled, purple-colored leaves.

She was so absorbed in her work that she flinched when someone called her name. A small light brown spot on the painted exterior of the shell became a stain that she quickly dabbed away with a scrap of toilet paper. She lifted her head and saw Raske coming along the path.

"Always hard at work?" Raske called. As usual he was wearing canvas shoes, light trousers and a shirt, this time faded blue, his hat and sunglasses. Despite the heat, he showed no sign of exhaustion that could be noticed or even observed; his stride was quick and his clothes impeccable.

"Well, I'm occupied," Megan said. She cleaned the brush in the toothbrush glass and dried it on her shirttail. Then she quickly put it into her mouth and pulled it through her clenched lips, so the hairs would retain their tapered shape.

"May I see?" Raske stood in the sun and put his hands on the railing.

"They're only simple studies, sketches." Only then did Megan notice the scratch, about two inches long, on Raske's right cheek.

"A branch," said Raske, who had not missed Megan's glance. He touched the scabbed wound briefly and smiled. "You have to be careful here, so nothing catches on fire." He walked over to Megan, took off his sunglasses and looked at the drawings.

"Do you know what this flower is called?"

Raske bent over the pad on Megan's legs. "I'm sorry," he said, and straightened up. "Botany has never held any interest for me."

"Never mind," Megan said. "I'll ask Tanvir." Then it occurred to her how badly Raske had spoken about Tanvir. "Or Miguel," she hastened.

"Nancy is familiar with flowers," Raske said, pretending not to notice. He stretched out his hand. "May I?" he asked, reaching for the shell. "You should drop in on her sometime soon anyway. Odin doesn't seem to be doing very well."

"Odin?"

"The dog. Nancy's Labrador. He's not eating like he should."

Megan saw the dog now and then, when he trotted behind Ruben or fell asleep on the floor in Nancy's living room, but had always failed to ask his name.

"I can take a look at him today," she said.

"Very good." Raske put the shell back, pulled a handkerchief from his back pocket, and polished the lenses of his sunglasses with it. "And everything else? How do you like the island life?"

"Still good," Megan said. She took the watercolor box, water bowl and brush off the second chair she had taken from one of the empty houses, and put everything on the floor. "Would you like to sit down?"

Raske seemed to reflect a moment, then pulled the chair by its back toward him and took a seat. "I have a few minutes," he said, and put the sunglasses in the pocket of his shirt. "The car is broken, this time probably for good. Now I have to walk, like everyone else." He grinned.

I like to walk," Megan said.

"It's just because my house is a little remote. Now and then I have to carry things. Gas canisters, for example."

"I could try to build a bicycle for you."

Raske laughed. "Build a bicycle?"

"My father did it once. From scrap parts."

"Well, we have plenty of those here," Raske said, still laughing. "Anyway, don't bother."

"I have a guilty conscience, because I don't do anything."

"Why? You're doing something. You treated Wesley's foot successfully."

"Well, you can hardly call that work," Megan said. She tried not to look at the scar that almost disfigured Raske's otherwise well-proportioned and undamaged face.

"Of course you can. Besides, I warned you. If you need frantic fifteen-hour days to be happy, you're in the wrong place." Raske grinned, folded the handkerchief carefully and thrust it back into his pocket.

Megan smiled. "I just don't want to give the impression that I'm a freeloader."

"Don't worry, you haven't. And you haven't been paid." Raske's grin grew even wider.

"I still need to write down the bank account number for you."

"Do that."

There was a pause. Raske chased a fly that was circling his head.

"May I ask you something?"

"Of course."

Megan cleared her throat and hesitated. "It's so . . . I was wondering what . . . what someone like you . . . " She paused, searching for the right words.

Raske laughed. "What someone like me is doing on this island."

"Yes. I mean . . . "

"I think I know what you mean. The answer is: I'm like you. I like the life here."

"Even now? After everything is so . . . so different."

Raske laughed, leaned back and crossed his legs. "Yes, even now," he said. "I've been locked up long enough in offices and laboratories. I thought of myself as an ape in a cage."

"You worked with apes?"

"Well, yes. Sometimes."

Megan waited.

"After graduation, I worked for various companies. Among other things, in genetic research."

"But you studied economics, right?"

Raske seemed to have to think about the question. "Yes," he said. "But my field has always been medical research. Where costs and profits also have to be calculated." He smiled. "Here, unfortunately, I miscalculated somewhat."

"Well, yes. Perhaps times will be better again."

"So you say." Raske looked at his watch and rose. "It's time. If I can do anything for you, let me know, okay?"

"May I go with you the next time you travel to the mainland?"

"Do you need anything?"

"A book about the flora and fauna of the Philippines. You can take me off your payroll."

"That might be a bit problematic. To find something so unusual, I mean."

"Of course. That was stupid of me."

"Not at all. I'll try to obtain the book."

"I can do that. Is there a bookshop, then, where you go?"

Raske laughed. "I suspect not. You need to imagine a place very small and very ... how shall I say it ... provincial."

"Sounds like the place where I grew up."

"I doubt it. Unless you grew up in a poor, dirty and not undangerous hick town. In any case, you shouldn't come with us if it isn't absolutely necessary."

"No. The book isn't that important." Megan now actually considered herself a little foolish, perhaps because of the fact she felt Raske was treating her like a child.

"As I said, I'll see what I can do." Raske stepped from the shadows into the sun and turned to Megan. "Is Esther there?"

"I think so." Megan knew that Esther was in her living quarters, but thought it better to act in front of Raske as if it did not matter to her where her neighbor was at the moment. No one on the island had to find out that they had spent the night together, for the second time, Raske least of all.

Raske walked the few steps over to Esther's and knocked. When the door opened, he entered.

Megan resisted the urge to sneak to the back of the building and listen at Esther's windows; she put away the art supplies and changed clothes. She owned two pairs of pants, one of which was already in dire condition, two shirts, one with a torn sleeve, three T-shirts, two of which were still somewhat presentable, and ample socks, panties and bras. Eventually, she would have to travel to the mainland with Raske, she thought, whether he liked it or not.

She washed a few things with soap and hung them in the sun. Then she turned to the window and waited. Because her watch was broken, she counted silently. About ten minutes later, Raske left. Megan watched him as he disappeared behind the bend in the road, and sat down on the bed to wait again.

Again ten minutes passed. Then another ten. Finally, Megan stood up and walked over to see where Esther was. She knocked and called, and when there was no answer, she opened the door and entered the room. She had only been here accompanied by Esther, and it seemed strange to stand alone in the middle of the chaos that made the room seem as small as a cluttered closet. And the absence of Esther's voice confused her; the absence of her laughter and her slow somnambulistic movements. Because the curtains were closed, the room was almost entirely in darkness. Megan looked into the bathroom and then let light in through one of the windows. On the bed there were clothes, toiletries, packs of chewing gum, stuffed toys, colorful pillows. From open dresser drawers even more skirts, blouses and colorful scarves overflowed, on chairs there were straw hats and cheap necklaces, lipsticks, disposable cameras, sunglasses and hair clips made of glittering plastic. Megan tripped over shoes, empty glasses and a radio. On the shelves there were souvenirs from Manila, disassembled flashlights, CD cases, perfume bottles, a stuffed blowfish. The walls were papered with pages from magazines, an apparently arbitrarily assembled mosaic of movie stars, cars and landscapes. Images of interior rooms and festive parties were hanging there, make-up tips with pictures and the map of a city in Lithuania. On the bureau Esther had kept one area for a few photos of family members: her parents, two brothers, a sister. A hand's width away, as if creating a respectful distance, hung several automat pictures that showed Esther and three girls, young and making faces, with red lips and more eye shadow than their childish faces could handle.

Megan sat on the bed and picked up the stuffed elephant, whose sides were bare, rubbed away by a childlike desire for closeness. It was as quiet as a museum. She would never make love in this bed, perhaps, she thought, because the parents and siblings could see her from their place on the wall.

She put the stuffed animal back, closed the curtains and went out.

It was warmer; the air began to whirl over the dry earth. Megan used the umbrella as protection from the sun, like Tanvir did. She went to the kitchen hut, but there was no one there, not even Rosalinda, and then she knocked on Carla's door.

"Yes?"

"It's me, Megan."

"Come in!"

Megan opened the door. "Am I disturbing you?"

Carla was sitting at a table between two open windows. "Oh, no." She took off her glasses and put down a pen.

Megan left the umbrella outside, closed the door and sat down on the second chair.

"Pretty hot, huh?" Carla poured iced tea into a glass and pushed it over to Megan.

"Yes." Megan took a sip. "I'm looking forward to the rainy season."

Carla hissed derisively through her lips. "Are you crazy? It's just as hot as it is now, only wetter."

Again it occurred to Megan that she was being naive, and she realized how little she was prepared for this continent. In her suitcase for Borneo, against Stuart's advice, she had packed only light clothing, a wool sweater, two pairs of tight jeans, and a pair of cowboy boots, things that were useless in this climate, and were now probably mildewed or had been thrown away long ago.

"What are you doing?" she asked, so she would give no more thought to Stuart.

"I'm writing to my parents. They're worried."

Megan nodded, as if she understood. She looked around. The room was bright and there were few pictures hanging on the walls; there was no wardrobe to take up space. One door led into the bedroom, another to

480

the bathroom. Nothing was random; everything had its place. While Esther saved and collected and adapted herself, it seemed that Carla had already packed her essentials and was always ready to go, if need be even in the middle of the night.

"And you? What are you doing?"

Megan shrugged. "Not much. I was drawing. Now I want to go to the beach."

"Swimming?"

"We'll see." Megan drained her glass and got up. "Thanks for the tea."

"There's beer in the evening." Carla grinned.

"Yes." Megan went to the door and opened it. Warm air was blowing toward her and the smell of dry grass. "See you later." She closed the door, took the umbrella and quickly crossed the clearing to the end where the path to the sea began. Small birds fluttered up in front of her and disappeared in a grove. Sadness seized Megan unexpectedly, like a cloud in a blue sky pushing itself in front of the sun. There is no reason for it, she told herself, shouted the sentence out loud and started to run.

In the afternoon she went to the villa to check on the dog. She had packed a couple of Raske's small presents in a bag: the stethoscope, the penlight, the latex gloves. As she approached the house she saw Ruben, playing on the lawn with Chester and Wesley. She waved to him and he raised his hand tentatively. The sight of the two apes who were wrestling in a hammock, cheered Megan up a little. She climbed the stairs, entered the house without knocking and went into the living room, where Nancy Preston was sitting in her chair and crying.

Megan stood in the middle of the room and waited for the woman to notice her presence. The dog was lying on the floor beside the chair, and, as far as Megan could tell, he was breathing. She took a step toward them.

"Nancy? It's me, Megan O'Flynn," she said as quietly as possible.

Nancy lifted her head and stared at Megan with red, swollen eyes. "Oh my goodness," she said, then cried again, and pressed a crumpled handkerchief to her lips with both hands. Her hair was a tempest-tossed nest from which extended three or four yellow hairclips like the beaks of birds.

Megan went to her chair, crouched down and put a hand on the woman's arm. "Everything is okay," she said softly. She felt Nancy's pulse, which was almost normal, then stroked her arm. "It'll be okay."

Nancy sobbed and shook her head slowly. The ashtray on the table beside her was empty, so great her grief seemed to be. There was just a glass of water, half full, with the red imprint of her lower lip.

"Should I take a look at Odin?"

Nancy looked at Megan. The make-up she had put on in the morning was smeared; from her eyes thin black lines ran down her cheeks. "Who?" she asked, without taking the handkerchief from her mouth.

"Odin. Your dog."

As if she had to sort out her thoughts for a second time, Nancy shook her head again. Then she blew her nose into the handkerchief and put her hands in his lap. "He's not called Odin," she said, and the clarity in her voice surprised Megan.

"No?"

"No," Nancy said firmly. "His name is Himself."

"Himself," Megan repeated flatly.

"Is there something wrong with him?" Nancy drew in air with a sob, as if she was about to start crying again.

Megan knelt down, hung her head and closed her eyes. After a while she took her hand away from Nancy's arm and opened her eyes again. From the corner of her eye she saw the dog's hind legs moving. She got up, took the bag from her shoulder and took out the stethoscope.

Nancy blew her nose again. "Tell me; is there something wrong with him?"

Megan knelt in front of the dog and listened to his heartbeat with the stethoscope. "This morning Torben Raske told me he isn't eating anymore."

"Oh that!" Nancy cried, apparently her old self again. "That's over."

"Does that mean he's eating normally again?" Megan touched the dog's wet nose and lifted his lips up to check the condition of his teeth and gums. The Labrador opened his eyes, examined her with a sleepy look and closed his eyes again.

"It depends on how you look at it," Nancy said. "Sometimes more, sometimes less. But he is eating."

Megan patted the dog gently and stood up. He sleeps a lot, right?"

"Yes, he likes to dream."

"He dreams?"

"Of course," Nancy said. "I don't know what he dreams about, but he dreams all the time. When I listen to a record he moves his front legs, as if he's conducting."

Megan put the stethoscope back into the fabric bag, carried a stool over to Nancy's armchair and sat down. She felt better, and she could see that Nancy had calmed down.

"He's okay," she said after a while. "You don't have to worry anymore."

"Worry?"

"About the dog."

"I'm not worried about him."

"I just thought, because . . . because you were crying."

Nancy looked at Megan with a furrowed brow as if she was wondering when she had been crying. "Oh," she said suddenly, raising her right hand, only to drop it again immediately. "That. —That was because our wedding anniversary is today."

It took Megan a moment to understand. "That's why you were crying?"

"I'll cry about the dog, too. But that can wait."

"Your husband's name was Bobby, right?"

Nancy nodded, her eyes directed at her hands, which clutched the handkerchief. Her lips trembled. Then she looked at Megan and smiled. "On our anniversary we always took a trip," she said. "Once we went to Disneyland. Like little children."

Megan smiled.

"He was a good husband." Nancy wiped the handkerchief over her eyes and smeared even more mascara.

"He certainly was."

"I miss him."

Megan was sitting too far away to be able to put her hand again on Nancy's arm again, so she stayed where she was, and clasped the fabric bag that was lying on her knees. She wondered if her parents had ever celebrated a wedding anniversary, and doubted it. The dog yawned silently, and later twitched his front legs as if he was scratching at an imaginary door. There was nothing to be heard from the two apes; they were probably taking their afternoon naps. Megan listened to the faint crackling of the wood, which contracted in the heat. She could not think of anything to say, and she hoped that, in the silence, Nancy would not begin to cry again. She would have liked to have known why Esther left without saying anything to her, but then she decided that she was thinking too much. Here, everyone moved in their own way, at their own pace. With the exception of Tanvir, no one was particularly talkative, as if everyone on this island had to keep their history a secret. A history, Megan was convinced, that was as mundane as her own: a divorce, the prospect of earning a lot, a chance meeting, a job abroad which one had never applied for.

"What's the name of my dog?" Nancy asked suddenly, and her voice sounded as firm as ever.

Megan emerged from her coma and looked at the woman, who seemed to her at first like a pale ghost in a fading dream.

"Odin," she answered, after the name came back to her again. "Torben Raske said that was his name."

"Oh, him." Nancy made a derogatory gesture. "He got me the dog. In Manila. He named him that. Odin." She exhaled contemptuously. "Look at him yourself." She turned her head toward the sleeping animal. "Does he look anything like a Nordic God?"

"Not really."

"He's himself. Himself."

Megan nodded.

For a while they observed the dog like a great mystery. Megan wondered if Raske would photograph the animal when it was dead, to add to his collection.

"If you don't mind, I would like to lie down now," Nancy said. She slid forward on the chair and fumbled for her slippers with her feet.

Megan hung the fabric bag on her shoulder and got up quickly.

"Of course," she said, and helped the woman get up.

"Thank you, dear." Nancy leaned against Megan for a moment, as if she would first have to get accustomed to standing upright. Then she went to the bureau, grabbed the mirror and studied her face in it. "Oh dear God!" she cried, and held her hand in front of her open mouth. "I look terrible!"

"Oh, no. Not at all." Megan carried the stool back to the spot from which she had taken it.

Nancy turned and looked at Megan, as if she had already forgotten that she was not alone. "Terrible," she said energetically. "Please go."

"Shouldn't I help you upstairs?"

"I'm going to lie back down here. On the sofa." Nancy flailed about with the hand mirror, whose handle and frame were ornate and gold-plated. "Please go now."

Megan wondered how she could ease the tension of the unpleasant situation, but then simply said: "Good-bye," turned and left the room.

485

Outside, she sat for a short time on the stairs before she went to the meadow where Chester and Wesley were sleeping in their hammocks. Ruben sat dozing in the shade of the trees, a piece of paper on his legs and a pen in the limp, open hand resting on the grass. Instead of waking the three of them, Megan decided to just stand still for a moment and try to enjoy the peaceful tranquility of this scene, but all she felt was a feeling of abandonment. She resisted the temptation to seize the sheet of paper and read what Ruben had written, touched Chester's hand instead and then walked away.

The sea lay quietly in front of her, a blue-green surface, floating in the sunlight. When she plunged in and the warm water enveloped her, she felt a happiness that she knew was fleeting and as barely tangible as the tiny blue and silvery shining fish that disappeared only when she came quite close. She swam far out and eventually had to force herself to turn back. When she raised her head she saw the bright strip of sand and the green of trees and palms and over everything the glittering sky. On the shore she let herself be rocked by the waves and stayed in the water so long the skin on her fingertips turned white.

Then she lay down in the sand and closed her eyes. Tonight she did not want to talk to anyone, ask no questions and hear no answers. She tried not to think about anything, and eventually she fell asleep.

7

The time of the monsoons came early. Megan woke up in the morning, and then it rained for months. If life on the island had previously been a calm river, it was now a lake, flat and unmoving. While the world around her seemed to sink, she sat in her room and wrote. She had put aside a supply of paper, so she seldom had to leave the room. In the morning she walked to the kitchen hut for breakfast under a big yellow umbrella. Mostly she was alone, and she liked not having to talk or listen. In the evenings she ate with those who were there. She often stayed in her room for days, working and reading. In the area next to the storage room, between the firewood and the coconut shells, she found some of the books that were damaged during the hurricane; among the perhaps fifty she did not find one that she knew, let alone had read. The diesel generator could not be repaired, so she spent the dark hours in the light of the petroleum lamp. It seemed that she even had to light a candle in the day time, to type or to identify the letters on the yellow, curled pages. The patter of the rain eventually turned into silence, white noise that drowned out everything by swallowing it.

Carla had missed the best time to leave the island and decided to stay until the end of the rainy season. In order not to die of boredom, she began to sew quilts, so she scanned every corner of the research station for rags and even used washed up scraps of clothing, life rafts and signal flags. It also seemed that Malpass was no longer thinking about an early departure. He showed his face less and less, and when he appeared in the kitchen hut once again, he was even more withdrawn and sullen than before. For some reason Rosalinda gave him the cold shoulder, which threw him completely off balance and caused him to turn pale at first and then transparent, as if he was turning into his own ghost.

Megan didn't know what Raske did. She suspected that he spent his time either sitting in his house or sailing the boat to the mainland. Several times she had resolved to ask him if she could accompany him, but then concentrated on writing again and surrendered to the sleepy, all-dominating rhythm of the rain. She eventually discarded the list of things she thought she needed. In one of the rooms in the laboratory building there were boxes from which you could stock up on shower gel, sham-poo, tampons, toothpaste, batteries, chewing gum and other seemingly indispensable consumer goods. Sometimes there were newspapers lying around the kitchen hut, but Megan had long ago stopped reading them. In the seclusion of the island, the colorfully illustrated reports about the unfortunate state of the world seemed to her even more ridicu-lous, the possibilities to change anything, even worse. She no longer wanted to keep up to date, no longer wanted to be fed with the pulp from the same old news, which made her sick and angry, stunned and powerless. She did not want to read about a sinking refugee boat from Africa and then scroll to an article which concerned a race between mil-lion dollar yachts, as if both events happened on different planets and as if none of them were the earth on which she, Megan O'Flynn lived.

She had set up a practice in Room 2 of the laboratory building, but she didn't have much to do. Wesley's fracture had healed, and Nelson's test results gave no more cause for concern than Chester's slightly elevated cholesterol levels. And the human patients did not keep her particularly busy. Esther had a thorn in her foot; Rosalinda cut her finger; Carla caught a cold; Miguel was stung by several wasps; Jay Jay dropped a brick on his toe. Even Malpass showed up, and complained about a painful shoulder, chronic heartburn and the weather. She gave him an ointment, pills, and the advice that he should find something to do. When he left, she suspected that he had hoped for more from the visit—a healing touch, comforting words, perhaps an emergency operation on his damaged heart, which he never mentioned.

Raske had entered the treatment room only once, on the day when he helped Megan set it up. He never seemed to be sick, never even slightly ailing. Should any injury have occurred in the time Megan had been on the island, he had probably treated it himself. Or he went to a doctor on the mainland. Once he brought her a copy of a bank transfer, which showed that Megan's pay had been deposited. That was when she noticed the bandage on his forearm that was not quite covered by his shirt sleeves. When she said something to him about it, he told her some story about an abrasion, harmless and almost healed, nothing worth talking about.

Nancy Preston, too, never took advantage of Megan's medical services. She enjoyed a remarkable robustness, and if she suffered even once from an ingrown toenail or an eye infection, she let Tanvir treat it. Unlike the rest of the research station staff, she relied on the medical capabilities of her friend and she was loyal to him. Ruben, about whom Megan could still not say whether he was Nancy's servant, pupil, surrogate grandchild, or everything in one, was also Tanvir's patient, which, given the confused feelings that the boy apparently harbored for her, was quite convenient for Megan.

After several weeks of continuous rain and typing the last fifty pages of a first draft of the book, Megan remembered the reason she had come to the island and visited Nancy in the villa. Ruben opened the door for her and disappeared after that. She could not tell whether he knew that Megan had hung the stolen T-shirt in his closet, but it gave her a secret pleasure, only slightly diminished by compassion, to see him still so embarrassed. She told Nancy how much it would mean to her to be allowed to help work with the primates, and offered to play with Chester and Wesley for a few hours every day and assist Nancy with her teaching.

Shrouded in smoke and equally radiating authority and benevolence, Nancy was enthroned in her chair and visibly enjoyed the fact that someone had approached her with an appeal. She wore an ankle-length dress that seemed to be made of numerous stamp-sized gold panels, a bracelet, a necklace and earrings with amber beads, black stockings, and on her feet flat solid gold patent leather shoes decorated with two gold lace stitches that looked like dragonflies.

After Megan had argued her case, Nancy was silent for a while. She had Ruben come running by ringing a small bell, and ordered coffee. Then she folded her hands, took a damp, crackling breath from the depths of her lungs, leaned back, as if only thinking about what was going to be said was already tiring, and began a lecture in the course of which she reviewed her first landing on the island, rhapsodized over the carefree days of research, lamented the gradual decline of the research station, and after nearly an hour of sober contemplation ended with the picture as it presented itself today. Nobody was talking about work with primates from a scientific point of view anymore, she said with remarkable objectivity. The occasional lessons only served to keep Chester and Wesley busy a little bit and discourage their intellectual dullness. For years now, Nelson wasn't interested in anything more than simple games, trips to the pond and hours of video consumption, which was partly due to Jay Jay's lack of skill and his work ethic. She praised Tanvir, who had taken care of Montgomery since the departure of the specialists and through much attention and regular practice had not only prevented the bonobo's intelligence from wasting away, but had even further enhanced it.

Last she thanked Megan for her offer, smiled like a glittering goddess of generosity and granted her permission to come over every other afternoon, to spend one hour in the playroom with Chester and Wesley. Then, by yawning, she declared that the audience was at an end, slipped off her shoes and put her feet up on the padded stool in front of her chair. Megan thanked her dutifully, stepped over the dog and went into the garden where Chester and Wesley, supervised by Ruben from the far distance of the veranda, were taking their afternoon naps in the shade between two trees. When she rocked Wesley's hammock back and forth, he opened his eyes and looked at Megan. She took his hand and began to hum a song softly, and after a while he was asleep again.

Until well into the afternoon she remained with the two chimps, sang to them, wove them wreaths from blades of grass and read in the lines of their hands happiness and long life. When she turned her head she saw Ruben, sitting with rumpled hair in a wicker chair on the veranda, secretly staring at her and seemed to desire nothing more ardently for himself than to be an ape.

In the fourth month of the rainy season, Megan revised her book and typed up the three hundred and forty pages once again. One afternoon in September she packed the stack of papers in two plastic bags and stashed them in the cavity under the window sill. Radio music drifted over from Esther's room, Miguel hammered nails into the outside wall of his hut, and when both eventually fell silent, there was only the whisper of the gentle rain and the musical scale of the drops that fell in puddles onto the wood or onto the already overflowing ground.

Megan went outside, opened the umbrella and walked toward the villa to spend an hour or more with Chester and Wesley. Last month she had limited her visits to Nancy's to two times a week, in order to finish writing the book. She had begun to doubt more than ever the meaning of her work, and had decided one day to either see it through to the end or

491

throw away what she had written so far. Now that the bundles of paper, heavy with the weight of thousands of words, lay in their hiding place, she felt neither satisfaction nor a sense of wasted effort; as she walked through the gray of the afternoon, she did not know whether it was quiet joy or infinite emptiness that made her footsteps lighter.

As she crossed the clearing, whose slightly sunken center had become a shallow pond, she ran into Ruben. Soaked to the skin by the rain and shivering despite the heat, he stood in front of her and cried, "You have to come! He's dying!"

Megan laid a hand on the boy's shoulder. "What are you saying? Who is dying?"

"Himself! Come! Quickly!" Ruben grabbed Megan's arm and pulled her along with him. He was wearing short, pale gray pants, a white shirt and white socks but no shoes, and he dragged Megan so violently behind him that eventually she dropped the umbrella so she could keep up with him.

While they ran the rain grew heavier, the shower started rushing down, and when they reached the staircase of the house it was pouring buckets. Ruben flung open the door and rushed into the house, and Megan stumbled after him, panting and wiping wet hair from her face.

Nancy stood beside her chair and Megan had barely entered the living room when she spread her arms and cried: "Dear me! It's so good that you're here!" She was wearing a light blue trouser suit and a white knee-length cardigan, and her feet were shoved into brown slippers. Her hair, formerly pinned up in an intricate style, looked less today like a massive tower than a besieged fortress, out of which several dark wooden sticks protruded like gun barrels. She had been crying; black makeup ran in blurred lines down her cheeks.

The dog was lying on the floor, as if he had not moved since the last time Megan was here. He had apparently stretched out his legs; one ear rested flat on the floorboards, the other was flipped back over his head.

Megan knelt down beside him and touched his warm, dry nose, pushed his eyelids up and then put her ear to his chest, to hear a faint sound of breathing and an even softer heart beat.

"What's the matter with him?" asked Ruben, who lay across the floor on his stomach and stroked the dog's side with one hand.

"He's very tired," Megan said, and almost laughed at the banality of her sentences; you didn't have to study veterinary medicine or spend much time observing this dog to see that he was patiently and apparently calmly nearing his end.

"How old is he?"

Ruben looked up at Nancy, who was a few steps closer and was suddenly holding a lighted cigarette in each hand.

"Almost as old as you, Rubinho; fourteen or fifteen."

"How long has he been laying here?"

"I wanted to go out with him after breakfast," said Ruben. "But not him. It was raining, and I thought he didn't want to."

"Did you go walking with him yesterday?"

"Yes, in the evening, since it wasn't raining."

"Has he eaten today?"

"In the morning. A little."

Nancy sat in the chair and put one of the two cigarettes in the glass ashtray next to a coffee mug and a cup that stood on the table beside her. "Look, he's conducting."

The Labrador was moving his front legs, slowly, like in a dream.

Nancy began to cry, but stopped again and went to the Gramophone to open the lid.

"I'll get my bag." Megan patted the dog's head. "Then we'll see what I can do." She stood up. "Stay with him and pet him, okay?"

Ruben nodded and stroked the Labrador's fur even more firmly.

"I'll hurry." Megan left the room and walked down the hallway. Music rang out from the living room behind her, a violin, a trumpet. She opened the door, took two steps at time and stepped out into the rain that was no

493

longer composed of large, heavy drops, but had become a dense spray that a light wind drove in her direction.

She ran the entire way. The ground was a single swamp; frogs squatted in the puddles. Once she slipped and fell. She swore, because she knew the dog would not die in the next half hour, and anyway there was not much she could do for him. When she arrived at the laboratory building she was out of breath and the rain had washed away the mud. Jay Jay and Nelson were watching a documentary film about hurricanes; on the screen, in any case, rooftops and billboards were flying through the air when Megan took a look into the dark room. She closed the door to the treatment room, gathered up a few things that would perhaps give Ruben the illusion that the dog could be helped, and packed everything into a doctor's bag. On the handle of the bag, fastened with a red ribbon, hung a card that contained the words ARTIFICIAL LEATHER! In Raske's handwriting. Megan pulled it off, left the room and locked the door. In the hallway she opened every door, looking for an umbrella, but she did not find one and set off for villa without it.

In the early evening it stopped raining. As if a dirty cloth was being pulled away slowly, the patch of brightness in the sky grew ever larger. It was still lead-gray and dark in the west, where the night waited, already starting again, and individual clouds formed on it like mildew on a damp wall, but rain did not fall from it any more.

Nevertheless, Megan carried an umbrella with her when she walked to Raske's house in the twilight, to bring him the news of the dog's death and to ask Raske in Nancy's name to obtain a Labrador puppy on the mainland, again a light brown male. The ground squelched beneath her feet, brooks flowed everywhere, rivulets trickled. In a murky pool tadpoles, water fleas, larvae and tiny crustaceans swarmed. Herons poked in the mud of the meadows for food and rose up, disturbed by Megan, with a few wing beats into the strangely clear air. Crickets rubbed their damp legs together.

A portion of the gravel had been washed from the path into the grass, into the beds and up to the front of the door. Leaves and branches were scattered about, flowers, severed by the rain, floated in the brown water of a ditch, which disappeared into the bushes. A pale gecko basked in the glow of the porch light.

Megan was just about to ring when she heard the voice. She lowered her hand and listened. From everywhere came the crackle of the earth, through which the water ran, the gurgle of hidden rivers. Suddenly music was playing so quietly that Megan did not know at first whether it was the sound of a piano or the jingle of falling raindrops. When a trumpet joined in, a bass, and finally the drums, she turned the knob, but the door was locked. She walked around the house and searched for a second door, but there wasn't one. In the back there were trees with shining wet trunks and leaves as big as two hands. Between them, on a carpet of leaves, there were fruits as red as cherries, whose foul smell filled the darkness.

Then she heard the voice again and this time she had no doubt that it was Esther's. For a while Megan just stood there and listened. Now and again she thought she heard Raske, but it could have been the sound of the bass, the beat muffled behind the walls and reverberating in the courtyard. One time she didn't know whether Esther was laughing or crying. In the heavy, mildewed air, she suddenly grew tired. She rolled her head and hung her shoulders, hunched her back and shook her arms, the way she used to before swimming. Then she climbed the tree that was so close to the house one of its branches touched the wall. The bark was slippery, and as Megan moved forward in a sitting position, she did it slowly and carefully, and her eyes were fixed straight ahead.

Now she saw the windows on the upper floor, two in darkness and one illuminated. The light was reduced to a pale yellow glow by a thin curtain, and disappeared in the blackness of the rectangular courtyard. Megan crouched motionless on the wall for a few minutes, her hands in a layer of rotten leaves which were growing out of thin twigs the size of matchsticks. Gusts of wind drifted down irregularly like the scraps of jazz music that came from the house.

Then finally someone came into the room, and although Megan could only make out the outline, she realized it was Raske. The figure that appeared behind him was undoubtedly Esther. The ceiling fan began to turn and move the curtain and with it the silhouettes of the two bodies, which looked as if they had been recorded during a subtle tremor. Megan's legs ached, and she sat down and let her feet dangle in the courtyard. She heard music and the two voices, but understood nothing of what was spoken. The window was about eight meters away from her and she pulled up her legs, placed her feet against the wall, raised herself up slowly and then balanced with outstretched arms and eyes fixed on the bright tips of her sneakers, moving forward in tiny steps.

Finally, she was so close to the house wall that she could touch the cool plaster. She crouched down, closed her eyes and tried to distinguish the voices from the scraps of music, but she could not. Not a single complete sentence reached her, only now and then a word or a name: Tanvir, Malpass, several times her own. When nothing more was said and the room released only light and music into the darkness, Megan went to the place where the wall formed a right angle, followed it a few meters to the center, sat down and waited.

After a while she felt like the lone visitor at an open air cinema; the screen was illuminated, but contained no images. Raske and Esther did not appear again. Eventually, the music stopped. Megan supposed that Esther would soon leave the house, but nothing happened. In the silence, she tried in vain to remember where Raske's office was, where the bathroom was, and where the bedroom was. She could feel the presence of the two of them; sense their movements behind the walls. She closed her eyes and breathed deeply in and out, ten times, twenty times. Her stomach cramped. She put her head back, opened her eyes and was startled to

496

see that the sky was full of stars for the first time in months. When she saw the moon, she howled at it. Somewhere a bird squawked, and she laughed. She wiped the tears from her face and saw the light go on in the second room, and Raske step to the window. In the second it took him to push the curtain aside, she swung her legs over the wall, pushed off with her hands and jumped into the darkness.

The wall was about three meters high, but she landed with her left leg first, and her ankle snapped. A short, searing pain shot through her foot. She let herself fall forward, and continued to lie on her stomach, clenched her fists and cursed softly. Then she clenched her teeth, got up and hobbled away. Behind her everything remained quiet, no slamming doors, no shouts. She had to put weight on the ankle, she thought, otherwise she would not be able to go any further soon. She started to run and the pain made her eyes water, but she did not stop. The ground was soft; in some places it bounced like the mats Chester and Wesley used for gymnastics; in others it caved in, as if she was moving in the bog behind Feargal Walsh's farm.

She ran, limping, and soon she hurt all over: her feet, legs, back, sides. Her entire body cramped and she walked slowly, taking in the air deeply and evenly and raising her arms at the same time. Just as she thought about taking a rest, she saw the plain at the end of the field lined with tall grass, and behind it, between the trees, the sea, and she decided to continue on and lie down in the sand.

The sea was still agitated and dirty, the beach littered with driftwood and trash. But the sky gleamed in dramatic perfection. An extravagant number of stars sparkled like diamonds tossed on a black velvet cloth. Megan sat down, took off her sneakers and rolled up her trouser leg. She touched her foot, moving it gently back and forth. The ankle was swollen but not discolored; no ligament appeared to be torn. After she had also taken off the second shoe, she walked through the wide strip of flotsam to the water and waded into the waves, approaching the brown foam, and even more wood and seaweed and garbage.

When she turned around after a while and headed towards the dry sand, she heard the engine. She screwed up her eyes and peered over the rippled surface of the sea, but she did not see a ship or boat. The chugging grew louder, and then quieter, seemed to grow completely silent and a little later penetrated the sound of the breaking waves. Megan sat down and put on her shoes. In front of her, on a bed of seaweed and twigs, there were plastic bottles; farther away shone the dull orange of a Styrofoam ball, like the ones hung from fishing nets.

She stood up, wondering which direction to take to get to the research station, and saw the light. First it was just a white point that disappeared after a few seconds, then, while Megan wondered if she had been mistaken, she saw it again. This was repeated so often that she was sure there was someone standing maybe two hundred meters away from her with a flashlight. She walked away from the beach up to the path that ran between the body of vegetation and the plain, and followed it for a bit.

Then she heard the hum of the engine loudly and clearly. The rain had washed away the earth from under the roots of a tree that was now lying prostrate in the sand, and when she reached it she ran, crouching, from the trunk to the crown, where a few withered leaves and a beard of seaweed and bits of plastic hung from the branches. She knelt down and observed the boat, which moved towards the slowly blinking eye of the light, eventually maneuvered alongside the waves and glided with them toward the shore. In the breaking waves of the surf the man in the stern turned off the outboard motor and raised it up, and two men jumped from the stern into the shallow water to pull the boat to shore. The only passenger remained seated until he could step onto dry land over a box that was placed in front of him. The man was tall and wore a white, knee-length shirt and dark pants and walked in long strides up to the figure with the flashlight, who was waiting for him next to a big stone. As the

498

two shook hands, the three-man crew sat in the sand in front of the boat hull, and a little later a match flared, and three cigarettes glowed in the dark.

Megan could not see the faces of the men and could not hear what they were saying, because they were too far away. It was not until the dark patch she had taken for a stone budged and walked across the beach, dimly lit by the moonlight, to poke with a stick at what had recently washed ashore, that she saw it was Montgomery. Now she also believed she could see Tanvir's shining bald head and even hear his voice, which was impossible because of the distance and the surf noise. She considered sneaking up to the men through the bushes and the trees, but then stayed where she was. The pain in her foot had slowed to a dull, unpleasant feeling, a hot traction when she moved it. She sat down and waited, without knowing for what.

After a while she leaned back against the trunk and stretched out her legs. She wondered who the men were and why Tanvir was meeting them, but she could not think of any plausible explanation. A queasy feeling began to spread in her stomach; she had not eaten since breakfast. She decided to rest ten minutes and then go back to the research station to see if Rosalinda had left something on the stove. After her watch stopped, she had grown accustomed to estimating the hour several times a day and had managed by now to come within half an hour. Now it was nine, she guessed, no more than half past nine. She remembered how she had often entered under the canopy of her room in the middle of the day, looked at the overcast sky and had loudly shouted out a time, whereupon Esther had shouted back the actual time.

The thought of Esther gave her a pang. She shouldn't have gotten involved in anything, she thought. She should have kept to herself, an island on the island. With this thoughtless step, guided by stupid desire, she had entered the circle of the castaways, the sordid circle of lonely hearts. Malpass and Rosalinda. Carla and Tanvir. Her and Esther. Esther and Raske. She bent her left leg, grabbed her foot with both hands and twisted it in all directions. The pain outshone every thought and every other pain. She gasped. Sweat flowed from her pores. She sat on the hill behind the house and cut into the skin of her foot with a knife, where no one would see it, shoved the blade under her toenail until everything went black, until she screamed like Holly, who did not understand what had happened to her and just knew that her life was over. Holly, who smiled and pricked up her ears when she heard music.

When someone put a hand on her, Megan opened her eyes and saw Montgomery, sitting in the sand in front of her. Once again, she was not frightened. The idea that from now on, whenever she was sad, Montgomery would come to hold her hand, made her sob. The bonobo took off his hat, moved closer to Megan, touched her cheek where the tears ran down, and pursed his lips. Then he drew back his hand and examined the wet tip of his index finger with a frown.

"I know," Megan said softly, "I cry too much." She leaned forward and rested her head on his chest.

Montgomery sighed, awkwardly patted Megan's shoulder and finally let his hand rest on her back. They remained in this position for several minutes. Megan did not feel any more pain, only a familiar despair, which for a long time she had known was a part of her, like her name. A plaything of her moods, Stuart had called it. Stuart, she thought, who had also been such a mistake. Had he ever heard the heartbeat of a primate without holding a stethoscope to his chest?

A barely perceptible jolt went through Montgomery. Then Megan heard it too. Tanvir was calling him. Montgomery sat up and took Megan's hand in his, drew gently on her arm. She turned her head and saw the boat travel out to sea through the waves of surf and the beam of the flashlight casting white lines on the beach.

Megan pulled her hand away. "Just go," she said.

Montgomery looked at her quizzically and grabbed her forearm.

"No. Go alone."

The bonobo looked in Tanvir's direction, then again in Megan's eyes. Above the noise of the sea and the singing of cicadas, his name sounded like the cry of a very unusual bird.

"Go to Tanvir." Megan made a shooing gesture with her hand and lay down.

Montgomery hesitated, but finally he touched Megan's knee in a helplessly tender gesture, put on his cap and went around the crown of the tree to Tanvir, who was only a stone's throw away. Megan waited for a while. Eventually, she raised her head over the trunk and watched as Tanvir and Montgomery, the light of the flashlight between them, disappeared into the dark cove of a small forest. She pushed herself up and groaned loudly as she put pressure on her left foot. In the strip of flotsam she found a branch that she used as a cane on the path where the ground grew firmer. Now she remembered the yellow umbrella she had been carrying and had left in front of Raske's house. She wondered if she should get it, decided against it, and then limped to the research station.

There was nobody in the kitchen hut, not even Rosalinda. Megan was going to take the key out of its hiding place, but she could not find it. Neither Carla's light nor Malpass' was still burning, and she knocked in vain at both doors. She went to the laboratory building and got a package of the strongest painkiller Raske had procured. In the first room she found a half-full bottle of water and washed down two tablets with it. There was a banana and a few pieces of dried coconut in a bowl. She sat down in the armchair Nelson always used when he watched videos, ate the banana and waited until the drug took effect.

When the muffled roar of the generator became a stutter and soon after that completely died and the lights went out, she went outside. Dark blue night surrounded her. The height of the celestial sphere was overwhelming. She took a few steps, imagined herself alone on the island. She could hardly feel her foot. Alone with Montgomery, she thought, and the rest could remain missing, even Carla, who would soon disappear anyway, now that the rainy season was coming to an end.

She walked on and on and eventually stood at the door of her living quarters. Esther's windows were dark; Miguel had probably been asleep for hours already. Inside, Megan lit the kerosene lamp, drank a glass of water and swallowed another tablet. It wasn't until she was sitting on the bed that she saw the sheet in the typewriter. She stood up and pulled the paper from the roller. I HAVE TO TALK TO YOU. ESTHER. She crumpled the paper and threw it into the trashcan in the bathroom. The light from the lamp scared away a gecko who had been sitting on the wall above the mirror. She washed her hands and face, gathered up her things and stuffed them into the backpack. Then she lifted the board of the window seat and convinced herself that the reams of paper, wrapped in plastic bags, were still there, and pushed the board back into its original position. When there was a knock on the open door behind her, she almost cried out and whirled around.

"We didn't want to scare you." Tanvir, who, instead of the dark clothing from the beach, wore white knee-length trousers and a saffron-yellow shirt with a round collar, raised both his arms to chest level and turned his palms forward. Montgomery, who was standing beside him, did the same.

"But you did."

"I do apologize."

"It's okay." Megan looked at the bonobo. "Hey, Montgomery. Come here." She sat down on the bed. "You too," she said to Tanvir, and tried to give her voice a cheerful tone.

Montgomery took his cap from his head and walked into the room. He still wore the long dark blue pants and a jacket of the same color. Tanvir took off his sandals and followed him inside. Montgomery stood in front of Megan, gently took her hand and looked into her face. If he had been a man, Megan would have braced herself for something more serious: an accident, or a marriage proposal.

"Montgomery has been worried about you."

"Really?"

Montgomery nodded, reached into the side pocket of his jacket, pulled out a sheet of paper and gave it to Megan. Megan unfolded it. It was the drawing with the many flowers that Montgomery had made for her.

"He showed me the paper and pulled me to the door. And here we are."

Megan stroked Montgomery's arm. "I'm fine. Thank you."

Montgomery shook his head.

"He doubts the veracity of your answer," Tanvir said.

"Oh, I sprained my foot. Is it possible that he . . . noticed it?"

"That or he has clairvoyant abilities." Tanvir pointed to the chair. "May I?"

"Of course."

Tanvir sat down. "I wanted to talk with you, Megan. Tomorrow, not now, in the middle of the night, but since I'm here now. . . " He cleared his throat. "You may remember our conversation. When I asked you to think about leaving the island." He looked at Megan.

Megan nodded. Montgomery crouched down, put both arms on her legs and rested his head on them.

"Well, I'm begging you once more to go," Tanvir said seriously. "I cannot tell you the reasons, but you should really leave. The sooner the better."

"You ask me to leave without telling me why?"

"Yes." Tanvir turned to the door to make sure that there was no one nearby, and then looked intently at Megan. "Please believe me, this island is not a safe place for you."

"But for you?"

Tanvir sighed, rubbing his bald head. "I can handle it."

"What were you doing this evening?"

"Doing? What do you mean?"

"Just what I said. What were you doing this evening?"

"Well, I cooked for Montgomery and myself. We ate. Then we played a few rounds of Memory. Listened to music. About two hours ago Monty was restless."

"Did you take a walk?"

"No. Montgomery doesn't like the rain."

"And tonight, when it stopped raining? Then did you take a walk?"

Tanvir looked at Megan, searching her face as if he was looking for a clue that would explain the reason for her question. "No. Why do you ask?"

"Why are you lying?"

Tanvir let out a laugh, but his face showed confusion and consternation. "What? I'm not lying. Why do you say that?"

"I saw you. You and Montgomery. And the four men in the boat."

Tanvir was now staring at Megan. His hands were on his knees, and he moved back and forth nervously.

"Do these men have anything to do with the alleged danger I'm in?"

It seemed as if, with a deep sigh, Tanvir let out all his energy, but also all his tension. He leaned back and let his arms hang down the side. For a while he fixed his eyes on a point on the floor next to Megan. Finally, he took a breath and said, "The man I met with is the leader of an Islamist separatist group. His name is Farid. In this area there are several gangs who are struggling for independence from Manila and the Islamization of the islands in the South. Farid is one of the moderate representatives, but there are others who are willing to use force. Farid has warned me against these dangerous and unpredictable hot-heads again and again."

"And what does this mean in concrete terms?"

"The hotheads are planning a raid on the research station. They don't want scientists from the West in their territory."

Megan thought for a moment. "They want to kill us?" she asked. At the last word Montgomery raised his head and looked first at her and then at Tanvir.

"It's okay, Monty," Tanvir said in a low, soft voice. "It's okay."

"Did he understand the word? Kill?"

"Yes. It alarmed him."

"Well, who wouldn't be?" Megan stroked Montgomery's hand and he laid his head back down on her legs.

"I see you have packed your things." Tanvir pointed to a backpack standing next to him on the floor.

"I want to get out of here."

"Why?"

"That's my business."

Tanvir nodded. "And where to?"

"Maybe the visitors center."

"You have to leave the island. Please. In answer to your earlier question: Yes, your life is in danger."

"Even if I wanted to, how would I get away?"

"Farid will send a boat. Tomorrow evening."

"What about the others?"

"Carla knows about it."

"Esther? Malpass? Raske? Rosalinda, Miguel, Jay Jay."

"Nothing will happen to Rosalinda, Miguel and Jay Jay."

"Who says so? Farid?"

Tanvir nodded. "Yes."

"The three of them are Catholic, right?"

Tanvir lowered her eyes. "They're Filipinos."

"But not Muslims."

"Nothing will happen to them. Farid promised."

"Farid, the moderate one. What about the hot-heads? Have they also

505

promised you something?"

"No. But if everyone leaves the island, no one will get hurt. Unfortunately, Raske and Malpass are not thinking of leaving. I don't know what Esther wants to do."

"She certainly doesn't want to be killed."

"Is she in her room?"

"I don't think so."

Tanvir got up, walked to the door, slipped into his sandals and went outside. A short time later Megan heard a knock and Tanvir calling to Esther. Montgomery sat up and listened. Megan patted his hand.

"She's not there," Tanvir said when he returned.

"I'll write her a message."

"Good. You should come to me when twilight falls. Then we will go to the beach together. Farid will wait."

"What about him?" Megan pointed her chin at Montgomery, who had dozed off. "And Nelson and Chester and Wesley?"

"They're staying here with me." Tanvir sat down again.

"With you? You're not going away?"

"Not just yet."

"Did you make a deal with them?"

"They'll leave us in peace, me and Nancy."

"Oh, I completely forgot about her! And what about Ruben?"

"He has nothing to fear, either."

For a while they were both silent. Montgomery was snoring softly. A moth circled the light.

"What kind of a deal is it?"

"I'm a doctor. They need one."

"And Nancy?"

"She doesn't want to leave."

"And the hot-heads will let her stay?"

"I only negotiated with Farid. I offered him part of the money that

506

Nancy's foundation sends every year, and he agreed. He wants to build schools, buy books, pay teachers."

"Naturally."

"He's not a bad person, Megan. Not a fanatic."

"If that's the case, I could stay. As your assistant."

A smile swept over Tanvir's face. "That won't work."

"I'm not a Catholic."

"You're a woman. A Western woman."

"I could wear a burka. No one would see me."

Tanvir sighed and stood up. "Promise me to come tomorrow." He looked at Megan. "Megan."

"Yes, all right." Megan bent her upper body forward and laid her cheek in Montgomery's palm.

"You really want to spend your last night on the island in the visitors center?"

"Yes," Megan said softly.

"As you wish. I'll help you with the move." Tanvir picked up the backpack and hung it on his shoulder. Then he put a hand on Montgomery's shoulder. "Hey, Monty, wake up."

The bonobo opened his eyes and blinked. He was warm and smelled like a closet full of clothes.

Megan smiled and gently squeezed his hand. "You don't have to help me," she said to Tanvir.

"We'd like to. Right, Monty?" He looked at the bonobo.

"Help Megan, okay?"

Montgomery nodded eagerly. He reached down, took his cap off the bed and put it on.

Megan took a few things from the bathroom and filled a plastic bag with them. The seahorse that Montgomery had given her was on the bedside table. She wrapped it in toilet paper and put it in the breast pocket of her shirt. Then she gathered the sheets and the pillow under her arm.

"And these here?" Tanvir pointed to the three colored pencil drawings, three pencil sketches and the two watercolors pinned to the wall above the bureau.

"I can get those tomorrow," Megan said. She put the bedding on the floor, rolled a sheet of paper into the Olivetti and wrote Esther a message.

COME TO TANVIR'S AT TWILIGHT. WE HAVE TO LEAVE THE ISLAND. MEGAN.

She pulled out the paper and folded it once. Then she picked up the bundle and the plastic bag, stuck the flashlight Tanvir had given her into the front of her waistband and stood in front of the door. She peered into the darkness and feared that Esther would show up, and wished for it at the same time.

"Do you have everything?"

Megan turned around. Tanvir had hung the backpack on Montgomery and held the kerosene lamp in his hand. Megan nodded. She thought about the manuscript, and resolved to retrieve it from its hiding place the next day. She went to Esther's room and slipped the folded paper under the door. Montgomery was standing on the path, a lonely wanderer in the night. She went to him and took his hand. In her room the lights went out, and shortly after that Tanvir appeared in the doorway with the rolled mattress under his arm and turned on the flashlight.

"Did you know that the dog died?" Megan asked, as he walked beside her.

"Himself? No. I haven't been to Nancy's for two days." Tanvir stopped suddenly, as if he only now realized the importance of the message. "Oh . . ."

Megan and Montgomery also stopped. "Heart failure," Megan said. "When I wanted to take care of him, he was already dead."

Tanvir stared at his feet, nodded. "He was old."

"Fifteen or sixteen, Nancy said."

"Poor thing. She was very attached to that dog."

"She wants Raske to get her a new one."

"Well, we'll see." Tanvir shouldered the mattress and began to move.

Megan and Montgomery also began walking. "We'd like to bury him. Tomorrow."

"He'll have to be cremated first. And the soil is too wet. It's impossible to dig a grave right now." Tanvir panted from the exertion; beads of sweat appeared on his forehead.

"Is there a cemetery on the island?"

"A cemetery? No. So far nobody has died."

"Not even primates?"

"Yes. They were burned. But their ashes weren't . . . well, not buried."

"I think the research station should have a graveyard."

Tanvir let out a prolonged groan. "You build a hospital, and suddenly, everyone is ill. Put in a cemetery, and suddenly people are dying." He moved the mattress to the other shoulder, and did not say another word until they were standing in front of the visitors center.

On a sunny day the room, with a floor of bright stone tiles, brick walls— some covered with bamboo and wood panel wainscoting—and the high ceiling, seemed grand; but now, in the light of the kerosene lamp that hung from one of the exposed roof beams, it looked tiny. In one corner there was a table, a storage unit and two empty display cases. On the table were broken picture frames and letterhead curled from the humid air and note pads. Cardboard boxes full of IPREC brochures were stacked against a whitewashed wall and above them were bright circular spots that served as reminders of the places where clocks had once displayed the time on the five continents. Under them the plaques with the names of cities were still attached: Manila. Dallas. London. Dakar. Sydney.

"You could also sleep in one of the rooms in the laboratory building," Tanvir said. "Or with us. It's very tight there, but at least comfortable."

Megan dropped the bundle of bedding on the mattress that Tanvir had put in the middle of the room. "No, thanks. That's nice, but I . . . "

"That's okay. You'd rather be alone."

Megan nodded. Montgomery threw an arm around her leg, and she patted him gently on the head.

"I'm very sorry that you're going."

"Yes. Me too."

"I'll miss our talks."

Megan looked at Tanvir. She wanted to ask him why he told people different stories about his life and whether he had also lied to her, but then it didn't seem important to her. "So then," she said, holding out her right hand. "Good night."

After a moment's hesitation, Tanvir took Megan's hand and squeezed it. "Good night."

Megan crouched down, placed two fingers on her lips and then to Montgomery's mouth. "Good night."

The bonobo's gaze hit her like a wave that knocked her off her feet, lifted her up for a split second into the brightness and then threw her down again to the lightless, fluctuating bottom. Montgomery let out a noise that sounded sorrowful in her ears and maybe disappointed, then he lowered his head, turned away and walked to the door.

"See you tomorrow," Tanvir said. For a moment he stood still, as if he was pondering how he could comfort Megan, and then followed Montgomery, who had already closed the door behind him.

Megan swallowed a painkiller and then slept for two hours. Now she sat on the mattress in the glow of the kerosene lamp and tried to write a letter to Tobey, but her imminent departure from the island prevented her from composing any clear thoughts. After she had filled half a notebook page with nonsense, she crumpled the paper and threw it into a corner. She took out the seahorse and looked at it for a while, then put it into an outer pocket of the backpack that Montgomery had taken off only after much persuasion.

The night was no longer starlit when she stepped out the door. A thin cloud cover suppressed what little brightness the moon had recently dispensed. Megan took the flashlight, pocketed the painkillers and went on her way to the beach. She did not feel the sprained ankle at all. The effect of the pain medication continued and even made her head light and every sensation pleasantly dull. Even from a distance she saw a light burning in the kitchen hut and heard Carla's voice and that of Malpass. The two were quarreling. Carla sounded drunk and Malpass tired and irritable, again and again words and phrases in Spanish and French tumbling out. Megan would like to have spoken with Carla and eaten something, but the thought of having to endure Malpass for even one minute held her back. To avoid being seen by the two, she left the path and crossed the clearing, where the puddles had disappeared and only the memory of the soft, slippery soil from the rain in recent months remained. In the grass belt that lined the plain like a shaggy fur collar on a threadbare coat, she turned on the flashlight. A heron flew up in front of her. His white feathers caught the shaft of light for a few seconds, and then he sank in the darkness without a sound.

She stood on the beach for a while, where the waves trickled out and the sand was firm, and looked out to sea. For the first time since Tanvir had suggested that she had to leave the island, she wondered whether she could trust him. Perhaps, she thought, the story of the Muslim freedom fighters was just another product of his imagination, a well-staged attempt to get rid of the woman who had ruined his last hopes for the post of physician at the research station. Perhaps he really was not right in the head, as Esther had said, and turned innocent fishermen into religious extremists, a few quirky islanders into a bloodthirsty gang that tried to kill her and the rest of the foreigners.

Then she shook her head, picked up a stone and threw it into the surf. No, she told herself, Tanvir was not crazy. He may be exaggerating the danger a little, but apparently he was truly concerned. And the thought that he might be envious of her because Raske allowed her to treat the research station staff in addition to the non-human primates was ridiculous. She thought she knew him now well enough to know that he had resigned himself to his position on the island and didn't consider anyone an enemy, not even Raske, with whom he seemed to have made mutually acceptable and profitable agreements. He enjoyed the protection of his lady friend, Nancy Preston, from whose foundation money Raske benefited, and who in turn was important for Nancy, because he represented IPREC.

If you looked at it from this perspective, the three formed a perfect symbiosis, and Megan wondered what Raske had planned to preserve this condition. She walked along the beach, which again and again was covered with floating debris. Now and then she bent down and picked up a piece of wood, a piece of plastic or a bottle that was empty and did not contain a message by a stranded sailor or a little girl, who had been waiting in Ireland for a response from the other end of the world. She wondered whether Raske actually planned in order to stay on the island, and she decided to ask him. Maybe everything was not so bad, she thought, and the men Tanvir had described as dangerous and unpredictable did negotiate.

The ship appeared in front of her so suddenly that she thought it was an optical illusion, a trick played by her eyes, tired from the light of the flashlight, and her brain, muffled by painkillers. She stopped, turned off the flashlight, closed her eyes and opened them again. The ship was still there. It was out in its anchorage spot, rocking in the light waves. A few lights were burning on board, white and yellow dots and dashes. The sight was somewhat amusing, as if a festival was being celebrated on the deck and music played at every moment.

At the end of the wooden pier, which jutted out to sea a bit at high tide, a rowboat was moored. A wave lifted it gently and Megan could see its white-painted side. As she approached the ship she looked around constantly, and was soon convinced that she was alone on the beach. If there was anybody on board, they stayed inside.

The ceiling of the sky had grown closer with every hour; the night grew darker. On the horizon clouds were billowing, vast scenery on the stage of the sea. The wind picked up and blew the smell of feculent seaweed and decaying wood into Megan's face. When she reached the planks that were lying in the sand and connected with wire, which only for the last twenty meters formed a kind of pier, she stopped again and waited. Apart from the noise of the surf in front of her and the whirring of the cicadas singing behind her, silence prevailed. She took off her shoes and walked to the end of the pier. There were a pair of oars and a life jacket in the boat; in a pool of water cigarette filters bobbed up and down. Megan only now saw the chain, secured with a rusty padlock that connected the boat to a post rising out of the water. For a while she stood there and regarded the ship, about two hundred meters out, then she took off her shirt, t-shirt and pants, wrapped the flashlight and shoes in them and put the package on her head. She stepped into the water, waded into the depths and began to swim. The farther she moved away from the shore the calmer the sea was, and although she had to hold the bundle in one hand, she made good progress.

When she reached the ship, she grasped the anchor chain with her free hand and rested. IPREC was written in large black letters on the bow. She looked up to the guardrail that was two or three meters above her. There was no sound from the steel belly, only the sloshing of the water could be heard, the scraping of the chain and the groaning of the hull, rising and falling in the waves. Megan pulled herself up out of the water a little on the chain, threw the bundle on the deck and waited. When nothing happened, she gathered her strength and climbed up the chain, but the metal frame was so smooth that she kept slipping. Finally she gave up and swam around the bow to the other side. At the stern the ship was secured with a rope to a buoy which, Megan assumed, was held in place by a steel cable and a concrete block resting on the bottom of the sea. The rope was slippery where it hung in the water, but a little higher it was dry and had a good grip, and when Megan reached the top she swung a leg over the guardrail, drew herself up with both arms and slid down onto the deck.

She lay there a moment in order to catch her breath, then got up and looked for the bundle of clothes. She found it next to a ladder and got dressed. The lights came from three white solar lamps fastened to the guardrail, and two lamps in the wheelhouse that Megan had perceived as yellow lines from the shore. Now, from where she found herself on board, the ship appeared smaller than it had from a distance. In the cold light of the solar lamps, it seemed to her almost unreal, kind of shabby, an inferior copy of the ships from her childhood. If a fishing vessel in the Dingle Bay was a steel box, this was a cookie jar. Except for a miserable and obviously useless mast at the bow, rigging of any kind was missing. The wheelhouse was made of wood, the floor she was moving on thin and rusted through in some places. In the wheelhouse, where the white paint was peeling all around and cables, intertwined and wrapped with electrical tape, hung from the walls, a staircase led into the belly of the ship. When Megan turned on the flashlight and shone it into the black hole, she was assaulted by the smell of diesel fuel and sea water. After she had taken a deep breath, she grasped the railing with her free hand and descended the steps.

Below, she found herself in a corridor that was confined on both sides by steel walls painted a light gray. Behind an open door was a storage room, half filled with poorly secured metal boxes and drums made of blue plastic. Neither the boxes nor the barrels were labeled. In the opposite room were two cots which contained bare mattresses and folded

514

blankets. On a table top that folded down from the wall on chains there was a bottle that had been used as an ashtray. Fresh air blew in from a barred air shaft opening in the ceiling. Megan picked up a piece of cardboard, which turned out to be a flat box for caliber 22 rifle ammunition.

Back in the hallway, she went toward the stern, and after a few meters the beam of the flashlight revealed a door that led to the engine room, a dark hole stinking of diesel, the floor covered with a film of oil and dirt. On the walls were filthy rags, wrenches, and technical drawings wrapped in plastic film. Megan knew nothing about engines, but even she could recognize that it would be a miracle if the monster in front of her, seemingly assembled out of unsophisticated spare parts, would be able to drive the propellers.

The two rooms in the bow were small and served as a kind of broom closet and pantry. In one of them water containers, tin cans and plastic boxes with rice, flour, sugar and salt were stored; in the other there were cleaning agents, tools and half a dozen fire extinguishers, not one of which looked like it would work. In the pantry there was a steel cabinet, taller than a man, locked and not yet infested with rust stains. Although she knew she would not find anything, Megan looked for the keys, picked up cans and groped in the gaps between the cans and the lids of the boxes on the upper shelves with her fingers. Before she left she swallowed a painkiller and washed it down with a cup of water.

On deck, she turned off the flashlight and filled her lungs with fresh air. There were still huge clouds on the horizon, their bellies already colored by the first faint light. The wind came in gusts; far out the sea was uneasy. Moon and stars were no longer visible. A gull flew away above Megan, and its increasingly high, sustained cry reminded her of the rat.

The two lights were like the eyes of an animal that had left the forest and crossed the boardwalk to the beach. When the bobbing points came nearer, Megan recognized Raske and Malpass, who carried a box, and ducked behind the railing. Through the hole in the anchor chain she saw

Malpass stumble and fall. She heard the breaking of the box on the boards, Raske's curses and the wailing voice of Malpass. Now there was still time to go to the stern, she thought, shimmy down the rope into the water and swim toward them. But then she went back into the musty bowels of the ship, crawled into the pantry behind the wall of wood and metal boxes and waited.

Not half an hour later the ship sailed. The engine roared, and caused the thin steel walls to tremble and every object to vibrate. Megan opened her mouth slightly so that her teeth would stop buzzing. At the stern, the propeller choked and howled like a wounded sea monster; in the bow each breaking wave resounded like cannon fire and made the bolts and rivets creak.

Raske and Malpass had placed the box on the deck and started the engine. It was ages before the monster started and the coughing and spitting had become a deafening noise, interrupted again and again by brief engine failures. Between futile attempts Raske, who was apparently in the engine room, had roared instructions to Malpass, who was standing in the wheelhouse.

Eventually the noise grew weaker and for a short time the pounding of the individual cylinders could be heard, then the engine seemed to flood. A little later the anchor chain rattled through the opening in the guardrail, which sounded in Megan's compartment as if one thousand hammers were beating against the steel wall. Raske and Malpass talked loudly, but even though Megan crouched under the opening of the air shaft, she could not understand anything except a few individual words. She was about to straighten up in order to let the blood circulate in her legs, when she heard footsteps on the stairs. Shortly thereafter, the door opened and the overhead light turned on. Megan froze and held her breath. She heard someone open the cupboard and remove something from it, and her heart stopped for a moment when she realized that

Raske or Malpass could lock the door to her compartment. Then the steps withdrew, echoed on the steps and eventually on the deck. Megan stretched, moved her legs and held her ear to the grille of the ventilation shaft, but now the two men were silent.

A few minutes later the roar of a boat engine swelled, and Megan heard as the wooden rungs of the rope ladder beat against the vessel wall and the box on the top floor was dragged. The last sounds she heard were Raske's voice and the gradually fading engine noise. When she was sure she was alone on board, she left her hiding place and went upstairs. Crouched behind the guardrail, she saw the boat that had been pulled ashore, and three men, two of them dragging the box. The third, who could only be Raske, walked in front of them and shone a flashlight on the path that someone had trampled into the sand, which disappeared a little further on between the trunks of a small forest.

Megan looked for a plastic bag in the pantry, did not find one and emptied one of the plastic boxes in which the food was stored. She ate a slice of shrink-wrapped bread, drank two cups of water and went back on deck, where she took off everything but her underwear. After she had closed the lid to the box which contained her clothes, shoes and flashlight, she climbed down the ladder into the water and swam, to the shore, pushing the box in front of her.

The island she landed on differed little from the one she had left. The vegetation seemed to be the same and the sounds of crickets chirping and frogs croaking also sounded familiar. Because she did not turn on the flashlight, Megan moved slowly through the forest she had reached after crossing the wide strip of beach, which was covered with driftwood. As she walked she got used to the rustling and cracking, the wing-flapping and excited croaking around her, but at every unusual sound she flinched and paused. Once she thought she heard shouting, then the sound of a starting motor.

As she stepped from the darkness onto a plain, a little light between the clouds, a hint of dawn, had already begun to spread. In the distance there arose a hill that Megan at first mistook for a formation of rain clouds that had lowered over the island. She was making better progress now and soon reached the end of an expanse the size of a football field, where the almost barren soil transformed into a shaggy lawn. In the dim morning light the low hills appeared less impressive to her. She stopped and looked at the gentle slope rise, flanked with bushes and small trees, the crest enveloped by mist, and then she continued to follow the muddy path, saw rocks and tree skeletons in a grassless field, left a palm grove behind her and finally came to a path that, with its deep water-filled troughs, looked like it moved vehicles on a regular basis.

Soon the first buildings appeared, gray, apparently windowless blocks which hardly stood out from the twilight of the surroundings. Megan sat down on the ground behind a tree, rested and listened to sounds. The pain in her foot made a return appearance, a diffuse throbbing that grew stronger the longer she did not move. She swallowed a pill and regretted that she had not brought along any water. While she waited for the pill to take effect, she leaned against the tree and closed her eyes. Tiredness crept from her legs up her back and into her head. What she heard was so familiar to her from the other island, that after a while she noticed the hum of the diesel generators. She got up and walked along the path to the blocks, which proved up close to be brick buildings, standing on circular concrete columns, with flat roofs made of corrugated iron, and in fact windowless. On the rooftops Megan saw solar panels, water tanks and rectangular air shafts. At the end of the building, about twenty five meters long, the generators were housed behind soundproof walls, and on each long side there was a steel door with an electronic lock protected from the elements by a transparent Plexiglas box. There was a large black number painted on each door and a sign warned against trespassing. Only now did she notice a flashing red light under the eaves and was glad she

518

had not touched the door.

She continued walking and came to a muddy spot rutted with deep wheel tracks around which three buildings were grouped. In the smallest, a wooden house on brick pillars, a light was burning; in front was parked a green Jeep with a trailer on which were piled a dozen or more metal boxes the size of steamer trunks. Megan hid behind a tree and studied the house, then ran in a wide arc toward the rear of the building where there were two bicycles leaning against a wooden railing. All over the place there were metal barrels full of rain water, stacks of tires, boards and bricks, numerous gas bottles, a wheelbarrow, and a dented refrigerator. She crept to the back door of the house, crouched under one of the windows filled with warm light, and heard Raske and Malpass and the man who had sailed the boat, and in between a metallic clicking, as if large padlocks were being unlocked.

Because she could not make out any of the conversation, she walked cautiously to an open side window. In that moment, the front door opened. Megan pressed against the wall and listened as the men loaded something into the jeep or on the trailer. The third man sounded like a Filipino. He had a high, hoarse voice, and answered only to Raske's instructions. A little later doors slammed, then the engine started and the jeep drove off.

When Megan no longer doubted that all three were gone, she entered the house. She looked into a room where there was a mattress on the floor, into a tidy kitchen and a small bathroom and finally into a room with a large wooden table, some stools, worn armchairs and a chest of drawers where, encircled by candles, dried flowers, playing card-sized pictures of saints and intertwined rosaries, there was a statue of the Virgin Mary made of colored plastic. On the wall above the statue hung a cross made of dark wood and a photo of a young woman. On the carpet under the table Megan found a cartridge and stuck it in her pocket. Now she understood that the click she had heard had been the noise of loading

519

weapons. She left the house and peered into the windows of another building, but saw only dark, empty rooms. Every door she tried to open was locked.

About a hundred meters away from the houses, at the end of a lane, she came upon a bunker-like building of concrete with a chimney towering out of its flat roof. Beside the bunker, under a corrugated iron roof, there were five containers and two wheelbarrows. Shovels, rakes and brooms leaned against the wall of a wooden hut, where oil-stained barrels were stored. Although a foul stench rose from the containers, Megan would have gladly looked into one, but chains and padlocks secured the lids.

To her surprise, the steel door of the bunker was unlocked. Megan pushed it open, turned on the flashlight and walked into the room, which smelled liked oil and cold ashes and was dominated by an enormous incinerator formed of brick walls and black iron parts. The door of the incinerator was open and there was a clear view of a horizontal spit, the base covered with a layer of gray ash. In a corner by the incinerator there were sacks made from nylon fabric that had once been white, crawling with flies. Megan took one of the long metal hooks from a wall bracket and poked through the cinders. At the very back of the shaft there were particles that had not completely burned, and she scooped some of them in her direction. Between charred chunks of wood she found something that she identified after a few seconds as the bones of an animal. She poked the nylon bags with the hook, opened them and shone the flashlight inside. The insides of the bags were filthy; at the very bottom of one, in a dark, partially dried layer of hair, maggots were moving. When startled flies began to buzz around her head, Megan threw the hook on the floor and ran outside.

Under a sky now illuminated by the mild morning light, she moved a few yards away from the bunker and took a breath of fresh air. Then she went back to the three houses, followed the path in the opposite direction, and after a short time reaching a long building standing on pillars; running along the side that faced her there were cages made of chicken wire. The cages, reminiscent of dog kennels and half-covered by a sloping roof, were empty. In one, a frayed rope hung from the roof; in another, there was a metal bowl filled with rainwater. Megan threw a stone against the wood siding of the building, hid behind the bushes and waited. When nothing moved, she looked for a door, found one that wasn't locked, and opened it.

The little light that fell through the narrow window was barely able to illuminate the room, which looked to Megan like an endless corridor. Against the wall along the windows there were rows of tables with black office chairs. After every second table, there was a green filing cabinet as high as the low ceiling. Megan walked on a carpet that absorbed the sound of her footsteps. A computer keyboard, a printer without a cover and a disassembled phone lay on the floor. At the end of the room, in front of a locked door, there were four metal boxes of the same make Megan had seen on the trailer. Each of the boxes was secured with two locks which could not be opened either with the rusty scissors Megan found, or with brute force.

In the plywood wall opposite the windows there were recessed glazed openings, through which you could see the cages. In the middle there was a door leading into the area between the building and the cages. Pages from calendars with photos of landscapes covered the free surfaces. One shot showed the Tower Bridge in London, and on a whim Megan pulled the page off the wall, crumpled it and threw it into one of the trashcans.

Most of the drawers in the file cabinets were empty. What Megan found were blank forms and worksheets with no entries, unused envelopes and clear plastic folders, empty hanging file folders and index cards. In one drawer there were forms with hand-written notes, and Megan deciphered blood types, body temperatures and weights, various date entries, and abbreviations that made no sense. Because the light was so bad and she did not want to use the flashlight, she went through the door in the plywood wall and sat on a folding chair in the inner court under one of the Plexiglas windows that replaced the corrugated metal every few meters and provided a little light.

She was puzzling over the meaning of some recurring abbreviations when she heard the sound. At first she was not sure if she was mistaken, but then she heard it again. A kind of barking, she thought, the faint barking of a puppy. She got up, put the pages on the chair and went to the far end of the building, past eight empty cages, until she was standing in front of the last one. This cage was larger than the others and not made of chicken wire, but from massive iron bars. In its center, on dry, sandy soil, there was a tree without bark, which reminded Megan of the climbing trees in zoos. Beside the tree there was a hole, like the entrance to a cave or the burrow of an animal. On a stone she saw corn, bananas and nuts, and water shimmering in a plastic container. There was a door, also made of welded iron bars, but it was locked.

To the right of the cage there was a brick room that contained a small table and a folding chair. A staircase led below the ground, and Megan turned on the flashlight and walked the five steps down into a narrow room that smelled of damp earth and faintly of feces. Half of the exposed -brick wall was taken up by a door with a viewing window. A cover made of plywood concealed the square peephole. Megan pushed it aside and moved her face close to the glass window to peek into the dark room behind, but she could not see anything and was about to go up the stairs when she discovered the switch. She flipped it and on the other side of the window a ceiling light went on and threw a faint bluish light on the stone walls of an artificial cave, its floor covered with a thick layer of straw and leaves. Megan turned off the flashlight and approached the peephole again. She saw the foot and half a leg only after a while, and it took twice as long before she realized that it was the limb of a human being and not that of a primate. A child, she thought suddenly, and the realization came to her with such violence that she staggered away from the door and banged her back against the wall.

After she had calmed down somewhat and was breathing normally again, she went to the door again and tapped the tip of her index finger against the glass. The leg twitched, and as Megan tapped her knuckles against the glass, it disappeared entirely from her sight. The straw was moving, and soon after she heard from above a prolonged cry, a kind of howling, and then barking, but this time louder than before. She ran up the stairs, rushed out of the annex and saw the creature that made these sounds, and the sight took her breath away. The child, a girl, was small and skinny and naked, her dark skin dirty and teeming with a chaotic pattern of scars and scratches, her head shaved and covered with scabs. Moving on hands and feet like an animal, it rushed to and fro, yelped and barked and jumped up to the bars of the cage again and again. When it noticed Megan, it froze for seconds. Its flat chest trembled and its eyes with black pupils were wide open. It crouched, let out a terrified whimper and then disappeared quickly into the hole.

Megan went to the cage and clung to the iron bars. She was struggling for air, closed her eyes and tried to concentrate on breathing. Her foot suddenly hurt. She vomited, but there was very little in her stomach. She wept and beat her fists on the grill until her skin cracked. When she turned, she was almost glad to see Malpass.

He stood there, staring at Megan, a stupid expression on his face. "What are you doing here?" he asked. He wore respectable shoes; brown pants with side pockets and a shirt of dark blue that made the lighter straps of a backpack stand out. A black scarf was wrapped around his neck.

Megan wiped her shirt sleeve across her mouth and said nothing. Suddenly all of the timber beams began to snap, but seconds later she realized that it was the sound of heavy rain falling on the roof. Now she also noticed the change of light; in the minutes she had spent in the room

523

below the floor, the brightness of dawn seemed to have disappeared.

"How did you get to this island?" Malpass asked in a louder voice. His round face was flushed and sweaty.

"I flew." Megan sat down. Only now did she see the gun that was hanging on Malpass' shoulder, a machine gun, like the ones gangsters in movies used.

"You're snooping around," Malpass said. He took the sheets of paper in his hand, waved them in the air and threw them back on the seat of the chair. "Stay in your seat!" he shouted as Megan was about to struggle to her feet. He took a step forward and pointed at her.

Megan got up anyway.

"You should stay in your seat!" Malpass released the safety lock on the gun and fired into the roof. The bullet smashed through the Plexiglas and a few tiny pieces of glass showered down.

Megan doubled over and put her arms protectively around her head. The blast left a roaring in her ears. When it grew weaker, she heard the girl crying from under the ground.

Malpass fired a second shot.

"Stop!" Megan shouted.

"Then do what I tell you," Malpass shouted back.

Megan sat down. She trembled; her heart raced.

Malpass stripped off the backpack and let it fall to the ground. Without taking Megan out of his sight, he toppled the stacks of paper from the chair and sat down. He untied the knot of the scarf and used it to wipe his face. Suddenly he threw his head back, spat something in French at the ceiling and groaned out loud.

Then he was almost calm for a while and just listened to the patter of the rain on the roof. No more sound came from the hole. Water dripped through the two bullet holes, forming small puddles on the cement floor.

"What kind of girl is that?" Megan asked at some point. Her voice seemed strange to her, fragile and quiet, and she didn't know if Malpass had heard her at all. She rested her back of against the bars and tried to take a deep breath in and out.

Malpass did not answer. He stared absently past Megan and seemed to wait. The machine gun with the shoulder strap lay across his legs like a strange musical instrument.

"Who is that girl in the cage?" Megan tried again and flinched when a nearby door opened and footsteps clattered.

Malpass rose to his feet, groaning. As soon as he stood up the door flew open, and a large, thin Filipino stormed in with a rifle at the ready. The shorts and the shirt of the man were completely soaked and his rubber boots left traces of mud on the bright cement. He stopped and looked back and forth between Malpass and Megan, panting and with his mouth open, in which glittered a gold front tooth.

"Where have you been, damn it?" Malpass barked at him.

"Making fire in the oven," said the Filipino. His hoarse voice sounded like an old man's. "What's wrong? Who is that?"

"Get a piece of rope or something," Malpass said. He hung the gun across his shoulder and pulled a pack of cigarettes out of the side pocket of his trousers.

"Rope?"

"Anything. We have to tie her up." Malpass fumbled a cigarette out of the box and tucked it between his lips.

"Who is she?"

"Don't ask questions, and just get the damn rope!" Malpass put the pack back in his pocket, lifted the paper bundle from the floor and held it out to the man. "There. This has to go. And look to see if there are any more of them lying around."

The Filipino leaned the gun, a carbine that looked like a relict from a museum next to the machine gun, against the chair and hurried, the stack of papers pressed to his chest with both hands, into the building.

Malpass sat down again. For a time he regarded Megan with a look that was as penetrating as it was veiled, then he suddenly seemed to remember the cigarette, took out a lighter and lit it.

"What happens now?" Megan asked, although she had little hope for a response.

Malpass enveloped himself in smoke and silence. His right leg jiggled nervously. The rain grew weaker, the patter lighter. Sounds drifted through the open door in the plywood wall as if all the drawers of the file cabinets were pulled out and closed again in rapid succession.

A little later the Filipino came in with a piece of cable in his hands.

"What are you waiting for?" Malpass shouted and stood up. "Tie her up!"

The man hesitated a moment, then walked slowly, with his head down, to Megan and knelt down beside her.

"Her hands," Malpass said.

Megan did not move. "What are you going to do to me?"

"You just do what I say." Malpass aimed the barrel of the machine gun at Megan. "Please."

"Otherwise, you'll shoot me?"

Malpass closed his eyes for the length of a sigh and then opened them again. "No. That's unlikely," he said, struggling for control. "But I'm getting fed up. It won't stop raining. I have a toothache. These Muslim assholes are threatening us. And as if that weren't enough, you suddenly appear." He crouched down and looked at Megan.

"Ramon is going to tie you up now, and it would be nice of you if you didn't fight back." He took a long draw on the cigarette and blew the smoke in Megan's face.

Megan turned her head to one side and stretched out her arms.

"Thanks." Malpass sat up.

Ramon kept his eyes lowered while he wrapped the cable, from which the plug still hung, around Megan's wrists and knotted the ends several times.

"Is it okay?" asked Malpass. "Not too tight?"

Megan did not answer. Her throat was burning, and a bitter taste filled her mouth.

Ramon took his gun. "Must work," he said, and went to the door.

"What?"

"Load boxes. Then the oven."

"Where is Raske?"

"He left. With the ship."

"That wasn't our agreement."

"He says he comes back. In two hours, maybe three."

Malpass mumbled something unintelligible.

Ramon stood there, hesitating, then he left and soon after that a door slammed.

"And now?" asked Megan.

Malpass turned to her as if he had forgotten that she was there. He seemed to think it over. "We wait," he said.

"For what?"

"Raske." Malpass collapsed on the chair. He folded the scarf and tied it around his neck. After the last puff, he threw the cigarette butt on the floor and stomped it out with the sole of his shoe.

Megan leaned against the bars. The pain in her hands diminished, but grew worse in her foot.

Malpass took a bottle of water from the backpack, unscrewed the cap and took a long sip. Then he put the cap back on and rolled it across the floor toward Megan.

Despite the fact that her hands were tied, Megan managed to pull the box of pills out of her pocket.

"What's that?" Malpass asked.

"Painkillers." Megan, put two tablets on her tongue, jammed the bottle between her feet, turned the cap and drank.

"What are they good for?"

Megan shrugged her shoulders, whereupon Malpass rose and signaled for her to give him the package and the bottle. He pressed two tablets out of the foil and washed them down, then sat down again, wiggled his foot and drummed his fingers on the gun.

"Are you going to kill me?" Megan asked, and a laugh stuck in her throat. She could only remember one question that was even more absurd than this one. She had asked her ex-husband, after he had betrayed her, whether he had ever truly loved her.

Malpass took a deep breath in and out, stared at the water stains that were spreading across the cement floor, and seemed absorbed in brooding over an answer. His brow was furrowed as he finally looked into Megan's eyes and said, "Not me."

Megan refused to fathom the meaning of these two words. She forced herself to think of something else, and landed, without wanting to, on a New Year's Day in her London flat, jam-packed with books. Hungover and without having adopted one good resolution, she had decided to kill herself by jumping out the window. But even after hours she had not had the courage or cowardice to do it, and finally resolved something for the New Year, namely to continue living.

Her eyes opened. Malpass' gaze, suddenly clear and attentive, went past her, and she turned her head to the cage and saw just at that moment how the girl disappeared into the hole.

"She's the drop," Malpass said softly.

"What?"

"That causes the barrel to overflow. Or whatever they say in your language. These religious idiots have never cared about what we do here. Until Raske had to buy his damn jungle child."

Megan waited, but Malpass said no more. He took out the cigarettes and lit one. Leaning back, he sat and smoked absent-mindedly.

"He bought a jungle child? I don't understand."

"The girl was found on an island. Further down in the south. The mother had abandoned it there. No intuitiveness. It's wild. It doesn't speak. It barks and howls like a dog."

"Raske bought it? From whom?"

"Well what do you think? From enterprising bastards!" Malpass coughed and wiped smoke away from his face with his hand. "They delivered the child here a few weeks ago. And duly took the money."

"And now?"

"And now?" Malpass cried, and his voice cracked. He leaned forward, emerged from the fog, red-faced and sweaty. "Now we have the sons of Mohammed at our throats! Because the little one is neither man nor beast, but she is a child of Islam! And must be freed!"

"I think so too."

Malpass laughed. "Of course you do! No animals behind bars, right?"

"She's a person," Megan said. "A human being."

"She bites. She catches birds and mice and eats them raw."

"All the same, she doesn't belong in this hole."

Malpass was silent. Bent forward, his elbows on his knees, he smoked the cigarette to the end, dropped the butt to the ground between his shoes and then seemed to be too tired to grind it out.

"What is this here?" Megan asked after a while.

Malpass raised his head.

"What's in the long buildings? What is the oven for? What are these cages?"

"You don't even want to know," Malpass said.

"What's in the metal boxes?"

Malpass leaned back and folded his arms over his chest. H looked at Megan for a long time, as if he was thinking over whether or not it was worth the effort to answer her. He groaned and shook his head, and just when Megan began to think he would sink back into silence, he said: "Documents. Lists. Test results."

"What tests?"

529

"You know what viruses are."

Megan nodded.

"I'm not talking about influenza viruses. Not herpes. Not kiddie viruses. I mean real viruses. Deadly viruses. Ebola. SARS. Nipah. Marburg. Retroviruses. Does that ring a bell?"

"And what does that have to do with this island?" Megan asked. She pulled her legs up and put her bound arms around her knees. The active ingredients in the pills took care of her system; a pleasant numbness blocked out the pain and even a part of the anxiety.

"On this island," Malpass said, spreading his arms out as if with great effort and them dropping them in exhaustion, "we collect viruses. We analyze them. We record them. We change them. We mix them. We breed them." He face, flushed and shining with sweat, was lit by a smile, then reverted to the shadows of nervous indifference. "At least we did, until a month ago."

Megan thought for a moment. "Why?" she asked.

Malpass groaned like an adult who has grown tired of a child's naiveté. "Why!" he said theatrically, as if the word was the epitome of ignorance and innocence. "So we won't be overwhelmed by a pandemic! So we're prepared when a virus mutates to an aggressive form! So we understand the mechanisms of an epidemic!" When he got up, the machine gun fell clattering to the floor. He bent down and put it on the chair. Then he took the scarf from his neck, wiped off his face and took a sip of water.

"I still don't understand all of this," Megan said. "What does IPREC have to do with all of this? Who is Raske? Who do you work for?"

Malpass stretched his arms into the air. When he stretched the small of his back, groaning, Megan realized that he was performing gymnastics.

"My spine," he said, put the scarf on the back of the chair and sat down again. "And a toothache. And heartburn." He laughed as if over a frequently heard joke, broke a pill out of the foil and drank some water. Then he held out the box and the bottle to Megan, but she shook her

530

head. He looked at the clock, took a cigarette out of the pack and leaned back. "IPREC is a . . . How do you say it in English? *Une Chimère*. A mirage? —We call it a front. IPREC is our official mission. What's happening on this island is the real reason we're here. —Talk to the chimpanzees?" He laughed, lit a cigarette and coughed after the first puff. "What's the point? We're not interested in what goes on in an ape's brain. We want to know what new diseases are emerging in their blood."

"Who are you doing this for?"

"For humanity," Malpass said and giggled. "For the survival of our species. —Oh, and of course for money."

"From Nancy Preston's foundation?"

"That's for IPREC. Extra income, so to speak. What we're doing here is funded by other sources."

"Let me guess. By the pharmaceutical industry."

"The pharmaceutical industry. Correct." Malpass grinned.

"Are there primates on this island?" Megan moved her fingers, which were numb from the cable and the pills.

Malpass tilted his head back and blew smoke toward the ceiling. The patter of the rain had become an almost inaudible noise, a crackling that sounded as if the wind was blowing grains of sand on the roof.

"I take that as a yes," said Megan. "Does everybody know about this place? Carla. Esther. Tanvir. Nancy."

Malpass laughed. "Nancy? Are you joking? She thinks she's saving the world here!"

"And the others?"

"Does it matter? This will all be over soon. Anyway, I won't be here long, you can believe me. We'll carry away whatever we can. Documents. Blood samples. All that stuff. Raske can stay, for all I care. He thinks he can negotiate with the jihadists. Pay them more money. But that won't work. Not this time."

"Because of the girl?"

531

"He already had one," Malpass said, so softly that Megan barely understood. "From Laos. Maybe ten, twelve years old. Maybe even twenty. It's hard to say."

"What happened to her?"

"An ape in the body of a human," Malpass said, as if he had not heard Megan. "Raske gave her a name. A name; no number. After three weeks she died." He coughed and took a sip of water.

"Experiments were done on it?"

Again Malpass did not respond to Megan's question. "I warned him. Monkeys. They don't interest these guys. But a child. Just a girl. Not of much value in this part of the world, as we know. But one from here. One of them. And suddenly, as they say, they're rattling their sabers."

"How do they know about the girl?"

"Nothing happens here that they don't know about."

"Why not just give her to them?"

"Nothing more preferable than that."

"What's stopping you?"

Malpass flicked the cigarette butt in the direction of the puddles, but it ended up on the ground where it was dry, and a wisp of smoke rose up from it until the fire reached the filter and went out.

"You give them the girl, and they leave you alone."

"And then everyone will live happily ever after." Malpass stood up and hung the machine gun across his shoulder. "They want to get rid of us. The little girl is only a pretext. A reason to kick us in the ass. They hate the West. We're the infidels. The devil." He drank the remaining water from the bottle.

"Is that what you are? The devil?"

"For them. —And probably for the apes."

"What do you do with them?"

Malpass looked at his watch. "End of question time."

"Just one more," said Megan. "What do you intend to do with me?"

Malpass evaded Megan's gaze. "I'll leave that decision to Raske." He stuck a finger in his mouth. "The toothache is gone." He smiled. Then he took a walkie-talkie from the backpack, turned it on and held it to his ear. "This fucking crap!" He shook the device, turned the knobs and struck it against his leg like a flashlight with a loose contact. "I hate this island. Everything is falling apart. Nothing lasts more than a year." He stuffed the walkie-talkie back into the backpack and took out a second bottle of water.

"Can I have a sip?"

Malpass rolled the bottle over the floor, and when it stopped a meter from Megan, he went over and gave it a nudge with his foot. Megan turned on her side and struck hard against his legs with both feet. Malpass was so surprised by the attack that he did not even cry out. It was only when he was on the floor that a whimpering sound escaped his throat. His upper body covered the weapon, and he reached out a hand to the shoulder strap and was about to sit up, but Megan was fast and kicked him in the stomach with all her strength. Malpass spat a stream of air and collapsed. He crawled away from Megan a bit and rolled over on his side to grab the machine gun with both hands. Megan hit him on the head with the toe of her shoe, and his jaw or his nose broke with a crunch. Then he was lying on his back, his arms stretched out sideways and his bloody mouth distorted.

When Megan bent over and took the gun, she was trembling all over. She no longer felt her foot or the wounds on her hands. She stumbled backwards a few steps until she bumped into one of the wooden beams that supported the roof, then leaned against it and tried to breathe normally. Malpass stared wide-eyed at the ceiling and coughed. His head rested in a puddle of water that looked like a pool of blood. Megan made a circle around him, took the scarf from the back of a chair, poured water over it and dropped it on his chest. Then she searched for the pills, found them in an outer pocket of the backpack, swallowed one and drank half the bottle. She threw the remaining pills into the bottle, shook it and placed it next to Malpass' head.

"I'm sorry," she said softly.

Malpass gasped; bloody bubbles of foam burst on his lips.

Megan hung the machine gun across her shoulder, took the backpack and walked through the door in the plywood wall and then went outside. The rain floating down from the depths of the sky was a fine drizzle, a dense fog enveloping everything and except for a faint, uniform rustle, soundless. Megan could only hear the great drops that fell from the gutters and the trees and burst into puddles on the leaves. After she had walked a few steps, she sank to her knees and wept. Sobbing, she put her face into the wet grass and dug her fingers into the soft earth. Her head felt hot and empty and light, her body cold and heavy. She was infinitely tired and at the same time wide awake; nothing hurt her, yet she was wracked with pain.

"I'm sorry," she whispered. Again and again.

Then she got up. She threw the machine gun into a field overgrown with bushes and walked along the muddy path toward the houses. Now and then she stopped and turned around, but Malpass did not appear. She saw smoke rise above the trees and mingle with the veils of rain and knew that it came from the fire Ramon had started in the oven.

In the barracks, lulled by the noise of the generators, she scraped the cable against the edge of an iron staircase, but she couldn't cut through the wire under the plastic cover and when the skin under the cable began to bleed, she gave up. In the backpack she looked for a knife and found the walkie-talkie, a pair of sunglasses, two packs of cigarettes, a candy bar, a small flashlight, a lighter, a bundle of dollar bills and a French passport in a Tupperware box, an empty box of pills, a pen and a notebook. She counted the money: seven hundred dollars in fives, tens, twenties and fifties. The photo on the passport showed the pale, round face of a man who was not comfortable being photographed. Guillaume Maurice Malpass, Megan read, born on fifth day of October one thousand nine hundred fifty-four in Lille, France, size one meter seventy-four centimeters, weight ninety-three kilos. She began to cry again, but then she pulled herself together, ate two bites of the chocolate bar, put on the backpack and stood up.

She kicked her foot against the doors of several barracks, disappointed that it didn't set off any alarms. The rain grew stronger and drummed on the sheet metal of the roofs. She took a direction where there were no paths, waded through a swamp and had to turn back when a barricade of thickets blocked the way. Small gray birds floated past her like the spots that danced in front of her eyes when she was unspeakably tired.

Eventually, she sat down on the ground under a tree and thought about where she actually wanted to go. To the beach, she thought, without being able to say what she would do there. She took the walkie-talkie from the backpack, turned the knobs and, when it emitted nothing but noise and crackling, threw it into the tall grass behind her. She continued walking, scanning the sky for smoke, but in the blur of the rain she could not see anything and ended up back at the barracks. Until she realized that there were other buildings than the ones whose doors she had kicked, she had almost nearly walked past them. She turned around and saw four buildings resting on concrete piles, each about twenty, maybe thirty meters long, the windowless walls covered with bright plastic elements and the flat roofs crammed with solar collectors, ventilation pipes, water tanks and light shafts made of Plexiglas. Here, the doors were not labeled with numbers but with the letters A to D.

Under the buildings there were plastic pipes, black and red, most of which disappeared in the earth. Every five meters a black one projected to the edge of the barracks. Megan leaned down to one and listened, but out of the barred opening, which had the diameter of a steering wheel, there was no noise that would have been louder than the hum of the generators. But she noticed a familiar aroma; despite the rain and wind and in spite of diesel and the damp mildew in the air, she smelled animals.

She searched for a stone that would fit in her hand and struck the electronic lock on one of the steel doors, but only managed to smash the sheet metal cover and expose a few colored wires which she could not do anything with. When no short circuit caused the door to open and no alarm went off, she sat down on the steps and ate the rest of the chocolate bar. Then she got up, threw the stone against the façade and went to the other end of the barracks, where she found a path in the high grass and decided to follow it.

The shape that emerged in front of her from the watery mist which the rain had again become, looked from afar like a flower. Too tired to run away, Megan stopped and examined the yellow flower that swayed slightly back and forth in the wind and, as she got closer, turned out to be the umbrella she had left beside Raske's door the night before.

Esther also stopped. Her face was pale, but that was possibly due to the light and because she wore dark blue trousers and a T-shirt of the same color. An aluminum suitcase, the size permitted on an airplane as hand luggage, hung on her shoulder; in the hand not holding the umbrella, a gun glimmered.

Megan found her voice first. "And now?" she asked.

Esther said nothing; she didn't even shrug her shoulders.

"What's in the suitcase?"

"Nothing," Esther answered flatly.

"Are you going to the apes?"

Esther was still silent.

"Can I come?"

Esther shook her head.

"Why not?"

"It's . . . " Esther stopped and looked at the ground.

"What?"

Esther raised her head. "You mustn't see that."

Megan could feel her abdomen contract, as if ice-cold water or hot acid filled her stomach. The little gray birds of fatigue fluttered in front her and she closed her eyes for a moment, opened them again and saw how dark it was above her and how large; raindrop fell, unaffected by any wind. She thought about the oven and the bloody bags and involuntarily jerked her head, as if the flies were buzzing around her.

Esther walked over to Megan and stood so close that the umbrella covered both women. "Who did this?" she asked.

"Malpass," Megan said absently, as if she was remembering a long-ago event that had lost all meaning.

Esther stuck the gun in her waistband, put down the suitcase and stuck the handle of the umbrella in the crook of her arm, then loosened the knots, one by one.

Megan watched her. She could not imagine ever again taking another step, she was so exhausted. She saw the plug dangling from her wrist and felt like a machine that someone had unplugged. When her hands were free, she did not know where to put them. The sound of the rain that struck the umbrella sounded deafening in her ears.

Esther wound the cable carefully, but suddenly she seemed to realize the absurdity of her actions and she dropped it on the ground. For a moment she stood there like someone caught doing something stupid, then she took a half step forward, and after a second's hesitation, she embraced Megan with desperate violence.

Megan let it happen. Just the thought of defending herself exhausted her. She felt Esther's heartbeat against her breast, but no longer her own.

"What are you doing here?" Esther whispered. The umbrella was tilted to one side and they were soaked with rain within a few moments.

"Show me the apes," Megan said quietly, seized the gun as if in a dream and held the barrel against Esther's temple.

Esther loosened the embrace, but she did not let go of Megan.

"No," she said after a pause while she and Megan stood there motionless, a strange pair of dancers waiting for music.

Megan broke away, took a faltering step back, aimed the gun in the air and fired. When nothing happened she looked at the gun and vaguely remembered the safety lock, and while she was looking for it, Esther grabbed her and threw her to the ground. She lay on her back and stretched out the arm with the weapon; with the other arm she fought Esther off. She closed her eyes and it was like the past, when her gasping brother had been lying on her, to tear something out of her hand, nothing of value, anything that gave him a reason to fight with her, to test his growing strength on her and to press his confusion, his hatred, and his love on her body in a secret pattern of bruises. She had always been stronger and still let Tobey have his triumph anyway, his miserable reward in the form of an apple, a crayon, a seashell and the stubborn certainty that he had achieved a victory.

The shot sounded as if the world hung on a rope that had broken.

For the length of a horrified breath, the bang made Megan and Esther stop in their tracks, and then Megan rolled to the side and pushed herself to her feet. She trembled, her head throbbed, and every raindrop that touched her made her unsteady. She turned the gun on Esther.

"I want to see them," she said.

Esther continued to lay there. "Don't shoot." Her voice was as clear as her eyes. A sandal had slipped from her foot and lay beside her in a pool of brown water.

Megan dropped her arm, tilted her head back and closed her eyes. The projectile still flew through the sky, a small, glowing piece of metal that, when the energy of the explosion was consumed and the resistance of the air was too great, lost speed and height and silently plunged into the sea and sank to the bottom in the darkness, and no one was killed.

She looked at Esther and put the warm gun muzzle to her head. "Show

538

them to me," she said.

When Esther straightened up, the shape of her body remained in the compressed blades of grass, which filled with water. She stretched out her hand. "Megan, please . . . "

"Show them to me," Megan screamed.

Esther jerked back as if from a blow. Her hands and knees in the muddy earth, she curved her back and tucked her head between her shoulders.

"I'm going to count to three!" Megan held the gun with both hands.

"One!"

Esther stood up. She put her foot in the sandal and began to cry when she lost her balance and nearly fell.

Megan thought of Briona Fanning, who had laid down with her child in the ice cold night, the woman who had walked into the sea with stones in her pockets, of Nunu, the orangutan girl who had used all her strength to end her life.

"Two," she said softly and closed her eyes.

"Stop!" shouted Esther.

Megan opened her eyes.

"You want to see them?" Esther yelled and brushed the wet hair away from her face. "Then come with me." She picked up the suitcase, stretched out her hand for the umbrella but then left it there, and eventually moved with slow, unsteady steps toward the group of trees, behind which lay the barracks.

Without putting down the gun, Megan followed her.

Behind the steel door that Esther opened with a magnetic card, there was a second one made of iron. To unlock it with a key that she wore on a string around her neck, Esther had to shut the steel door first, and the two women shared a long moment immersed in darkness. They had said nothing along the way, and even now they were silent in the half-square meter between the two doors. After the iron grille door was locked behind them again, they entered a room the size of a changing room, just sufficiently lighted by a fluorescent tube recessed in the ceiling. Warning signs and safety regulations covered two red-painted steel doors, and as if the illiterate or those who didn't know English very well would sometimes get lost in this place, each and every rule was repeated by a pictogram. In an open cabinet hung white protective suits, and on a shelf there were yellow rubber boots and a container with masks and gloves. A rifle and a fire extinguisher were hanging on the wall. A yellow panel contained the words EMERGENCY GENERATOR in black letters and another one said PUMP.

Esther put the suitcase on the floor. "You can put the gun away. I'll show you everything." She wiped her hand across her wet, dirty face. "Put it away. Please."

After some hesitation, Megan secured the gun and put it in her pocket. Then she took off her backpack.

Esther pushed the card into the lock of one of the two doors, entered a numeric code and pulled the card out again. A green light flashed and the door was unlocked with a click. Esther pushed it open and entered the room in which burned a few lamps.

Megan followed her. She could feel her heart beating in her throat and the icy, burning sensation in her stomach returned. She stared at Esther's back, the hum of generators and the gentle clatter of the blades of the ventilation system in her ears. When Esther stopped and stepped aside, a passage of fifteen, maybe twenty meters long, opened in front of Megan; tiled boxes ran along the walls, stacked floor to ceiling, each about two meters wide and deep, and each one along the aisle was supplied with a sheet of transparent plastic which contained a recessed door and a feeding hatch, both equipped with several bars. In a metal frame on the door there was a card on which a large number and a were displayed and several entries were recorded.

The first three boxes on each side were empty and dark, but in the next one diffuse light was smoldering and Megan went toward it with bated breath. In the first occupied cell, huddled in a corner, an animal sat, which from her studies she knew was a rhesus monkey. He seemed to see, but it was impossible to tell whether his gaze out of the staring eyes passed through her, or whether it actually reached her. He had bent his legs and wrapped his arms and tail around them, and his breathing was so shallow that Megan could not detect it. On the clean floor there was a plastic bowl of food, and at a stainless steel tube protruding from the wall the animal could quench his thirst. Out of two openings in the ceiling covered with rigid plates came a barely audible humming, a breath of air stirred the fine hairs of the ape's fur. Along the back wall of the box was a channel which ended in a grated drain.

In the boxes right next to it and on the opposite side sat another rhesus monkey, followed by two long-tailed macaques and several pig-tailed macaques. The fur of many animals had bald spots, a pig-tailed macaque had a bandage on his arm, a thin-tailed macaque had a scabbed wound on his leg. Some seemed to be asleep or dozing; others sat awake and motionless, their empty gazes focused on something behind Megan, behind the wall of the building and the edge of the world.

"What are you doing with them? Megan asked, and only now realized that she was crying. In the slaughter house in England she had moved in a dark nightmare of noise and smell, blood and corpses, and believed she had seen the worst thing people could do to animals; in this dim tunnel suffering and death were quieter and cleaner, but no less terrible.

"Experiments with their blood," said Esther, who was sitting on a white box near the door.

"They all have some kind of virus?"

"Most of them."

"Where do they come?"

"Out of Africa. And from breeders."

"How many do you have?"

"Once there were about three hundred. Now just twenty."

"Why?"

"We're going away from here."

"Where?"

"Torben wants to go to Africa. Senegal. Maybe Cameroon."

"Are you going with him?"

"I don't know."

"What happens to the apes?"

Esther hesitated before she answered. "We're putting them to sleep," she said, rising.

Megan saw that Esther had not been sitting on a box, but on a pile of white bags, like the ones that were stored near the stove.

"And the jungle baby?" she asked. "Are you also putting her to sleep?"

Esther was pale, her eyes glassy. For a moment it seemed she would lose her composure, but then she closed her eyes and breathed deeply a few times in and out. "Torben," she finally managed to say, laboriously and in a feeble voice. "He really wanted it. We were against it. But he didn't care. A few years ago he also had a girl like that. Lara. It was no longer alive when I came to the island."

"You haven't answered my question."

"He wants to take it with him."

"How are you getting out of here?"

"With the ship."

"When?"

"Soon. - And you? What about you?"

"I wanted to leave this this evening. But now . . . "

"Leave? How?"

"It doesn't matter," said Megan.

Esther went to Megan and stood two steps in front of her. In this light, she looked exhausted; the rings under her eyes were even darker. "Stay here," she said softly, and then, a little louder, "Please." She stretched out his arm and lowered it again.

Megan turned and went to the boxes along the end of the room where a a shelf made out of stainless steel and a refrigerator stood in front of a white wall. On the shelves were boxes of medicines, blank index cards, pins, a stethoscope. The refrigerator was empty except for a few bowls of fruit. It wasn't until Megan shut the door that she saw the ape in the back box. It was a chimpanzee. He was sitting there with his knees bent, leaning against the back wall of his prison, staring at the floor in front of him. Megan crouched down and looked at him. He was young, younger than Wesley, but he had as little resemblance to the chimpanzees that lived in Nancy's house than a tattered rag doll had with a living being. His little body was gaunt, his hair sparse and dull, and a pale gray film had settled over his pupils. A spot on his left arm was shaved and the dark red of a puncture wound from an injection shone on his bright skin.

He was not staring at the floor. He was watching a tiny black beetle that had strayed into his cell and was crawling over the tiles. With a motion slowed by weakness or caution he pushed a hand in front of the insect and waited for it to climb on his finger. To raise his arm seemed to strain him beyond words and he put his hand on his knee and moved his head closer to look at the beetle.

The sight broke Megan's heart, and she sank to her knees. Her face was burning, her scalp felt, as if she was freezing. What tears she had left ran down her cheeks.

She heard the clicking sound of the lock only after Esther was gone. For several minutes she stared at the red rectangle before she got up and walked to the door. She did not even bother to call or hit against the steel panel. Seized by boundless weariness and resignation, she slid to the floor, curled up and fell asleep within seconds.

When she opened her eyes, she had no idea how much time had

543

passed. For a while she lay on her back and looked at the ceiling, where a few lamps still threw a faint light across the room. Finally she got up and looked for a window, but there was not one. She squirmed and entered one of the empty boxes, only to find that even though she had removed the grille, she could not climb to the roof through the narrow shaft. The pain in her feet and hands came back, and she regretted having left Malpass all the pills. The medicines on the shelves were all antibiotics, anti-inflammatory drugs and sedatives. She swallowed a pill that, according to the leaflet, had about the same effect as Valium, took a bowl of fruit from the fridge and sat down on the stack of bags. While she ate, she remembered the gun. She took it out and tried to estimate what would happen if she fired at the electronic lock, and rejected the idea for the time being.

The animals were silent and listless. Megan gave them pieces of fruit through the hatch in the box, but they did not appear to be hungry. Every now and then the ceiling light flickered, a silent storm. The bags were unused and clean, and even so Megan only reluctantly spread a few of them on the floor and lay down. Rain drummed on the roof. The active ingredients of the sedative shot through her bloodstream. She imagined how it would be if Esther did not come back and release her. With closed eyes she watched as a half-baked plan formed in her head, in which the sedative and the gun played an important role. She did not know if she would have the energy, the mad courage of despair. In London, the sight of the cars parked far below had sufficed to make her climb off the windowsill. But there, she thought, she had had a choice, and here, she would eventually have no more.

She heard the shot while she sat thinking with the gun barrel at her temple. She opened her eyes and stood up. A second shot was fired, then a third and fourth. She stood in one of the empty boxes where the sounds penetrated through the ventilation shaft, but outside it was quiet again.

Minutes later shots rang out again on the island, this time fainter, more distant. Megan counted and came up with eleven or twelve. At some point she thought she heard an explosion, a muffled bang, like the times Tobey would explode an inflated paper bag on the other side of her door to frighten her.

She did not want to picture what had happened. She swallowed another pill, lay down and cocked the weapon. The metal of the gun was warm, the trigger just a little resistant. Perhaps that would not be such a bad way to die, she thought: to pull the trigger while sleeping, dreaming.

Around her there was silence and darkness, but she was not dead. The diesel generator was not running anymore; there was no light and no fresh air. Megan rolled over from her back to her belly. Her arms and legs felt numb. She knelt down and hoped in vain to discover something other than the deepest black. Then she saw a tiny red light flashing at the door and crawled toward it on all fours. She rose and pulled on the handle with both hands, and when she managed to open the door she was seized by relief like a wave of cool water.

She stood in the pitch-dark hallway for a while and waited until she was able, despite the lack of oxygen, to stand on her legs. She remembered the backpack with the flashlight, but Esther seemed to have taken it. Finally, she felt her way to the iron grille door, and although she had expected it would be locked, she fell into a silent panic. She sat on the floor and tried to think clearly. She did not understand much about technology, but suspected that the power failure had knocked the electronic locks out of service. What she knew for sure was that the mechanical lock could only be opened with the key or with force. She remembered the gun and scanned the wall beside the closet, but the holder was empty.

It seemed to take an eternity for her to find the gun and an index card. She took two cloth masks off the shelf and blocked her ears with them. She slid the index card between door and the frame, and found the bolt she would have to hit with the bullet. She put the gun barrel on that point and took a step back. Blocking out thoughts of ricochets and holding the weapon with both hands, she pulled the trigger.

Despite the fabric in her ears she felt the bang rip threw her head. It seemed to her as if the flash of the muzzle bathed the entire room in bright light, as if the sound waves bounced off the walls and submerged her. She waited a moment and then kicked her foot against the iron bars, but the door did not move. The metal glowed where the bullet had blasted it. Megan thought she saw a flash. An acrid, sulfurous smell filled her nostrils as she was preparing to shoot a second time.

After the third bullet, the magazine was empty. Megan threw herself against the door, which creaked and groaned but did not budge. She took a fire extinguisher from the wall and slammed it against the lock, and finally broke the latch. Megan was so exhausted that when the steel door opened, as if by itself, she stumbled down the steps, fell on the wet ground and lay there.

It was evening, perhaps seven or eight o'clock, maybe later. Megan looked at the sky, from which a fine rain was falling straight down. Her mouth was open, the noise escaped slowly from her head. In a hollow beside her water had collected and she turned over on her stomach and drank it. She thought of Tanvir and the man who would supposedly come with a boat to take away her and Carla and everyone else who did not want to die, and the fact that she was on the wrong island.

She got up and went back to the barracks. The locks of the steel doors were apparently programmed in such a way that if the generators failed and the emergency power generator did not function, they opened automatically. The room Megan entered looked exactly the same as the one across from it, but all the boxes and the refrigerator were empty. A few unused bags were lying on a shelf, there was a plastic bowl full of shrink-wrapped gauze, bandages and needles, and against a wall leaned something Megan only recognized as a blowpipe for anesthetic darts when she took it in hand and noticed the plastic mouth piece. She threw it on the floor and went to the apes in the other room. There, she pushed back all the locks on the doors to the boxes and opened them. Then she sat down in the darkness of a corner and waited.

The animals moved as little as before; none made a sound. At some point a long-tailed macaque stretched his arm out timidly as if to check whether the transparent wall in front of him was truly no longer there. It seemed the others had not even noticed that the doors of their cages were open. Megan left the corner and knelt down on her knees in front of the chimpanzee's box. He raised his head and looked at her, and Megan slid closer to him, waited and then carefully slid a hand across the floor until it was lying on the tiles of the box. The chimpanzee looked down and saw the hand. In his eyes there was nothing, no curiosity, no confusion, no fear, just an apathetic emptiness. He sat there leaning against the back wall, his hindquarters in the gutter, which was now covered with a layer of excrement and urine, and breathed as if he no longer had any spark of life left inside him.

When Megan touched him gently on the leg, the monkey flinched. With an amazingly quick movement he grabbed Megan's hand and bit her on the forearm. Then he let her go as fast as he had grabbed her, thrust himself into a corner and threw his arms around his bent legs. He did not tremble, seemed not even to breathe. Only the frightening glittering under the cloudy grey of his pupils betrayed that he had not yet lapsed back into the old, seemingly indifferent and resigned lifelessness.

Megan had not found disinfectant anywhere and let the rain, which by now had grown stronger, wash out the wound. She went from one barracks to the next and opened all the steel doors, but because the iron lattice doors blocked her entrance, she could not tell whether there were animals in the boxes. She remembered the machine gun, and she made her way to the building where she had left Malpass, to search for the weapon. Despite the rain and the almost total calm, she believed she could smell a whiff of burning in the air and was surprised when she found the furnace abandoned and no smoke rising from the chimney. One of the containers under the corrugated iron roof lay overturned on the ground. From its dark interior the dirty white of the bags gleamed. A half-laden wheelbarrow stood beside it. Megan stared at the open container for a while, and then she continued walking.

At the building with the cages she paused behind a tree long enough to be sure there was no one nearby. Then she tried to remember where she had thrown the machine gun. She turned in a circle, thought she recognized a few shrubs and combed the area in the vicinity of the high grass. Eventually she gave up, went to the end of the building and entered it through an open door. The metal box in the office was gone, and there was no sign of Malpass except the cigarette butts on the floor. The door to the room beneath the floor had been broken open and the girl had disappeared. There was dry grass and a piece of rope on the floor. Megan bent down to press her finger tip into something she thought was blood.

She went back outside and through the heavy rain to the three houses. Out of habit she ducked behind the broken refrigerator, listening for sounds. She took an empty Coke bottle and threw it against the wall of the small wooden house where Raske, Malpass and Ruben had loaded their weapons. When nothing happened, she went around the house to the front door. In the middle of the muddy clearing, surrounded by deep vehicle tracks, there was a motorbike and a single pair of light green rubber boots.

Inside the house she was enveloped by warm, stuffy air. She slammed the door behind her and paused in the hallway, waiting. Then she went past the kitchen, where the cupboards had been emptied, into the dark living room. Here again, everything had been removed: the furniture, rugs, lamps, pictures. Only the thin curtains still hung over the windows. In one corner she found the fragments of the Virgin Mary, a few wooden beads of the rosary and candles.

At first she thought it was the sound of a rising wind, the whispering of a breeze that came through a wall crack, the soft moans of a roof beam. Then she heard it again and followed it. At the door that led into the small bedroom, she stopped. She did not want to enter the room, but did it anyway.

Esther was lying on the mattress. She opened her eyes as Megan knelt down beside her and took her hand. A thin blue blanket was spread over her. Near her head the flashlight from Malpass' backpack dispersed a weak, colorless light.

"What happened?" Megan asked and ran her free hand over Esther's forehead.

Esther looked at Megan a long time from under half-closed, fluttering eyelids. "I wanted to come," she said softly, as if she had just recognized Megan. "To get you."

"I know."

"Honestly."

"I'm here now."

Esther closed her eyes. "Yes," she said. Her lips were bloodless and cracked. Blades of grass were hanging from her hair.

Megan pulled the covers down a bit. Esther's upper body was naked. Her right arm lay on her stomach, her hand holding a crumpled, blood-soaked T-shirt. A sound of dismay escaped Megan's lips, and Esther opened her eyes in confusion. Megan cautiously lifted the hand with the T-shirt. The fabric parted from the dried blood and revealed a hole, black and no bigger than a cherry pit.

Megan touched the bluish skin around the wound. "I'll get help," she said.

"No," Esther whispered and held Megan's hand firmly. "Stay."

Megan covered Esther and stroked her cheek. Only now did she realize that the key and the string were gone.

549

"Torben . . . " Esther said and then fell silent, as if she had used the last vestiges of her energy to pronounce the name.

"What about him?" Megan leaned forward and felt Esther's breath on her skin.

"He left without me," Esther murmured.

"Maybe the ship's engine broke down," Megan said. It didn't matter how stupid it sounded. "He's sure to come."

Esther shook her head so slowly that it was hard to perceive it as movement.

"Who shot you?"

Esther eyes closed. Megan held her cool hand, stroking it. The patter of the rain grew louder. Spots formed islands on the mattress. Esther's blood was a continent. An insect floated in the circle of light from the flashlight, its wings shimmered silver. When Megan lay down beside her, Esther sighed. Megan pulled the ring from her finger and exchanged it with the one on Esther's. Esther's hand and her own were like those of twin sisters. Esther looked at the ring and smiled, but perhaps Megan only imagined it, because the lights flickered before they grew weaker and eventually went out.

At dawn Megan began to take doors off their hinges, to knock down kitchen cabinets and to pry boards from the floor with a piece of iron that she had found behind the house. She got even more doors from the empty, adjoining houses and dragged them to the meadow next to the clearing. It had stopped raining. Although a light wind was blowing and the air was almost cool, Megan was sweating. When she was shaken by an outburst of tears, she jumped up and down on the doors until they splintered. The wound on her forearm looked bad, but Megan did not feel it any more than she did her feet or her hands.

After she had piled the wood in a flat heap, she laid the mattress on top. She ripped a curtain into shreds and soaked it with gasoline from the

550

tank of the motorbike. Then she went back inside and sat down for a while on the floor of the bedroom. The notebook full of French phrases, the pen, the empty pill bottle and the lighter were the only things that were still left in the backpack. Megan put the lighter in her pocket, wrapped Esther in the blanket and carried her outside. To counter the shabbiness of the wood pile and the mattress, she gathered a handful of flowers from the meadow and decorated the corpse with them as best she could.

It occurred to her that she had never been to a funeral, not even her father's. As a child she had buried countless animals in the garden, but she refused to enter a cemetery. She had fragments of obituaries for blackbirds, mice and rabbits in her head and she remembered a few sentences from the eulogy for a baby orangutan, but she did not know what last words to deliver for a dead person.

Finally, she whispered the two lines from William Butler Yeats' gravestone, lit the shreds of curtain soaked with gasoline and threw them between the wood. Because she could not watch as Esther's body went up in flames, she ran away when the fire reached the mattress and black smoke rose into the sky. She ran to the end of the meadow, crossed a marshy field, lost a shoe in a ditch and threw the other one away. Soon she was standing on the beach and watched as the rain came over the sea. She lay in the sand, took a deep breath and screamed her brother's name up into the clouds.

She was not tired anymore when she got up, took off her pants, T-shirt and shirt and went out into the dirty surf. She rolled her shoulders as she had done in the past, stretched out her arms, pushed her feet off the ground and dived into the warm water and swam away.

News from Tobey

The dogs are barking, because it's dark. No sooner do you lie down and think about how quiet it is at last, than they begin. As if they waited until the last diesel generator and the last light and the last damn radio has been turned off. All day they lie in the shade of the trees and in the hollows between the shrubs. If we lie down, they get up, slowly and reluctantly, as if they have a dreary chore ahead, a job they hate. One begins to bark and the others start. Occasionally they rest, and you doze off, even though you know they will not let you sleep. Most likely you will get used to it eventually. Then it will no longer disturb you, as it disturbed you that first night, and the second and third and fourth, and on this one.

You would like the dogs. You would play with them. You would feed them. You'd think up names for them. You would talk to them.

For five days I have been waiting for these bastards to get the damn motor afloat. After two days I thought they had cleared off with the money I gave them for spare parts. But then they came back and actually started to work. They sit under a corrugated iron roof at the edge of the water and screw and weld away at the rebuilt engine block. Twenty people look on; there are many children. Two of the three men who own the boat work; the third, a skinny old guy with bad teeth, squats there and smokes and from time to time makes a comment. I have shown them a photo of you, an old one. They did not recognize you, but I'm sure that you have changed. But they did remember you, the young woman who wanted to go to one of the islands. When I ask how long the repairs will take, they suddenly don't understand English any more and talk all at once until I'm fed up and go back to my room.

My room. Four by four meters, a bed and a chair. No table. Two windows. The one faces the wall of the house next door; through the other I can see into the courtyard with the chickens. The chickens are like the damn dogs, except they annoy you during the day instead of at night. When it's hot and I'm lying on the bed, I can hear them. You know, I always used to wonder what these stupid creatures have to cackle about all day. You said they could actually sing like birds, but because they are so shy and inhibited, they just stutter. And you said sometimes when they feel they're not being observed, they sing better than a nightingale. When I was five, I believed you. I snuck up on our damn chickens and listened to them for hours, but I never heard them sing. I think they were talking to themselves. They teeter around the farm from morning to evening and comment on every damn kernel of corn they find, every damn worm they get hold of. And if they don't find anything, they comment on that too. Chickens are old, stupid women, babbling to themselves. But at least they rest at night.

Five days in this damn hole. I know I should not use words like *damn* and *condemned*. You thought that it was wrong when we were children, and that probably hasn't changed. But I'll be honest, until a few months ago things were still pretty lousy for me, and since I'm sitting in this hole and things aren't working out, all the bad memories are coming back. If I tell you about everything I've experienced, maybe you will understand me. But where should I begin?

How about the night that I ran away to Dublin? You know, after you came into my room. Christ, all I have to do is close my eyes and I see everything in front of me again. Why did you do it, Meg? Ten minutes later, and I would have been gone. Did you think you could hold me back? Did you really believe I would stay? And don't just tell me now that it wasn't all that bad because we're not real siblings. At the time I didn't know that! Until a few months ago I didn't know that we have the same mother, but not the same father. I had to figure that out myself. Thanks a lot! Cait sends you her regards, by the way, but you probably don't care about that. She doesn't really send you her regards; she said only that if I see you sometime, I should tell you that she's sorry and that she made a big mistake back then. She said she always wanted to get in touch with us, but then she didn't have the courage to do it. She thinks we hate her, and as for me, she was damn right for a long time. She told me who my father is, and maybe I'll meet him sometime. Not soon, but some day. Back then he worked in Killorglin, at the bank. They were together for over five years. She ran away to Dublin because of him. He now lives in Dundalk. I saw a photo of him, and now I finally know why you have so much of Seamus in you and I have nothing. Well, I must have gotten some of his damn obstinacy somehow, even if it wasn't through his blood.

But back to that night. I went to Nenagh, which is about half the distance to Dublin. It was pouring buckets of rain, and I swore the whole time. I was afraid that the case wasn't closed, and the guitar on my back would get wet. In the morning I was totally exhausted and chilled to the bone and drank about ten cups of coffee at a gas station shop. The woman behind the counter took pity on me and gave me the key to the toilet. I stood for an eternity there in front of the hand dryer and more or less warmed myself up. Shortly before Dublin the motorcycle bit the dust and I had to push it through the country for an hour before I found a shop that was open. I asked the owner if I could use his tools, for a fee of course, but he refused. I was completely worn out and pretty much in the bag and not in the mood to mess with the guy and I gave him a twenty and said I'd come back as soon as possible to get the BSA. Then I took a seat on the next bus to Dublin.

If I were to start writing about the time in Dublin now, there would not be enough paper. Barry has probably told you a little or written. Why did you really have a post office box? Why did you have to make your life such a damn secret? Barry was constantly babbling that I should go to London and look for you. Or that I should at least write letters. But I would not. I was so damn angry at you, Meg! One time Jason and I were completely drunk and got tattoos; him a flaming heart and me a cross with barbed wire. The next day he asked me why it had to be a fucking cross. And I said, just because. But eventually I thought I probably chose it because you have such a huge problem with the church. Pretty crazy, I know. A cross, holy shit! Father MacMahon would have loved me!

Aidan told me that you write him a postcard now and then. And he didn't understand why you never gave an address or phone number. We talked with each other on the phone regularly since I moved to Dublin, and when he was traveling and came to a city, he sent me an email. Three weeks before Seamus died he disappeared to Canada, just like that, without saying anything to me. His secretary said he had cracked up again and had to get out. Of course, he was untraceable, and so it happened that I was the only member of the family at the funeral. Cait didn't come either, and I can't tell you how fucking angry I was at her. And you.

Aidan returned two months later. He had been traveling somewhere in the wilderness, and when he got to a city and read my mail, it was too late to fly to Ireland. He visited me and proposed that I accompany him on his next trip. But I didn't want to. Things were going pretty good with the band. Barry had come to Dublin. We were together again. We had plans.

You probably heard somehow what happened then. After Dermot shot a bullet in his head in the rehearsal room, everything fell apart. Mick drove straight home. A shrink helped him come to terms with the images of Dermot's exploding head. Barry stayed for two months and watched how Jason and I pumped ourselves with drugs. Then he left. One day he just disappeared. He wrote me a letter a week later, from Mizen Head, somewhere in the southwest. A month later he called from home, but that day I was so out of it that I didn't understand what he was saying to me. Three months ago we saw each other, in Tralee. He is training to be a nurse there. His parents don't care very much for that. But he doesn't care.

Do you know what I think? Maybe Barry coped with Dermot so well because of the butcher shop. The blood, the flesh, the bone fragments, the tufts of hair; he had already seen all that. Those were animals, but still. Maybe he's a bit like you and has more pity for a pig or a cow than a man. Maybe he heard about an earthquake with 10,000 dead on the radio, and it bothers him a little, and then his father kills a calf and he's devastated.

Jason and I have also disappeared. As a duo, we were still there, only different; you could see us. But actually we were gone, farther away than you can ever travel. Jason began to shoot up at some point. Sometimes, if my brain wasn't totally confused, I tried to dissuade him, but I couldn't. We had money. Jason's mother gave it to him. After the thing with Dermot, he told her he wanted to fly to India to recover from the trauma, and she sent him a check for five grand. At first I thought we would lay off the drugs at some point, it was just our way to forget that damn day, but of course that was nonsense. Eventually Jason stopped going out of the house. He got the stuff from a guy who rode a bicycle and wanted us to call him Mr. White. From time to time I went out to shop for bread, sardines and fruit for Jason.

On a nice day, after many weeks of rain, I forced Jason to go out. We went to Mount Pleasant Tennis Club and sat on one of the benches from which you can see the seats. A few girls were playing, thirteen, fourteen years old. Jason was always blown away when he saw them, even on that day. He called them elves and fairies and wanted to write a song about them. We sat there until the evening. We had iced tea and chocolate, and for the first time in ages I thought we could manage to get out of the whole mess. That night Jason listened to music, just like every night. And the next morning he was dead. An overdose. A mistake. He was probably in such a good mood because of his elves and fairies that he injected too much of the shit. So somehow his death was also my fault; I was the one who should have gotten him out.

Crotty, our old landlord, was not exactly thrilled when the first ambulance pulled up outside his house and then the cops came. What had happened in the basement had already been quite stressful for him, even though the police had closed the file on the case very quickly. But two deaths within a year were too much for him. He sold the house and said I could stay until the new owners start to rebuild.

Then suddenly Aidan appeared and took me to Klonakilty, to his house by the sea. Although I didn't want to go anywhere. I wanted to stay in Dublin and get drunk every day. But Aidan outsmarted me. He let me drink until I passed out. Then he packed me into his Volvo and drove off. When I came to, I was already on his damn couch. And Rotten, who Aidan had also brought along, lay across my legs.

Two days later was Jason's funeral. He had always said that his final resting place would be in Morocco or India. He found that somehow cool and romantic. Now he lies in the cemetery in Killorglin, next to his father, and there is nothing on his grave stone cool or romantic, just *Beloved Son*. Barry and Mick and their parents came to the funeral and a few people from class. Some wept. It was terrible. I didn't want to stand beside this grave. I did not want to listen to Father MacMahon again. I wanted to lay in my room in Dublin and think of nothing, not about the past, not about the present and certainly not about the future. Later I went with Aidan, Mick and Barry to Delaney's and let myself get plastered. It was pretty weird to see them again. Mick was hardly recognizable. He boozed quite a bit and didn't want to talk about Dublin, or the band, or music. At some point he got up and walked out.

The next day I woke up in Aidan's former workshop. The shed was completely empty, except for the cot I was laying on, a table and a chair. Then Aidan brought me something to eat, a pot of tea and a book. And you know what? He pushed the stuff through a hatch, like I was a prisoner! At first I thought he was kidding me, but he said he'd let me out again when I was sober and promised to stay there! Can you believe it? Gathered all together, my previous temper tantrums were a mouse fart compared to what I cried out in this damn shed from rage and frustration. First, I smashed the table and the chair, and then I broke the pot and tore up the book. Of course I tried to get out, but Aidan has turned the shed in a damn fortress. He planned it, Meg! Do you remember the toilet at the very back next to the bandsaw? He installed a shower there! I don't want to tell you the whole story now, just this much: I was in there for 58 days. During the first three days I was raging until I couldn't anymore; then came the withdrawal symptoms, and I cried and begged and threatened. Then I slept for nearly a week. Aidan brought me fruit juice, clean clothes, books. At first I screamed at him when he pushed something through the hatch, then I ignored him. At some point he gave me the CD player and the CDs that he had taken out of the room in Dublin with the rest of my stuff. I think after about three weeks, I told him that everything was good; I didn't want anything to drink; he could let me out. But he said I wasn't ready yet. I insulted him again and ranted and threw the CD player against the wall. I didn't want to listen to any more music anyway, never again in my life.

One day Aidan pushed a pile of letters through the door. They were all from you. When I was in Dublin, Barry told me that you sent him letters for me. But I didn't want to read them. I didn't want to know anything about you. Barry kept them all. There were only copies, Aidan was probably afraid that I would tear them up. And I wanted to, at first, but then I read them, back and forth and again and again.

At some point we started playing rummy, through the hatch. Aidan told me about his travels. On the evening before he let me out, he brought me food and two bottles of beer. I didn't drink them. I know it always sounds a little crazy when someone says it, but I learned a lot in the 58 days, especially about myself. Of course I wasn't a new, better person. But at least I was no longer the crazy guy in Dublin, who lies in his room and drinks away the little bit of sense that he has. I was cured, healed, saved. At least for now.

Aidan offered me a job in his furniture factory, and for a while I worked there. On weekends when the weather was good, we drove to the sea or went hiking. Sometimes Barry came with us. Do you know that he loves you? Of course he has never said it, but it's as plain as the nose on your face. We also go to the farm regularly. Every time we drove into the yard Barry and I hoped that you would be there, that you would be sitting in the barn with the chickens and reading them poems out loud. But you were never there.

I hadn't had anything to drink in a couple of months, when Aidan said that I should visit my mother. I didn't want to; you know why. But Aidan came back to it again and again. The fact that we only have one mother and that I would regret it later if I didn't go to her now, and so on. He annoyed me so long I eventually went. Aidan called her in advance, and Cait welcomed me with coffee and cake. She lives in Glasnevin now, in a four-room apartment. The guy she lives with is named John. They've been a couple for four years, but they're not married. He's still working, something with shipbuilding. When I arrived, he wasn't there. Cait said he wanted to leave us alone for our first meeting. She showed me a photo of him. He looks pretty nice. She kept asking me what I was up to, but somehow I couldn't open my mouth. Then she told what had happened to her during all those years, and I just listened to her and drank coffee. I couldn't eat any of the cake. She said that in the past she was often depressed. When I came into the world, it was especially bad. One day she wondered how she could kill us and herself as painlessly as possible, and then she knew that it was time to leave. She said it: It's time to go. Her friend, the guy from the bank—my father—rented her an apartment in Dublin. For an entire year she left the apartment only once a week, to shop, she said. But who knows if it's true. Maybe she went out every night and celebrated her new freedom. She has also explained to me why she didn't come to the funeral, but they were just excuses. She doesn't want the farm; she is giving it to us. Great, huh? Eventually she didn't know what else to say and we just sat there. Every night as a child I had worked out a million questions that I wanted to ask her, once and now I couldn't ask a single one. The woman that I saw was my mother and still a stranger. Maybe this will change, sometime soon or in the distant future. I don't know. She wanted to give me money for a taxi to the station, but I didn't take it. I offered her my hand when we parted, and while I was standing in the hallway I could hear her crying behind the door. I wondered if I should knock again, but then I left.

After I was sober and rational and had seen my mother, Aidan brought down two suitcases from the attic. They had once belonged to a man whom I had regarded as my father for 20 years. And they had never traveled beyond the borders of Ireland. I asked what I was supposed to do with them and Aidan said: fly to the Philippines and look for you.

And that's what I'm doing now. Before I left, I tried to find as much as possible about Jeffrey Salter on the Internet. I came across one of his books at a Dublin bookstore: *Values: a Critical Consideration*. I'm sure you know it. I read it from the first page to the last and didn't even understand half of it. Aidan called the publishing house in Canberra and asked if he could have Salter's address or telephone number, but they didn't give them to him, neither in Darwin nor in Manila. So I just left. In both of the suitcases I had a bundle of dollars, copies of your letters and the name of an old man who, instead of Manila, might also be in Darwin, or maybe even no longer alive. But I was lucky. Jeffrey Salter was actually in Manila. Aidan had advised me to ask the philosophy students at the university about him, and after two days I found a student worked for the professor now and then.

When Salter heard that I was your brother, he invited me to dinner. Over fried noodles and vegetables, he told me about the island he was on many years ago. He seemed very friendly and helpful but also very old and forgetful. Once he called me Tommy, another time Robert. Anyway, he remembered that you wanted to go to the island and that he had told you approximately where it was. It wasn't until I looked at a map later, that I had any idea what I would be getting into with this search. The area Salter told me about was at least twice as large as Ireland. And the map showed only a fraction of the islands which exist in the region.

But now I'm here. For five days I have been sitting in this godforsaken . . . nest on the coast and waiting until we finally leave. The dogs are still barking. I will give this letter to a man who has a scooter. I already bought stamps for the envelope in Manila. I don't know what to expect. The boat the three guys want to use to bring me to the island has not made a particularly confidence-inspiring impression on me. If we drown on the way to you, you will hopefully get these lines sometime. I am sending them to Barry; maybe you will get in touch with him sometime in the future.

In one of your letters you asked if I miss you. Yes, I do. Very much. In another you ask if I hate you for what you did. No, I do not. For a while I did, but not anymore. I hope I find you, Megan. I hope more than anything in the world.

Who loves you?
Tobey!

EPILOGUE

Tanvir Raihan traveled by boat from Manhattan to Brooklyn. He thought it was the most appropriate way to handle the last part of his journey. After leaving the water taxi, he paused on the pier for a moment and looked out into the bay, where the Hudson mingled with the sea. A light rain fell; the wind carried inland. Clouds pressed over the city on the other side, causing houses and bridges to disappear. Lights and sea gulls emerged from them and disappeared inside them again. Nothing here reminded him of the radiant heat and the light blue serenity of California, which he had left the day before, and yet Tanvir had been smiling since he got out of the plane.

He took a taxi and got out at Prospect Park West to take a walk along Carroll Street, despite the bad weather. At the airport he had bought a yellow jacket which ballooned with every breath of air. He still had more than three hours to kill, so he mingled with the people who were walking their dogs, jogging and bicycling, a maze of colorful umbrellas and rain coats and furs. When he saw a light-colored Labrador it reminded him of Nancy's dog, and of the cemetery, which he had created, even though the ground was wet and not yet ready to receive the dead.

He left the park and sat in a small restaurant that advertised on a board outside the fact they had no television. There were five tables and a dozen chairs in the room; pictures and posters and handwritten menus hung on the walls. All the tables except one were free. An old man was sitting at it and reading a newspaper, which he put down when Tanvir took a seat beside him. He had a small round head with large ears and kind gray eyes. His white hair was just long enough that the hat, which hung together with a jacket on the back of the chair, had left behind a semi-circular imprint. The hostess, an overweight woman in her forties, brought Tanvir a cup of coffee and recommended the homemade apple pie. A little later a boy came to his table and put a piece of warm cake in front of him. He was about ten years old, wore a New York Yankees T-shirt and a pair of glasses with thick lenses, which definitely did not make his life as a child more bearable.

"Is that your mother?" Tanvir asked when the boy made no move to leave.

The boy nodded.

"Tell her the cake tastes very good."

The boy turned his head toward the counter, behind which the woman was putting cups on a shelf. "Mom, the man says the cake tastes good," he cried, and then he turned back Tanvir again with a serious expression, as if expecting another order or a tip.

"Leave him alone!" the mother cried back.

"He's not bothering me," Tanvir said out loud, but the boy walked away and disappeared through a door behind the counter.

"He plays guitar," the man said abruptly. "Electric guitar. It sounds like someone roasting a radio over the fire."

Tanvir laughed. The cake had a hint of vanilla.

"May I ask where you're from?" The man had turned to Tanvir, his face bright and open like a door to a sunny landscape. His tweed jacket was brown and old; the shirt underneath white and perfectly ironed.

"San Diego," Tanvir said.

"Oh. And what brings you to Brooklyn in this weather?"

"I'm meeting with a publisher."

"Oh. Good for you." The man pursed his lips and nodded approvingly. "And what is he publishing?" he said, still nodding.

"In this case, a friend's book."

Now the man raised his eyebrows in admiration. "You don't say. What is the book about, if I may ask?"

"A childhood in Ireland. And a thousand other things."

"That's quite a bit. And what is the book called? Or is it a secret?"

"Music in the Dreams of Dogs."

The man closed his eyes for a moment, as if he was letting the words linger in his head. Then he held out his hand to Tanvir. "Stanley Bogdanovich."

"Tanvir Raihan."

The men shook hands.

"I came to America from Serbia in 'fifty-two. The Promised Land, you know."

"I've been here since 'sixty-four. I fled back them from an arranged marriage in Malaysia."

"Seriously? I'd certainly like to hear more about that."

Tanvir looked at his watch. "The short version or the long one?"

"The long one," said Stanley Bogdanovich, without a second's hesitation.

Tanvir smiled, ordered two cups of coffee and began to tell his tale.

ABOUT THE TRANSLATOR

 EUGENE H. HAYWORTH is a librarian and Associate Professor for the University Libraries at the University of Colorado Boulder. He holds an MA in English Literature from the University of Rochester and an MLS from Syracuse University, and he has studied German language and literature at the University of Colorado Boulder, as well as the Goethe Institute in Berlin. His first book, *Fever Vision: the Life and Works of Coleman Dowell*, was published by Dalkey Archive Press in 2007. In 2010, he lived in Berlin, Germany, where he taught at Humboldt Universität as the recipient of a Fulbright scholarship. His English translation of Günther Freitag's novel *Brendel's Fantasie* was published by Owl Canyon Press in 2011, and in the United Kingdom by Haus Publishing in the spring of 2012.